Kissing Comfort

Jo Goodman

BERKLEY SENSATION, NEW YORK

THE BERKLEY PUBLISHING GROUP
Published by the Penguin Group
Penguin Group (USA) Inc.
375 Hudson Street, New York, New York 10014, USA
Penguin Group (Canada), 90 Eglinton Avenue East, Suite 700, Toronto, Ontario M4P 2Y3, Canada
(a division of Pearson Penguin Canada Inc.)
Penguin Books Ltd., 80 Strand, London WC2R 0RL, England
Penguin Group Ireland, 25 St. Stephen's Green, Dublin 2, Ireland (a division of Penguin Books Ltd.)
Penguin Group (Australia), 250 Camberwell Road, Camberwell, Victoria 3124, Australia
(a division of Pearson Australia Group Pty. Ltd.)
Penguin Books India Pvt. Ltd., 11 Community Centre, Panchsheel Park, New Delhi—110 017, India
Penguin Group (NZ), 67 Apollo Drive, Rosedale, Auckland 0632, New Zealand
(a division of Pearson New Zealand Ltd.)
Penguin Books (South Africa) (Pty.) Ltd., 24 Sturdee Avenue, Rosebank, Johannesburg 2196,
South Africa

Penguin Books Ltd., Registered Offices: 80 Strand, London WC2R 0RL, England

KISSING COMFORT

A Berkley Sensation Book / published by arrangement with the author

Copyright © 2011 by Joanne Dobrzanski.
Excerpt on pages 381–391 by Jo Goodman © by Joanne Dobrzanski.
Cover art of man by Paul Hakimata Photography/Shutterstock.
Cover art of fence by David Young/Shutterstock.
Cover art background by Balcioglue/Shutterstock.
Cover hand lettering by Iskra Johnson.
Cover design by Rita Frangie.
Interior text design by Tiffany Estreicher.

ISBN: 978-1-61793-005-8

BERKLEY SENSATION®
Berkley Sensation Books are published by The Berkley Publishing Group,
a division of Penguin Group (USA) Inc.,
375 Hudson Street, New York, New York 10014.
BERKLEY SENSATION® is a registered trademark of Penguin Group (USA) Inc.
The "B" design is a trademark of Penguin Group (USA) Inc.

PRINTED IN THE UNITED STATES OF AMERICA

For Yvonne, for everything

Prologue

October 1850
Sierra Nevada Foothills

They were still miles away when they noticed the buzzards circling. Newton Prescott pulled up his mare, tipped the brim of his hat back a notch, and glanced sideways at his companion. Tucker Jones met the glance, the right side of his mouth already turning down at the corner, foreshadowing his scowl.

"What d'you think?" Newt asked.

"You don't want to know."

Newt reasoned that was probably true. Tucker had an unnatural sense for when events were going to take a turn. It would have been helpful if Tuck knew whether the turn was right or left, up or down, good or bad, but that kind of foresight didn't accompany his gift, at least not that he'd ever shared. Newt was inclined to believe that Tucker Jones always knew a bit more than he let on, but had decided a long time ago that it was a burden best shouldered alone.

Newt watched one of the carrion feeders swoop low and disappear from sight, only to reappear as if shot from a cannon. "Something scared him off."

"Something ain't properly dead yet."

Nodding, Newt replaced his hat at the proper angle and

blocked the red-orange glow of the lowering sun. "What's your pleasure, Tuck? Circle around or advance?"

"I reckon circling makes us no better than the buzzards."

"True enough."

They rode on in silence. It suited them. Newton Prescott possessed no unnatural senses, but he had a head for facts and figures. He knew about probability and the odds of drawing an inside straight, and right now it was a good bet that he and Tuck were going to be flush with trouble.

They'd known about the wagon train eight days ago. Tuck had pointed out the tracks as they came across the emigrant trail from the north. It was a small party, five, maybe six wagons, some cattle, and a few spare horses. There were women in the group. Newton had recognized the way certain footprints were misshapen by the drag of skirts along the ground. They reckoned there might have been as many as twenty people in the party, but judging from the way the wagon tracks often strayed from the route, no one in the group knew how to read the trail or had a good head for their destination.

It was reasonable to assume this party had been separated from the main group, cut out, perhaps, for differences with the wagon master, or left behind because of illness or bad blood or by choice. Newton arrived at sixteen possibilities for the separation, and Tuck didn't have an opinion about any of them. Newt was curious. Tucker Jones was not.

They'd discussed catching up with the train, maybe offering their services as guides to San Francisco—because Newt had figured the chances of that being their destination as near ninety-six percent—but neither of them had called for a vote, so it just remained a discussion. As a consequence of this decision not to decide, they spent two nights a few miles from Beattie's Trading Post near the Nevada-California border to make certain they missed the train entirely.

But here they were anyway, advancing on what was surely the same party they'd spied evidence of better than a week ago. Newton thought the tracks had probably stopped cold for one of the settlers since he and Tuck had first seen them. That was the story the buzzards seemed to be telling.

The problem was, the buzzards didn't know how to count.

Newt and Tuck did. They made it to be seventeen souls; eighteen when they got in a little closer and saw a woman lying on her side with an arm and shoulder hunched protectively around her dead child. Leastways, they supposed it was her child. There was no way of knowing for sure, but the fact that there was only a single bullet wound suggested it was a mother's selfless love that kept them joined in life and death.

Newt tied his kerchief around the lower half of his face as the odor of putrefying flesh assaulted his senses, carried as it was on the back of a gentle evening breeze. Out of the corner of his eye, he saw Tuck jerk up on the blue-and-white kerchief around his neck until it covered his mouth and nose.

They would be gravediggers now, Newt supposed, even if they looked like they meant to hold up a stage.

It took better than four hours to bury the dead. They struck at the hard ground with shovels and picks they took from the wagons. The tools that had been purchased to mine for gold in the California hills were put to practical use, one that didn't account for a man's dreams. They buried the mother and her child together and dug separate plots for everyone else. They covered the shallow mounds of dirt with rocks to keep predators from dragging bodies from the graves.

Newton found a Bible among the ransacked treasures, and he opened it at random to read a short passage over each grave after the last stone was set in place. Tuck listened, but he didn't bow his head, and he didn't offer any words of his own. He always waited for Newt to finish before he hefted the shovel he'd been leaning against and struck the ground again.

They finished by the light from half a dozen lanterns. Newton closed the Bible and slipped it under his arm. Tuck pitched the shovel as hard as he could. It clattered against a wagon wheel. He dropped to his haunches and set his hands on his knees. It wasn't the physical labor that left them tired and aching; it was the nature of the labor. They'd discarded the kerchiefs hours earlier, having gotten used to the stench, and took them out now to mop their brows. Their shirts were damp with sweat, and the cool night air raised the unnatural, bone-deep chill to the surface of their skin.

Tuck looked up at the sky. It was a clear night, hardly a

cloud. The stars hadn't strayed from their familiar pattern, and Tuck found solace in that. He always took calm where he could find it.

He put his hands at the small of his back and rose. Tall and rangy, he unfolded slowly, grimacing slightly as he felt the pull of muscle across his shoulders. "I guess we both know what happened here," he said finally.

"I guess we do." Newt carried the Bible over to the wagon where he'd found it and put it inside. "The question in my mind is now that we've buried the dead, what are we going to do about it?"

"Two of us. I make it to be five of them. Could be six."

"Six," said Newton. He'd looked over the tracks, same as Tucker, but he'd been a bit a longer at it. "That'd give us three men apiece. Not bad odds. Just about even, I'd say."

That raised Tuck's smile. "Folks are always saying how you got a head for numbers, but I don't get how they figure that."

Newt shrugged. He was half a head shorter than his friend, with shoulders half again as broad. He used the kerchief to swipe at his throat before he stuffed one corner into the waistband of his trousers. "They probably have two days on us, wouldn't you say?"

"About that."

"They went northwest."

"It looked to me like they rode out in pairs. Real precise they were. Probably couldn't help themselves."

Newton had seen that, too. "Soldiering leaves it's own kind of mark on a man, I reckon. They took all the horses. I suppose they mean to sell them." He looked to where a couple of cows still grazed on the hillside not far from the center of the attack. "What I can't figure is why they killed everyone."

"Ain't there a saying that dead men tell no tales?"

Newt nodded slowly, rubbed his chin. "They must have come from the same direction they left. They weren't following the train. They were waiting on it."

"I had the same thought. You come across a strongbox anywhere when you were poking around?"

"Didn't see one."

Tucker Jones grunted softly. "Neither did I. These people don't seem to have much in the way of valuables left."

"There're all kinds of buzzards."

Tucker grunted. "Can't sleep here," he said. "I don't mind saying so."

"One of us had to say it." Newton whistled softly for his horse. The mare had meandered to an outcropping of rocks and was snuffling between two boulders and scratching at the ground. "You take care of the lanterns while I get Dulcie before she gets herself stuck."

For the rest of their lives they would disagree about who heard the hollow cry first, but they sprinted toward the source of the sound and reached the outcropping at the same time.

Newton grabbed Dulcinea's reins and pulled her away while Tucker pressed his face against a narrow crevice in the rocks.

"What do you see?" Newt asked, quieting Dulcie.

"Shh. Can't see anything." Tuck turned his head and gave the opening his ear. At first he was met with silence, but he knew something about patience, and he counted out twenty-two long seconds in his mind before he heard the sharp release of a breath held too long. He straightened. "I need one of those lanterns."

While Tuck was retrieving it, Newt bent over the crevice and put his head in the same position. "Did you hear something?" he called after Tuck. "I don't hear it now."

"That's because you're talking."

Newt gave way a few inches to let Tuck dangle the lantern over the crevice. Both men tried to peer in. They bumped heads, swore softly, and it was Newton that gave way, but not before he glimpsed a pair of dark, expressionless eyes staring back at him. "Mother of God," he said under his breath. "That's a child. Is he alive?"

Tuck watched the pupils constrict in response to the light. "Alive."

"How'd he get in there?"

"A better question is how are we going to get him out."

True enough. Newt went in search of a crowbar while Tuck kept the lantern light above the child's upturned face.

"Dulcie must have startled him," Tuck said when Newt

returned. "I think he was sleeping. He's got some of the sand-man's grit about his eyes."

"What do you know about the sandman?"

Tuck shrugged and pointed to where Newton should set the crowbar. He explained to the child what they were going to do, but there was no reaction. Other than the soft cry when Dulcie surprised him, he hadn't made a sound. Other than blinking, he hadn't twitched.

"He puts me in mind of Lieutenant Carmichael," Tuck said, setting the lantern down. "Remember?"

"Monterrey," Newt said. "I remember. It's only been four years and a bit. That was the battle that struck him dumb. He was never right after his brother was killed. Are you saying that's what happened to this little fellow?"

"I'm just sayin', is all." Tuck helped Newt apply weight to the crowbar. "Just sayin'."

Both men grunted as the boulder shifted. Newt held it in place long enough for Tuck to reach inside the widened crevice and extract the child. As soon as Newt let go, the precarious arrangement of rocks began to slide. Tuck jumped out of the way of a boulder that would have rolled over his feet if he hadn't been alert to the danger. The lantern was crushed and the light extinguished.

Newt caught Dulcie's reins before the mare strayed too far. He led her across the loose rock to follow Tucker back to the wagons. He hitched Dulcie to the first wagon he came to while Tuck plucked another lantern from the ground and carried it and the child well past the freshly dug graves, the overturned and scattered belongings, and the eerily silent covered wagons.

It was anyone's nightmare.

Still shaking his head, Newt came to stand beside Tucker. His friend was on his knees in front of the child and looking about as helpless as Newt felt. The child they'd both assumed was a boy was wearing a red-and-white gingham dress.

"He's a girl," Newt said.

"I'm not disputing it."

"Does she have name?"

"Of course she has name. She's just not saying what it is, is all."

"We need to call her something."

"We'll come to that by and by."

"Has she said anything at all?" asked Newt.

"Not a word."

Newt also dropped to his knees. While Tuck was still a little taller than the girl in this same position, Newt met her at eye level. "How old are you?"

The child blinked but remained silent. She stared back without defiance or interest, not so much seeing him as seeing through him. It occurred to Newt that she was an empty vessel. Soulless. Her hair was as black as her eyes; pulled back from her forehead to make a tight braid that was coiled at the nape of her neck. Bits of dried blood dotted a scrape on her cheek, and there was a bruise just beside her right eye. The rocks were to blame, no doubt. She was just a wisp of a thing, skinny more than slender, all of her fragile boned, yet somehow still steady on her feet. The shoulder seam in her dress had a small tear, and her black leather boots were scuffed and layered with dust. Perhaps someone had hidden her away among the rocks for safety, but Newt was inclined to believe she'd found her own way there. She hadn't understood those boulders could become a tomb. She would have died under them if Dulcie hadn't come across her.

"Maybe some water," Newt said finally. "A little food. That might help." He started to rise and noticed for the first time that she was clutching something in her right hand. It looked like a tin. Slim and rectangular, slightly longer than the small fist she made around it, the side that he could see was painted red and white like her dress. "What's that in her hand?"

"I've been wondering myself."

"Have you asked her for it?"

"She's got no reason to give it to me. Way I figure, it's all she has in the world, so I'm lettin' her keep it."

"Somehow looks familiar to me," said Newt. "Could be I've had a tin like that myself." He finished straightening and it came to him. He snapped his fingers above Tuck's head. "Dr. Eli Kennedy's Comfort Lozenges. That'd be the peppermint she has. Spearmint comes in a green-and-white tin."

"Well, she can keep them," said Tuck. "In fact, she can keep the name, too."

"Eli? Now that makes no sense."

Looking up, Tuck gave Newton a withering glance. "Not Eli. We'll call her Comfort until she tells us different. Comfort Kennedy."

Newton thought about it, shrugged. "It'll do, I suppose. It's bound to be a puzzle trying to figure out who she is. Could be there will be kin back East; someone who will want to know what happened."

"Water first. Like you said. Get the jerky out of my bag."

Newt started to walk away, stopped, and then turned on his heel. "You're not thinking about keeping her, are you? We don't know anything about raising a baby. What are we going to do with her while we're prospecting?"

"A fool can see she's not a baby, and we can't leave her behind."

"We can take her back to the trading post."

"And leave her with strangers? That doesn't set right with me."

"*We're* strangers."

"But we can trust us," Tuck said practically. "Name someone else you can say that about."

Newt couldn't. "She's a *girl*."

"So? You told me you grew up with four sisters."

"You're making my point."

"It's only until we can find her kin."

"*If* there's kin."

"You said yourself there's bound to be kin."

Caught, Newt's mouth snapped shut.

Tuck arched an eyebrow. "Too late to take it back. Get her something to eat, and then you can nose around for clues. In the meantime, Comfort and me are going to sit right here quiet as snowfall and contemplate the stars. Seems like she needs a little peace. I know I do."

"This is the plumb dumbest notion you ever took into your head, Tucker Jones, and I haven't forgotten the time you drank half a bottle of tequila and proposed to that Mexican whore in Vera Cruz."

"True enough," said Tuck. "But I wasn't the one who married her."

Chapter One

Except for the fact that the guest of honor had failed to make an appearance, everyone who'd gathered to celebrate his birthday agreed he was missing a splendid affair.

Comfort Elizabeth Kennedy stood with her back to the granite balustrade on the portico and surveyed the activity in the grand salon. She'd closed the French doors behind her when she made her escape to the portico, but she didn't have to strain overmuch to hear the lilting melodies of the stringed orchestra or the titter and tattle of so many voices rising and falling in concert with the music. Woman after woman was led in a graceful arc past the beveled windows, blurring the definition of each gown until Comfort saw them as a single piece and held their luminescence in her eye as she would a rainbow.

One corner of her mouth lifted as she saw her Uncle Tuck taking his turn across the floor with Mrs. Barnes. He was duty bound to do so, as Uncle Newt had already danced with the widow. It wasn't competition that prompted each of them to invite every eligible woman to dance; rather, it was the very opposite of that. Neither wanted to show the least favoritism or become the subject of speculation in regard to any particular female.

Smile fading, Comfort turned away from the house. Torches lighted the circuitous path to the fountain situated squarely in the center of the wide expanse of lawn. She considered leaving the portico for the relative privacy of the garden, even moved a foot in that direction, but then came up short as she realized she didn't want to be that alone. For a moment she let herself do more than hear the three-quarter time of the waltz; she let herself feel it. She swayed, feet rooted, her side-to-side bent so slight as to merely suggest motion. Raising her head, she studied the night sky and found calm and order and the peace that had been snatched from her when Bram made his ridiculous announcement. And it *was* a ridiculous announcement. Spectacularly so.

She couldn't bring herself to place all the blame on his shoulders. Hadn't she gone along with him? Trusted him as if she had no mind of her own? Where was the sense in that? His own mother would have counseled her against it. Abraham DeLong meant well. That was at the crux of the problem. He always meant well. Comfort rarely felt as easy in anyone's presence as she did in Bram's. That was his effect on people, his special talent, and tonight, when she'd needed to keep her wits about her, he'd managed to make her forget the most fundamental truth: there were invariably unforeseen consequences for following Bram's merry lead.

The doors behind her opened. Comfort stiffened as the music momentarily swelled, and she wished that she had acted on the impulse to leave the portico in favor of the fountain. It was too late, of course. She was standing in a pool of torchlight and couldn't hope to slip unnoticed into the shadow of a marble column.

"So this is where you've gone," Bram said, closing the doors.

Comfort shrugged and purposely did not glance over her shoulder. If she didn't look at him, the odds improved that she would remain firm. Bram's reckless smile had caused hearts stouter than her own to seize.

"You're angry." He stood directly at her back and placed his hands on the balustrade on either side of her. If he dropped his chin, he could rest it in the curve of her neck and nuzzle her ear with his lips. He did neither of these things. "I can tell you're angry."

"Then there's no need to comment, is there?"

He chuckled softly. "How is it possible that you can be flush with heat and frigid in your sentiments? Butter won't melt in your mouth, but I could boil water for tea on the nape of your neck." Bram tilted his head to gauge her smile and saw that there was none. "Oh, you *are* mad."

Comfort lifted Bram's right hand from the balustrade and stepped sideways to elude capture. "I thought you understood that was a given." She turned and showed him her most withering look. True to form, he remained undaunted. Worse, she was afraid his smile was actually deepening. "You might have warned me that you intended to announce our engagement."

"You would have had no part of that."

"Precisely."

"Then I fail to understand how informing you would have helped. Everything would be just as it was at the outset of the evening when there was hardly an utterance that did not include the name of our sainted guest of honor. When is he coming? Where has he been? Will he be surprised? What could have detained him?" Bram's gaze slid from the fountain to Comfort. "I can tell you, Mother is mortified by his absence."

"Your mother is made of stronger stuff than that. I do not think she has the capacity for mortification." Comfort was tempted to point out that it seemed to be a DeLong family trait. "Even if you're right in this instance, Bram, what possessed you to make such an outrageous statement?"

"Didn't I just say? Everyone was talking about *him*. What is unreasonable about giving Mother's guests something else to discuss? And if you'll permit a small immodesty, I want to point out that Mother's event has been saved by my quick thinking. Our engagement put her over the moon."

Comfort took a slow, calming breath and chose her words carefully. "I appreciate that you want her favor, but did you consider even for a moment what her reaction will be when our engagement is summarily ended?"

Bram's gaze sought out the fountain again.

Comfort sighed. "I didn't think so." As there was nothing to say beyond that, Comfort simply joined Bram in his deep study of the torch-lit garden. She did not mind the silence settling between them, but experience told her it would be short-lived. Bram's inclination was to fill the void.

"Summarily," he said. "Why summarily?"

"Pardon?" Her mistake, she supposed, was that she turned to look at him in the same moment his grin was breaking wide, changing his features from merely handsome to indecently so. His pale blue eyes met hers with unwavering directness and issued a challenge that still managed to be boyishly charming and full of mischief. She found herself asking the question she did not believe she had the courage to voice: "You intend our engagement to end, don't you?"

"Of course."

Comfort was glad that she had steeled herself for just such a careless reply. He'd answered with no discernable hesitation. It was better that way, she told herself. She had nothing to grasp at, nothing that she would question later and perhaps attempt to interpret as uncertainty on his part. If he were uncertain, she would have cause to hope. Nothing good could come of that.

"Then summarily seems entirely appropriate," she said. She was relieved to hear herself sound so sensible. She concentrated on schooling her expression to be equally imperturbable. "As we are in agreement that the engagement must end, it should be done without delay."

One corner of Bram's mouth kicked up. Reaching out, he tapped Comfort on the tip of her nose with his index finger. "There it is again. Why should it be done without delay? Who says that's the better course?"

"I do."

"Well, yes, but I don't think you've thought it through."

Indignation made Comfort stiffen. "*I* haven't thought it through? You're saying that to *me*?"

Bram tapped her nose again. "Careful, dearest. You'll put this out of joint, and your lovely countenance will not be improved for it."

She slapped his hand away. "Stop acting the fool, Bram. I *am* angry with you. Do not test the limits of my patience."

Dutifully dropping his arm back to his side, Bram stood sharply at attention. Although he made the effort, he could not quite manage to affect a contrite mien. His mouth twitched.

Comfort stared at him. He'd recently run his fingers through his blond thatch of hair, and she quelled the urge to make the unruly runnels right again. Her fingers curled into loose fists at her side.

"If it will make you feel better," he said, "you can blacken my eye."

"Do not tempt me." She relaxed her hands. "What makes you think I'd blacken only one?" She was gratified to see that gave him pause. Gathering the unraveled threads of her composure, Comfort said, "If you don't believe our engagement—our *sham* engagement—should be ended quickly, then you'd better explain yourself. What you've begun involves more than just the two of us. I am also thinking of my uncles. They did not welcome your announcement with the enthusiasm of your mother."

"That's because I did not approach them first to state my intentions and ask for your hand. I grant you, that was an error of judgment on my part. There was no time to take them aside and do the thing properly."

"And *that's* because you acted on the engagement the moment you thought of it. Why *me*, Bram?" She waved a hand toward the salon, where his mother's guests continued to chatter and laugh and spin themselves about the floor oblivious to the small drama unfolding just beyond the doors. "Look there. Amelia Minter." Out of the corner of her eye, she saw him follow the sweep of her hand. She pointed again. "Deborah Brush. Oh, and there is Miss Arleta Ogden. All have something to recommend them besides the fact they're unattached. I know any one of them would have been pleased to participate in your scheme. I cannot think why you chose me."

Bram's eyebrows rose. He regarded her with surprise. "I believed that was obvious. Aren't you my friend, Comfort? I should have been well and truly snared if I'd put myself in reach of any of those young ladies. You were my only choice. I trust you."

There it was, Comfort thought. In her own way she was as predictable as he was. He'd never been disappointed by depending on her steadiness and good sense. "I should insist that you marry me," she told him. "It would serve you right if I took offense to my own nature and behaved as rashly as you." She took some solace from the small crease that appeared between his eyebrows. It would not last long, she knew, but he was momentarily wary.

"You wouldn't, would you?"

"God forbid."

Relieved, he leaned forward and bussed her on the cheek. "*This* is why I adore you."

Comfort was tempted to raise her palm to her face and make a shelter for the lingering imprint of his mouth. Resisting temptation was part and parcel of her long friendship with Bram DeLong. "And I adore you," she said, meaning it. "That doesn't release you from making a full explanation, however. If our engagement is not to be ended summarily, you will have to say how you mean for us to go on. Further, do not suppose for a moment that I will keep the truth from my uncles. You may say what you like to your mother, but Newton and Tucker will hear the truth from me."

Bram blinked. "Then I am a dead man."

Unmoved, Comfort shrugged.

"Although that will summarily end our engagement," said Bram.

For the first time since Bram joined her on the portico, Comfort smiled.

Bram chuckled. "Very well, I can hardly stop you from speaking freely to them. I hope you will find a way to soften the blow."

"And I hope you will not be offended, but I believe they will be relieved by the news. You are not what they hope for me, Bram. If they were still prospectors, they wouldn't stake a claim on you."

"A man who does not know his shortcomings as well as I do would take offense to your candor. It is to my credit, I think, that I am fully aware that my moral fiber is dangerously frayed."

Comfort laughed. "Only you can manage to turn a slight upon your character on its head. Enough. You have one more chance to state your intentions before I announce to everyone in the salon that you were only pulling their collective leg."

"Six months," he said quickly. "We will allow our engagement to run its course in six months. You will end it in whatever manner you choose, publicly if you wish."

"I would never do that."

He ignored her. "You may humiliate me, make me the villain, turn me out for being the fool that I am. It would serve me right."

"I'm sure it would, but you fail to appreciate how I would become an object of speculation and pity. We will end it quietly by simply dropping a word here and there with our most sympathetic but reliably indiscreet friends. The engagement will be ended that easily."

"All right."

"But six months?" she asked. "That is too long, Bram. You cannot manage to keep up appearances for so long, and I will not be made a fool while you troll the brothels for female companionship. Everyone knows where you take your entertainments."

Bram's lips twitched again. "Plain speaking, Comfort, even for you. Is your objection to brothels in particular or me having female companionship in general?"

His amusement twisted her heart, but she brought up her chin and narrowed her eyes in a way that put him on notice. "It is my opinion that perhaps you can abstain from visiting your usual haunts for six weeks."

"Only six weeks? Is it your contention that I behave like a satyr?"

"If the horns fit . . ." When he merely continued to stare at her, she added, "I said 'perhaps.' I am not confident you can stay away from the Barbary Coast that long."

"Are you challenging me?"

"No."

"It sounds as if you're challenging me."

"That's because you are filled with ridiculous notions this evening."

"Six months, Comfort. I can do it. I tell you, I am flirting with responsibility. It wasn't so long ago that I was dispatched to Sacramento to attend to matters of business for Black Crowne. I held my own with the governor. I sat at the same table with railroad men and their Pinkerton agents and didn't blink. Six months is nothing compared to spending an evening with legislators who require money for favors but aren't nearly as straightforward about it as whores." He realized his own speech had become rather plain, and he apologized.

She rolled her eyes. "I'm not asking for six months. Six weeks is sufficient. Moreover, people will expect that I come to my senses before then. If I wait as long as six months to end it, they will wonder at my discernment, and the public relies on my ability to recognize a good investment from a bad one. Jones Prescott is successful in part because of my facility for discriminating the levels of risk."

Now it was Bram DeLong who rolled his eyes. "Not everything you do is a reflection on the bank."

"You're wrong."

"I'm not, but I see that you believe it. I do not accept the same yoke, and it *is* a yoke, Comfort. Everything I do is *not* a refection on Black Crowne. I am a person separate from the family enterprise, and if you do not know that to be true, then ask my brother. He will tell you the same."

Comfort chose not to press him. Hadn't he just described his trip to the capital as a flirtation with responsibility? As far as she was concerned, Bram had made her point for her. "Six weeks," she said.

"Four months."

"Six weeks."

"Three months."

"Six weeks."

"Two months."

"That's eight weeks, Bram."

"Yes, I know."

"Very well." She was not gracious in concession. "But if I learn before then that you've been a visitor anywhere in the vicinity of Pacific Street, I will break the engagement immediately. If there is gossip about you, whether it's whoring or gaming, I will break your thumbs. You understand that would be painful, I imagine."

Bram had sense enough not to laugh. There was nothing in her expression to indicate that it was an idle threat. Comfort rarely spoke about her childhood, and there were likely only a dozen or so people who knew some of the truth, and only three that knew all of it, but in spite of the success of Jones Prescott, or perhaps because of it, there was always talk. The fact that the talk was mostly whispered seemed to lend it credence. It was possible that Miss Comfort Kennedy, she of the well-modulated voice and correct manner, might indeed know a thing or two about breaking a man's thumbs.

"Painful," said Bram. "Yes, I understand."

Comfort did not indicate that she was satisfied. She simply gave him her back and began walking toward the garden.

"Comfort."

She didn't turn. "Don't follow me, Bram." She could almost feel his hesitation. He wasn't used to being held at bay, and she had never had cause to do it before this evening. She was afraid the balance of their easy friendship had shifted, and if that were so, it fell to her to keep Bram from realizing it. She could not make herself that vulnerable. "Make some excuse for me. You'll think of something." Well outside of his hearing, she added, "You always do."

Even before she stepped onto the garden path, she heard the music swell and then recede as the door to the salon was opened and closed again.

She wondered how Bram would explain her prolonged absence, but the thought didn't occupy her. He had a gift for making explanations, and one would come to him far more easily than one would have come to her. His knack for making the most outrageous behavior seem reasonable, even acceptable, fascinated her. She could admit, at least to herself, that she was a little envious of his talent. Except in matters of virtually no consequence, she had an almost compulsive tendency to tell the truth. Lying came hard to her, and there were times when that was more curse than blessing.

Comfort veered away from the fountain. The steady rush of water was pleasant to her ears; the spray was not. She circled to the far side and followed the flickering torches all the way to the back of the garden. A hedgerow, carefully tended to take on a shape that was probably painful to its leaves and branches, bordered the rear of the property. Comfort removed one of her elbow-length gloves and ran her palm along the top of the hedge as she skirted the perimeter. She walked slowly, occasionally stopping to breathe deeply from the scent of the bay far beyond her. The ocean called to her from the opposite direction, still farther away, and in her mind she called back, taking the first tentative steps to the water's edge. A ship was waiting for her, a Black Crowne ship, bound for . . .

Adventure, she supposed. Yes. Bound for adventure.

"You look as if you wish yourself anywhere but where you are."

Startled, Comfort instinctively shied away from the voice. She required only a moment to recover her wits and the glove she'd dropped. Straightening, she stared down at the intruder, a circumstance that was made possible because he was lounging on a stone bench some three feet away.

"I might say the same of you," she said. It was difficult not to show her agitation as she pulled on her glove.

"I'm exactly where I wish to be."

"Your place is inside, Mr. DeLong. Your mother is expecting you. Her entire guest list is expecting you."

"And yet, I am here."

She noticed that he didn't stir. He remained in a half-reclining position in the corner of the bench, an arm extended across the scrolled back, one leg drawn up at the knee and the other stretched and angled in her direction. He regarded her without any particular interest, as if he were already bored by their brief exchange. It made her wonder why he'd spoken in the first place. She might easily have passed without noticing him. Almost immediately, she corrected herself. For reasons she did not entirely understand, failing to notice Beauregard DeLong had never been possible.

Comfort was glad of the shadow play across his face. His eyes were a most peculiar shade of blue-violet, and to be the subject of his study was to be pinned in place by twin points of light glancing off polished steel.

"Are you going inside?" she asked.

"I haven't decided. Are you?"

"I've been inside all evening, Mr. DeLong."

"Bode."

Comfort acknowledged this preference with a slight nod. She couldn't imagine that she'd ever be that familiar with him. From Bram she knew that his older brother's name had been too much of a mouthful, even for a child as precocious as Beauregard was alleged to have been. He repeated what he thought he was hearing all around him. Beauregard DeLong. Beau DeLong. Bode Long. The most difficult part of the story for Comfort to imagine was that Beau DeLong had ever been a child.

"Would you like to sit?" asked Bode.

As he didn't move, Comfort considered the invitation suspect. She had never thought of him as someone who embraced formalities, so perhaps it was only that he was tired of looking up at her. "No, thank you."

"As you like."

Bode didn't shrug, but it was as if he had. Comfort wondered that he could communicate so much carelessness in so few words. Nodding again, this time as a parting gesture, Comfort took the first backward step to remove herself from his presence. She came up short when he spoke.

"I noticed you and Bram in earnest discussion on the portico."

Comfort stared at him and said stiffly, "You should have made yourself known."

"Perhaps. I thought it impolite to interrupt."

"It is far more impolite to eavesdrop."

"It is. And so I came over here." A short, soft laugh rose from the back of his throat. "You don't believe me."

She didn't deny it. "I suppose I'm wondering at what point you left."

"Do you imagine listening to your conversation with my brother was a temptation? I assure you it was not. My only thought was escape. I saw you, and I left. And why wouldn't I? Your presence there gave me another opportunity to avoid that crush inside. Who are all those people?"

"Your friends."

"Do you think so?"

"Your mother and Bram say they are."

"Then they must be."

Comfort sighed. "You've known about this party, haven't you? For how long?"

"Just about as long as my mother."

She smiled a bit ruefully. His answer was not unexpected. "I suppose her excitement made all the secret planning perfectly transparent."

"Something like that."

Comfort had hoped for a less enigmatic reply. "You'll be appropriately surprised, won't you?"

"Is it important to you?"

Not understanding the question, she frowned. "To me? It's important to your mother."

"I'm certain it is, but that's not what I asked."

"I don't see why it matters." When he said nothing and let silence become a burden, she answered. "It's important to me because it will give your mother pleasure. She deserves that."

"We are all deserving."

"I hope so."

Bode tapped the back of the bench with his index finger. "What has your part been?"

"My part?"

"Mother elicited your support. She can't have a secretary to help her manage her affairs, so she relies on those trusted people within her sphere of influence." He paused, arching an eyebrow. "Are you going to tell me she didn't rely on you?"

"I assisted her with the guest list." One corner of her mouth lifted. "And the menu." The quirky line of her lips became more defined. "And the seating arrangements." Laughing softly, she added, "And I auditioned four separate stringed orchestras before I hired this one."

"Then you're also invested in the success of this party."

"I suppose I am."

He considered her answer for a long moment before he made his decision. "Then you'd better help me up."

Comfort stared at him. "Help you—" She stopped talking and rushed forward to lend assistance when he began to push himself to his feet. There was no mistaking that standing required his full attention and effort.

Comfort took his right arm and brought it around her shoulders, supporting him as best she could. She was tall, but he was taller still, and the fit presented no difficulty for either of them.

"What happened?" she asked. "Where are you injured?"

"My back."

She glanced at him, saw his grimace when he stepped forward, and paused to allow him to catch his breath. "Can you make it with only my assistance? Perhaps I should summon more help."

"I hobbled here on my own. Your support is sufficient." To prove it, he took a more confident step. This time his lips didn't twist into a perversion of a smile. "By the time we reach the doors, I'll be able to walk unaided."

Comfort kept her doubts to herself. She slid an arm around his waist to steady him. "You haven't said what happened."

"No, I haven't."

Recognizing that she held the upper hand, no matter how briefly, Comfort decided to take advantage. She stopped cold and halted his forward progress. For the first time since happening upon him, torchlight bathed Bode's face, and when Comfort's glance swiveled sideways, she saw clearly what the shadows had concealed.

His face was distorted by the swelling in his left cheek. It was only a matter of time before it took over his eye. Dried blood defined a slash just below and a little to the right of his chin. A cut on his forehead disappeared into his hairline.

She sighed with great feeling. "Did you give as good as you got?"

"At least that good, I hope."

"The police? They were notified?"

"And further delay my arrival? No. I didn't make a report."

"I see. What happened to the miscreant who assaulted you?"

"Miscreants," he corrected, offering a slim smile. "All away, I fear, run off by a gang of young ruffians who then relieved me of my money and what remained of my dignity."

"Then you'll have no justice."

"It seems unlikely."

Comfort braced herself to take Bode's weight again. "I think we should use an entrance other than the salon."

"That was my intention before I came upon you and Bram. The first side door I tried to use was barred."

"Bram insisted. He was concerned that with so much attention on the salon, the rest of the house was ripe for plunder.

I think we'll find the servants' entrance open. If not, I can slip inside the salon and find someone who will open it." She slowed their progress as they reached the fountain and invited him to rest for a moment.

Bode refused the offer. "Too many kinks to work out," he said. "It's better if we keep going."

"Very well, but if your back seizes again, allow me to shoulder more of your weight." She was uncertain of his response. It might have been laughter; it might have been a growl. Neither communicated cooperation. When she considered it, it was rather astonishing that he'd asked for her help at all. That must have pained him every bit as much as his back.

"Where were you assaulted?"

"Not more than fifty yards from the Black Crowne warehouse."

"So you were on your way home."

"I was on my way here."

The distinction was not lost on Comfort. Bram lived in the family home with his mother. Bode lived above the shipping offices on Montgomery Street and had done so since returning from the war. Comfort was not privy to the reason Bode chose to live apart from his family, and Bram was often uncharacteristically tight-lipped where Bode was concerned. Her encounters with Bode had always been brief, mostly in passing, and for her at least, accompanied by a fine element of tension that annoyed her and appeared to amuse him. Bram made a point of steering her clear of Bode when he was around, but she had a niggling suspicion that this was done more for Bram's sake than hers. "Will you recognize your assailants if you see them again?"

"Which ones?"

"The ones that waylaid you first."

"Then no, but I think I know where to find the young ruffians. They might be able to identify the others, if they can be compelled to talk. On principle, they're against speaking out."

"Honor among thieves?"

"More likely fear of retaliation if any one of them talks. And by retaliation, I mean disfigurement or death. My attackers were probably Rangers."

The Rangers were the most fearsome of the gangs operating in the Barbary Coast. No one faced them down, although the newspapers regularly pointed out their vices, reported the harrowing accounts of their victims, and called for them to be rounded up and expelled from the city.

Comfort felt Bode's eyes on her again, as though trying to decide what she knew or had heard about the Rangers. Had he meant to shock her or prove to himself that she could not be shocked? If it was a test, she had no idea whether she passed or failed. She was relieved when they reached the portico and Bode indicated that they would go on. They were more than halfway to their goal.

"You were fortunate to have survived the encounter," she said evenly. "I've never heard of the Rangers being run off by anyone."

"That occurred to me also, but those boys swarmed like locusts." He gestured toward the servants' entrance. "The kitchen will be as crowded as the salon," he said. "But I think I know all of the staff. I can't say the same for the guests."

Comfort ignored that. If the guest list included people he did not count as his friends, he was still acquainted with them. They were business associates, men of power and influence, traders, bankers, railroad men, politicians, and speculators, and Beau DeLong stood shoulder to shoulder with them. They'd come to wish him well, and quite possibly to use the opportunity to settle some bit of business, but mostly they'd come to wish him happy on his thirty-second birthday.

"There is considerably less hesitation in your step," she said.

Bode nodded. "You can ease away if you like."

"When we reach the door."

They negotiated the stone steps that led down to the kitchen with considerable care. Comfort was glad she hadn't abandoned him. He was favoring his left leg, and she suspected the injury to his back was now radiating pain as far as his knee.

"I understand the bruises and cuts to your face," she said. "But what happened to your back? Were you kicked?"

The truth was less palatable. "Tripped."

"You tripped or you were tripped?"

"Is that an important distinction?"

"Perhaps not to you, Mr. DeLong, but I would like to know if there's amusement to be had at your expense or if I must continue to feel sorry for you."

"I stumbled over my own feet trying to avoid the point of a knife."

"Well," she said, vaguely disappointed. "It's difficult to know how to respond to that." Comfort reached for the door and turned the knob, testing whether she'd be able to ease it open. At first she thought it was barred, but a second push made it give way. "If you don't want to be seen, I can manage to distract the staff long enough for you to take the back stairs to your old bedroom. I'll send Hitchens to you. He'll see to your cuts and draw you a bath."

"Send Sam Travers. Hitchens will report to Alexandra straightaway."

It struck her oddly that he referred to his mother by her Christian name, but she didn't comment. "All right." She looked him over, gauging his ability to manage the staircase on his own. The narrowness of the passage would assist him, because he could brace himself on either side as he climbed. "Shall I tell Bram that you've arrived?"

"No." He touched his swelling eye. "There will be no hiding this. Does any reasonable explanation come to mind?"

"I'm afraid not." Comfort wondered what it was about his brief, mocking smile that drew her attention away from his eye. "Bram is the one you should ask."

"Yes, he is." He fell silent for a moment. "No matter. Something will occur to me."

Regarding the whole of his battered face again, Comfort meant her smile to be encouraging, but she suspected it lacked confidence. She had never heard anything about Beauregard DeLong that led her to believe he had a facility for telling less than the bald truth. It made him feared. Indeed, all evidence to the contrary, now that he'd set his jaw tightly enough to make a muscle jump in his cheek, he was not a man who had been beaten. She did not think he had ever needed her help, or perhaps anyone's.

Disquieted by his steady, frank regard, Comfort felt her smile fading. For the second time in the course of the evening,

she wished herself anywhere but where she was. Giving him
the faintest of nods, she turned away to slip into the kitchen,
where the activity remained loud and furious. She hadn't taken
a step when she felt Bode's fingertips brush her elbow. She
wanted to ignore him. Instead, she looked back.

"Does my brother know that you're in love with him?"

Of all the things he might have said, this question was easily
the least expected. Comfort knew what it was to have the blood
drain from her face, and she felt it again now. A chill crept
under her skin, and beneath the smooth crown of her ebony
hair, her scalp prickled.

"Yes," she said. She spoke quickly, too quickly, and it made
her wonder how he would interpret it. She swallowed, all but
choking on the lie, and was unnaturally pleased that she
could meet his gaze directly. On the heels of that hubris, she realized that it was truer that she couldn't look away. She did
what was left to her and made her features expressionless.
"That is, I should hope so. He announced our engagement this
evening."

Bode's expression merely became thoughtful. "Did he?"

"Yes."

"Then you have my con"—an infinitesimal pause—"grat-
ulations."

Comfort felt certain he'd wanted to say con*dolences*. That
tiny pause had been deliberate, pregnant with meaning, and
she should have bristled in defense of Bram, or at least in
defense of herself. What she did, though, was incline her head
and accept his words at face value. "Thank you."

"That remains to be seen."

Comfort's nostrils flared slightly, but she made no reply.

"I saw you," he said simply. "On the portico. I told you that."

Comfort understood then that she had no better evidence
that Bode hadn't overheard any part of her conversation with
his brother. His eyes told him a story his ears wouldn't have.

"I saw *both* of you."

Now Comfort had his full meaning. "I've been told to expect
more directness from you, Mr. DeLong. Say it. Say all of it."

"Bram doesn't love you, Miss Kennedy."

Having it put before her so bluntly, even though she'd

demanded that he do so, still had the power to make her heart falter. "I believe your brother will disagree with you."

"I'm sure he will. He frequently does. It doesn't mean I'm wrong." He leaned his shoulder against the inside wall, not casually, but for support, a small concession to his injuries. "Don't misunderstand. I'm aware you and Bram have been friends for years. He probably cares more for you than he does for anyone else of his acquaintance, and he could well mistake that circumstance for love, but you should know that it's not."

"Perhaps what it is," she said, "is enough."

He was quiet for a moment before he conceded, "I hadn't considered you might take that view."

"Now you know." She spoke with a certain directness that effectively ended their conversation. Careful not to give Bode any indication that she was in full and hasty retreat, Comfort swung her skirts to the side and left the entry alcove for the relative calm of the kitchen.

Newton Prescott slipped a finger between his stiff shirt collar and his Adam's apple and tugged. He'd probably been more uncomfortable in his life, but just now no specific memory was coming to him. The salon was warm, and for some reason that defied good sense, the doors to the outside remained closed. He had always suspected that Alexandra DeLong's blood ran cold, and here was proof. Lord, but he could think of no greater pleasure right now than sitting in his own home with his slippers on and feet up.

He surveyed the gathering as best he could without finding a box to stand on. Mrs. Rodham's smooth, white shoulder kept getting in the way. In any other circumstance, it would have been a pleasure to look at, but right now it was a distraction and an obstacle. Although Newt was not engaged in conversation with his present company, he nevertheless excused himself from their circle and maneuvered sideways to reach the inner perimeter of the dance floor.

Across the room, he saw Tucker engaged in a similar scan of their surroundings. Tuck had the advantage of height, and he was able to make his survey from deeper in the crowd. Newt noticed that Michael Winter was yammering in Tuck's ear, oblivious to Tuck's attention being elsewhere. Newt caught Tuck's eye when that dark gaze came around to him. Their communication would have been imperceptible to anyone looking in their direction, but the exchange of nods and glances had them moving simultaneously toward the overflow of guests in the hallway, and then to the front parlor, and finally to the relative quiet of what had been Branford DeLong's sanctuary within the house when he was alive: the library. It was also the place where Branford regularly cornered and groped the prettiest of his house servants, willing or not. Newt had once overheard Branford confide that the walls of books deadened the sound of so much sweet moaning. Having it from the horse's mouth, Newt never questioned the gossip about Branford DeLong's interest in women outside of his marriage, an interest that necessarily came to an end when Branford was killed running a Union blockade near Hampton Roads, Virginia.

At the time of his death, it was rumored that Alexandra Crowne DeLong made peace with her husband's affairs and indiscretions, but that she would never, *ever* forgive him for taking up the Confederate cause. Newt reckoned it was true. Alexandra's family probably built the *Mayflower* before they boarded it.

Newt leaned against the library door to keep other guests out. Tuck was already hitching a hip on the edge of Branford's massive mahogany desk.

"Where d'you suppose she's gone?" asked Newt. "I haven't seen her for the better part of an hour."

"Bram disappeared for a while. Did you notice?"

Newt nodded. "I thought he'd come back with her."

"Our little girl has a mind of her own."

Their little girl was a woman full grown, twenty-five on her last birthday, but Newt didn't remind Tuck of what he already knew. "Six proposals of marriage," he said instead. "Six. And *this* is the one she accepts. That must be the very definition of a mind of one's own."

"Must be."

Newt frowned. "Is it our fault?" he asked suddenly, rubbing his broad brow. "Something we did?"

Tuck folded his arms across his chest. "Something we did

that made her stubborn? Or something we did that made her stupid?"

"Oh, I know she gets her cussedness from us."

"Then I expect we also have to take some responsibility for stupid."

Newt accepted that Tuck was right, but he wasn't happy about it. His broad brow remained furrowed. "Remind me, what was it about that McCain boy we didn't like?"

"Shifty."

"And Fred Winslow's oldest son?"

"Shiftless."

"Theodore Dobbins?

"Full of shift."

Chuckling, Newt felt the tightness in his chest ease. "Who does that leave?"

"Jonathan Pitt."

"Over my dead body."

"And Richard Westerly."

"Over your dead body."

Tuck nodded. "There you have it. We've come to Abraham DeLong."

"She didn't ask us what we thought."

"Could be she didn't want to know, or could be she knows and didn't want to hear." He drew in a deep breath and released it slowly. "You harbor any doubts that she loves him?"

Newt tugged at his shirt collar again. "There's a couple or three ways to look at that, so hell yes, I have doubts. We agree our girl has a mind of her own, but that doesn't mean she knows her own mind. I can't figure if she loves him or just thinks she does."

"Does it matter?"

"Maybe not. I can't find a way to make anything good come of it, and when it's all said and done, and her heart's brittle and breaking, she'll blame herself."

"That's her way," said Tuck. "Always has been. Remember how she was when we found her, all hollowed out, nothing but empty black eyes and a shell of body that looked like it would shatter if she sucked in enough air to catch her breath?"

"I remember."

"And all those years going by while she carried around that

little red-and-white tin like it was something real special, when what she was doing was reminding herself that it was her fault for what happened to those pilgrims."

"I recollect that, too."

"That's her nature," Tuck said. "We can't undo her nature, so I suppose what we can do is take her in when it all goes to hell in a handcart."

"I reckon that's right." Newton's cheeks puffed as he blew out a breath. "Did you suspicion things were going to take a turn tonight?"

"I had a feeling."

"You should have told me."

"I thought it was indigestion. I had the clams."

Newt made a sound at the back of his throat that communicated his displeasure. "Seems like there's no choice but to go along with this engagement."

"Seems like."

Newt kicked the door hard enough to make it shudder. "Damn it, Tuck. Bram DeLong should have asked us for Comfort's hand. The way he did it, it was disrespectful."

Tucker put out a hand. "Easy. We don't need company on account of you causing a ruckus." He waited for Newton's shoulders to go from hunched to brooding. "Bram's spoiled."

"I'm not arguing that."

"Comes from having a face like an angel, I expect."

Newt stared at Tucker. "He has a face like an angel?"

Tucker shrugged. "I've heard women say that. He looks regular to me."

Newt just grunted.

Tucker pushed himself away from the desk and stood. "We'd better go back. If Comfort's not with Bram by now, you look for her outside. I'll look around upstairs. Maybe Alexandra's cornered her and they're planning the wedding."

And because Newt looked as if he wanted to kick the door again, Tucker hurried over and opened it.

Bram went to Comfort's side the moment he saw her on the threshold of the salon. Before anyone close to her could remark on her absence, he captured her wrists and held them out on either side of her. Smiling warmly, he cocked his head and made a thorough study of her.

"Your gown has been repaired beautifully. Didn't I tell you that Mary Morgan was extraordinarily talented with a needle and thread?"

So that was the explanation he'd given for her disappearance. It was rather uninspired as excuses went but thoroughly serviceable. "Indeed," she said, turning slightly to show off the sixty-five-inch train that was de rigueur for a proper ball gown. "I defy you to find the rend."

Bram chuckled. "You know I cannot." He released one of her wrists and drew the other forward until he had her arm secured in his. With a brief apologetic smile to the guests closest to them, Bram led Comfort onto the floor and swept her into the waltz with a grace that made it seem effortless.

Comfort smiled up at him. "I am always a better dancer when you're my partner."

"I know. And I'm a better partner when I'm dancing with you."

Her smile reached her dark, coffee-colored eyes. "Have you always known the right thing to say?"

"I think so, yes."

She laughed.

The sweet sound of it washed over Bram like a cool, cleansing spring rain. For reasons he did not entirely understand, it sobered him. "I'm sorry, Comfort. I mean it."

She could have said that he always meant it. Underscoring that point seemed petty. "I know," she said. "We'll manage. It is only for six weeks, after all."

"Eight," he said. "That was the hard bargain you struck."

"I was merely confirming that you remembered."

Bram regarded her in a way he hadn't done before. His last study had been for the benefit of his guests, and he realized he'd barely seen her. This he did for himself, taking in the upsweep of her thick black hair and the exposed vulnerability of the nape of her neck. Comfort did not meet any standard of beauty. Her mouth, especially her bottom lip, was too generously proportioned; her eyes, a fraction too widely spaced and a bit too large for her face. Her nose was unremarkable, neither turned up prettily nor refined in the manner of the blue bloods. Tall and slender, she had no curves to speak of except those that were compliments of the construction of her evening gown. Beneath the red-and-white-striped silk dress, a pannier crinoline exaggerated the definition of her hips and derriere, while the formfitting cuirass and décolletage gave the impression of fuller breasts than she'd been endowed with by nature.

And yet, he thought, while no single feature would inspire the poets to put pen to paper, Comfort Kennedy could inspire a man to be better than he was. Newton Prescott and Tucker Jones believed that. They credited her with all their success. Looking at her now, with her darkly solemn eyes and slim, reserved smile, Bram realized he believed it as well.

Who would he be, Bram wondered, if he were a man better than himself?

And the answer came to him: Bode.

It was like a blow, and Bram's breath hitched. His timing off, he made a misstep and could not catch himself quickly enough to steer Comfort clear of the same mistake. She stumbled. He corrected their course by lifting her slightly and then steadying her on the downbeat.

Comfort regarded him curiously. "What is it?"

"Nothing. That is, nothing that matters. A stray thought, is all. My mind wanders."

"Yes, it does," she said.

Bram heard no accusation in her tone, only acceptance. Was that how she did it? he wondered. Did she make a man better by embracing who he was until he expected something more of himself?

"You're really very lovely, Comfort," he said, and realized he meant it.

"Pretty compliments?" she asked, her indifferent tone at odds with the creeping color in her cheeks. "Save them for someone who will truly have you, Bram. You know I am not that woman."

Chapter Two

Bode stood back from the mirror and regarded his reflection critically. Travers had done what he could to make the evening clothes presentable, but a thorough brushing had not removed all of the mud spatter from the trousers or erased the dark droplets of blood near the collar of his starched linen shirt. Travers had also drawn a hot bath for him, and while the soak and scrubbing helped revive him to a near human state and eased the stiffness in his back, it couldn't erase the swollen and blackening eye or the scalp wound.

"Get me one of Bram's shirts," he said. "I can't wear this." He started to shrug out of his jacket, grimaced, and murmured his thanks when Travers stepped forward to help him. "You don't think I should join the party, do you?"

"It's not for me to say."

There was no mistaking that it was a tart reply, and Bode noticed that Bram's valet was careful to avoid eye contact. That was answer enough. "I imagine I'll never be forgiven for leaving you behind when I moved out."

"No, sir."

Chuckling, Bode began unbuttoning his shirt while Travers placed the jacket over the back of a chair. "That's more like it. I value your opinion, you know."

A proper valet might have offered a haughty sniff. Travers

snorted. He was a small, wiry man who had once moved through the rigging of the majestic Black Crowne clippers with the agility of a monkey. The collapse of a burning mast had crushed his right leg some fifteen years earlier, and while there were those who said he'd been fortunate not to lose it, he still chafed at the brace that helped support his weight and often wondered if he'd have been better off with a peg. He knew men who still worked the ships with a peg. The brace made him ungainly. Worse, it made him rattle. He remembered what it was like to move with the stealth of fog. Now his comings and goings were announced by creaks and clanks, and no amount of oil to the hinges silenced all that racket at once.

Bode's fingers paused on the last button. "You heard Bram's engaged?"

"I heard."

"What do you think?"

Travers lifted an eyebrow. "I think you might have left it to too late. That's what comes of taking care of everyone but yourself." He pointed to Bode's swollen eye. "Look at what you have to show for it. Bram's stealing Comfort and you're getting none."

Bode supposed he deserved the opinion he asked for. "She loves him."

"Of course she does. Bram wouldn't have it any other way."

Bode shrugged out of his shirt. "She might even be good for him."

"No doubt about it. Still, I had it in my mind that you need her more."

It wasn't a new idea to Bode either. He said nothing.

"And would be better for her, too." Grinning widely, Travers held out one hand for Bode's shirt. "This is for the rag bin." He swung around, dragging his leg slightly.

"I have a plan, Sam."

Samuel Travers paused and rubbed his bony chin with his knuckles. "Never occurred to me that you didn't. You always were a real good thinker, Bode."

Bode gave him a pointed look and gestured toward the door. "The shirt, Sam." It wasn't until Travers was gone that Bode allowed himself the indulgence of a sympathetic smile. He'd known when he left home that he was abandoning the man who had mentored him more than his own father, but leaving Sam behind had been done for a purpose. Bram needed mentoring now, although judging by tonight's behavior, Bode had good reason to wonder how much his younger brother was open to influence.

He leaned toward the mirror and examined the cut on his scalp. Ruffling his thick, dark copper hair around the wound, he attempted to hide it. His mother would notice, though perhaps the other guests wouldn't look past his eye. *That* was going to be a shiner. He only remembered having had one like it before, and he'd been about twelve on that occasion. At least he'd been proud of that one, earned as it was for defending Bram from a trio of bullies. That was twenty years and three thousand miles ago. Most often the score of years seemed less distant than the geography. He was still looking out for Bram.

Travers's return brought Bode out of his reverie. He accepted help slipping into the shirt and put up with Travers fussing about the fit of the jacket until the valet began making soft clucking noises. Stepping away from the mirror's unforgiving reflection, Bode put out a hand.

"Enough," he said. "There's no more that can be done. Certainly no one's going to blame you if I'm turned out like a sow's ear instead of a silk purse."

"A lot you know. Your mother will say I shouldn't have turned you out at all. Send for the doctor, that's what she'll want to do."

"Well, there are probably three of them downstairs, so it's more likely I'll be trampled when they rush forward to do her bidding."

"There is that." The momentary gleam in his eye said that he approved. Sobering, he looked Bode over, and then tilted his head toward the door. "Go on. Have a care you don't upset your mother more than you can help it."

As advice went, it was exactly what Bode knew he needed to hear.

Alexandra DeLong captured Comfort as soon as Bram released her at the end of the waltz. She crooked a finger at her son and kept him from slinking off. "Come with me, both of you. There are still more guests that want to congratulate you, and I won't have you slipping away again either alone or together. Do neither one of you have any sense of what is expected?"

Very much afraid that Bram would be unable to conceal his amusement, Comfort did not hazard a glance in his direction. Alexandra was a formidable presence, a force of nature on the order of earthquakes and tidal waves, and she did not suffer anyone opposing her for long. Determined and forthright, she made her opinions known, and for those who lacked her clarity of purpose or principle, she was entirely capable of making her opinion theirs.

Comfort dutifully allowed herself to be moved through the guests lined six and seven deep close to the ice sculpture and lemonade drinks fountain and deposited next to her uncles. Their expressions told her they'd been swept up in Alexandra's wake as well.

"Apparently we haven't accepted everyone's best wishes," Tucker whispered as Comfort leaned in to kiss him on the cheek.

When she did the same to Newt, he said, "If I die right here, don't let them bury me with this idiotic smile on my face."

Comfort tamped her own smile as she turned to offer herself for Alexandra's inspection. At her side, she felt Bram's fingers close over two of hers and squeeze gently. Comfort had always suspected that Bram might be a little afraid of his mother, and she accepted that his gesture was as much to steady his own nerves as it was to steady hers. She'd never told him that while she sometimes stood in awe of Alexandra Crowne DeLong, she wasn't afraid of her.

Alexandra looked over her impromptu receiving line with the gimlet eye of a shipmaster examining his crew. Behind her, the ice sculpture at the center of the fountain dripped steadily, but its shape was still recognizable as the flagship of the Black Crowne fleet, the *Artemis Queen*. Alexandra might have been the inspiration for its figurehead. She stood like the immortal huntress, shoulders back, chin up, prepared to challenge anyone who did not meet her approval. At fifty, she was a handsome woman, though in her youth she had never been beautiful or even what passed for pretty. She'd once confided to Comfort that she'd grown into her features, and given the length of her nose, the narrowness of her face, and the bony definition of her jaw, it was the best she could hope for.

Her hair was her vanity. Thick and lustrous, it was a deep shade of red and only beginning to reveal threads of silver. For tonight, it had been arranged in a smooth coil and artfully accented with white rosebuds. More rosebuds, this time in silk, trimmed the tiered flounces of her ball dress.

"You'll do," she said at last. She speared Newt with a second glance. "Stop fussing with your collar."

Newt's hand dropped to his side with such alacrity that even Alexandra was moved to smile.

Inclining her head toward him, she said quietly, "Ask Bram for the name of his tailor. A thick-necked man like yourself can benefit from a good fitting." She straightened, nodded her approval a second time, and moved into position beside her son. Almost immediately there were guests advancing on them.

Comfort, suddenly recalling Bode's description of the young ruffians as a swarm of locusts, had an urge to take a step back. These people were much better dressed, but Comfort believed they were capable of picking her bones clean, even if they'd leave her pockets untouched. A sideways glance at her uncles warned her they felt similarly, and probably weren't as confident that their pockets were safe.

Feeling every bit the pretender she was, Comfort nevertheless managed to accept the kind sentiments expressed by Alexandra's guests. While her response tended to be reserved, she couldn't help noticing that Bram was considerably more at his ease, cheerfully managing the fraud as though it were sport. She was not endeared.

Had she not been so aware of his good humor, Comfort wouldn't have sensed the change in him as quickly as she did. It was not a difference of tone or manner, but one of temperature. Where their fingers touched, his had gone cold. She was still trying to think what to make of it when the orchestra abruptly stopped playing.

Her attention, like everyone else's in the room, was drawn to the cause of the disruption. Bram's fingers threaded in hers, and this time it seemed to Comfort that he wasn't offering what might pass for encouragement. It seemed, rather, that he was clutching her.

Perhaps he was, she thought. His brother looked like hell as he straightened from having the violinist's ear. Whatever efforts Bode took to make himself presentable, they weren't sufficient. On the other side of Bram, Comfort heard Alexandra inhale sharply. This was followed by a similar intake of breath from many of the female guests. To Comfort, it seemed as if the air had been sucked out of the salon. Seeing Arleta Ogden weave unsteadily, she supposed it was a good thing Bode took the time to scrub away the blood. There might have been fainting otherwise.

Comfort was tempted to curl her lip at Miss Ogden's dramatics. Instead, she remained politely fixed on Bode as he prepared to address his mother's guests. She felt certain that she knew what he was about to say. Her lips moved around the word even as he spoke it.

"Surprise."

And just like that, there was air to breathe. Bode's voice might have been a stone skipping across the glassy surface of a pond. Tension broken, light laughter rippled through the salon. Even Alexandra was able to give up a faint smile. Bram's hand felt warm again.

"I apologize for the lateness of my arrival," Bode said. He pointed to his swollen eye. "I don't know what explains this except for the lowering truth that I should not go poking around my own warehouse with a walking stick and no lantern when there are boxes and barrels so precariously stacked that a mother cat and a litter of kittens can push them down on my head."

Comfort blinked. The lowering *truth*? What happened to the Rangers and the ruffians? She watched as Bode scanned the gathering with his good eye. Before she could look away, he found her. He only held her gaze for a moment, but she knew a warning when she was given one. Bode's cautions were as sharp as darts. He'd learned something about a gimlet-eyed stare from his mother and showed he could use it to good effect.

"Please," he said, gesturing to the musicians to pick up their instruments. "I hope you will forgive the interruption and go on as you have. It seemed prudent to make one explanation rather than dozens."

"More like a hundred," Newt said in an aside to Tucker. It came out more loudly than he'd intended, but then again, he was a thick-necked man and had a voice that touched all the bass notes before it left his lips. He smiled unapologetically as Alexandra turned a disapproving eye on him.

"Thank you, Mr. Prescott," Bode said. "It is easily a hundred." As though in sympathy, he mirrored Newt's unconscious gesture of tugging on his collar. He was glad for an excuse to do it, because Bram's shirt was an uncomfortably close fit. "And nearing a hundred degrees. Let's open the doors, shall we? Mother? You don't object?"

Alexandra capitulated graciously. "Whatever you like, Bode. It's your birthday."

"Well then, I do like." He extended his hand toward her. "Will you take the floor with me?" When she nodded, he stepped forward to go to her. Guests parted for him. He permitted Alexandra a moment to frown and fuss as she examined his face before he took her arm and led her into the clearing made for them. "Everyone," he called out just as the music began. "Pretend you've wished me happy and go about the important business of enjoying yourself."

Comfort watched Alexandra as Bode turned her on the floor. Her smile was unrestrained and her skin fairly glowed. She looked a decade younger than her fifty years.

Bram jerked his chin in the direction of his brother. "He looks just like our father. She loved the good-looking bastard."

"Mind your language," Tucker growled.

"Pardon me," said Bram. "You're right. I forgot myself. I meant to say handsome bastard."

Comfort set her jaw so she wouldn't laugh out loud, but her eyes warned Bram that he needed to apologize. It wasn't that Tuck objected to blue language, only that he objected to it being said around her. When he thought he was outside of her hearing, he favored certain expressions that would put color in a sailor's cheeks. She might have given in to her amusement if

Newt hadn't stepped away from his post and invited her to take a turn with him. She accepted his offer gratefully.

"Tucker can be a bit of a prude at times, and that's nothing I've not said to his face," Newt told her. "Not that I approve of Bram's language either, but I would have taken him aside and said as much, not made a point of it in front of you. That's not the way it's done."

"His father was a thorough bastard, though."

Newt gave a shout of laughter. "That's my girl." Comfort had to guide him through the next few steps while he recovered his timing. "Do you think Bode knows about your engagement to Bram? He didn't mention it."

"I imagine his mother is telling him now." It was odd, Comfort thought, how she could manage to avoid an outright lie by not quite answering the question that was asked.

"Tuck and I were surprised by Bram's announcement," Newt said.

"I saw that."

"We were thinking he should have said something to us beforehand."

"I told him that. He thought he was being modern."

"Is that what he's calling it?"

Comfort thought it best not to make any response. Uncle Newton was a single syllable away from a tirade.

"How do you suppose Bode will take it?" asked Newt.

"I haven't thought about it."

"Perhaps you should. He's steering Alexandra this way, and unless I miss my guess, we're about to change partners."

Comfort's distress was real, although she forgave her uncle for thinking she was merely flattering him by pretending not to want to leave his side.

"Chin up, Comfort," he said, bussing her on the cheek before he turned her over to Bode. "At least you won't have to worry that he'll tread on your toes."

Overhearing this, Alexandra looked alarmed at the prospect of Newton doing as much to her beautifully shod feet. She made one last appeal to her son as Newt led her away. When it was clear Bode wasn't going to change his mind and rescue her, she flung the accusation of heartlessness at him.

Comfort observed that the epithet had no impact. It didn't come as a surprise. "Perhaps you *are* heartless."

"This can't be the first time you've thought it."

It wasn't, and she realized she must have shown that in some small way, because he gave her a smile that hinted at superiority. "Smug is an expression not suited to a man with only one useful eye."

"Your point is well made."

"Oh, I know I made it well. It begs the question, was it taken?" She heard him laugh softly. The sound lingered at the back of his throat, aging like a fine wine before it touched his lips. Realizing that she was staring at his mouth, she quickly lifted her gaze. His pathetically swollen eye looked painful; his good one looked amused. "Is there something particular that you want, Mr. DeLong?"

"Bode. I'm going to be your brother-in-law."

"Bode," she repeated. "Now, will you take me back to Bram?"

"In a moment. It doesn't hurt for my friends to see that I'm pleased with the engagement."

"You told me you don't have friends here."

"I'm making some."

Comfort had never heard that Beau DeLong possessed a shred of humor. His reputation was for working hard and then working harder. She didn't trust this man holding her. She wasn't even sure who he was. Her regard grew suspicious. "Did they club you on the head?" she asked.

"They?"

"The mother cat and her litter."

"Oh. I might have a lump or two at the base of my skull."

Comfort peered more closely at his good eye to see if the pupil was contracting properly. She couldn't tell without holding a candle flame close to it.

"What are you doing?" he asked.

"Trying to determine if you're concussed." She thought it was to his credit that he didn't ask why. Some part of him must know he was behaving strangely. "You've danced with me longer than you danced with your mother," she said. "And done so beautifully in spite of your injuries. I imagine everyone is convinced that you are over the moon at the prospect of having me become a member of your family. Now, please, escort me back to Bram."

"When this piece is ended." He glanced in his brother's direction. "Bram appears to be deeply engaged in conversation with Tuck."

That did not ease Comfort in the least. "If they're talking politics, it can't end well."

Bode didn't disagree. "Why do you think Bram chose tonight to announce your engagement?"

"You should ask him."

"I will, but I'm asking you now. Didn't you discuss it?"

"Not before this evening." Even as she said it, she wondered if Bram's answer would support her or make it seem as if she were lying. Just now, she wasn't certain that she cared.

"Bram takes some odd notions into his head."

Comfort didn't hear a question, so she kept quiet. Perhaps if he only talked to himself, he'd grow tired of the company.

"You've always impressed me as a sensible influence. Mother says the same. How long have you and Bram known each other?"

"Since my coming-out."

"That's right. The party. You were what? Sixteen?"

"Yes."

"And he was seventeen. Nine years, then. You wrote to each other, I believe, when he went east to Harvard. And didn't you later attend some seminary for young ladies?"

"Oberlin College," she said. It was difficult not to grit her teeth at his condescension. "In Ohio. Men also attended."

"Did your uncles realize that when they packed you off?"

Now she understood he was purposely trying to rile her. Although she was unclear as to his motive, it made it easier not to give in. "You know them," she said lightly. "Do you think they'd let me go anywhere without sending three Pinkerton men in advance of my arrival?" He surprised her by chuckling again. "Actually, Uncle Newton accompanied me there and remained until he was certain I was settled. Uncle Tuck attended my graduation and escorted me home."

"I see. You and Bram corresponded while you were both away?"

"Yes."

"As friends."

"You say that as if you cannot fathom it, but it's true."

Bode did not trouble himself to pretend he believed her. He made a small shrug to indicate it didn't matter. "How many proposals of marriage have you had, Miss Kennedy?"

"Mr. DeLong," she said deliberately, "if you persist on being rude, I'll make you wish you were still fighting off the Rangers."

"I think it must be four," he said. "Perhaps five. What was wrong with—ahhh!" Bode's right knee buckled as pain arced jaggedly down his leg. It was like electricity crackling between two copper leads, only this was a jangling nerve between the base of his spine and his kneecap. It made no difference that Comfort was responsible for crippling him; his only choice was to accept her support when she offered it or fall flat on his face.

Several men rushed forward to lend their assistance, but Bode put up a hand and held them off. "Something to sit on," he said. "That will be enough." Almost immediately he felt the seat of chair pushing against the back of his knees. Comfort bent with him, easing him down. Through a haze of pain, Bode saw she was actually smiling. Those attending him might mistake her expression for sympathy and concern, but he knew she was sincerely pleased to have put him so firmly in his place.

"He was fine," she said by way of explanation. "Until he wasn't." Comfort backed away as more guests crowded in. When she saw that Alexandra had reached Bode's side, she ducked out and went in search of Bram.

She came toe to toe with Tucker Jones first. He smiled, slipped his arm in hers, and would have dragged her out to the portico if she had not accompanied him willingly.

"I saw that," he said without preamble. "You wedged your foot between his, stepped sideways, and bore down on him."

Comfort sighed. "He was annoying me. Do you think anyone noticed?"

"Other than Bode? I doubt it. You moved as smoothly as Chin Fong clearing opium eaters from the back room at the Snow Palace." Tuck shook his head. "That was an observation, not high praise."

Her mouth twitched.

"Oh, very well. It was an observation *and* high praise. Bode's not likely to forget what you did. How did you know he'd go down so easily?"

"I knew his back was bothering him," she said honestly. "And I took shameless advantage."

Tucker didn't care about that. "How was he annoying you? Was he improper?"

Comfort was trying to decide how to answer that when Bram appeared at her elbow. "Oh, I was looking for you. Do you mind, Uncle Tuck? I wanted to take some fresh air with Bram."

Tucker waved them off, but not before he made Bram shift uncomfortably under his most implacable stare.

"Why did he look at me like that?" asked Bram as he escorted Comfort off the portico and into the garden. "Did you already tell him?"

"I'm not going to do that here," she said. "So, no, I haven't said anything. He looked at you like that so you aren't tempted to annoy me."

"Oh. Do I? Annoy you, that is."

"Frequently."

"Well, I'm less likely to do it now that I know your uncle can turn me into a pillar of salt."

Comfort flashed him a grin. "Did you see Bode? Is your brother all right?"

Bram shrugged. "I couldn't get close. I think Mother intends the servants to bear him upstairs on a chair like he's the Pharaoh Ramses. I wanted to make certain that you suffered no injury."

"Me? No, I'm fine. It was sudden, and I suppose he could have pulled me to the floor if I hadn't been quick or strong enough to support him, but I was, so that's that."

Bode looked her over, gauging that what she said was true. "He asked you about the engagement, didn't he?"

"Yes. He's curious about the suddenness of it. I told him we hadn't discussed it before this evening."

"True enough. I'll remember that."

"I think he means well," she said, surprising herself. "He's accustomed to looking out for you."

"Cleaning up after me, you mean."

Comfort could have told him that if he didn't take his position as society's—and his mother's—fair-haired bad boy quite
so seriously, Bode wouldn't have to carry a broom and dustpan.
She held her tongue. "I didn't say that."

"You don't have to. I did." He sighed heavily. "What can he
possibly find objectionable about me asking for your hand? You
are educated and even-tempered, possess sound judgment, and
exert a reasoned influence."

"Maybe he thinks I will bore you," she said dryly. She was
all the things Bram said she was, and more than a little bored
herself by so much in the way of good sense and moderation.

"Maybe you would, but I believe he'd be glad of it." The
words were out before he properly heard them. "I'm sorry. I
meant no offense. That came out in a ridiculous fashion."

"It's all right," she said.

But there had been a hitch in her step, and Bram knew that
he'd bungled it. "You *don't* bore me," he said. "You couldn't."

"I could," she insisted. "If we were married." She stopped
in a pool of torchlight and waited for him to turn to face her.
"Eight weeks, Bram. You'll wish at the end of it that I'd won
the negotiation. We're friends, certainly we are, but we've
never—what's the old expression?—oh, yes, we've never lived
in each other's pockets."

"It's true that we haven't, but you'll see that it doesn't matter.
You're looking on the wrong side of things, Comfort. Hasn't it
occurred to you that at the end of two months you'll be the one
wishing you'd accepted my original terms? I intend that we
should have such a fine time as an engaged couple that you will
put aside your reservations about my character and want to
accept my proposal in earnest."

What Comfort wished was that she could duck into the
shadows. It required a great deal of effort to keep her expression
guarded and skeptical. "We'll see," she said. She took his arm
and led him away from the light and toward the stone bench
where she'd found Bode. "But I'm doubtful."

Alexandra DeLong paced the length of the rug in front of the
fireplace in her son's room. Bode lay on a chaise brought in for

him from one of the guest rooms. It was a necessity when it became apparent the bed did not offer enough support or comfort for him. He claimed there was less pain in a partial recline than either standing or lying flat on his back.

The door had just closed on the retreating servants when she spoke. "This is why you should come home," she said, gesturing broadly to indicate the length of the damask-covered chaise.

"I *am* home," Bode said reasonably.

"Do not pretend you are obtuse. You know perfectly well what I mean."

"Yes, I do. It's a familiar argument."

"I prefer discussion."

"So do I, Mother, but surely we know by now that this will end badly."

Alexandra stopped pacing, regarded her son for a long moment, and finally sighed. "You shouldn't assume I'm surrendering my position just because I'm choosing not to continue this *discussion*."

One corner of Bode's mouth kicked up. "It never occurred to me."

Sweeping her train to one side, Alexandra dropped into the wing chair closest to the chaise. She plucked several rosebuds from her hair and dropped them on a side table. When she saw Bode giving her a look while pointing to his chest, she glanced down at herself and saw a cluster of white petals clinging to her bosom like snowflakes. She carefully collected them and dropped them on the table.

"The roses were Mrs. Dufré's idea. She showed me illustrations in one of her pattern books from Paris. I think perhaps it was too much. Rosebuds are for young women, not matrons, and certainly not widows."

Bode arched an eyebrow at her. "And not for mothers who are marking their son's thirty-second birthday."

"That's right."

He rubbed his chin, a reserved half smile still playing about his mouth. "I wonder what a proper response might be."

"Bram would know."

"He certainly would."

Alexandra fell quiet, waiting. When Bode didn't fill the silence, she did. "You could try, you know."

"Very well. I don't think I'll mention you were skirting dangerously close to self-pity."

"No. Don't mention that."

"Then perhaps what I should say is that you are an arbiter of good taste and your tastes influence fashion. You've made rosebuds extraordinarily popular this evening, and Mrs. Dufré should thank you for carrying off her design with such confidence."

"I'd rather you didn't say any of that either."

He chuckled. "All right. The truth, then. You made the rosebuds want to be the rose."

She stared at him. "My God," she said quietly. "You have his silver tongue."

"Bram's?"

"No, your father's."

"You'll understand if I don't accept that as a compliment."

Alexandra nodded, her expression momentarily sad as she reflected on the past. "I don't think I meant it as one." She forced a smile. "Still, it was lovely what you said."

Bode returned her smile. The fire crackled beside Alexandra and light flickered in her hair, accenting the deep red color more beautifully than the rosebuds had. His mother deserved to be happy. Wasn't that what Comfort said to him this evening?

"Are you happy, Mother?"

Alexandra did not mask her surprise. "What an odd question. Did you take a blow to the back of your head?"

"No," he said. Because she looked as if she might get up and verify his denial for herself, Bode put a hand to the base of his skull and rubbed hard. He managed not to grimace. "I swear it, no." He watched his mother deflate slightly and ease back into her chair. "It's not an unreasonable question, you know. Are you happy?"

"Are you living at home?"

"No."

"There is your answer."

He sighed. "Your happiness cannot be dependent on that."

"Who says? Show me where it's written."

"Now who is pretending to be obtuse?"

She returned his stare pointedly.

"Me?" he said. "You think I don't understand?"

"I know you don't. You're not a parent."

"How does one explain Father? His happiness never depended on the choices his sons made."

"Nothing explains your father. He sired you. He was not a parent. And I would challenge your assertion that he was happy." Diamonds glittered as she waved one hand dismissively. "But all that aside, it remains a truth that raising my sons is my singular achievement. If I want to rest my happiness on their choices, then that is my prerogative."

"God, but I wish you'd had half a dozen children. Your happiness is a considerable burden for two sons to shoulder."

"Two sons. Four shoulders. It seems adequate, if only you and Bram would share it evenly."

Groaning softly, Bode closed his good eye and let his head thump against the back of the chaise. The contusion at the base of his skull throbbed. He shouldn't have rubbed it quite so hard. He picked up the covered icepack Travers left for him and held it over his shiner.

"Bram seems to be doing his part to help," he said.

"You mean his engagement?"

Bode turned his head a fraction and risked a narrow glance at her. "Has he done something else?"

"That will always be a question, won't it?" Her rueful smile said she accepted it. "But, yes, I'm pleased with his announcement and his choice."

"His timing?"

"It was unexpected, I grant you that. I think if you had arrived on time, he would have chosen another venue to make the engagement public, but a celebration had been planned, and he saw an opportunity to give our guests something else to talk about besides your absence."

"Then perhaps I should have apologized for showing up at all."

"Nonsense."

"I was being facetious, Mother."

"Oh. I don't usually miss that. I must be more tired than I thought." As if to underscore her point, she yawned abruptly. "Well, there you have it. I'm going to bed. I'll send Travers back to assist you with your nightclothes. Do you mean to sleep on the chaise?"

"Yes. I think I will."

"Whatever is most comfortable," she said, coming to her feet. She approached the chaise and bent to kiss him. His forehead was cool beneath her lips, and she looked to the ice-pack as the cause. "Sleep well, but make sure Travers leaves a bell with you so that you can call for help if you need it."

"I shall," he said dutifully.

Straightening, Alexandra gave Bode one last head-to-toe study. "I cannot understand how the collapse of a stack of boxes and barrels simultaneously injured you at the front and the back."

Because it seemed as if she didn't expect an answer, Bode didn't supply one. "Good night, Mother."

"Good night."

After the disquieting events of the previous evening, Comfort embraced the sense of peace she felt when she woke in her own home. Not far off, the sound of church bells could be heard calling people to Sunday services. Realizing the ringing meant she was already too late to attend, she lay back and allowed herself the luxury of a lazy, feline stretch. Her movement disturbed the cat that had been tucked in the warm curve of her knees. Thistle sank his claws into the cotton coverlet and then into Comfort's flesh. She jerked her legs away and made a grab for him.

"Come here, bad boy." She chuckled softly when he didn't even make a show of resisting her. Turning on her side, she cradled him close and rubbed her chin between his ears. His long gray-and-white hair tickled her. "We missed church, but I'm guessing we weren't the only ones. Uncle Tuck might be up, but he'll be having breakfast in his room, and I imagine Uncle Newt is still snoring."

She remained in bed a little longer, rising only when she felt she was in danger of drifting back to sleep. She did not want the day to slip away from her, not when she had explanations to make. The carriage ride last night had afforded her the only real opportunity to present the facts to her uncles, and she'd been loath to disturb the quiet calm that was their blanket on the journey home.

She rang for assistance and asked for a bath to be drawn. Suey Tsin moved about as quietly as the cat, occasionally causing Comfort moments of alarm when she rounded a corner and came upon the girl unexpectedly. While Comfort soaked, Suey Tsin presented day dresses for her to wear. Communicating in truncated English, rapid-fire Chinese, and a flurry of gestures, her maid presented a compelling argument for the ice blue dress being more suitable as evening attire, for a dinner party perhaps, or for the theater, and as a result, Comfort chose the lemon yellow pinstripe.

By the time she arrived in the breakfast room, Newton was sitting in his usual place at one end of the table and studying the paper folded in thirds beside his plate. Although he rose slightly at Comfort's entrance, and gestured to her chair, his eyes never left the account he was reading.

Amused, she kissed the cheek he absently offered and took her seat. She had just unfolded a linen napkin over her lap when Tuck joined them. She looked up in surprise. "I would have wagered that you'd already taken breakfast in your room."

"That's why Newt and I have always cautioned you against making wagers. You don't have the head for it." He sat, snapped a napkin open with considerable flourish, and laid it protectively over his chest like a bib. Ignoring Comfort's mild censure, he leaned forward and sniffed deeply. He immediately ferreted out the covered platter that was hiding the bacon and reached for it. After placing three crisp strips on his plate, he passed it to Comfort and then poured himself a cup of coffee.

"I make wagers all the time," she protested. She permitted herself one bacon strip, put four on Newt's plate, then thought better of it and took one back for herself. "Every time I make an investment for the bank, in fact."

"That's different."

"What he means," Newt said, still staring at his paper, "is that mostly you're wagering other people's money. You're more clearheaded when it's not your own."

Comfort bit off one end of a bacon strip and waggled what remained of it at her uncles. "Are you two ever astonished that you made your fortune in banking?"

"Always," said Tuck.

"It passeth all understanding," said Newton.

"Well, as long as you know it." She took the platter of scrambled eggs from Tuck and spooned a heap onto her plate. She left it to Newt to serve himself. He did not always take eggs if he judged them too dry. Comfort poured coffee, added cream, and spread a dollop of orange marmalade on a triangle of toast. "Are neither of you going to say anything?" she asked, raising her cup to her lips.

Attention on his paper, Newt merely grunted, but Tuck asked, "About what?"

"You know very well. Bram's announcement. Our engagement. Plans for the wedding."

"Oh, that. Newt and I decided that it was for you to say."

"Say what?"

"Whatever you like, dear."

Newt finally pushed the morning paper away and looked up. "It was unexpected," he said. "Even Tuck didn't have an inkling that it was coming. You could speak to that first." He examined the eggs, decided they were to his liking, and added them to his plate. "If you want to, that is."

Comfort tried to recall a time when the pair of them had tiptoed around anything. They'd always been considerate of her feelings, but this was excessive. "I wasn't expecting Bram to make an announcement either."

"I wondered," said Tuck.

"There was a moment—just as quick as a finger snap," said Newt, "when I thought Bram might have steered his ship aground. You saved him, though."

"I did. It would have been embarrassing to all of us if I hadn't."

Tuck snapped a bacon strip between his fingers. The sharp crackle of the sudden gesture caught all of them off guard, and

Comfort gave a start. Tuck looked at the part of the strip dangling from his fingertips and just shook his head. He muttered an apology because it seemed he should, although he was uncertain what he was apologizing for.

Newt spoke up. "Tuck and I don't mind a little embarrassment. It's more concerning that Bram didn't speak to us first, and apparently not even to you."

"When did he propose?" asked Tuck. "Just last evening, or were you keeping secrets for upwards of a day or so?"

"I can keep a secret from you for longer than that." She glanced at Newton. "From both of you."

Neither argued. They merely regarded her politely, waiting.

"He's *never* proposed," she said, giving it all up at once.

"Hah! I *knew* it," said Newt.

"You did not," said Tuck. "You were apoplectic. You *kicked* a door."

"You kicked a door?" Comfort's dark eyebrows climbed her forehead.

"He did," Tuck told her. "We were holed up in Branford's library deciding what to make of the news, and he kicked a door."

Newt bit off a corner of dry toast and made a face, partly because he disliked dry toast, and partly because just now he disliked his partner. "What happened to our decision to support her?"

"Of course we'll support her. We always support her. But there's been no proposal, so we don't have to support her in that."

"But there *is* an engagement," Newt said. "In his usual Bram-handed manner, he's put the cart before the horse."

Tuck frowned deeply. His eyebrows made a V above the narrow bridge of his nose. He directed his question to Comfort. "What does it mean exactly that there's an engagement and no proposal?"

She slowly released the breath she'd been holding. "In this case, it means that the engagement is a fraud. I told Bram that you would be relieved."

Newt and Tuck exchanged glances, and it was Newt who

spoke. "Relieved? I don't know about that. This situation has about as many prickles as a porcupine with her back up."

"I'm going to break it off in eight weeks."

"Eight weeks?" Newt stopped drizzling honey on his toast. "How was that decided?"

"We negotiated terms," she said. "I had to. He wanted to continue the charade for six months."

Tuck lifted his eyes heavenward. "Thank you, Lord, for giving us a child with more sense than a bag of hair."

"Uncle Tuck!" Comfort quickly raised her napkin to her lips to stifle her laughter.

"What? I told Newt from the first that you'd be a comfort to us, and you are. I don't know why he worries."

Newt swallowed a mouthful of coffee. "I worry so you don't have to, and you should thank me for it." He regarded Comfort with concern. "So you're willing to pretend to be Bram's fiancée for the next two months. Did I hear that right?"

"Yes," she said, staring at her plate. "It did not sound quite so ridiculous when Bram said it."

"I'm sure it didn't. There's something you can learn from that in the event you haven't already figured it out."

She smiled ruefully. "I think I've got it."

Newt was confident that she had. "Well, then, I'd like to know what possessed him to make the announcement in the first place."

"I'm not sure that I even understand it," she said. "The best I can explain it is that he felt a need to do something when Bode didn't show up."

"He could have put a half-dozen dinner plates on sticks and kept them spinning," said Tuck. "I never get tired of seeing that."

"And broken plates," Newt added, unable to resist another caution, "aren't as messy as broken hearts."

Comfort chose to deliberately misunderstand. "Do you really think I can break Bram's heart?"

Newt gave her a sideways look, telling her in no uncertain terms what he thought of her response. Tuck, though, chose to answer as if she meant to be taken seriously.

"You could," he said, "if you helped him find it first." He

looked up from his plate to find Newt glaring at him. "Not a challenge," he added quickly. "And it would be cruel."

"Yes," said Newt. "Like finding a splinter in Thistle's paw, pulling half of it out, and leaving the rest to fester."

Comfort and Tuck stared at him.

Newt shrugged. "Someone has to say it." He used his knife to point at Comfort. "I'd feel better if I knew that Bram couldn't do that to you."

"My heart's my own."

Newt wanted to be convinced. He saw it was the same for Tuck. They both nodded slowly in unison.

Tuck tore off a bit of toast the size of his thumbnail and held it under the table for Thistle. The cat wound around his legs twice before he took the treat. "Does Alexandra know?"

Comfort had been dreading the question. "No. Bram doesn't want to tell her he made it all up."

"That's not fair to her," Tuck said.

"He thinks it would be worse if he told her."

"For him," said Newt. "In eight weeks, when you break off the engagement, it will be worse for you."

Comfort hadn't considered that. "I have to believe she'll be understanding. She knows engagements don't always end in marriage. Look at Emma Farmer and Leland Broderick. They were engaged for two years before they decided they didn't suit."

"That marriage was arranged for purely mercenary reasons," Tucker told her. "The families ended it for precisely the same reasons. I'm not sure that Emma or Leland had any say in the matter."

"I didn't realize. But it doesn't negate my point. They were engaged, and now they're not."

"Did you see the Farmers this evening?"

"No. They weren't on the guest list. Neither were the Brodericks."

"That's how Alexandra handles people who don't conform to her expectations."

Newt nodded. "And she didn't even have a dog in that fight. You have to consider how she'll react when it's her son."

"She isn't blind to his nature."

"She wasn't blind to her husband's nature either, but she never failed him in public. Even when he threw his support to the Johnny Rebs and put the Crowne fortune at risk, she stood at his side."

Tuck patted his knee and let Thistle jump on his lap. He stroked the cat, feeling its contented purr as a vibration against his palm. "I reckon Alexandra DeLong can suffer just about any indignity without blinking her public eye, but I don't believe she's ever not had her private revenge."

Chapter Three

Comfort was reading at the window bench in her room when Suey Tsin brought in a message from Bram. Thistle remained curled in her lap while she looked it over, and he required more push than nudge to vacate his cozy post when Comfort wanted to rise.

"My leaf green jacket, please," Comfort said, glancing up from Bram's broad scrawl to look out the window. "That will be sufficient, I think." The sky was cloudless, and sunshine had warmed her pleasantly while she read, but when she cracked the window earlier, she discovered she'd been deceived as a chilling breeze slipped into the room. "And the matching gloves."

She folded the note in quarters and laid it on her nightstand beside the red-and-white tin that had been her bedtime companion for as long as she could remember. Her fingers trailed over the cool, smooth surface of the tin. It was inevitable after so many years of fingering it in a likc manner that some of the paint had worn away. She could still make out all of the letters, but that was largely because while the paint had faded over time, the engraving in her mind had not.

Dr. Eli Kennedy's Comfort Lozenges.

She felt her fingertips tremble slightly and removed her hand before the tremor was visible to herself or Suey Tsin. Stepping back from the bed, she crossed the floor to where her maid held out her jacket.

"Will you let my uncles know that I've left?" she asked.

"I tell Mista Barkin. He tell uncles."

Comfort didn't think that Suey Tsin had spoken more than a hundred words to her uncles in the four years she'd been working in the house. "All right. You tell Mister Barkin. He'll know better when they can be disturbed." It was her uncles' practice each Sunday afternoon to hole up, as they called it, in their study on the pretense of discussing business for the upcoming week. It was not a well-kept secret that what engaged them was a couple of shots of whiskey each and a nap.

"You not want to tell either," Suey Tsin said.

Comfort couldn't deny it. "You're right."

"Where you go?"

"Pardon?"

Suey Tsin's sloe-eyed glance slanted in the direction of the bedside stand. "Message come. You go. But where you go?"

"Oh, of course." She held out her hand for Suey Tsin to assist her with the buttons on her gloves. "The note's from Bram. He's invited me to join his mother and him for tea."

The maid nodded. "I tell Mista Barkin."

"Yes. Good."

"You take carriage."

"No, I'm going to walk." She was looking forward to fresh air and stretching her legs.

"Too far. You take carriage."

Comfort shook her head. Bram's house wasn't far at all. A few blocks and a steeply inclined street were all that separated their homes. "I'm walking," she said firmly and accepted Suey Tsin's jerky nod as acquiescence. "Now, what have I done with my reticule?"

Bode plucked the damp and dripping bundle of shaved ice from his eye and tossed it at Travers. The valet had just enough warning to prepare for the pitch by cupping his hands together. He caught it easily and carried it to the bathing room, where he deposited it in the sink.

"Mind you," he called back to Bode. "You were supposed to keep it in place another ten minutes." He dried his hands and returned to the doorway in time to see Bode using his shirtsleeve to dab at his eye. Reaching around the corner into the bathing room, Samuel grabbed a towel and flung it at Bode's head.

Bode caught the tail of it before it fluttered to the floor. "Thank you." He gingerly pressed the towel to his eye. "Given the proximity of my eye to my brain, the latter was in danger of drowning or freezing."

"Neither one of those things explains stupidity."

Bode lowered the towel and gave Travers an inquiring look from his good eye. "I see we're speaking frankly."

"Something has to be said."

"You're not referring to the icepack, I imagine." When Samuel simply stared back, Bode sighed. "Ah. It's the note, then."

"O'course it's the note. And I don't hold with you making me party to your scheme."

"Scheme lends the plan more deviousness than it deserves, don't you think?"

"Scheme," Travers said firmly.

Bode shrugged and finished wiping down his face. He folded the towel neatly and held it out for Sam. "She's not here yet, so maybe she saw through it. I never tried my hand at forgery before, and Miss Kennedy has more than a passing familiarity with Bram's penmanship."

"She'll be here. I can't explain it, but she likes your mother. She won't turn down an invitation to tea."

"Then perhaps we should have some. You'll see to that, won't you?"

"Only because I live to do your bidding."

Bode's sardonic look matched Travers's tone perfectly. "The tea," he said. "And some of those little sandwiches Alexandra likes."

Travers nodded once. He collected a few damp towels and slung them over his forearm before he turned to go. To make certain he had the last word, he waited until he was closing the door behind him before he said, "Maybe you should have thought on this plan a little longer."

Bode's firm mouth lifted at the corners as the door clicked into place. He appreciated Sam's concern, but he didn't share it. He merely wanted to speak to Comfort. He was hardly sowing the seeds of scandal. That was the kind of gardening that Bram did.

Resting his head on the back of the chaise, Bode closed the only eye he could and listened for some sign that would indicate that Miss Kennedy had finally arrived.

"I don't understand," Comfort said as Hitchens opened the door wide enough for her to step inside. "I thought Mrs. DeLong would be at home. I'm sure that's what Bram wrote."

"I can't speak to that, Miss Kennedy." Even when the house was operating smoothly under his direction, Hitchens had a wrinkled brow. Now, with the calm waters stirring slightly, the wrinkles were pressed into sharp creases. "Mrs. DeLong and Master Bram have not returned since leaving for church. Their plans included a repast with Reverend Asbury and his wife following the service and a carriage ride out in the direction of Lands End. I do not expect them for several hours."

Comfort pressed her lips together, thinking. "Perhaps I misread the invitation and it was extended for another day."

"I don't know what else explains it," said Hitchens. The tightness in his features eased a bit as he could find no reason that responsibility for the error should be dropped on his stooping shoulders.

A movement at the top of the stairs drew Comfort's attention. She saw Samuel Travers cross the landing and disappear into the west wing. He had been carrying a large silver platter in front of him. She didn't think she imagined that it was Alexandra DeLong's prized tea service that he was balancing.

Her nostrils flared slightly with the strength of her exasperated exhalation. "Never mind, Mr. Hitchens. I think I know what happened. You'll excuse me, won't you, but since I'm here, I may as well make a sick call on Mr. DeLong."

Hitchens stiffened slightly, drawing back his shoulders. Even with this adjustment, he was not quite eye to eye with Comfort. "Allow me to inquire if he's taking visitors."

"There's no need. Mr. DeLong and I don't stand on that sort of ceremony. He'll receive me. In fact, I believe I'm expected." She neatly sidestepped the butler's attempt to interfere with her advance on the stairs. She pretended that his intention was to escort her. "Don't trouble yourself, Mr. Hitchens. I know the way."

Bode sat up when he heard Travers fumbling with the door-knob. A moment later the valet entered, the tea service balanced gingerly on the fingertips of one hand. "Careful with that," Bode said unnecessarily. "Put it on the table beside that chair."

"I'm not sure she'll be sitting down," Travers told him. "Could be this platter is holding a whole lot of weapons she'll be launching at you."

Bode ignored the warning and focused on what was salient. "She's here?"

"Just arrived."

"Well, send her up."

"Oh, I think she's on her way."

"Really?" He had intended to ask Travers how that had come about so quickly, but Comfort's sudden appearance on the threshold of his room made the question unimportant. Bode started to rise, clenching his jaw when his back began to spasm.

"Stay where you are, Mr. DeLong. I told your butler that you and I don't stand on ceremony."

"He doesn't stand at all," muttered Travers. This aside earned him a withering look from Bode and Comfort's appreciative smirk. He pretended he was unaware of either and set the tray down. "Is there anything else, sir?"

Bode indicated the bell on the floor at his side. "I'll ring if I need you."

Travers restrained the retort that came to mind and addressed Comfort instead. "May I take your jacket and gloves?"

"No."

"Your bonnet, then."

"No, Mr. Travers. I won't be staying long."

"Very well." He made a point of not hurrying from the room, leaving both parties to stew in silence until he shut the door and moved out of their hearing.

Comfort glanced around the room, noticing the bed was turned down but too neatly pressed to have been slept in. She went to the foot of the chaise, liking the superiority of height and the safety of distance.

"Well, Mr. DeLong, I'm here, and it seems you went to some trouble to make that happen."

"I went to surprisingly little trouble. Travers delivered the pen and paper and lap desk, and Billy Powell delivered the note. I did compose the message, however, but that only required a single draft."

"Your handwriting is very like your brother's."

"I expect that's because we had the same tutor."

Flattening her mouth, Comfort let her impatience show. "What do you want?"

"Company."

She blinked. "Company?"

"Yes. Is that so astonishing? My mother and brother abandoned me, and you heard Travers for yourself. His idea of biting wit is to sink his teeth into my flesh. So, yes, I want company."

She regarded him suspiciously. "*My* company?"

"You're the only one I invited."

"I can bite, too."

"And I know it." He waved a hand to indicate his position on the chaise. "How did you manage it exactly? As I heard you tell everyone within earshot, I was fine . . . until I wasn't."

"So you brought me here for an apology."

Bode shook his head. He made a pass through his dark copper hair with his fingertips. "You may make one, of course, if you are moved to it, but I'd rather hear how it was done. Better yet, I'd like you to show me."

"You're serious?"

He inclined his head a fraction in her direction and simply regarded Comfort until her skeptical expression faded.

"It's a ridiculous idea."

"Perhaps."

When it didn't appear that he would waver, she reluctantly agreed. "I suppose I can demonstrate, but you will have to imagine that I have an adversary."

"Perhaps not." Leaning over, he grasped the teak handle of the bell and shook it. "Give him a moment."

Comfort raced forward and snatched the bell from Bode's hand, silencing it against her midriff. "What are you thinking?" she whispered harshly. "Mr. Travers wears a brace."

"It's for the purpose of a demonstration only. I don't want you to hurt him."

She set the bell well outside of Bode's reach. "I won't do it, and if he heard your summons, I want you to send him off."

"Oh, very well, but I'm telling you, he'd be game for it."

"I don't care." She watched the clock on the mantelpiece, and when two long minutes passed without Travers appearing, she finally relaxed. "He didn't hear it."

"More likely he ignored it."

Comfort thought she'd be wise to do the same but found herself unbuttoning her gloves and jacket. For good measure, she removed her bonnet and laid it on the seat of a wing chair. She raised her arms as they had been during their dance.

"You were holding me so," she said. "And taking me through a turn. You made it easy for me to stay in the cat stance."

"The cat stance?"

As she lowered her hands, the line of Comfort's mouth turned uncertain. "You know. Like a cat. Light and ready to move."

"Show me."

She hesitated. She would have to raise her skirts.

"You didn't do it with your hands. You used your feet."

"Actually, I used both."

Bode looked pointedly at the hem of her walking dress and waited her out. When she lifted it high enough to reveal soft kid boots and a pair of finely turned ankles, his expression didn't change. "All right," he said. "Now what?"

"Do you see how I'm bearing my weight on my rear foot?" she asked. "Notice how it's angled. The tip of my forward foot is raised and the heel rests lightly on the floor. That's the cat stance."

"I see. And you were moving around me like that while we were dancing?"

"Only the once," she said. "Only after I warned you."

He remembered. "And then what?"

Comfort looked around again and spied a ladder-backed chair behind a writing desk. She went over to the desk and moved the chair back and forth to gauge its weight before tipping it on its rear legs. The carpet rippled as she dragged the chair to the chaise.

Raising her hem and assuming the cat stance once more, Comfort glided effortlessly through a graceful circle step and demonstrated how quickly she'd caught Bode off guard by upending the chair. Her reflexes were sound, and she grabbed the chair before it thumped to the floor, much in the way she'd grabbed and supported Bode.

"Show me again," he said.

She compressed her lips, considering. "Just once more," she said finally. Looking away from him, she began humming softly, repeating several measures of the waltz the musicians had been playing when she and Bode danced. She held up her skirt, this time not hampered by a train, and made two elliptical revolutions around the wing chair and the writing desk before she moved in on the ladder-backed chair. Comfort had considerable momentum this time, and her glide and kick lifted the chair more than six inches off the carpet before she caught the front lip of the seat and set it down gently.

Flushed, as much from the pleasure of her performance as the exertion of it, she turned on Bode. The flush became the color of embarrassment when he began to applaud.

"Don't," she said, shaking her head. "The worst thing I've done is shown you how very little encouragement it takes for me to behave so foolishly."

He stopped clapping but kept his palms pressed together and rested his chin on his fingertips. "Your engagement to my brother aside, I don't believe you've ever done anything foolish in your life."

"You don't know me very well."

He turned thoughtful. "Why is that?"

Comfort shrugged. "That is the sort of question you have to answer for yourself."

"Fair enough." He nodded to the wing chair. "Will you sit? There are tea and sandwiches." When he sensed her hesitation, he added, "Please. I would like it. Really."

"All right. For a little while." She returned the ladder-backed chair to its place and removed her bonnet from the seat of the wing chair. She laid it beside her jacket and gloves on the chest at the foot of the bed. "Do you take sugar? Cream?"

"Neither."

"You probably prefer it with a touch of whiskey the way Uncle Newt does."

"More like a touch of tea with my whiskey."

She poured the steeped tea from the pot into a delicately fluted china cup. "That's more like Uncle Tuck." She extended the cup to Bode and made sure he had it securely in his palm before she released it. Taking both cream and sugar for herself, Comfort tested the taste before she sat. "Would you like a sandwich? Mrs. Deltry makes excellent ones."

"No, thank you. But help yourself." He waited while she selected a petite watercress sandwich. "Do you know all my mother's staff?"

"Not all, I'm sure. But many of them."

"How does that happen? I'm not sure Alexandra knows them."

"I know the ones that have accounts at our bank."

Bode's short laugh made the cup rattle in its saucer. He steadied it. "So it's business, then."

"Good business."

"Perhaps. Black Crowne's never done business with Jones Prescott."

"I know."

"Do you expect that will change once you and Bram are married?"

"I don't see why it would, and you should know that Bram and I don't discuss money."

"I'm sure you don't, but you might consider having that conversation before you exchange vows. It could be . . ." He paused, searching for the right word. "Illuminating."

"There's no point. I doubt Bram could shed any light on Crowne Shipping and the DeLong finances if he held a candelabra over the book of accounts. Everyone knows you and your mother make all the decisions, and as you've chosen to work with Croft Federal just as your father did, I don't see Bram's marriage influencing the relationship you have with Mr. Bancroft."

Bode's left eyebrow lifted. "A candelabra?" He appreciated the picture she brought to mind. "If only you exaggerated," he said, his mouth twisting wryly. What Bram knew about figures mostly related to the female form. That education was compliments of dance halls and brothels, and perhaps from observing their own father in pursuit of what was under every woman's skirt. He hadn't learned it in the classrooms at Harvard.

"What did you study at Oberlin?" Bode asked suddenly.

Comfort couldn't follow the change in subject, but she supposed that didn't matter. "Mathematics."

"Really."

"Really," she said, repeating his intonation precisely. "Statistical calculation and analysis. Probability. The evaluation of risk. Applications for business, economics, and engineering. My degree says liberal arts, but all of my concentrations were in math."

"Remarkable."

Comfort felt another warning was in order. "It's just that sort of condescension that contributed to you lying on that chaise."

Bode arched an eyebrow at her but said nothing. He sipped his tea.

Comfort took another dainty sandwich, cucumber this time. "Your eye looks worse than it did last night."

"I know."

"Did someone give you ice for it?"

"Ice. Beefsteak." He pointed to the plate of sandwiches. "Cucumber slices."

Comfort regarded her sandwich uneasily.

"A different cucumber entirely, I'm sure."

Hungrier than she was skeptical, she plopped what was left of the bite in her mouth. "What about your back? You couldn't rise when I came in."

"It will be fine. I'm going to work tomorrow."

"Do you think that's wise? It doesn't appear that you were able to sleep in your own bed."

"That's not my bed. At least it hasn't been for years. My bed has some support, like this chaise."

"Then it's true what they say about you?"

"Enlighten me."

"You sleep on a bed of nails."

"I eat them, too. And spit rust."

She laughed and realized quite suddenly that she was enjoying herself. Perhaps it was that he only had one steely eye. The intensity of the blue-violet glint had been reduced by half, and he hadn't so much as turned it on her once.

"What do you do at your offices?" she asked.

"As little as possible," he said. "I prefer being away from them. My interest is the ships. Talking to the masters. Inspecting. Looking over the cargo."

She was certain he had employees for those things, so if he did them, it was because he really wanted to be out of doors.

"There are meetings, I suspect."

"Mm. Too many. Deals. Contracts. Agreements to be settled with a handshake." He felt his jaw tighten. "Or with the turn of a card."

"That really happens?"

"Sometimes." He wanted to shrug, but his shoulders were suddenly too tight to make it appear careless. He sought a neutral tone instead and was glad to find it. "It's San Francisco."

She nodded, understanding. She'd seen lots of valuables traded or sold in the gambling tents and mining camps, and she'd been witness to what never should have been bought or sold in the cribs and whorehouses.

"Bram told me you used to be master on the *Artemis Queen*," she said. "Do you miss it?"

"Sometimes." Almost always, he could have said. Admitting it would have been indulgent. "What do you know about the *Artemis*?"

"What everyone knows, I suppose. She's your flagship. The most beautiful ship in the fleet. At least I think she's the most beautiful. I don't know if that's what makes her a flagship."

Bode wondered if she'd accept an invitation to go aboard. He didn't extend the offer, though it would have been interesting to see her reaction. The *Artemis Queen* was weeks out from completing her China run. There was still plenty of time to consider it. "What do you do at your offices?" he asked. "Besides learn the name of every person who has an account at Jones Prescott."

"I review the city papers from the previous day so I can follow up on the important stories. News out of the legislature and governor's office, for instance. Railroad expansion. Who is getting federal land grants. All of the things that influence interest rates and investments."

"What else?"

"Well, I read and approve loan applications. Uncle Tuck and I decide how we'll deliver payrolls to the mines. What routes, which stage drivers we'll use, or if we'll send the money by train. We always have to consider robbery. Uncle Tuck has a special sense for it. Not robbery," she said quickly. "But for avoiding it."

"I had no idea," he said. "About any of that."

"Uncle Newt and I discuss investments. That has always been his strength. He can look over fluctuations in the market and know exactly what funds he wants to transfer. With the telegraph the market is no longer just local. We can make transfers with our agents in Chicago, St. Louis, and New York."

"Is he ever wrong?"

"Of course. More often than he's right. But it's not like he's pushing all his markers to the center of the table and betting against the house. The distribution of money over a variety of investments of varying risks helps soften the blow of a single failure. Even a catastrophic one." Comfort realized she was rattling on about a subject that would have had Bram plotting his escape. It wasn't fair that she'd taken advantage of her captive audience. "I'm sorry. You didn't deserve that. It was probably every bit as painful as the stitch in your back."

"Hardly."

She wondered if he was sincere. There was no inflection in his voice and no expression on his face to guide her.

"You're the only woman I know who works." He knew immediately that he'd said something wrong. Comfort Kennedy had her hackles up. Before he could determine what made her bristle, she was letting him know all about it.

"That's not true. In this house alone there is Mrs. Deltry, Mrs. Patrick, Mrs. Eversly, and no less than seven girls employed as housemaids and kitchen help. And dare I mention your mother? She'd have something to say, I'm sure."

Bode was equally sure that was true. He cleared his throat and made an attempt at looking contrite. Apologies did not come as swiftly to his lips as they did to his brother's. "Allow me to amend that. I was trying to say that you're the only woman I know who works outside of her home—or anyone else's for that matter."

She conceded the point, and she didn't want to make another

using dance hall greeters, actresses, pretty waiter girls, and whores as further examples. Comfort inclined her head, acknowledging his correction. "Men seem to have a difficult time recognizing the contributions of women."

"I never thought of myself as one of those men," Bode said. "Until now. Consider me corrected." He finished his tea and held out the cup and saucer for Comfort to take. The awkward stretch put his back into spasm again. He swore softly as the saucer slid from his nerveless fingers and the teacup followed.

Comfort caught the saucer in her free hand and the cup on the toe of her shoe. Pretending she didn't see Bode's look of astonishment, she carefully set her own cup and saucer on the tray and then added his saucer. She bent forward and removed his teacup from the tip of her kid boot.

"What do you do when you're asked for an encore?"

She made a dismissive gesture that was at odds with the amusement playing about her mouth. "I had to make the attempt," she said. "That is your great-grandmother's china."

"I know. I didn't realize you did."

Comfort shrugged lightly. "Your mother's shared stories on occasion. She remembers the tea service from when she was a little girl."

"She really does like you, doesn't she?"

"I hope so. You seem surprised."

Not surprised precisely. Alexandra had said much the same thing to him. What he was, he thought, was suspicious. He remained quiet on that count. It was simpler to accept Comfort's statement than to explain his differences with it.

Comfort couldn't surmise the direction of his thoughts, but she recognized that he was in considerable pain. Because she couldn't be sure how much her actions on the dance floor had exacerbated his injury, she felt compelled to offer him some relief even if he didn't entirely deserve it.

"Lie on the floor," she directed without explanation.

Bode stared at her.

Comfort repeated herself, but this time with a deliberate pause between each word.

"I heard you," he said. "I even understood. What I don't know is why you want me to do it."

68   Jo Goodman

"You'll have to trust that I mean to help." Her eyebrows lifted a notch. She said, "Well?"

Bode recognized the challenge in her expression. What he honestly didn't know was whether or not he was up to it. Until Comfort arrived, Travers had attended him throughout the day, bearing some of his weight as he hobbled to the bathing room to see to his morning ablutions and personal needs. Travers suggested that he remain in the borrowed nightclothes, robe, and slippers while he recuperated, but he insisted on dressing because he'd woken up with a plan already fully formed that would bring Comfort around.

Setting his jaw to keep from grimacing, Bode pushed himself as upright as he could manage and swung his legs over the side of the chaise. He caught Comfort staring at his feet.

"You really should remove your shoes," she said. "Shall I help you?"

"I'd rather keep them on."

"All right." She tucked her smile on the inside of her mouth. How many times, she wondered, had Bram told her that his brother could be fastidious? Is this what he'd meant? Whether it was a demonstration of manners or modesty, or simply that he didn't want to reveal a hole in one of his socks, Comfort found it an unexpectedly appealing aspect of his character. Then again, perhaps it was only that he meant to be difficult.

Bode got on the floor by sliding off the chaise and going straight to his knees. He began to lean back, but Comfort put out an arm to stop him.

"You'll have to take off your jacket," she told him. "That's not negotiable. And lie on your stomach. I'll find a towel for your head."

Bode watched as she stood and disappeared into the adjoining bath. She never looked back, obviously expecting that he wouldn't make any sort of protest. He didn't. In a careful series of shrugs, he managed to push his black frock coat over his shoulders so that it was hanging loosely at his elbows by the time Comfort returned. Without asking his permission, she freed his trapped arms and put the jacket on the chaise.

"Your vest," she said. "Come on. In for a penny, in for a pound."

"Spoken like a banker."

She didn't believe he meant it as a compliment, so she didn't thank him, and since his fingers had begun to fiddle with the buttons on his gray silk vest, she didn't goad him to do the job more quickly. Judging where his head would be when he stretched out on the carpet, Comfort folded the towel and then placed it on the floor.

"Walk forward using your hands for support," she told him, taking his vest away.

Bode couldn't come up with a single good reason to do what she said. "I don't think I—" Out of the corner of his eye he saw her skirts flutter. She was actually beating a tattoo against the floor with the toe of her boot. He glanced up. Sure enough, her impatience was also visible in the flat line of her mouth and in the tight fold of her arms across her chest. "Is it generally known that you have tendencies toward the tyrannical?"

Comfort unfolded her arms and let them fall to her sides, but her mouth did not soften appreciably. "I am only discovering it myself."

Bode didn't miss the hint of accusation in her tone. Apparently he was responsible for revealing this unpleasant facet of her nature. It almost made the ridiculousness of his position palatable. He began easing forward exactly as instructed.

Comfort perched on one arm of the wing chair and began unlacing her boots while Bode made his painful way to the floor. He would never return to his offices tomorrow, she thought, not without intervention. No matter that he wanted to believe it could be accomplished by sheer force of will, she knew better. She removed her boots.

"Turn your head so you can rest your face on your cheek," she said. "But move your arms to your sides."

He did as he was told, because, really, what choice did he have at this juncture?

Comfort regarded the stiff line of his long frame and shook her head. It wouldn't do. "Try to relax." This had no appreciable impact. She sighed. "Begin by closing your eyes." Since she could only see his swollen one, she had to trust that he was doing as she asked. "Imagine a stream of clear, cool water flowing under your skin. Imagine the sound of it as it slips over muscle and sinew. You can only hear the sound of the water and the sound of my voice, and they become one, a single quiet current that lifts tension and carries it away."

Her voice became incrementally softer as she went on, and also more insistent. "You feel the water at the back of your neck, cool rivulets running over your skin. The water is pooling across your back. Your shoulders are pleasantly heavy under the weight of the water. You feel some of it trickle down your spine. There is no part of you that is untouched by it. The water is everywhere. It lies against your back, your legs, the soles of your feet. You feel it slipping along your arms, across your palms, and between your fingertips. You cannot stir it. It stirs you."

Comfort lifted the hem of her dress as she moved to Bode's side. "The water is a satisfying weight. You don't fight it. You don't want to." She stepped onto his back. "You accept it." Her toes curled into the muscles on either side of his spine. She moved slowly, carefully, her skirts brushing Bode's arms as she walked the length of his backbone. Her steps were small, her carriage balanced, and she moved with the grace and confidence of a tightrope performer. Her voice remained quiet and steady, and exactly as she'd told him it would be, at one with the current.

Her toes worked especially hard at the base of his spine where his muscles were so tight it was like standing on a board. Or in Bode's case, at the edge of a gangplank. She bent her knees slightly, pressing more deeply, looking for the spring in the board. She thought of the water, her form, and the power of her dive, and then she pushed off.

Even before she heard his soft grunt and the subsequent blissful moan, Comfort knew she'd found and released the pinched source of his pain.

Landing lightly on the balls of her feet, she pulled her skirt clear of him and turned away so she could sit in the wing chair. She picked up one of her boots, loosened the laces a bit more, and started to slip her foot inside. It was not surprising that Bode hadn't yet said a word. When she did the same thing for Tuck, he often napped right where he lay.

She didn't glance at Bode until she'd finished lacing both boots. He hadn't opened the one eye he could, but she could tell from the faint twitching of his fingers that he hadn't fallen asleep.

"You don't have to move," she said.

"I don't think I can." Even as he said it, he knew it wasn't accurate. He didn't *want* to move, and for the moment he appreciated the difference. "What did you do to me?"

"I can't properly pronounce it, but you can inquire of almost any Chinaman and he will be able to tell you. Not every Chinaman can do it, though, so you should be careful not to let just anyone make the walk."

"I'll keep that in mind."

Comfort looked around the wing chair to the clock. "I should go. You've had your fill of company, I think, and I prefer to be elsewhere when your mother and Bram return home."

"Why? There's nothing improper about you paying a sick call." Now he opened his eye and gave her an inquiring look. "Unless, that is, you mean to tell them how you came to be here."

"I don't believe I'll mention it, although Mr. Hitchens might say something. Before I understood what was going on, I told him I'd been invited by Mrs. DeLong."

"Let me deal with Hitchens."

Bode would have to, Comfort thought. She certainly had no intention of doing it. She got to her feet.

"Stay," he said.

"I'm quite certain I'm expected at home soon. And I walked, Mr. DeLong, so I have to account for the time it will take to walk back."

"I'll arrange for a carriage."

"You're treading dangerously close to petulance."

Was he? Probably. "Are you always so forthright?"

"No. No one is any one thing always."

Bode got his hands under his shoulders and pushed himself up. He drew in his knees and then sprang from that position to his full height. All of it was accomplished without the slightest twinge of pain. "Amazing," he said under his breath. Even more softly, he said, "Witch."

Comfort was already at the foot of the bed retrieving her jacket from the chest. She pretended she hadn't heard. The characterization did not displease her, though, and she suspected that was because she'd had her fill recently of being called sensible.

Bode came up beside her and held out his hand for her jacket. She gave it to him and turned so he could help her into it. "Thank you," she said, her hands gliding over the buttons. "I can manage the rest." When he didn't step back, she slipped sideways, taking her gloves and bonnet with her. She couldn't have said what made her uncomfortable. She was fine . . . until she wasn't. "Good day, Mr. DeLong."

He smiled narrowly at her. "You've called me Bode before."

She had, but she couldn't remember why. She didn't want to call him Bode now. Comfort inclined her head politely. "Good day."

Bode didn't reply. He watched as she secured her bonnet, wondering if she would be clumsy with the ribbons. She wasn't. She did equally well with her gloves, pulling them on smoothly and managing the buttons with the deft precision of one who did not always wait for the assistance of a maid. He grabbed his waistcoat as they passed the chaise and put it on while he escorted her to the door.

"You don't have to see me out. I know the way."

"I realize that, but I'd like to test the limits of that correction you made to my back."

"Unless you throw yourself off the landing, or try to somersault down the stairs, you'll be fine." She shrugged when he kept pace with her. "But please yourself."

Bode gave Comfort the banister side of the staircase. There wasn't a step that he took that made him want to reach for her or reach around her for support. He was almost sorry for that. Almost.

Hitchens came hurrying into the entrance hall when Bode and Comfort arrived. Bode waved him off. "It's all right, Mr. Hitchens. I'm walking Miss Kennedy out."

"But your frock coat . . . your back . . ." He frowned more deeply. "Your hat."

"I can't tell if your concern is for my health or my wardrobe." Beside him, he heard Comfort laugh softly. "It's fine," he told the butler. "I'm only going as far as the street."

Comfort opened the door before Hitchens decided to throw himself across it and bar their exit. She slipped out, Bode right behind her. "I don't think he'd have let you leave if you hadn't already put on your vest."

"Probably not. He's fussy." He caught her quicksilver smile. "What is it?"

"Bram says something similar about you."

"Really?"

"Fastidious is what he said." Clearly, Comfort saw, it was a word Bode had never applied to himself. "Maybe he meant it in the sense that you are particular and difficult to please." She saw he wasn't bothered at all by that description. It made her wonder again about his reluctance to remove his shoes.

When they reached the street, Bode hung back. "You'll be careful?"

"I always am."

"No one is any one thing always."

Comfort didn't miss his gently mocking tone or her own words coming back at her. "I've heard that also." She pointed across the street to where a young Chinese girl appeared suddenly from the shadowed, narrow passage between two great houses. She carried a basket over her arm and wore a dou lì, the traditional conical straw hat, on her head. Her long queue had fallen over her right shoulder and lay like a rope of black silk against her white tunic. "That's Suey Tsin. She's been waiting for me."

"What, there? All this time?"

"I'm afraid so, but that was her choice. She didn't accompany me here. She followed. She disagreed with my decision to walk rather than take a carriage."

"You could have asked Hitchens to show her to the servants' entrance. She could have waited for you in the kitchen." He was aware that Comfort was regarding him oddly. "What?" he asked.

"Let me say only that she wouldn't have been welcome and leave it at that." She waved to Suey Tsin. "I'm glad you're feeling better, Mr. DeLong. I wish you well." With that, she stepped off the curb and began walking across the street to where Suey Tsin waited for her.

The Jones Prescott Bank was located on Powell Street in the block between Post and Sutter. The bank had an imposing granite front, but the rest of the building was brick construction, most of it salvaged from structures that had collapsed in the tremblers that plagued the city. If one examined the bricks closely, there was charred evidence that fire often followed the quakes. Still, from any side, the bank looked impressively solid, which was exactly how Newton Prescott and Tucker Jones wanted it to be seen. Their last names were chiseled deep into the frieze above the doorway, the order having been decided eighteen years earlier, not alphabetically, but by the flip of a coin.

Bram DeLong strolled into the bank on Monday morning and waited his turn at one of the teller cages to inquire after Comfort. He knew she had an office on the second floor, but he had never visited her there. In fact, he'd only been to Jones Prescott on two previous occasions, one time to seek a loan that would not come to the attention of his mother or his brother, and the second time to repay it. He couldn't depend on Mr. Bancroft at Croft Federal to keep the transaction confidential, and it was only prudent that Alexandra not learn the extent of his gambling debts.

Bram dealt exclusively with Tucker Jones, not only repaying the loan, but all of the interest. His mistake had been to pay the loan back immediately after his luck turned at the tables. He knew the quick repayment had confirmed Tucker's suspicions that the loan was for gambling debts, not to buy into a railroad venture. The next time Bram needed funds, he applied for them at Wells Fargo.

Bram passed one large empty office with two desks turned to face each other. It was the office where he'd sat with Tucker Jones to discuss his loan, but he felt safe in assuming that it was the one that Tucker shared with his partner. He passed several other rooms, all closed off, that he thought were probably for files and general storage.

He found Comfort's office at the end of the hall. Her door was open, as were both windows. A light breeze ruffled tendrils of hair that had the good sense to escape the chignon at the back of her head. That nest of hair, Bram noticed, appeared to be held in place by a tortoiseshell comb and two pencils. There were several documents fanned out in front of her, one held down by the corner piece of a charred brick, another by the weight of a book, and in one case, by an actual crystal paperweight. She looked over the reports—and even from where he stood, Bram could see they were boring—while twirling a pencil against her lips and occasionally nibbling it like a dainty beaver.

She was so entirely engrossed in what she was doing, he realized she had no idea that he was standing just some eight feet away.

"I can't say that I enjoy being so completely irrelevant."

Comfort gave a start. She fumbled with the pencil at her lips so clumsily that she nearly poked herself with it.

"Careful," said Bram. "If you do injury to your eye, you'll only be good as a bookend with Bode."

"Lord, but you scared me." She tossed the pencil away from her and sat back in her chair. Her expression remained startled. "Where did you come from?"

"Downstairs. I spoke to one of the tellers. That was all right, wasn't it? I mean, you do occasionally take visitors in the inner sanctum."

She laughed at the drama and mystery he infused into "inner sanctum." "Occasionally. But this is a first for you."

"It is." He looked around. Besides the desk there were two plain wooden chairs, three file drawers, and a small table littered with more detritus of her work. The back wall held her framed diploma from Oberlin, and between the windows there was a watercolor of a Pacific coast sunset. He lifted his chin toward it. "Is that your work? I didn't know you had any talent for painting."

"That's because I don't. And if I did, I still wouldn't display it here. Uncle Newt painted that. He gave it to me before he left me at Oberlin. There was never the slightest chance that I wouldn't come back to San Francisco, but Newt is convinced his painting had something to do with my return." She smiled slyly as she swiveled in her chair. "Uncle Tuck's threats were equally unnecessary."

"Did I ever write that I thought about staying in Boston?"

"No. Never." She would have remembered because it would have broken her heart. "Did you consider it seriously?"

He turned a charming and falsely modest grin on her. "Now, Comfort, what sort of question is that?"

"A serious one."

"And?"

"And you don't answer those."

"That's right."

She just shook her head, amused, but perhaps not as amused as she would have been before he announced their engagement. "What are you doing here? That's not too serious a question, is it?"

"No. I'm here to suggest that you accompany me to the opera house next Tuesday. It's the opening of *Rigoletto*, and I have it on good authority that no expense was spared in the production."

"Which opera dancer told you so?"

"Amusing, but you're wrong. It was one of my mother's friends. Newland Jefferson. He's one of the producers."

"I know Mr. Jefferson." She considered what it would be like to sit beside Bram in his family's box for the length of *Rigoletto* and be the recipient of envious, covert stares and hushed asides. Attending the event would make their engagement more real to the public. "Will your mother be there?"

"Yes. A proper affair, with chaperone."

"I do like the opera," she said wistfully.

"I know. And your uncles hate it."

That decided her. "All right, but if this is the beginning of your campaign to extend our engagement beyond eight weeks, I feel compelled to remind you it won't work."

"It's one evening, Comfort."

That was true, she thought, but he was already grinning like he'd pulled a gold nugget out of a claim he'd just staked. Before she could think better of her answer, he was pivoting on his heel and heading back down the hall. She thought he might be whistling.

Shaking her head and smiling softly to herself, Comfort picked up her tooth-marked pencil and returned to reading. She'd just found her place when her chair listed sideways and the floor rumbled under her. She dropped the pencil and grabbed the lip of the desk to steady her. She held on until the thump and crash coming from the direction of the stairwell shot her to her feet.

Chapter Four

Comfort could see that Bram was in a bad way before she reached him. He lay at the bottom of the steps with his left leg turned out at an unnatural angle. Grasping the banister in the event another trembler made her lose her footing in the same way this one had done to Bram, she hurried down the stairs to his side.

There was a low buzzing beyond the stairwell, as though someone had thrust a stick into a beehive and disturbed the industry and order of the inhabitants. Comfort doubted anyone else had heard Bram fall. She knelt beside him just long enough to determine if he was conscious. He wasn't, but his chest rose and fell steadily, and when she glanced at his broken leg, she thought unconsciousness might be a blessing.

Running her fingers over his scalp, she felt a tender spot at the back of his head. She had imagined what it would be like to tidy Bram's ruffled and unruly thatch of sunshine yellow hair, but the circumstances in her mind's eye had been significantly different. Comfort snorted softly, impatient with herself for raising that silly, girlish memory.

She placed a hand on Bram's shoulder and spoke as if he could hear her. "I'm getting help, Bram. I won't be long." Standing, she grasped the door handle. The door to the lobby opened into the narrow stairwell, and there was little room for her to maneuver without disturbing Bram. She inched the door open, nudging aside one of his outstretched arms with the toe of her boot, and slipped sideways through the opening as soon as she judged it was wide enough.

There were no obvious signs of damage to the bank lobby that Comfort could see at a glance. Five patrons were milling around the open doorway, chatting among themselves while they observed activity in the street. The three tellers on duty were still at their posts, but no longer making transactions. Newt and Tucker had put certain procedures in place in the event of shakers, and the tellers had evidently followed them. The reinforced door that led to the bank's Boorstein & Durham safe was closed, and the cash drawers in the cages were locked. Once thirty minutes passed without an afterquake, the tellers would open for business.

She hurried over to the cages and joined the men's huddle. They ended their hushed conversation abruptly, and Mr. Tweedy, head teller these last five years and with the bank for more than eight, regarded Comfort over the top of his gold-rimmed spectacles.

"I was just saying how I was going to go up and see to your welfare since you didn't come down straightaway," he told her. "Are you all right? It was only a little quake, but rules is rules."

"I know, Mr. Tweedy, and I'm perfectly fine. Mr. DeLong, however, is lying unconscious in the stairwell. I'm certain his leg is broken. I need one of you to summon a doctor and another to go to the Black Crowne Shipping Office and inform Mr. DeLong's brother. If he's not there, you'll have to go to the warehouse."

Mr. Appleby was quick to volunteer to find a doctor. No one in their small group doubted it was because he wanted the easier of the two assignments. "Dr. Winter was at my cage not twenty minutes ago. If he was on his way home, I bet I can catch him."

Comfort wanted more certainty from their newest teller. "You *will* find him, Mr. Appleby, whether or not he's on his way home, and you *will* bring him here even if you have to sling him over your shoulder. You understand?"

Appleby's jug ears reddened at the tips, but he straightened and pulled his narrow shoulders back, meaning to show that he had the strength to do it. "I won't be long." He ducked out of the huddle before Comfort could change her mind about letting him go.

"Mr. Tweedy? Mr. Harte?" Comfort looked from one man to the other and saw only reluctance in their features. "Well, I will go then." When the men made what was obviously a perfunctory objection, she merely raised an eyebrow. "I appreciate your reluctance, and I'm not going to insist you do something that I am not willing to do, so one of you will remain at Bram's side, and one of you will manage the bank until my uncles return from the exchange."

Mr. Tweedy shook his head. "You can't go, Miss Kennedy. It's not safe even in daylight for you to venture into the Barbary Coast."

"It's only eleven o'clock, Mr. Tweedy. The sots and sailors are either sleeping or still passed out. Most of gambling houses are just opening their doors. Even the Rangers are resting after a long night of brawling and thieving. That little quake wasn't enough to make them leave their whores." She watched Mr. Tweedy blink so owlishly that the effect was comical. It was a good indicator of her frustration that she didn't laugh. "There. I've shocked you. If you don't report my language to my uncles, I won't mention that I gave you and Mr. Harte an opportunity to go to Crowne Shipping in my place." She turned on her heel and offered one last piece of advice over her shoulder. "You'd do well to make sure Mr. Appleby doesn't give you up."

Comfort crossed half the lobby before Mr. Tweedy caught her. "I'll go," he said, holding up his hat to prove that he was prepared. "The warehouse only abuts the Coast, doesn't it? And the Crowne Office is a few blocks from there. I can go around."

"Go whichever way you like," she said, out of patience. "Just go." Turning away, she thought she should probably feel guilty for shaming him into it but couldn't find that emotion for all the worry covering it. She caught Mr. Harte's eye as he was heading toward the stairwell and directed him back to the cages with a jerk of her head.

Comfort slipped into the dim stairwell and turned up the gaslight to better evaluate Bram's condition. Stooping, she touched his shoulder and tapped it gently. "Bram? Bram, can you hear me?"

She thought his eyes might have flickered behind his lids, so she held her breath, studying them for a moment but realizing it was only the play of shadows across his face. Afraid to move him, Comfort took advantage of his unconsciousness to leave his side and find what she could that would give him some ease when he woke. She discovered half a bottle of whiskey in one of Newt's desk drawers and some crumpled, paint-spattered sheets in a storage closet.

She was close to the bottom of the stairs when she realized that something had changed. Bram's body lay nearer the door than it had when she left. "Bram? You're awake?"

He didn't open his eyes, but he answered her from behind clenched teeth. "God, yes."

She almost cried with relief. "I'm coming. I have some sheets to put under your head and whiskey for the pain."

Bram looked up at her through a slit under his lashes. "Good. Hit me with the bottle and cover me with the sheet."

Comfort marveled that he could find humor in his situation. It seemed excessive, even for him. Looking down at him, she simply shook her head. Ten minutes couldn't have passed since he'd told her that he never took anything too seriously. There were some things she could accept at his word.

Comfort set the bottle on the lowest step and let go of two of the sheets. She folded the one in her arms into thirds and slipped it under Bram's head. "Can you look at me?" she asked.

He opened his eyes. "Twins." He gave her a groggy smile. "Very nice."

She couldn't tell whether he was having her on. She held up three fingers and demanded that he tell her the truth. Although he answered correctly, she wasn't convinced that he hadn't guessed. "I swear if I learn that you're pulling my leg, I'll pull yours."

"The broken one?"

"That's the only one worth pulling."

"Hard-hearted woman," he said under his breath.

"Yes." She looked him over again. "Can you extend your good leg? Wiggle your fingers?"

He did both those things. "See?"

She thought he was inordinately proud of his accomplishment, but then again, she wasn't the one in what had to be excruciating pain. "I need you to move away from the door. You're blocking it."

He looked sideways and saw what she said was true. "I was trying to get out."

"I know. And I'm sorry I wasn't able to stop you. I only left you for a few minutes."

"It's all right."

"I can help you."

"No. I'd rather you didn't."

Comfort nodded, understanding. In his position, she didn't think she'd want anyone touching her either. She moved out of his way and sank her teeth into her lower lip to keep from making unhelpful wincing noises. She grimaced several times, but he was concentrating on inching away from the door and paying no attention to her. When he'd moved far enough that even a man possessing the girth of Dr. Winter could get through, she told him to stop.

Comfort readjusted the makeshift pillow under Bram's head. "Have you ever had a broken bone?"

"No." He raised his head and looked down the length of his body at the unfortunate positioning of his left leg. "God, no." His pant leg was stretched tight across his knee. "I think I fell on it."

"What?"

"I think I fell on my own leg." His voice was rough but clear. "The stairs slipped out from under my feet, and I couldn't catch myself. I landed with all of my weight on my knee and . . ." His voice trailed away as he tried to recall what happened. "I don't remember after that."

"That's because you also hit your head."

"What about my face?"

She smiled. "Untouched. As beautiful as it ever was." Comfort thought he seemed satisfied with that. Bram was nothing if not confident of his fine looks. "Dr. Winter's been sent for."

"I don't know him."

"He's more than competent to handle your injury, and he wasn't far away. In fact, I expect that he'll be here shortly." Whether or not Mr. Appleby would make it so was out of her hands. "I also sent Mr. Tweedy out to notify your brother."

Bram groaned, but pain had nothing to do with it. "Why would you do that?"

"Because I thought he should know."

"Did you send someone to tell my mother?"

"No. Your brother's closer."

"Yes, but *she* would do something. Bode will thank your messenger for the information and return to what occupies him: his goddamn ships."

She blinked. "I'm sure you're wrong."

Bram's grimace veered toward derisive.

"I can't send anyone out with a message for your mother. I have only one teller here, and my uncles are still at the exchange."

"It's all right," he said after a moment. "She'd come with three doctors and six servants to bear my litter. It would be a farce of enormous proportions." He raised one hand to indicate their small space. "They couldn't possibly all fit, and God knows, she would insist that they try."

Comfort didn't have any trouble believing that. She laid her knuckles against his cheek. His skin was cool to the touch. She reached behind her and gathered the discarded sheets. Snapping them open, she covered Bram from his feet to his shoulders. "You're going to live," she said. "It's not a death shroud."

He smiled weakly. "I think I'll take that whiskey now."

She opened the bottle and held it to his lips. He placed a hand over hers and made certain she gave him more than a medicinal swallow. She let him have another swig before she took it away. She'd just put it back on the stairs when footsteps approached the other side of the door.

Comfort scrambled to her feet and kept the door from being pushed open with too much force. "Dr. Winter." She held up one finger to delay his entrance a moment longer. "Thank you for coming. Let me open the door from this side. You'll have to squeeze through, I'm afraid."

"I'm sure I'd have to do that in any case," he said, beaming and patting his protruding belly. He wore a brown wool jacket buttoned only at the top, as was the current style. It was meant to show off his yellow-and-green-checked vest but did a better job of showing off his love for rich desserts.

Comfort pulled the door open as far as she was able without

disturbing Bram before she motioned the doctor inside. "Thank you, Mr. Appleby," she said when the teller continued to hover near the door. "You can go back to your station. It's time to resume business." She climbed a few stairs to give Dr. Winter room to move and sat down.

"Let's see what we've got here," Dr. Winter said, drawing back the sheets. "You're the only injury I've heard about, Mr. DeLong. Seems nothing buckled, or if it did, people got out of the way. Oh my. I'd say that's broken." He opened his black leather medical bag and took out a pair of scissors. "But let's make sure."

Comfort knuckled her mouth to keep from laughing at Bram's genuine look of horror. If Dr. Winter noticed that his patient wanted to object, he wasn't having any of it. He sliced through Bram's trouser leg from the ankle to just above the knee and spread the material open. Comfort squinted at the misshapen flesh around the break. The skin was angry red and pulled taut over the swollen knee. She didn't need the doctor's quiet whistle to know it was a serious injury.

Winter dropped the scissors back in the bag and handed it off to Comfort. "Well, it has to be set, of course, but I don't want to do that here. I'd prefer my office, but I can manage if there's a place with some privacy in the bank. The lobby is acceptable if you remove your customers. We still have to get him out of this stairwell, of course."

"We can move him to where we keep the safe," Comfort said. "That's just behind the tellers' cages."

"Good." The doctor continued his examination, checking for bruising and other injuries. He made Bram answer more of the same questions that Comfort had already put to him, and then settled awkwardly on the bottom step once he was satisfied. He contemplated the door and the logistical problem of moving his patient.

Winter reared back as the door suddenly opened. There'd been no indication that anyone was approaching. Behind him, Comfort jumped to her feet and threw out a hand toward the door to protect Bram from being shoved aside. The doctor bent forward when Comfort stretched out above him and grabbed the door.

"Bode!" It wasn't until he smiled at her with a certain smugness that she realized she hadn't called him Mr. DeLong. It made her want to put her fist through the opening with the express intent of blackening his good eye. That would have certainly been unfortunate for him, because he was now wearing a black patch over his injured one. The rakish effect would not have been improved by wearing two. "You can't come in. There's no room."

"Let go of the door and allow me to have a look."

Comfort pushed away, teetering slightly over the good doctor until her heels rested solidly on the step. "Be careful."

Nodding, Bode poked his head in. "Winter. You're here. That's fortunate."

"Hello, Bode. What happened to your eye?"

"Nothing interesting. How's my brother?" He glanced down at Bram and made his own assessment. Although he didn't know it, his soft whistle was an echo of the doctor's. "Hello, Bram."

"Hello, Bode. Good idea to use the patch. Very piratical."

"Travers's idea." He met Bram's lopsided grin with one very much like it. "Odd, isn't it, that providence should restore balance to our situations so quickly?"

Even Bram's pain couldn't mask his startled expression. Seeing it, Comfort frowned. "What does he mean, Bram?"

It was Bode who answered. "I'm reminding my brother he shouldn't have had so much amusement at my expense."

"You're saying he deserved this?" she asked. "That's cruel."

Bram hushed her. "He's teasing me, Comfort. It's what brothers do. It's what I did to him."

Her eyes darted between them and could find nothing in their expressions to support the uncomfortable feeling that they were lying. "We need to move Bram," she told Bode. "Dr. Winter can set his leg in the back room. We're just not sure how to get him there."

Bode nodded as he glanced around. "What do you have in the medical bag, Doc? Anything like a chisel?"

"I have a file." He opened his bag and showed it to Bode. "To keep my scissors and scalpels sharp."

"That could work. Give it to Miss Kennedy. I have a hunch she can move more nimbly around your patient than you can."

"Very well reasoned," Dr. Winter said. He passed the file over his shoulder to Comfort.

"What am I supposed to do with this?" she asked.

Bode slipped an arm through and around the opening and pointed to the hinges. "Use it to pop the pins. If you have to loosen the plates, the point of a scalpel should work on the screws. Don't fret, Doc. I'll see that you get a new set if one of them is ruined."

Comfort didn't care overmuch about the doctor's scalpels. She examined the file, turning it over in her hands, and thought that Bode had happened upon a good idea. It could work. She got up and carefully picked her way around Bram's sprawled form until she came to stand near his head. She yanked her skirt close around her feet so the fabric wouldn't fall all over Bram's face. Taking a substantial breath, she applied herself to removing the hinge pin from the middle plate. She slipped the flat edge of the file against the divot under the pinhead and pushed up. When it didn't budge, she used the heel of her hand like a hammer to steadily pound the file in the direction she wanted it to go. She gave a little yelp of surprise when it gave way.

"You see?" Bode wiggled the fingers of his outstretched hand. "Here, I'll take it."

She dropped the pin in his palm and proceeded to attack the uppermost hinge. It came out with considerably less effort. Her challenge was the bottom one. She couldn't get under it to apply enough force to push on the pin. She bent the tips of two scalpels trying to turn the screws in the hinge plates before she gave up.

"Perhaps if I lie on the floor," she said. Before anyone could dissuade her, she twisted into the corner and began sliding down the length of it. Bram cocked his head to one side to make room for her as she kept lowering herself to the floor until she was on her back. The width of the stairwell was too short for her to lie flat, so she made her feet climb the opposite wall. The hem of her dress slid past her ankles and pooled around her knees. She didn't raise her feet any higher. Thus braced, she slipped the file in place and pushed upward as hard as she could.

The pin gave a mere fraction of an inch. She grunted with her next effort. "I don't know," she said. "I don't think I . . ."

"Yes, you can," Bode said quietly. "Imagine all of you is the hammer."

She glanced sideways and caught Dr. Winter's quizzical expression. Lifting her head just a bit, she was able to make out Bram's skepticism. She gripped the file again and closed her eyes. *I am the hammer.* She shoved the file upward with such force that the pin shot from the hinge plate as though fired from a cannon.

She caught it neatly on its way down, mere inches from Bram's open mouth. It was all very satisfying.

Bode grabbed the door and shimmied it free of the frame. He tipped and angled it so he could pull it toward him. He passed it to the men standing in a semicircle behind him and reached across the threshold to help Comfort to her feet. She managed it with considerably more grace than any other woman of his acquaintance who had occasion to find herself on her back.

"Excellent work," he told her. Without asking permission, he put his hands on her waist and lifted her out of the stairwell. He did not, however, pass her to his men. He knew them each well enough to see they were disappointed. "Where are we taking Bram?"

The question distracted her and kept her from poking him with the file. She thought that distraction was probably the point, since she'd already told him about the back room. Shifting her attention to it, though, reminded her that it was still locked. "There. Behind the cages," she said. "I'll open it."

"Take this," Bode said, picking up one of the sheets that covered his brother. "I assume there's a table. Put this over it. We'll use the other sheet to make a sling. And you'll still want to clear the lobby."

Comfort nodded. The patrons might be curious, but no one needed to hear Bram scream.

Alexandra DeLong sat at her younger son's bedside and read *Innocents Abroad* while he slept. Occasionally she smoothed hair away from his brow, glad that it resisted her efforts to tame it and continued to fall forward. It gave her something more satisfying to do than rearrange covers that really didn't require straightening.

Bram was heavily dosed with laudanum and had been since Dr. Winter set his leg. She was grateful that the doctor had used an ether mask on Bram while he manipulated the bones, but now there was only laudanum and sleep to ease the pain. They only worked in concert. Without the laudanum, Bram couldn't sleep, and outside of sleep the laudanum could only reduce the pain, not erase it.

She looked up from her book as Bode entered the room. "You're still here," she said, marking her place with a finger and closing the book over it. "I didn't expect that."

"Obviously." He went to her side and laid a hand on her shoulder. "I thought I would spend the night. Take one of the watches, as it were."

"That's not necessary. I don't think I'll be leaving his side."

"Mother."

"Don't reprove me, Bode. I'd sit with you if you were in such a state as this." Alexandra smiled ruefully as she examined his eye. "You almost were. How is your back?"

"It's fine. *I'm* fine."

"If I'd had any inkling that my boys would be made of such fragile stuff, I would have had girls."

Bode chuckled. "I just bet you would have."

Alexandra was mollified enough to reach back and lay a hand over the one Bode had on her shoulder. "Thank you. I appreciate that you went to be with Bram when you heard what happened. I know it's not always easy to be his brother."

"Not always, no."

She let her hand fall away. "At least he didn't bring it on himself this time. I can take some solace in that."

Bode didn't say anything. He left his mother's side and went to Bram's. He studied his brother's pale face with its perfect symmetry of features. There was no denying that Bram possessed the face of an angel. It had been remarked on since the moment of his birth. Bode remembered, though he hadn't agreed at the time. At first glimpse he'd only seen a squealing, pink-and-wrinkled piglet and hadn't changed his mind until Bram was four and had more blond curls springing from his head than a girl. Bode decided it was better for his brother to be an angel than a girl and handed Bram a pair of their mother's sewing shears.

Bode had never encouraged Bram to trouble after that. Bram had always been able to find it easily enough on his own.

"He was at the bank to invite Miss Kennedy to the opera," Bode said.

"I know. Comfort told me. Is she still here?"

"Downstairs."

"How like her." Alexandra looked at the clock. "It's late. Already after nine. You should see that she gets home safely."

"It occurred to me. If I can get her to leave."

"Tell her I insist. She's not to blame, and I don't blame her, even if the accident did happen at Jones Prescott."

Bode thought he would leave that last part out when he spoke to her. He turned around, bent, and kissed his mother on the cheek. "I'll be back after I take Miss Kennedy home."

"Are you going to stay?"

"Yes, I told you I would. For the night."

"Forever," she said.

"No, Mother. I don't live here any longer."

"Then there's no point, is there?"

She was being called. The voices, and she was certain there were more than one, came to her first on a delicate, undulating thread of sound. They said her name; she knew they did. How else could they hope to find her if they didn't use her name?

She cupped one hand to her ear to funnel the sound. It was something she often did when she heard them calling. They never spoke all at once. They were an undisciplined chorus, and what they said came at her in rapid succession, the words separated by half measures, each one an echo of another. All of it indistinguishable.

All of it frantic.

She sensed new urgency in their cries. She was touched by it, but not in a tender, yearning way. This urgency had physical presence and sharp claws that dug into her flesh. She bled where they pierced her. She sniffed. That faintly metallic scent, was it her blood? She wanted to wet her lips but was afraid she'd taste blood on them. She swirled her tongue around her mouth instead and swallowed her own spit. Raising her knees to her chest, she made herself small, then smaller yet. Her hiding place was dark, but she closed her eyes to make it even darker. She could still hear them calling her, crying out, though perhaps not as loudly as before. She couldn't be sure. What they wanted from her was a mystery. Was there something she was supposed to do? She always wondered if there was something she was supposed to do.

What she did was flatten her cupped hand against her ear. She raised her other hand and clapped it over the other ear. She could almost not hear them now. She only had to wait them out and then it would be done. They could not go on forever. No echo lasted an eternity.

She had the sense of time passing, though she could never be certain how long. She sensed she was older when they found her, not merely by a few minutes or hours, but by years. She couldn't understand it but accepted it as the truth.

She didn't open her eyes right away. Even when she felt the heat of sunshine on her face, she kept her eyes closed. She could hear breathing, whispers, but she wasn't curious about these sounds. It didn't matter. They weren't part of the chorus. Every word was distinct.

"Christ. It's a kid. Goddamnit, I can't do another kid."

"You got to. Someone's got to. I figure I'm up two or three on you. Maybe four if you count that woman and the baby like they was separate."

"Ain't you got sense enough not to remind me? You wanna see me puke? This ain't what I signed on for."

"Ain't what I signed on for either, but I reckon it's what we're in the middle of. Now, you gonna jaw about it or get it done?"

She opened her eyes. The light hurt them, and she blinked rapidly. The men moved closer together, blocking sunshine. Their faces were indistinct, protected by shadow and a penumbra of sunlight around their heads. They might have been angels, but she didn't think so. They wore hats. She'd never seen a picture of an angel wearing a hat. They didn't always have halos, but they never wore hats.

"What the hell are you two doing? You find something?"

She gave a start. The two men were joined by a third. His voice was hoarse. It scratched her skin, making it prickle. She stopped flattening her hands against her ears and hugged herself.

"It's a kid," One said. "A girl. Damn me if somehow that don't make it worse."

Three bent and peered into her rock shelter. "Christ." He straightened, reached into his pocket, and withdrew something that fit neatly into his palm. After a few moments spent fiddling with it, he raised a hand to his mouth. When he spoke, his voice didn't scrape her skin quite so much. "Leave her be," he said.

"But you said no survivors," Two said.

"And now I'm saying leave her be. Do you have a problem with that?"

Two hesitated before he said, "No, sir."

"Seems like you do."

"No, sir. Not really."

One spoke up. "She's gonna die here. We're takin' most everything."

"So it would be a kindness to kill her now, is that what you're saying?"

Neither One nor Two said anything. They didn't shrug. They didn't move. They didn't make decisions.

"That's what I thought," said Three. He stared at the object in his palm, turning it over and over while the others waited for him to speak.

She waited, too. It would be important, what he said.

"Leave her," he said at last. "And leave her this."

She didn't have time to prepare for the thing that was tossed in her direction. It was an afterthought, and it landed in the cradle of her dress between her knees. She stared at it and had one clear image of the afterthought before she was plunged into darkness.

And then the voices began calling to her again.

"Miss Kennedy." Bode touched her shoulder, shaking her more forcefully than he had moments earlier. "Comfort. Wake up."

Comfort rolled her shoulder, trying to avoid the insistent and disturbing fingers that crawled over her skin like fire ants.

"Wake up. You're dreaming. It's a dream." By quickly stepping to one side, Bode managed to narrowly avoid hard contact with Comfort's head when she bolted upright. Watching her, he rubbed his chin as if he could feel the blow that hadn't happened. He wasn't certain she was awake. Her stare was vacant. The dark eyes, so beautifully expressive even when she did not mean them to be, were almost frightening in their perfect emptiness.

He put himself in front of her again and hunkered down. That positioned him below her eye level in a way that he hoped didn't threaten her. A single swift kick aimed at his chest, and he would be sitting on the floor. He tried to draw her attention to him by fanning his palm in front of her face.

Comfort blinked. "What are you doing?" She put out one hand to stop him before her eyes crossed.

Bode withdrew his hand but didn't move away. He studied her face. Her cheeks were sleep-flushed. Her slightly parted lips looked as soft and plump as pillows. Wisps of hair framed a smooth brow and brushed her temples. He thought that if he touched the cord in her slim neck, he'd feel only a steady pulse. Searching her eyes, he found them changed as well. What had haunted them had fled, and she now returned his regard as if he were the peculiar one.

"You were dreaming," he said.

"Was I?" Her eyes darted away, embarrassed. "I didn't realize I was tired enough to fall asleep."

"You don't remember?"

"What? Falling asleep?"

He shook his head. "The dream."

"No."

"Really?"

"Really." It was the only lie she could tell and have a reasonable expectation that she would be believed. She'd been practicing it for years, and when Bode didn't press her further, she was glad she'd made the effort.

Bode stood. "I was going to have a glass of whiskey," he said. "Would you like a sherry?"

Comfort touched her throat and nodded. She was parched. It was not possible to recall a time when she'd awakened from the dream and hadn't felt as if she had a mouthful of dust. Swallowing was painful as she watched Bode pour the drinks.

Looking away, her gaze slid over the gilt-edged clock that rested squarely in the middle of the mantelpiece to the oil painting that hung above it. A clipper ship, one with all of her gleaming white sails straining before the wind, ran high in the water, her bow cutting sharply through foamy crests like a knife through meringue. It captured a single moment in time, but looking at it, one couldn't fail to appreciate the artist's mastery of motion. The clouds were ellipses, casting long shadows as they rode on the back of a swift wind. The ship drew a narrow wake, exposing the cleft in the churning water to sunlight and throwing out a thousand glittering crystals of spindrift. Her sails were stretched to their full allowance, each one of them cupping the following wind, and at the top of her foremast her colors were unfurled in a rippling, snapping line.

Bode held out a glass of sherry to Comfort and followed her gaze to the painting when she didn't immediately take it. "Do you have an opinion?" he asked.

She shook her head. Out of the corner of her eye, she saw he was holding her drink. She took it, sipped only enough to keep her tongue from cleaving to the roof of her mouth, and then told him, "I have a reaction."

Curious about the distinction she made, Bode arched an eyebrow.

"I'm moved by it," she said simply. She held the stem of her glass between her palms and rolled it slightly. "It's a portrait, isn't it?"

"I don't know what you mean."

"That's a Black Crowne clipper. I recognize her colors. And the artist has taken some liberties with the scale of the ship against the waves. It makes me think this painting is more personal in nature. So many seascapes are about the artist's study of light. There's an attempt to capture reflection and distinguish the gradations of color in the sky and the sea and create a horizon that is real and yet insubstantial." She lifted her eyes to the painting again. "This artist was trying to capture speed. Perhaps supremacy. To the extent that such things can be caught, I think he succeeded."

"He? Are you so certain it was a man who painted it?"

Comfort tilted her head a little to the side as she studied the painting again. "No," she said. "I don't suppose that I am." Her head came up sharply, and she stared at him, faintly open-mouthed. "Your mother is the artist, isn't she?"

"No," he said, smiling slightly. "My mother is not as wildly romantic as that painting would suggest, but I think she would be flattered if you thought so. Your assumption that a man painted it was correct. The artist was my father."

Now Comfort's eyebrows lifted. "I never heard anyone describe your father as an artist." Nor a romantic, she thought, but she didn't say so.

"Well, no." His thin smile didn't falter. "That isn't what anyone talked about. He gave them other things to discuss." Bode chose the chair opposite the overstuffed sofa where Comfort sat. He leaned back and slid his long legs forward, crossing them casually at the ankle. "Many other things."

Comfort didn't think she was expected to respond to that. She was familiar with the gossip that accompanied Branford DeLong wherever he went and always suspected there was more than was ever repeated within her hearing. Except for a stray comment now and again, Bram remained largely silent about his father. Alexandra was equally reserved in discussing her late husband. Their reluctance to talk about him, even to appreciate his talents, made it stranger yet that Branford's striking oil painting was displayed prominently in their home. It was of the romantic style with its vivid colors and bold, sweeping brushstrokes, but perhaps it wasn't the artist they were admiring, but the subject, the seductiveness of the sea and the Black Crowne ship that could bring that temptress to heel.

"This isn't the first time you're seeing the painting, is it?" asked Bode.

"No. I've had tea with your mother in this parlor several times. If she noticed me staring at it, she never inquired after my thoughts."

"And Bram? Did he never ask?"

Amused by the idea, she said, "Your brother doesn't discuss art unless the subject is . . ."

"Naked and female?" he ventured when she fell silent.

Comfort nodded. She could have said exactly that to Bram, but his brother caused her to be strangely tongue-tied. She couldn't put her finger on why that would be the case, but she suspected it might have something to do with his impenetrable blue-violet stare. That did not stop her, though, from adding another salient feature of the only art that Bram was likely to discuss. "And plump," she said. "He waxes poetic if she's plump."

Bode's lips didn't so much as twitch. Instead, a small crease appeared above the bridge of his nose. He absently fingered the top edge of the silk eye patch. "What *do* you and my brother find to talk about? Or for that matter, what did you find to write about for so many years?"

"When you ask that question, I can never tell if it's your brother you mean to insult, or me."

"Bram cannot be insulted."

She pressed the lip of her glass against her smile before she sipped. "It cannot have escaped your notice that Bram has adventures. I don't. That's what he wrote about, what he talks about. And he does it with a great deal of wit. It is a rare moment that he fails to entertain. That is something to be appreciated, I think."

"You value him as your court jester, then."

She felt her hackles rise sharply. It required considerable effort not to place a hand to the back of her neck and smooth them over. She wondered if she should point out that *she* could be insulted. "I value Bram's friendship for what he brings to it that is out of the ordinary."

"I see. And what would he say he values about you?"

Comfort considered that for a long moment before she answered. "Perhaps that I don't judge him."

Bode studied her and then nodded slowly. "I think you're probably right." He finished his whiskey, set the tumbler aside, and pointed to the clock. "I'm surprised one of your uncles hasn't sent a carriage for you."

She blinked. "That can't be the right time. I thought the clock must have wound down."

"I'm afraid not."

"But it's twenty minutes after eleven." Comfort jumped to her feet. A cashmere shawl pooled around the hem of her dress. She stared at it. "Where did that come from?"

"Most recently it's been in your lap. Before that, it covered you while you slept. And before that, it was folded across the back of this chair."

She stooped and picked it up, closed the short distance between them, and handed over her glass and the shawl. "I have to go. Where is my jacket? My hat?"

"A moment," he said. "And a few deep breaths." It was good advice for himself as well. He put her glass beside his tumbler and tossed the shawl behind him. "Let me ring for Hitchens. He will make everything right. He frequently does." He stood and crossed the room to summon the butler.

Comfort's hand flew to her mouth. "I didn't even ask about Bram."

"You asked about him every other time I came in here," he said, pulling the cord. "One oversight does not make you careless."

"You're not telling me anything."

Bode managed not to sigh. "His condition is exactly the same," he said patiently. "He's sleeping. He's comfortable. He's drugged."

"I wish you would have awakened me right away," she said. "Perhaps I could have visited him one more time before I left."

"You were obviously exhausted. Vigils are wearing."

He was right about that. "Your mother's still with him?"

"Yes."

"You'll relieve her, though, won't you? She won't leave his side otherwise."

She won't leave his side regardless. He did not voice what went through his mind. The words would have tasted bitter on his tongue.

Rigoletto was a disappointment, but she could hardly blame her uncles for that. They'd succeeded in surprising her with tickets to the performance, and knowing how deeply they loathed opera, she was touched by their gesture and unable to refuse it. They were aware of Bram's invitation, of course, and equally aware that after his accident the DeLong family box would be empty. That wasn't quite how it turned out, however, and every time Comfort's eyes strayed from the stage, she saw Beauregard DeLong looking back at her.

Most disconcertingly, he didn't try to pretend he wasn't watching her. He wore the eye patch, and while she heard the explanation that he'd given at the party bandied about, no one seemed to think he was a charlatan for affecting the raffish, slightly dangerous look even though he'd only earned it by running afoul of a mother cat and her kittens. It was just as well, she thought. If the truth got about that he'd tangled with the Rangers and a band of ruffians and lived to tell the tale, there would be swooning.

She had run into him several times in the week since Bram's accident. It was inevitable, she supposed, that she would see him coming or going from Bram's bedside. He was invariably polite, though perhaps a little distant. It was hard to account for the feeling she had that he was there for her, not his brother, and she found herself thinking about him at odd moments, remembering a snippet of conversation, or more disturbing, the feel of his tautly muscled back under her feet. He never once mentioned that he would be at the opera tonight, and she wondered if she would be here if she'd known.

At the break, Newt and Tucker escorted Comfort to the lobby for refreshments. They had beer. She drank lemonade.

"Are you feeling well?" Tucker asked as they retreated to a stand of dwarf potted palms with their drinks. He hoped he could duck under the fronds and stay hidden there during the third act. "There's not much color in your cheeks."

"Isn't there? I don't know why that would be."

"I think she looks flushed," Newt said. "I noticed it while we were still in there. The Duke was singing. Gilda was singing. Rigoletto was singing. I was wishing they would just talk like regular folks, and I noticed Comfort looked flushed."

"Would you like to leave?" she asked, getting to the heart of so much concern for her looks and health.

"Oh, no," said Newt. "Promised myself that I'd stay to the end, bitter though it might be."

"Might be?" asked Tuck, scratching his chin. "They always end bitterly. I think the Italians must be the most dyspeptic people on earth."

Newt nodded sagely. "Probably comes from ruling the world once upon a time and then losing it all at the gambling table. That's enough to make a whole race of people disagreeable."

Comfort nearly choked on her lemonade. "What are you talking about, Uncle Newt?"

"That Caesar fellow. He put his empire on the table and rolled the dice."

Tucker winked at Comfort. "*The die is cast.*"

She laughed, and her enjoyment of the moment put genuine color in her cheeks. It lasted until Bode joined them.

He nodded to Newton, then Tucker, before addressing Comfort. "Miss Kennedy."

"Good evening, Mr. DeLong. I didn't realize you would be here this evening."

"A decision at the last minute when I learned that my mother was not going to attend."

"How is your brother?" asked Newt.

"Miserable."

Newt sighed heavily. "I'm more than passing familiar with that state."

Bode chuckled. "I noticed that you did not seem to be enjoying yourself before the break."

"Did you catch me napping?"

"No. I didn't see that."

"Then you're right. I wasn't enjoying myself."

"Uncle Newton." Comfort tried to him give a cross look, but his expression was so comically forlorn that she couldn't manage it. "He dislikes opera," she told Bode. "So does Uncle Tucker. They're here for me."

"Ah. I see." He inclined his head toward Newton. "Then what would you say to joining me in my box? All of you, I mean. I can have another chair carried in. There's plenty of room to add one. Mr. Jones, you can sit with Mr. Prescott at the rear. I know for a fact that you can sleep there undisturbed by anything except the sound of your own snoring."

Comfort saw immediately that her uncles were tempted by Bode's offer, and that she was at the root of their hesitation. Tuck witnessed what she'd done when Bode annoyed her at the party, and she had every reason to expect that he'd told Newt. They were probably as concerned for Bode as they were worried about what she would do if it happened again.

"It's a generous offer," she said. "I know my uncles would be delighted to join you."

"And you, Miss Kennedy?"

"Of course I'm coming." She accepted his arm as warmly as if she'd had a real choice, and then confided, "I don't like to let them out of my sight."

Tucker and Newton fell into step behind them. "I heard that," Newton said. "So did Tuck."

"But I'm not grumbling about it, am I?" Tucker said.

Comfort allowed Bode to maneuver them through the crowded lobby. Ruby stickpins and diamond-encrusted hair combs glittered in the gaslight. Silk and satin rustled noisily as evening gowns and crinolines were reshaped in the press of so many bodies. There was chatter and talk, but it seemed that no one was discussing the opera. Comfort understood that for most of the patrons, the performance was an excuse to gather, to see and be seen, and that didn't diminish her enjoyment.

She noticed that while Bode was polite to everyone who spoke to him, he did not pause to engage in intimate conversation. It would have been different if she'd been on Bram's arm. In contrast to Bode, Bram had an uncanny ability to greet everyone familiarly and make each person feel important in his life, and then never give them another thought until their paths crossed again. She rather admired Bode for the way he did it. There was no element of performance, no staging, no asides.

He was merely genuine, and it was relaxing.

Comfort paused at Bode's side as the couple in front of them began to negotiate the stairs to the upper level. The woman's train was so long, the flounces so elaborately detailed, that she required her escort's help to keep from stepping on her own skirt.

The gentleman fumbled with something in his hand as he lifted his companion's train. He could not close his fingers over the object and lend assistance at the same time. It fell out of his palm.

Comfort bent more quickly than Bode and scooped it up. "Here, sir. You dropped this." She held it out before she had a proper look at it, and when she saw what it was, tiny sparks darted up the length of her arm. They danced on her shoulder and her fingertips went numb.

Bode caught the red-and-white tin before it fell more than a few inches. "Here you go, sir. Almost dropped twice."

The gentleman smiled. His mustache lifted at the edges. "Thank you. I assure you, everyone sitting around me will be glad I didn't lose this. I am cursed with an annoying tickle in my throat the moment the soprano begins her aria."

Comfort didn't hear what he said as much as feel his words. His voice scratched her skin, making it prickle, and darkness closed in from all sides.

Chapter Five

The time that Comfort was unconscious of her surroundings could be measured in seconds, not minutes; therefore she was doubly distressed to find herself already being carried toward the outer lobby doors when she woke. Because drawing more attention was not what she wanted, she remained quiet in Bode's arms and allowed him to transport her from the heavily perfumed and cloying confines of the theater into the brisk evening air.

"You may put me down," she said when they reached the sidewalk. "Tell him to put me down, Uncle Tuck."

Tucker ignored her. He continued to wave his arm in a wide arc to summon their driver, who was waiting with the carriage down the street.

With no help likely to come from that quarter, Comfort applied to Newton. "Please, Uncle, explain to Mr. DeLong that I am fully prepared to stand on my own."

Hovering close at Bode's shoulder, Newton heard her and nodded. "Comfort's prepared to stand on her own," he said. "But if you put her down, I'll cut you off at your knees."

"Uncle Newt!" Comfort felt Bode's silent laughter rumble in his chest. The threatening glare she gave him was ineffective because he refused to look at her.

Tucker trotted off to meet the carriage and hurry the driver along while Newton continued to hover. Bode repositioned himself to better secure Comfort, and she surrendered to the inevitable and slid her arms around his neck so he wouldn't drop her.

It wasn't until the carriage arrived and Tuck opened the door for them that Bode set Comfort on her feet. Newt lowered the carriage step, and Tucker reached out to take her hand. It was then that Bode eased away.

"I'd like to call on her tomorrow," he said to Newt. "If I may?"

Preoccupied with getting Comfort safely in the carriage, Newt nodded. "Yes, of course. She'll be at home."

"I'll be at the bank," Comfort said before she realized that her answer made it seem as if she welcomed Bode's call.

Tucker pulled her the rest of the way into the carriage and poked his head out. "She'll be at home." He gestured to Newt to get inside. "Thank you, Bode. Good night."

Bode flipped up the step after Newt climbed in. He tapped the carriage to alert the driver that it was safe to leave, and then he stood at the edge of the sidewalk, watching the carriage until it turned the corner on Montgomery Street.

"Good night," he said softly. Hunching his shoulders against the breeze coming up from the bay, he began walking home.

Comfort knew she could not hope to put off an inquiry until she arrived home. She was mildly surprised that the carriage made it as far as Montgomery Street before her uncles began to pepper her with questions.

Tucker leaned into the space that separated the bench seats and took Comfort's hands. He squeezed them lightly and regarded her calm, dark eyes. He still took peace where he could find it, and just now it was in the gentle tightening of her fingers in his.

"Are you all right?" he asked.

She nodded. "Perfectly fine. It was unexpected, is all."

Newton knuckled his chin, thoughtful. "For us, too. You've never fainted before. Why do you suppose you did?"

"I've been thinking about that," she said. And she had. "I bent very quickly to pick up what the gentleman dropped."

"You did," said Tuck.

"And then I stood just as quickly."

"True enough," said Newt.

"So it was probably just that. The blood rushing in and out of my head." When Tuck and Newt said nothing, she added, "It was overly warm in the lobby, I thought. And did you notice that every time a gentleman emerged from the cloakroom, a fog of smoke accompanied him? I suspect all of that contributed to my light-headedness."

Tuck nodded once, released Comfort's hands, and sat back against the thickly stuffed leather seat. "That seems like a reasonable explanation. Newt? What do you think?"

"Except for leavin' out the part where she got a good look at that tin, it sounds about right."

"That tin? What do you mean?"

Tuck and Newt exchanged vaguely troubled glances. "Dr. Eli Kennedy's Comfort Lozenges," Tucker said.

Newt added, "The red-and-white tin."

Comfort's eyes darted between them. "I don't understand."

Tucker frowned. "The gentleman dropped a tin identical to the one you keep at your bedside."

"No, he didn't," she said. "He dropped a glove. I picked up his glove."

"Comfort." Newt said her name with a certain amount of reproof in his tone. "It wasn't a glove."

"You and Uncle Tuck were standing behind me. I don't know how you saw anything, but please, ask Mr. DeLong. He was right there. He saw it all." Comfort maintained a steady gaze. Clearly it wasn't what they expected to hear. If anything, they looked more troubled.

"It *was* a tin," Tuck said.

Comfort didn't know what to say. "I believe you think so, and even if it's true, I don't understand why you think it's significant. I've seen tins like it before. You know I have. Many times. I've never fainted."

Newt pursed his lips and wiggled them back and forth as he considered her answer. "I don't know, Comfort. I can't explain that myself, but it seems like something about it is significant. I saw what Tuck saw. You dropped like a stone."

"You dropped the tin first," said Tuck. "Do you remember that?"

"I remember dropping the glove. It slipped right out of my fingers."

Tuck frowned. "I don't understand this." He looked at Newt. "You understand it?"

"Nope. Not a thing."

Their genuine concern was more troubling to Comfort than her fainting had been. She tried to think of something that would ease their minds, but short of admitting that she'd picked up a tin, nothing came to her. It was tempting to retract her story and tell them what they seemed to want to hear, but the thought of lying, even with good intention, settled uncomfortably in her belly.

Comfort chose to stare out the carriage window instead, thus avoiding the worried expressions they wore all the way home.

Waking parched, Comfort reached for the carafe of water on her nightstand and poured a glass. The first one hardly quenched her, and she poured a second. By the time she satisfied her thirst, she had all but drained the carafe.

She'd made the decision the night before that she wasn't going to argue with Newt and Tuck about going to the bank. Not distressing them further influenced her decision, but it didn't explain it in its entirety. There were things Comfort wanted to learn for herself, and to make certain she could do it, she had to reach Beau DeLong before her uncles.

Since they expected her to remain at home, she thought it was safe to assume they would open the bank and visit the exchange before going to the Black Crowne Shipping Office. More immediately concerning was the likelihood that Suey Tsin would follow her if she got wind of what was being planned.

To allay her maid's tendency to be suspicious of any change in the routine, Comfort followed what had been established as normal for those infrequent occasions that she was feeling under the weather. That meant she didn't bathe or dress her hair and was uncharacteristically snappish each time Suey Tsin crept into the room to check on her.

On the third such inspection, Comfort played possum and garnered herself enough time to wash at the sink, plait her hair, and manage the strings that flattened the front of her simplest day dress. She chose a large straw hat trimmed with a black grosgrain bow that sat on her head like a mushroom cap. To make it plainer, she snipped off the ribbon streamer and removed the tiny tuft of field flowers that decorated the top. Instead of a jacket, she selected a thin brushed cotton shawl that had only a few hand-painted red poppies on it to recommend it as fashionable. She left her parasols in the stand. An elaborately decorated parasol was just the sort of accessory that would draw the notice of someone who coveted the money or status it would bring.

She timed her exit to coincide with the household help gathering in the kitchen for breakfast and their daily meeting and had no difficulty walking out the front door. When Suey Tsin realized she was gone, the maid would assume she'd sneaked off to work. Comfort hardly felt a twinge of guilt for her deception.

Black Crowne Shipping occupied a building set a block back from the wharf and south of Pacific Street. Unlike the warehouse, which abutted the lawless frontier known as the Barbary Coast, the shipping office where business was regularly conducted had not yet been swallowed up by the vice and violence of that district. It was, however, close enough to give a woman on her own reason to worry. Comfort clearly remembered Mr. Tweedy's reluctance to venture through the area and knew his concerns were not without foundation. She also recalled what she'd told him to ease his fears.

The Coast *was* quiet, at least relatively so this early in the morning, but in a few hours it would be a hive of activity. That was no different than it had been when she was younger and new to the city, although no one had yet called it the Barbary Coast. She'd known it by the name "Sydney Town," and for a brief period of time, it had been home.

There were mostly tents then. And shanties. Rough wooden pallets in the open air were what passed for boardinghouse accommodations, and the men who paid for the privilege of sleeping there were glad to be off the ground. After a hard rain, the mud was so deep in the streets it could suck in a horse. Sometimes it trapped a rider as well. Miners lived hand to pan and hand to mouth. All of them had dreams of the rich strike that would take them home on a golden ship. The ones who became successful, though, were hardly ever the ones panning the streams and digging out ore. Those that realized wealth got there by recognizing other opportunities and making the miners pay.

It wasn't much of an exaggeration that a man with three shovels, a couple of pickaxes, and a pound of nails could sell it all off and make enough money to open a hardware store. An enterprising merchant from Pennsylvania brought enough flour, salt, and bacon grease with him to start a cookery and, later, a dry goods emporium. There were men who sold rivets to repair dungarees, and who understood eventually that there was even more money in making and selling the denim trousers. And so it went for the men who had entrepreneurial skills, although perhaps no one was as committed to the success of their endeavors as the gamblers and whoremongers.

Newt Prescott and Tucker Jones came to banking the way a bear comes to be trapped in a pit. They fell into it on their way to somewhere else. Unlike the bear, they didn't try to get out. Once they understood their good fortune, they worked hard to make certain they'd earned it.

Comfort knew that Newt and Tuck believed it was her presence that was responsible for the trust other miners showed them. Children were so rarely seen that miners occasionally offered her uncles money just to ruffle her hair. They'd offer more to hear her laugh.

Newt swore they never took so much as a mote of gold dust in response to these offers. Tuck said it was because she would have bitten off the fingers of a man who dared touch her hair, and she laughed so infrequently that they would have been taking the money with no hope of keeping it.

What really seemed to engage the miners' trust was how close Comfort stayed to her uncles and how much regard they showed for her welfare. The first miner who asked them to hold his small bag of gold because he feared being rolled and robbed on his way to his claim discovered they could be counted on to return what they'd been given and a little something else besides.

While the miner worked his claim, Comfort accompanied Newt into town, where he bought three pounds of nails. She helped him sell the nails in smaller quantities, sometimes one at time, and when they returned to the mining camp, they had parlayed the miners' trust into gold and interest and a modest profit for themselves.

That was the beginning. After that, Comfort assisted Newt every time he went into town. She stood at his side and helped him hawk whatever he decided to purchase that day. Sometimes it was apples or eggs they got from a farmer before he could bring them to market. They sold wheat flour and salt pork, tea and coffee, and occasionally loaves of stale bread and slices of cheese. Whether they sold the wares on muddy corners or went from tent to shanty to tent again, at the end of the day they had gold to show for it.

Tuck accompanied them, but he didn't have the temperament for selling. His role was to follow them around and protect their investment. Neither he nor Newt considered that it was the gold.

Eventually they earned enough to set up a storefront, where they lent money for very little interest and offered to manage accounts for a small return to their customers. They lifted their first safe from an abandoned ship in the harbor, and it was good enough to survive the fire that leveled the town a few years later. They rebuilt, this time with a grander vision in mind, and began to make real investments in property, the Pacific trade, and the mining companies that were moving in. In 1859, when the Comstock Lode was discovered on the eastern slope of the Sierras in Nevada, they were among the backers of the quartz mills and mining machinery that eventually opened up the greatest veins of gold and silver anyone had ever seen.

Jones and Prescott became millionaires.

They never got entirely used to it, but occasionally they enjoyed trying. They built a house on Nob Hill as grand as any that existed at the time. Newt wrote to each of his four sisters back in New York and asked for their advice about books for his new home, especially those suitable for the edification and proper deportment of the odd little girl, now fourteen, whom he and Tucker wished to raise as a lady. And, he wrote on, recommendations for two old soldiers who were now required to stand toe to toe with society's best-heeled mavens and industrialists would also be welcomed. His sisters were helpful in all aspects of the venture, and he purchased over two hundred books to begin their library. Tucker put in a conservatory, not so much because he was interested in rare or beautiful plants, but because he wanted a room that opened to the sky.

That was how Comfort left Sydney Town with its cruel brothels and treacherous gambling houses. Newt and Tuck had done their best to protect her from the vices, but it had been a long time since they'd experienced the world at the eye level of a curious child, and when they needed to make certain there was shelter for her, they had all lived for a time at the rear of a saloon that was no more than a large tent with rooms cordoned off by blankets hanging over a hemp line. Some games of chance went on in those rooms, but mostly it was drinking and whoring, and while the girls who worked the rooms were always kind to her, the customers were not always kind to the girls. Comfort learned the difference between the moans they made when they lay with a man and the moans they made when a man laid them out.

Lost in reflection, Comfort almost passed the unassuming office for Black Crowne. She did miss the doorway and had to stop and back up a few steps. The tinkling of a bell fastened to the door announced her entry. She stood just inside, but no one came from the back to greet her. A long counter and the gate attached to it split the room in half. The gate was closed, an obvious attempt to keep the customers in one area and the clerks in another. At least temporarily. Rather like the lions and the Christians, she thought, and wondered which she was.

After several minutes of waiting, she approached the counter and rapped hard on it. She thought she heard something, but no footsteps followed the rustling, and that caused her to wonder about wharf rats. There was not very much that made her squeamish, but rats could do it. She gathered her skirts a little closer and pressed against the counter.

There was a spindle filled with notes at her side. For want of something better to do, she began to leaf through the messages. When that proved uninteresting, she counted the cubbies on the wall behind the counter and tried to guess at which ones contained important documents such as bills of lading and passenger manifests and which ones were the repository for things forgotten about long ago, like a schedule for a ship no longer making the Pacific run.

There was a small stove on the clerk's side of the counter whose warmth would have been welcome this chilly morning if someone had thought to tend to it. The clerk was obviously more warm-blooded than she. Rubbing her hands together—she hadn't worn gloves because she had none sufficiently plain—Comfort took a slow turn about the room. There were no chairs, no stools, no amenities for the customers. For the first time she wondered if the business was done by appointment. She felt a little better about being ignored after that and was able to stretch her patience all of five minutes. When rapping on the counter did not provide her with assistance and opening and closing the door several times was equally ineffective, Comfort opened the gate and stepped into what she was sure now was the lion's side of the room.

"Hello?" she called, entering the back room. "Is anyone—" She stopped because it was plain to her that there was no one around. It was a large room, much of it taken over by the storage of boxes and barrels and crates. There was one open corner with a desk and several chairs positioned directly in front of it. The surface of this desk had nothing in common with hers. It was clear of everything except a pen and inkstand, an oil lamp, and a blotter. She suspected she'd found where Bode worked.

Knowing that he had his own rooms somewhere in the building, Comfort began picking her way around the stacks. It was considerably more challenging than a garden maze. Even when she stood on tiptoe, she couldn't see over the top of or around most of the pyramids. She followed a course that she hoped would take her to a set of stairs at the back or to the rear exit and a set of stairs on the outside of the building.

What she found were steps so steep they might well have been a ladder. She recognized them as something that would have served that purpose on a ship's gangway and probably had done so at one time. "Ridiculous man," she said under her breath. Grasping the rope railings on either side of the stairs, Comfort began to climb.

Bode sat on a stool with his heels hooked on the lowest rung and his elbows resting on the edge of his drawing table. He studied the sketch in front of him, not satisfied, but not yet clear on what it was he didn't like. Perhaps it was her lines that were wrong. In his mind, she was sleeker than what he'd been able to draw. More fluid. Slippery.

One corner of his mouth lifted, tempering his frustration with humor. Slippery. She should be without friction, without resistance. She should be . . .

He began to furiously erase the changes he'd made in the last hour.

Comfort didn't know if she was expected to knock on the hatch or throw it open and then announce she was aboard. Courtesy dictated her response. She knocked.

Lost in thought, Bode mistook the direction of the sound and glanced up at the skylight overhead, expecting to find a gull pecking at the sash. When the sound came again, he correctly determined the source of it.

"I told you I don't want to be disturbed, John. Handle Mr. Roman's complaint yourself. If you can't manage that, I don't see the use of employing you any longer."

Feeling rather sorry for John, and hoping that managing Mr. Roman was what explained his absence from the front office, Comfort decided she should show herself. She pushed open the hatch wide enough to poke her head through. She felt rather like a prairie dog cautiously gauging the safety of leaving his hole.

"You won't get many visitors here, Mr. DeLong, although I understand that might be part of the appeal."

Dropping his pencil, Bode swiveled around and stared at Comfort. "What are you doing here?"

She pushed the hatch open wider and raised herself up another step. "That should be obvious. I've come to speak to you."

Bode slid off the stool and crossed the room quickly. He threw back the door, reached down to take the hand she extended to him, and helped her up.

Comfort was aware that she did very little of the work herself. He practically hoisted her out of the hole. When he set her down, she straightened her bonnet and shawl and smoothed the front of her dress. She gave a little start when he let the hatch slam shut.

"Well," she said, striving for a brisk, businesslike tone. "This is unexpected."

He frowned and pinned her in place with a narrow, steely look. "I think you have our lines confused. That's what I should be saying."

"Oh, I wasn't referring to the fact of seeing you as unexpected. How could it be? I came looking for you." She waved a hand airily about the room. "No, I meant this place. Your quarters. They are quarters, aren't they? As on a ship. The gangway. The hatch. Shipmaster's quarters." She bent a little sideways to peek around him when he didn't move. "It's quite large. A stateroom, I believe. I didn't expect that. It's not as big as the entire floor below, but that would be excessive. You have several rooms, I see. Cabins. Is that what you call them?"

"I call them rooms." Bode shifted and planted a foot firmly on the floor when she tried to step around him. "Who knows you're here?"

She shook her head. The look he gave her occupied the range between incredulity and fury. Knowing that she deserved at least some part of it, although perhaps not with the intensity of his present expression, Comfort found the grace to look sheepish. It wasn't her fault, she thought, that he believed she was being disingenuous.

Bode put his palm directly in front of her face. He was satisfied when she flinched. Good. She deserved to be a little afraid of him. "What about your maid?" he asked. "Suey Tsin."

Comfort's eyebrows lifted, surprised he remembered Suey Tsin's name. "She probably thinks I'm at the bank." She disliked talking to his hand but was loath to nudge it aside. Touching him did not seem to be advised, and in truth, she was averse to the idea on general principle. The general principle being that she didn't put her hand in fire.

Bode lowered his palm. "And where do your uncles think you are?"

"At home." She watched him close his eyes briefly and supposed he was dipping into his well of patience. When he looked at her again, she surmised the well wasn't very deep. "I'm certain they will try to visit you sometime today. I thought it was better if I arrived first."

"You mean I can expect that they will find you here?"

"No. No, I don't mean that at all. Not unless you continue to ask questions that delay me from explaining the point of my visit."

By God, she was taking *him* to task. "By all means, explain yourself."

She exhaled softly. "Well, I'm sure it will seem that a lot of fuss is being made about a misunder—" She broke off. "Can't you invite me in?"

"You are in. I dropped the hatch, didn't I?"

Comfort supposed his intention was to remind her that he could have dropped her through it. That he could *still* drop her through it. Her legs felt a little wobbly. "May I sit, then? You can put the stool right here. I won't move. I promise."

Bode didn't answer immediately. One corner of his mouth flattened as he pushed his hand through his hair, thinking. "You can sit over there," he said, stepping aside at last and pointing to the ball-and-claw-footed upholstered bench beneath a pair of windows. "I will hold you to your promise not to move."

Comfort was careful not to brush him as she crossed the room. She paused briefly at the drawing table, curious, but Bode's back-of-the-throat growl was like the sharp point of a stick in the small of her back. She kept moving.

Sitting down, she pressed the dove gray fabric of her dress over her knees and managed a small smile. "The walk here took longer than I expected." She shrugged. "But that is not—"

"You walked here?"

Bode's well wasn't merely shallow, she realized. It was bone-dry. "I did."

"Christ."

His language surprised her. The fact that he didn't apologize for it did not.

"Do you have any idea what might have happened to you?"

She looked pointedly at his eye patch. "I think I do, yes."

He tapped his eye. "This is the least of it. How far did you venture into the Coast?"

"Not far." She ticked off her route on her fingers—and all the reasons she considered her journey not to have been as dangerous as he supposed. When she was done, he was sitting as well. She folded her hands in her lap. "The important thing is that I've arrived safely. There's no point in reviewing all the things that *might* have happened. They didn't, and because the hour will be later when I return, I intend to hire a hack. I made certain I brought enough money with me to do that."

Bode swore again, this time so softly that it was hardly satisfying. "I won't let you leave here in a hack without an escort."

"Then maybe your clerk can accompany me. John, is it?" When he looked at her oddly, she explained, "You thought he was the one at the hatch, remember?"

Bode wondered if anything ever escaped her notice. "Mr. Farwell has another matter to occupy him. I'll take you back."

"That's very kind, but not necessary."

"I was going to call on you today." He added facetiously, "Remember?"

"Yes, but by then my uncles would have met with you, or if they hadn't been able to get away from the bank, they certainly would have cornered you upon your arrival, and I would have to hear all about it secondhand."

"What you just said made sense to you?"

Comfort gave him a withering look.

He didn't smile, but he appreciated that she had regained her footing. Now it was up to him to do the same. "Very well," he said. "What is the nature of this discussion that I am apparently going to have with your uncles?"

"They're going to ask you for your recollection of last night's events."

"I don't suppose they'll be inquiring about the third act of *Rigoletto*."

"No. They had already figured out that Gilda would be murdered. It's their contention that operas don't end well. I've told them that . . ." Her voice trailed away when Bode cocked an eyebrow at her. She hadn't expected that it would be so difficult to come to the point. It made her wonder if she was really as confident of what Bode would tell her uncles as she had supposed. Her palms were clammy and her heart had begun to thrum uncomfortably. She did not think she was going to faint, but she hadn't known it was going to happen the last time either.

"Miss Kennedy?"

The change in his voice from contemptuous to concerned brought her around. She blinked. "I'm sorry. I think this was a mistake." Offering a wan but apologetic smile, she began to rise.

"Sit. Down."

Comfort sat.

"That's better," he said. He stood and crossed the room to the sideboard, where he measured out a finger of whiskey. He carried the tumbler to her and pressed it between her folded hands. "Sip."

She did.

Bode stayed where he was, watching her until some color returned to her ashen face. "All right," he said when he returned to the stool. "I agree that you being here is a mistake, but since you've come rather late to that realization, you might as well carry out your intention. What is it in particular that Newt and Tucker will want to know?" A small crease appeared between his eyebrows. "Do they think I said or did something that caused you to faint?"

"No! No one said anything like that." Her dark eyes widened a fraction, and she asked softly, "You didn't, did you?"

"No."

She nodded. "That was my recollection also."

"Reassuring," he said dryly.

Comfort watched Bode plunge his fingers through his hair again. Sunshine from the skylight directly overhead gave his hair a metallic copper sheen. She realized she was staring when his eyebrows lifted a fraction. Rather than quickly look away just as if she'd done something wrong, Comfort took a careful sip of her drink.

"The gentleman in front of us," she said after the whiskey slipped warmly past her throat. "The one helping the woman with her train. Do you know him?"

"No. Is that what this is about?"

"Perhaps. I'm not certain." She drew a shallow breath and released it slowly. "Do you recall what it was that he dropped?"

"A tin. The kind that's sold in drugstores. I didn't get a good look at it. Is it important?" Apparently it was. There was the faintest tremor in Comfort's hands. He thought about taking the tumbler from her but decided against it. Perhaps clutching it was all that was keeping her upright.

"You're not mistaken? It wasn't a glove?"

He disliked quashing the hope in her eyes. He held up his hands, turning the palms over in a helpless gesture. "It was a tin."

"Oh." She nodded slowly and sighed. "I remember a glove."

"What do Tuck and Newt remember?"

"A tin. The same as you." Leaving what remained of her drink in the glass, she set it beside her on the bench. She pressed her palms against her knees as she'd wanted to earlier. "I was so convinced it was a glove that I think my uncles began to doubt what they saw."

"Which is why you suspect they'll want to speak to me."

"Yes. I invited them to. For confirmation." And then for confrontation, she thought. They would have to say something to her. No matter how distasteful they would find the chore, it couldn't be helped.

She looked forlorn. That troubled Bode. "Do you want me to tell them it was a glove?"

"Would you do that?"

"I don't know. Probably not."

She smiled a little at his answer. "It doesn't matter. I don't want you to. They saw what you saw."

Leaning to one side, Bode rested his elbow and forearm on top of his drawing on the table. "How do you account for remembering it differently?"

"I can't. I still see the glove. You can't imagine how disturbing it is to learn I can't trust my eyes."

"I don't think that's the problem. You can trust your eyes. It's your memory that's failing you."

"Thank you for clarifying, but the distinction hardly makes it any less disturbing."

"I understand." He rolled a pencil back and forth with the tip of his index finger. "What I don't understand is the importance you and your uncles are attaching to it. You haven't explained that."

Comfort supposed that she hadn't, not really. "I have a tin like the one the gentleman dropped. You remember the color?"

"Red and white."

"And what was written on it?"

He shook his head. "I didn't study it. You had it in your hand a moment, dropped it, and I picked it up. I barely glanced at it before I returned it to the gentleman. There was candy in the tin, I think. Maybe cough drops."

"Lozenges," she said. "Newt and Tuck recognized it at once. Dr. Eli Kennedy's Comfort Lozenges."

"Well, I don't know about that. I'll have to take them at their word." Bode considered what she told him. "Is that why you have a tin like it? Because of the name?"

She hesitated. "What do you mean?"

"The name. It's a little like yours, isn't it? Kennedy. Comfort. Do you have a middle name? Eli, perhaps?"

"Elizabeth."

"Close enough." He picked up the pencil and waggled it between his fingers. "I would have collected a tin like that myself, supposing it was named Dr. Beauregard DeLong's Royal Lozenges, or some such thing."

"Is that your middle name? Royal?"

"No. Crowne. My mother's maiden name. I thought Royal sounded better. For a lozenge, that is."

Comfort smiled. It was a slight one, and in the end, slightly sad. "I didn't find and keep the tin because of the name. I have my name because of the tin."

Bode's fingers stilled; the pencil stood at attention. "How is that again?"

"I was holding the tin of lozenges when Newt and Tucker found me, so they named me Comfort Elizabeth Kennedy. Elizabeth was a name they attached later. That was Newt's idea. Tucker is credited with having thought of the other."

"All right," he said, nodding slowly. "That explains one thing."

"You have other questions, I imagine."

"I do, but you tell me what you want me to know." When Comfort stood, reneging on her promise not to move from the bench, he didn't stop her. He let her wander and pretend interest in her surroundings while she considered what she wanted to say, and more importantly it seemed, got over her reluctance to say it. She was quiet as she passed from one area of his stateroom to another. There were no walls defining the interior, but she recognized the flow and function of the space. Bode had an area for study, for conversation, for eating, and for cooking. The part of his home that was closed off to her by doors, she assumed was for storage, sleeping, dressing, and bathing. He could have lived in a mansion on Nob Hill with dozens of rooms, some of them larger than the one he occupied now, but he'd chosen this. She glanced at the hatch, remembered what she'd said on arrival, and realized she'd been right. Bode wanted to be alone. She wasn't as sure that he liked it.

"Newt and Tuck aren't really my uncles," she said. She picked up one of the ebony knights from the chess set on the dining room table and rolled it lightly between her palms. "They explained to me early on that I could tell people whatever I liked about how I came to be with them, but if I didn't want to say anything, they were prepared to let on that I was their niece. Newton drew up a family tree that we all learned to explain our connections."

"The devil is in the details."

"Precisely. My mother was Tucker's sister. Newt was my father's older half brother. That was to explain the difference in our last names." She glimpsed Bode's mouth twitch. Hers did as well. She felt lighter in the moment and set the chess piece down. She'd never thought of their story as any kind of burden, yet saying just one small part of it aloud made her feel as if she'd shed a weight.

"I've never told anyone. No, not even Bram. And I feel

confident that Newt and Tucker have been silent as well. In some way, I suppose we've come to believe what we invented. Certainly, we've lived as if it were so. The truth is that I don't know who my parents were. I have the tense right, though. What I do know about them is that they're dead. I was part of a wagon train heading west that was attacked and robbed in the Sierra Nevada foothills. I was the only survivor. Newt thinks I crawled off on my own sometime during the raid. We can't be sure, because I don't remember any of what happened before Tuck found me wedged between some rocks."

Comfort smiled a trifle crookedly. "Actually it was Newt's mare Dulcie snuffling around that made Tuck investigate."

"Newt reminds you and Tuck of that, I take it."

"He hasn't for a long while," she said. "But in the beginning, yes. Frequently." She walked over to the table where Bode sat and studied the drawing under his arm. She said nothing about it, picking up the thread of her story instead. "We think I was five. I told them I was. It was about the only thing I would, or *could*, tell them, and they chose to accept it as fact. There was some discussion about whether they should take me with them. Apparently there was a trading post a ways back. If they'd been willing to retrace their steps, they could have left me there. They didn't really argue about it, not that I remember. It was mostly Tuck who decided and Newt who went along."

Bode had tried not to ask any questions, allowing Comfort to set the pace, but he was afraid she wouldn't mention the thing that had brought them to this point. "How does the tin figure in this?"

"I was clutching it, and I wouldn't give it up. I had no interest in anything they brought me from the wagons. Dolls. Combs. Books. Newt said that if I recognized any of it, they couldn't tell."

Bode nodded, understanding. After every battle, there were soldiers who couldn't have recognized their own mothers. They barely knew that the hand at the end of their arm was their own. "I saw it sometimes," he said. "During the war."

"I wasn't like that, Mr. DeLong. I was hiding. I didn't see the shooting. I didn't see bodies. Newt and Tuck buried everyone before they found me."

"You don't know what you saw. You don't remember."

Comfort returned to the bench at the window and sat. "No," she said. "I don't. That's at the very crux of the matter, isn't it?"

"He dropped a tin," said Bode. "A red-and-white tin."

She closed her eyes and rubbed them with her thumb and forefinger. "I can't see it." Unwelcome tears suddenly pressed against her lids. She didn't have a handkerchief.

"Here." Bode pushed one corner of a handkerchief into the center of her fist.

The ache in her throat prevented her from speaking. She simply nodded and accepted the gift.

Bode returned to the stool. "Perhaps you'd like to finish your drink?"

Dabbing at her eyes, she shook her head.

"All right, then I want to ask you about a week ago Monday night."

"Monday?"

"Yes. Bram broke his leg earlier in the day."

"Well, I certainly remember that."

He went on as if she hadn't spoken. "And you fell asleep in the parlor waiting for me to return from speaking to my mother. I chose to let you sleep because it was clear you were exhausted. I didn't wake you because you were dreaming. I woke you because you were terrified."

"I'm sure you've had nightmares. Everyone does."

"Not like that. At least not since I was a child."

She shrugged. "It doesn't matter. I don't recall it anyway."

Disappointed, Bode shook his head. "This is the first time since you've arrived that I don't believe you."

"I can't help that."

"You could tell the truth."

"You told me I could tell you what I wanted you to know."

"I didn't ask you to tell me what the dream was about."

Comfort twisted the handkerchief. "Very well. Then, yes, I remember some of it. Not everything."

"Do you have it often?"

"No." She hesitated and then admitted, "I had it again last night. I didn't wake during it, but I know it happened while I slept. This morning I woke thirsty."

"Thirsty?"

"Yes. I always need something to drink when I wake after I've had that particular dream. You gave me sherry."

"You only sipped it."

"That required a great deal of restraint, I assure you. Before then, my throat couldn't have been dryer if I'd swallowed a handful of sand."

"You could have asked for water. Tea. Whatever you liked."

"No, I couldn't. I wouldn't have been able to resist drinking my fill, and that would have put your eyebrows at the level of your hairline. It was better that you didn't see."

Bode didn't smile, but nevertheless, his blue-violet eyes softened. "Have you ever tried Dr. Eli Kennedy's Comfort Lozenges?"

It surprised her that she actually shivered. "No. It never occurred to me."

"Apparently not. Was the tin empty when they found you?"

"Yes."

"Then perhaps you tried them once before and didn't like them."

"I don't know."

"Why do you think you fainted last night?" he asked.

Comfort untwisted the handkerchief, smoothed it out on her lap, and began to fold it neatly in quarters. "I thought it was the warmth and the press of people and the fact that I stooped and stood so quickly when the gentleman dropped his glove." She stopped, hearing what she said, and sighed inaudibly. "Dropped the tin, I mean. After what I've told you, I expect you put the same construction on what happened as my uncles. You think it was because I saw the tin, don't you?"

"Haven't you seen others like it before?"

"Yes. Exactly. That's what I told Newton and Tucker. I don't faint when I walk into Donahue's Apothecary and see those exact tins displayed behind his counter."

"I'm sure you don't. That would have attracted some notice before now." He picked up the pencil on the table again and started to tap it lightly. "But your hand had a fine tremor in it when you held it."

"It did?"

He nodded. "I saw it. That's why you dropped it." He could see that she'd been unaware of it. Her expression was genuinely nonplussed. "Besides the tin you were holding when they found you, have you ever held another like it?"

"No."

"Ever purchased the same lozenges?"

"No. There are other kinds."

"But Dr. Kennedy's are still popular and have a reputation for effectiveness. I would have recognized the tin if I'd given it more than a cursory glance."

"Well, I've never used them," she said stiffly.

"And before last night, apparently never held one that wasn't your own."

Exasperated with his reasoning, she said, "Then you *do* think it prompted me to faint."

"No. It prompted you to let it drop as if it were a hot coal, but that's not when you fainted."

"No, it's not, is it? You caught it and gave it back to the gentleman."

"That's right."

She frowned. "I'm not clear on what happened next. He took it, didn't he?"

"He did. He thanked me on behalf of himself and everyone who was sitting near him."

Suddenly agitated beyond her ability to remain in her seat, Comfort jumped up. She put out a hand to stop Bode from continuing. "You don't have to say any more." There was an odd ringing sensation in her ears. Her skin began to crawl. "Actually, I'd prefer if you—"

The stool under Bode thudded to the floor as he leaped to his feet. He was quick, but not quick enough. Comfort's knees folded under her before he crossed half the distance, and she was lying crumpled on her side when he reached her.

Bode bent, scooped her up, and placed her on the bench, knocking the tumbler of whiskey out of the way. He took the shawl from around her shoulders, folded it, and put it under her head. She was already coming around, blinking rapidly against the bright sunlight streaming through the windows. He stood and drew the curtains. The skylight kept the room from being dark.

He removed Comfort's hat and laid the back of his hand lightly over her forehead. Her skin was cool but not clammy. "Perhaps we should think about other things that could have contributed to your fainting spell."

"What things?" she asked dully. She tapped his wrist to encourage him to remove his hand. When he did, she placed her forearm across her eyes. "I believe I mentioned the crowd, the heat, the stooping and standing. None of those apply here."

"You did jump to your feet."

"I don't think that was it."

"All right. What if it *is* me?"

"It's not."

He didn't think it was, but he was gratified to hear her say it with so much conviction. What he had to say next was more difficult. "Are you carrying Bram's child?"

Comfort tore her arm away from her eyes so quickly that Bode had no chance to duck out of the way. She hit him in the head with the back of her hand. "Oh, God. I'm sorry. Did I miss your eye at least? Please tell me I missed your eye."

He'd managed to grab her wrist before she drew it back, and now he held on, surrounding the loose fist she made with his fingers. "You missed both of them," he said.

The clasp of his fingers was firm and warm. Comfort didn't try to remove her hand from it. She had the odd sensation of complete calm. Given the question he'd just put before her, it was an unreasonable response.

"I'm not carrying your brother's child," she said. "Or anyone else's."

"I guessed that when you tried to blind me."

She started to object and then realized Bode was teasing her. That seemed an equally unreasonable response. "You're different than I expected."

"Since I imagine most of what you know about me came from Bram, I hope that means I've exceeded your expectations."

She smiled faintly and nodded.

"Good."

He held her gaze, and Comfort didn't look away; she didn't want to. His eyes no longer reflected the violet-blue spark of light glancing off steel. What she saw were deep, warm pools that invited her to stir their perfect stillness.

Without quite knowing why, she accepted their invitation. She raised her head. Her lips parted. She waited.

She understood what she hadn't in the moment before he touched her mouth with his.

Bode's eyes had been the calm before the storm.

Chapter Six

It began with a spark. Only that. The first inkling of what a kiss might be. The spark skittered lightly across her lips, delicate as dandelion fluff. It teased and tickled, this dance of a sprite over the curve of her mouth. She was smiling at the exact moment the spark became a flame.

Heat licked her lips. Fingers of fire slipped under her skin. She was boneless suddenly, melting like candle wax before the flame, and it was his mouth that shaped her, his hands that gave her form.

One of his palms cradled the back of her head. The other lay flat against her abdomen. Each one of his fingertips was a point of heat. There was no weight, no pressure. It was as if his touch had no substance, and the proof that it existed at all was the raised flesh that it left in its wake.

Her fingers folded around the front of his jacket. She didn't hold it as much as clutch it. It was something substantial, something quite real in the face of everything else that seemed otherworldly.

This kiss, *his* kiss, was far and away exceeding her expectations.

His tongue flicked her upper lip and touched the underside. She slid her tongue forward, touched his. She'd been tentative, but his response made her bold, and she sucked on his tongue, deepening the kiss, opening her mouth and his to the current of liquid fire.

She heard a sound, one she didn't recognize as coming from herself until she felt the vibration deep at the back of her throat. She realized she was purring as contentedly as her cat. Or almost as contentedly, she thought, because what she wanted was something more than being scratched between her ears.

Restless, she arched her back. Her heels dug into the upholstered bench. He pressed her back with the flat of his hand before she could turn on her side. She loosened her fingers where they gripped his jacket so they could climb his chest. She slipped them around his neck, lacing them together. She held his head, held it there, afraid he would end the kiss too soon.

His mouth hummed against hers. Her lips trembled. Her tongue quivered. She tasted a hint of coffee in the kiss. Like his tea, he took it without cream or sugar. She didn't shy from the faint bitterness. It had the opposite effect. She wondered if they could make it sweet.

They did.

He drew in a sharp breath. She moaned. The sounds mingled. Overhead, a gull tapped at the skylight, its tattoo identical to the one that her heart beat against her chest. She felt the thrum of the pulse in his neck. It had the same cadence. The very same.

His hand moved from her abdomen to just below her breast. The heat was almost intolerable, yet she couldn't move away. She stroked his neck and wound dark copper threads of hair around her fingertips. She wished she had not plaited her hair. She wished she had combs and pins and ribbons for him to remove. He would take them out one at a time, as slowly as he liked. She wouldn't shake her head; she'd let him sift her hair between his fingers and tug so gently that her scalp would tingle.

It tingled anyway. And then so did the rest of her. It was like the first shiver in the face of a fever; the one that slipped along every muscle. She seemed to contract all at once, folding in on herself so that her skin was no longer a comfortable fit.

She did not expect him to swear, but somehow it was appropriate, more reverent than blasphemous, and when he broke off the kiss and laid his forehead against hers, she knew she was right.

Bode was still on his knees. Raising his head, he sat back slowly, slipping one hand out from under Comfort's head, and the other, the one that rested near her breast, he let fall to the edge of the bench. She had to surrender her hold on his neck, and her fingers trailed over his shoulders as he moved away. Her eyes remained closed a moment longer, and when they opened, their focus was the ceiling.

"Comfort?"

She held up one finger, cautioning him to be quiet.

He didn't mind. He stayed where he was and watched her breathing ease. There was a like response in him, a settling in his chest that made him aware of his slowing pulse.

Comfort turned her head to the side and studied his face. None of his features had shifted from their symmetrical plane. There was no eyebrow arched with inquiry, no lift to one corner of his mouth. His jaw was relaxed so no muscle could jump in his cheek. He looked neither happy nor unhappy, nor any other emotion she could name. She thought she must be staring into a face of extraordinary tranquility, the face of a man at ease with himself, a man without regrets or misgivings.

She smiled then, because she knew he wasn't sorry.

Sitting up, she inched her way down the bench until she could put her legs over the side. She smoothed her dress over her lap. She could still feel the warmth of his hand where it had come so close to cupping her breast. Her skin smoldered with the lingering heat until it ignited in a flush that spread from her chest to her face. She pressed her palms to her cheeks and was grateful when Bode didn't comment.

Bode swept up the fallen tumbler of whiskey in his hand and stood. "Careful that you don't drag your skirt through what spilled. Give me a moment." His mouth twitched. "I'll swab the deck."

Comfort relaxed. It really would be all right. They would have a conversation that embraced what was usual, even mundane, and they would go on from there. There would be no regrets and no recriminations. Likewise, there would be no discussion.

"Well, it *is* very much like a ship," she said.

He glanced over his shoulder on his way to the broom closet and asked, "Have you ever been on a ship?"

"No." Her eyebrows knit, forming a neat vertical crease between them. "That is, not on one that was bound for anywhere."

Bode retrieved a mop. "One at berth in the harbor, then."

"Mmm, not precisely berthed."

"Ah," he said, understanding. "You were on one of the ships abandoned during the early days of the rush. My father said that until the hulks burned and sank, it was possible to walk across the bay and never touch water. Was that true?"

"I don't know. I never tried. But it seems as if it might have been true. There was more wood on the water than there was on land. Men fled the ships as soon as they arrived—even the men who sailed them."

"I know. My father and the other masters lost entire crews to gold fever. They had to pay exorbitant wages in excess of fifty or even a hundred dollars a month to keep enough men to make the return voyage." He finished wiping the spill and set the mop in front of him, holding it in a two-fisted grip that turned his elbows out. "So if you weren't using the hulks like lily pads to traverse the bay, did you live on one?"

"No. Some people did, of course, but not us. Newt and Tuck like terra firma, they would say." She saw Bode's ironic smile and appreciated it. "I know. They have long since recognized the contrariness of making San Francisco home, but they're settled now, and will tell you they still prefer shifting land to shifting seas."

"Then I don't have another guess," he said. "Why were you on one of the ships?"

She didn't answer right away, considering whether this was something she wanted to tell. In the end, she decided it hardly mattered. The deed had been done so long ago that no one was in danger of being punished for it. At the time, no one thought of it as a crime.

"Uncle Newton heard there was a safe on one of the ships that could be had if it could be taken off. He told Uncle Tuck about it, and they decided it was worth looking into. They were preparing to open a lending store and had enough business that they needed a safe."

"But not so much business they could buy one."

She shook her head. "No, they were just being thrifty."

Bode started to chuckle and then swallowed it whole when he realized she was serious.

"It also would have taken too long to order anything like it and have it transported west. Enterprising men looked closer at hand for the solutions to their problems. The most successful found them."

"They always do," he said. "You accompanied them, obviously."

"I accompanied one or both of them almost everywhere. It wasn't safe for me to be left alone, or at least they didn't think so."

"They were right." He paused. "They still are."

Comfort ignored him. "Uncle Tuck rigged some kind of contraption that enabled them to hoist the safe out of the hold. They came close to sinking the rowboat *and* the safe because that part of their plan was not well thought out, but eventually they managed to get it on board without drowning themselves. There was an old mule and a travois waiting for us onshore, and the poor animal earned its feed that night for pulling that safe through Sydney Town."

"That's a good story."

"It's true."

"That's what makes it good." He let the handle of the mop sway back and forth. "What kind of safe was it?"

"A Hildesheim."

"No, I meant what kind of locking device did it have? Padlock? A combination?"

"It had a pin and tumbler mechanism."

"How was it opened?"

She smiled. "I did the job on the box." Surprise made Bode lose his grip on the mop handle, but he caught it before it hit Comfort on the head. He was too stunned by what she'd told him to offer an apology. "You were only a child."

Comfort clapped her hands together once, delighted with his reaction. "I made it a better story, didn't I?"

He realized he'd been taken in. "All right," he said. "I believed you. And yes, it made for a better story, but tell me what really happened. How did you get the safe open?"

"It was already open. The ship's captain emptied it before

he left his command. Tuck worked on it for a long time—weeks, not hours—before he was able to reset the pins and tumblers so they operated on a new combination of numbers. He and Newton got stumbling drunk the night he finally figured it out."

"I imagine they did. What did you do?"

"Filled and refilled their glasses."

He eyed her suspiciously. "Really?"

"Really. I liked to take care of them. I wanted to be useful." As soon as the words were out, Comfort wished she could call them back. The slight tremor in her voice caught her off guard and somehow attached a deeper meaning to her words, one that she hadn't meant to reveal or, having revealed it, one she didn't intend to examine.

Bode considered asking her if wanting to be useful was the reason she worked in the bank. It wasn't a fair question, he decided, because she was already looking away, obviously regretting that she'd let him see vulnerability. He also decided against asking her because it wouldn't have been easy to stop with that single question. He'd want to know if being useful to her uncles, to the men who were in every way her saviors, was the reason she'd been so long in accepting a proposal.

He picked up the mop and carried it back to the closet. The last time he tried to ask her about proposals, she'd crippled him.

Comfort picked up her hat and ran her fingers back and forth along the straw brim. When Bode turned away from the closet, she said, "I'd like to leave now, Mr. DeLong."

"Mr. DeLong? Is that truly how you want to address me?"

"It's your name."

"It was my father's name, too. I prefer Bode."

Comfort felt leveled by the stare he turned on her, and perhaps it was only her imagination, but she believed he was threatening her with a discussion of their kiss as well. "Bode," she said, and butter wouldn't melt in her mouth.

He looked her over, waiting. "Imagine that," he said when nothing happened. "Lightning didn't strike you."

Comfort rolled her eyes. She fixed her bonnet on her head and picked up her shawl. After snapping it open, she cast it around her shoulders and stood. "You don't have to accompany me home. As I said, it was a kind offer but unnecessary."

He pretended she hadn't spoken. Sometimes that was the smoother course, he was learning. Opening the hatch, he crooked his fingers to motion her over. The dilemma that presented itself was whether he should assist her through the hatch and follow her down or whether he should go in first and make certain she made the descent safely.

While he was being uncharacteristically indecisive, Comfort took the matter out of his hands and put her right foot on the first step. She held on to the open hatch for support and brought around her left foot. She made a graceful pivot, grabbed the ropes, and started down the stairs in the same position she'd made the climb.

Bode was impressed. After two years in his employ, his clerk still hadn't mastered the steps, unwisely choosing to use them like stairs instead of ladder rungs. Bode watched Comfort until she was only a few feet from the bottom before he lowered himself through the hatch and followed.

Alexandra regarded Bram over the rim of her teacup. "I don't know how this will change things," she said. "But I'm certain it will."

"It was an accident."

"I know that." Her tone was crisp with a hint of impatience. "Even I can acquit you of doing something that is foolish *and* painful."

"Painful is inadequate to describe what I'm feeling, Mother."

"As foolish is often inadequate to describe so much else that you've done."

Bram conceded the point. His head was supported by two large down pillows, but his splinted leg was supported by three. This morning he'd been visited by Alexandra's choice of physicians. There was a frightening discussion about weights and pulleys that went on around him and that he tried not to hear. The laudanum made that easier. He did learn that whatever Dr. Harrison intended to do to him, it wasn't going to happen today.

Gritting his teeth, Bram pushed himself up to his elbows. He carefully supported himself on one and reached for the bottle of laudanum at his bedside. He was aware of Alexandra's eyes following him. She would only give him the drops as the doctor prescribed, but if he could manage to get them for himself, she didn't try to stop him.

He unscrewed the stopper, raised it, and allowed three drops to fall on his tongue. When he'd closed the bottle, he returned it to the nightstand. His elbows slid out from under him, and he collapsed back onto the pillows. The movement jostled his leg. He groaned.

"I don't see that it's worth the trouble you take to get it," Alexandra said.

"It will be," he told her. "In a few minutes, it will be."

She sipped her tea and said nothing.

His mother's silence was sometimes her hardest censure, and Bram didn't bear it well. "Did I hear Dr. Harrison mention *Rigoletto* when he was here?" he asked.

"He did. He attended the performance we missed."

"And? Was it the success Newland Jefferson predicted it would be?"

"It's Harrison's opinion that it was. I haven't looked in the papers yet." She set her teacup aside. "I don't think you heard the more important part of my conversation with the doctor."

"The weights and pulleys. I heard."

"Not that. It seems your brother attended the play."

"Bode?"

"Do you have another brother?"

Her tone, as dry as dust, made him chuckle. "A brother that you bore? No. But I can't speak for father's bastards."

"I should have had Dr. Harrison put a splint on your tongue."

He grinned, unabashed. "Why do you suppose Bode went? I know he enjoys opera, but he doesn't enjoy opening nights. I don't think he's been at one for years. Probably not since he moved out."

"If I have to hazard a guess, and it seems that I do, Bode was there because Miss Kennedy was there."

"She was? She went without me?"

"Apparently, yes."

"She didn't sit with Bode, did she? That would be odd. I'm not sure she even likes him."

"She was escorted by her uncles and sat with them."

"Good. I'm glad she didn't forget herself. She's *my* fiancée."

"Hmm. The doctor says she left in Bode's arms."

"You mean, *on* Bode's arm."

"I said what I meant." Alexandra absently fingered the cameo brooch at her throat. "Harrison didn't see what happened, otherwise he would have lent assistance, but he had it from someone who was present that Comfort fainted during the break between the second and third acts."

Bram shook his head. "I don't believe it. That someone got his story wrong."

"She might have been ill, Bram. Fevered. It can happen, you know."

"If she was ill, then it came on her suddenly. She wouldn't have left the house if she didn't feel well, not even for the opera, not when she knows how much her uncles dislike it."

"I wondered about that." She shrugged. "I don't suppose we'll know until we ask. She'd tell you the truth, wouldn't she?"

"Yes. What reason would she have to lie?"

Alexandra's steady glance fell on her son. "Perhaps she would if she's pregnant."

Bram reared back slightly, pressing his head more deeply against the pillows. "Comfort is *not* pregnant. Who would the father be?"

"I thought it might be you," Alexandra said, arching an eyebrow at him.

"Well, it's not." Reaching behind his head, he plumped the pillows. "It's not anyone. She's not pregnant. If she fainted, and I still have my doubts that Harrison or the person he listened to got it right, it's not because she's carrying a child."

"I believe you're offended on her behalf."

"I'd like it if you weren't so surprised. Comfort is my friend, Mother."

"How easily you forget yourself, Bram, and I find that I'm offended on her behalf. She's your fiancée. It's natural that you should offer a stout defense of her character, but I think you should base it on this new development in your relationship, not the friendship that came before."

"Very well," he said, closing his eyes. He could feel the

laudanum beginning to work. "I expect she'll come by today, or send someone around to ask about me. I'll inquire about the opera then."

"I was thinking you should send a note inquiring after her. That's the proper response given what the doctor said."

"All right. I will. Later, though. I'll do it later."

Alexandra frowned. "This is precisely why I have no liking for those drops."

"I know, Mother."

She sighed and leaned over to brush away the hair that had fallen so predictably across his brow. "I cannot stay out of patience with you," she said. "Your brother either. I admit I've been unhappy with him, but I'm going to invite him to dinner this evening."

Bram gave her a wan smile. "You're curious."

Alexandra didn't deny it. "You'd be just as curious if your brain wasn't a potato."

He supposed she was referring to the soporific effects of the laudanum. "You'll let me know what he says, won't you?"

"Yes." Standing, she drew up the covers so they fell over Bram's shoulders, then she stroked his head again. "I know you care about Comfort's welfare. I do, too. That's what makes it difficult to know how to think about Bode's involvement, whether it's blessing or curse."

When Bram offered no opinion, she realized he'd fallen asleep. It was probably just as well. She knew which side he'd take in the blessing versus curse debate. Outside of his brother's hearing, Bram did not often miss an opportunity to pronounce Bode the devil incarnate.

Bode didn't wait for Newton and Tucker to come to him. After escorting Comfort home, and seeing her all the way to the front door, he directed his driver to take him to the Jones Prescott Bank.

He was shown to the second floor, where the partners shared an office, and was announced with deference that he didn't require or believe he'd earned. He supposed the head teller's behavior had something to do with Bram's accident. Perhaps he believed there were still repercussions to come.

"Mr. Tweedy, is it?" asked Bode.

"Yes, sir."

"Thank you. My mother also wishes for me to thank you for your assistance when Bram fell." His mother had no idea who Mr. Tweedy was or that he'd been of any particular help, but Bode was grateful, and he knew Alexandra's thanks would send the other man along quickly, if for no other reason than to tell his coworkers. As expected, Tweedy hurried off.

Newton and Tucker were getting to their feet as Bode approached. He shook their hands and waved them back in their chairs. "I apologize for arriving unannounced. I appreciate that you're busy."

Tuck folded his rangy frame back into his leather chair and stretched his legs under the desk. "Take a chair," he said. "I had a feeling you'd come by today."

Newt frowned. "You did? You didn't say anything. How many times do I have to remind you that you gotta start telling me when you get one of those feelings?"

"You've been sayin' it since we fought at Monterrey, so I guess if I was counting, that'd be quite a few plus a bunch."

Bode had never been privy to the sparring between these men. They were well known from San Francisco to Sacramento for being careful but canny investors. There had been a time when their reputation for turning a profit led to undisciplined speculation among less scrupulous financiers, but after watching the opportunists drive share prices to heights that had nothing to do with their real value, Tucker Jones and Newton Prescott changed the way they conducted business. To protect their depositors' savings—and their own—secrecy was their holy grail.

Bode wondered if perhaps their best-kept secret was that they were still foot soldiers at heart.

"Newt and I were going to pay you a visit later, so I guess you saved us the trouble of getting there." Tuck rubbed the back of his neck when Bode remained standing. "About that chair . . ."

Bode glanced around and chose one that straddled the invisible line dividing the partners' office.

"It's always telling where a person sits," said Newt. "That's why we insist on it. You want to hear what your choice tells us about you?"

"Actually, no."

Tucker gave a shout of laughter. "Good for you. I believe that's the first time someone's declined. People generally like hearing that sort of nonsense. Newt says pretty much the same thing no matter where someone sits, but it makes most folks think he knows them real well."

Newt's mouth curled in disgust. "Now, you didn't have to tell him all that."

"Think I did," Tuck said. "You started it." He gave Bode his full attention. "Are you here about our niece or some other matter?"

"It's Miss Kennedy," said Bode. "She visited Black Crowne Shipping this morning. I came here to let you know that I delivered her home safely. It is impossible to know whether she'll remain there, although I believe Suey Tsin will take extraordinary measures to see that she does."

Bode had not given much thought to how Comfort's uncles would react except to hope that they would not throw him out. Given an eternity to contemplate what they might do, he still couldn't have predicted that Newton would stand and reach across the desks to Tucker with his palm out.

"Didn't I say she would?" asked Newt. "That'll be twenty."

Tuck opened a drawer on his left and counted out the bills. He laid them in Newt's hand. "Best use of that would be to hire a keeper for her."

Newt nodded as his fingers closed over his winnings. He darted a significant look in Bode's direction, one eyebrow arched in a dramatic fashion, his mouth curled in a half smile.

Bode held up his hands, palms out. "No, sir. Not for twenty dollars." In the event they misunderstood and thought he had a price, he added, "Not for all the tea in China."

Disappointed, Newt sat back down and put the money away.

Bode's glance darted between the two men. "I don't understand. If you suspected she would make the trip to my office, why didn't you make some effort to stop her?"

Tuck tugged lightly on his earlobe, his narrow features thoughtful. "Frankly, we didn't discuss it until we were here, and you saw for yourself that I lost a bet because I depended on her to show more sense. Newt gauged her worry better than I did."

Newt slid his hands along the arms of his chair. His fingers curved around the ends. "We both figured that if I was right, we could count on you to look after her. Seems we could."

Tuck nodded. "I don't know that we would have felt that way if we hadn't seen you with Comfort last night, but you were gentle with her, and a gentleman."

Bode was certain he didn't deserve their unconditional trust, but he wasn't going tell them about kissing their niece to illustrate the point.

"And we noticed you didn't annoy her," Newt said. "Leastways not so much that she put you on your backside again."

Bode couldn't have imagined that he'd be grateful for that reminder, but it was helpful in pushing the kiss from the forefront of his thoughts. Evenly, he said, "So you saw what she did while we were dancing?"

"I didn't," Newt told him. "Tuck did. He told me. Comfort said she had cause. Did she?"

"I'm afraid so."

"Well, now you know. She does all right looking after herself, although we've never known her to do what she did to you outside of a lesson with Chin Fong." He tapped his fingers lightly against the chair. "We'd appreciate it, though, if you didn't let that become fodder for a good story."

Bode's smile was faintly ironic. "It's only a good story if she tells it. I wasn't the one left standing."

"True." Sitting back, Newton crossed his legs. His slight smile faded as he set his arms across his chest. "Tuck and I want to know what you caught and returned to that fellow last night."

"It was a tin. Red and white. I told Miss Kennedy the same thing."

"How did she accept it?" asked Tuck.

"With difficulty. She believed me . . . believed what you told her . . . but she can't remember it any differently than she does. She still sees a glove."

Both men sighed audibly. Neither spoke.

Bode breached the silence. "It's confusing to her."

Newt nodded. "It's confusing to us."

"I understand. I can't explain it, and neither can she."

Tucker pushed back his chair, rose, and went to the door to close it. He didn't return immediately to his desk. He crossed the room to the safe. Bending in front of it, he carefully turned the dial, and then twisted the handle. He withdrew a bottle of whiskey and three glasses. He held them up so Bode could see. "You'll join us?"

Bode nodded. "That's a Hildesheim safe, isn't it?"

"Yes? You're familiar with them?"

"Not them," he said. "That one specifically, I think."

"Huh." Tucker used the heel of his shoe to shut the safe's door. "Comfort told you about it, did she?"

"Yes."

Tuck set the glasses on his desk and poured a couple of fingers in each. "I don't know that she's ever told anyone how we came by that safe. Surprises me some that she told you." He distributed the drinks and sat down again. "What else did she say?"

Bode understood that they needed to hear it from him. They would be naturally cautious about telling him anything that Comfort didn't want him to know. He wasn't confident they'd answer questions that she hadn't. "I think you will agree that she was extraordinarily candid," he said, and then proceeded to recount what Comfort had shared.

Tuck and Newt listened without comment. When Bode finished, their glasses were empty and his was hardly touched. He sipped his whiskey while they continued to think about what they'd heard. It was Newt who finally stepped into the silence.

"It seems she *was* candid," he said in a manner that indicated he accepted it. "Do you know, last night was the first time in years that the three of us—Comfort, Tuck, and me, I mean—talked about anything connected to the night we found her. Seemed to Tuck and me that she went east to college and came back with it all settled in her mind."

"You're aware she still has nightmares, though." Bode was uncertain what the look that passed between them meant. He thought they might have been surprised that *he* knew about her dreams, but then Tuck reached for the whiskey bottle and tipped it ever so slightly over his glass. Bode watched him add a splash to his tumbler and then pass the bottle to Newt to do the same. "You didn't know," he said. "Neither of you."

Tuck shook his head. "Not a word from her. Best of my recollection is that she was quiet about them for a couple of years before she went to Oberlin." He lifted his glass and used it to point to Newt. "She was, what? Sixteen? Seventeen?"

"Sixteen. Just before the coming-out party, remember?"

"That's right. Sixteen, then." He addressed Bode again. "That's the last time she said anything."

Newt continued the explanation. "She was a real Nervous Nellie about the party. Didn't want any part of it and told us so, but my sisters said it was the proper thing to do to bring a young lady out in society, and Tuck and I made up our minds we would do it. As the day got closer, we began to notice that her sleep was more troubled. The night before her come-out, she had such a spell that we decided that no introduction to society was worth putting her through so much hurt." He shrugged. "She talked us out of canceling the party, didn't she, Tuck?"

Contemplating the drink he poured, Tuck nodded slowly. "She sure did. And naturally, we thought we'd done right all around because we never heard anything after that."

"We didn't just accept her silence," said Newt. "We'd ask her about it from time to time. She led us to believe the nightmares were gone. Of course, growing up, she never remembered what they were about. Tuck and I always figured we knew, but she couldn't tell us. After her come-out, she didn't say another word. Maybe we should have been more suspicious." He rolled his glass between his palms. "It's the damndest thing to think about it now, but back then we thought it had something to do with Bram."

"Bram?" asked Bode. "Why would you think that?"

"She met him at the party," Tuck explained. "And he showed a particular interest in her. You must have seen it. You were there, remember?"

Bode gave no indication that he did.

Tuck went on, watching Bode closely. "Of course, Bram danced with her; you didn't. If recollection serves, he asked her more than once. We both remarked that the only time she seemed to genuinely enjoy herself was when he was close by. He could make her laugh, and that counted for something."

Newt nodded. "Bram, being Bram and all, well, we didn't figure that he'd remember Comfort the next day, let alone pay a call. He was just a boy full of wildness then, so we—" Newt abruptly stopped as he realized that he was talking to the wild boy's older brother. "No disrespect meant, Bode, but that's how it was."

"I understand," Bode said. Bram was not significantly changed from that boy, and they all knew it. Newton Prescott was showing restraint by not pointing that out.

Newt went on. "So we paid as much attention to him as he was paying to Comfort, but best as we could reckon, he was good company for her. We knew her feelings were attached, but—" He broke off again, this time in response to Tuck shaking his head. "Well, I don't suppose she'd want me to be saying anything about that." He shrugged. "What's more important is that they became friends. Stayed that way, too."

Tuck rested his chin on his fist. "I don't know what to make of what you're telling us now. Seems we credited Bram with more influence than was rightly his due, but that's because we wanted to believe our girl was doing better. She just got real quiet about all the bad that was still going on inside her. That's something she chose to do on her own. We probably should be careful about thinking Bram's responsible for that."

Bode wanted to knock back what remained of his drink. Instead he set it on his knee and turned the tumbler slowly, hoping the gesture appeared more absent or thoughtful than it was. "No, you're right. Bram's not responsible." Bode decided he'd let them put whatever construction they liked on his statement. "And Miss Kennedy's not entirely honest. That makes for a fragile friendship, I think, and for an even more fragile marriage."

Tuck and Newt were careful not to exchange glances. It was now clear to them that while Comfort had revealed a great deal to Bode in relation to the red-and-white tin, she'd told him nothing about the engagement being false. Her omission made it awkward to defend her against Bode's charge that she was not entirely honest, and pointing out that no person was *entirely* honest was inadequate justification for her behavior.

Tuck shifted all six feet of his rangy frame as he settled back in his chair. "This is the first I'm getting wind of any concerns about the engagement from a DeLong. Does Alexandra feel the same?"

"I have no plans to discuss this with her. I also won't be sharing any part of my conversation with Miss Kennedy with my brother. It's her place to do that. More than that, her acceptance of his proposal makes it her responsibility. I hope you will persuade her to be forthright with Bram."

"You can be confident that Newt and I will be having a conversation with her," said Tuck. "Whether she is persuaded by anything we have to say is something else again." He tilted his head to the side, his expression more considering than it had been. "Of course, you're welcome to tell Comfort yourself that she has a responsibility to Bram. It would be interesting to see how that turns out."

Bode knew when he was being baited. He left what Tuck was dangling on the hook and sipped his drink instead.

Newt clasped his hands and rested them on his chest. He tapped his thumbs. "What makes you so certain Comfort's still having nightmares? Did she tell you she was?"

"I observed it."

"You probably should explain that, 'cause from where I'm sitting, it doesn't sound quite right."

Bode told them about Comfort falling asleep in the parlor the evening of Bram's accident. "She denied she remembered anything about the dream."

Newt nodded. "That's true. She's never been able to recall what they're about."

Tuck caught the fractional lift of Bode's brow. "Wait a minute, Newt. I think Bode has a different idea about that. Is that right, Bode?"

Bode's gaze encompassed both men. "She remembers. She admitted as much. Talking about what she remembers doesn't seem possible for her. And I wouldn't suppose that she remembers all of what she dreams or even that what she dreams is an accurate account of anything that happened before you found her. It's tempting to say her nightmares are about the robbery and murders, but do you really know that?"

In unison, Tucker and Newt shook their heads.

"I don't know it either. What she told me was that she wakes up thirsty. She described it as having swallowed a mouthful of sand. It struck me that it might have something to do with the lozenges, but I couldn't walk softly enough on those eggshells to keep Miss Kennedy from hearing me."

"We know the feeling," said Tuck.

"There's one last thing," Bode said, and he told them the circumstances around Comfort fainting a second time.

Newton's cheeks puffed as he blew out a long breath. "I can't make any sense of it. You say it happened when you were telling her about that gentleman thanking you?"

"That's right. I don't know how you recall what happened last night, but I don't think she fainted until he turned to thank me."

"So she recognized him?"

Bode shook his head. "I don't know. Maybe. She couldn't explain it."

"Or wouldn't," said Tuck. "I'm entertaining doubts about which it is."

"What did he say?" Newt asked Bode. "Exactly."

"I don't remember exactly. I recall the gist." He repeated it as best he could, but no one, including him, was enlightened by his recitation. He removed the tumbler from his knee and set it on the corner of Tuck's desk. "If it's agreeable to you, I'd like to make some inquiries and discover what I can about the gentleman who dropped the tin. It shouldn't be difficult to find out who he is, but I'm not confident that it will come to anything when I do."

"Every stone needs turning over." Tuck looked at Newt. "You agree with that?"

"I do. Comfort won't."

"I'm not asking her permission," said Bode, getting to his feet. "I'm asking yours."

Newt pushed back his chair and stood. He held out a hand to Bode. "You have it."

Bode clasped his hand. They shook. Tuck rose a moment later, and the ritual was repeated. "Gentlemen." He nodded to each in turn. "Good day."

Comfort stood outside her uncles' study for a full minute before she entered. She was tempted to press her ear against the door as she'd often done as a young girl when summoned to this room. Being called to their study didn't necessarily mean that she'd done something wrong and that a scold was imminent, although that certainly happened now and again. More often she was asked to sit here with Newt and Tuck when they wanted to tell her something they'd decided was *significant*. The emphasis was hers.

Announcing their intention to give her a coming-out party was *significant*. Acceptance to Oberlin was *significant*. Learning that she would have a position of responsibility at Jones Prescott was *significant*. Comfort had often wondered if the rows and rows of heavy leather-bound tomes contributed to the solemnity of the room, because when they were inside it, her uncles spoke as if every word had weight.

Lifting her chin, Comfort braced herself for what she suspected was waiting for her on the other side of the door, that most dreaded combination of punishing lecture and grave pronouncement: the *significant* scold.

"Good," Tuck said as she stepped into the room. "You're here."

What he meant, Comfort knew from experience, was "Good. You didn't keep us waiting." The hint of annoyance in his tone confirmed her suspicions of why they wanted to see her. Tucker was only ever impatient when he was facing a task he found distasteful, and whatever he had to say to her clearly fell into that category.

Her uncles were sitting like bookends on either side of the cold fireplace. Without being told, Comfort took her usual seat in the middle of the dark green velvet sofa facing them. Folding her hands in her lap, she regarded them expectantly and tried to remember she was no longer five, but twenty-five. The need not to disappoint them, though, was still the same.

"We spoke to Beau DeLong today," Newt said. "I imagine you knew we would." When Comfort nodded, he went on. "He came to us before we got around to paying a call on him."

Comfort wasn't successful at concealing her small start.

"Yes, well, we were surprised also. He gave you up, Comfort."

She swallowed. "Gave me up?"

Newt nodded. "Told us everything."

Everything? she wondered. What did that *mean*?

"I didn't threaten him," said Tuck. "In case you're wondering."

"I wasn't," she said. "Did he do something that made you think you would have to?"

"Not at all, but I wanted you to know. If there was a bargain struck between you, he went back on his word."

Comfort realized that Tuck was simply trying to protect her. "He didn't betray my confidences, Uncle Tuck. I didn't ask him not to speak to you."

"Somehow I doubt you meant for us to know that you visited him at Black Crowne."

Comfort had regained enough poise not to show her relief. If they believed her conversation with Bode had taken place in his office, then they didn't know she'd been in his apartment above it. More importantly, they didn't know about her indiscretion. Or his. He hadn't told them *everything*. That gave her the confidence she needed to say, "Mr. DeLong is free to report whatever he likes. I wouldn't suppose that I could restrain him from doing that."

Newt knuckled his chin. "Bode restrains himself. He has no intention of telling his mother or Bram about your ill-advised trek through the Coast to reach his office."

Tuck picked up that thread and continued. "Just as he has no plans to reveal anything you told him to his family."

"That's good, isn't it?"

"We think so," said Tuck. "He does have one expectation, however. He expects that you will tell Bram."

"And we expect," said Newt, "that you'll be honest with us about these dreams that are still troubling you."

Comfort stared at them. She had forgotten there'd been any discussion with Bode about her dreams. That wasn't part of what she thought he'd told her uncles. Equally disturbing, but easier to discuss with Tuck and Newt, was Bode's expectation that she relate the whole of it to Bram.

"What I say to Bram, and whether I say anything at all, is my decision, isn't it? Bode can't dictate to me."

Newt cleared his throat. "He hasn't. Not precisely. Tuck

misspoke. What Bode expects is that *we'll* persuade you to speak to Bram."

"Then I am sorry you've been put in that position. I'm not telling Bram. Further, there's no reason that I should."

"From Bode's perspective there is," Tuck said. "He believes your engagement is quite real. I think you can appreciate that he's uncomfortable with you marrying his brother while keeping so much from him."

"He made an excellent point," Newt said, "about your long friendship with his brother. Isn't it reasonable to suppose that over the years you should have shared at least some of this with Bram?"

"Reasonable to whom? Has everyone but me forgotten that Bram tends to act first and apologize later? I might as well place an announcement in the *Chronicle* as share a confidence with him. The nature of my friendship with Bram does not extend to telling him anything I don't wish at least ten other people to know. How could you not understand that?"

"I think I do, but maybe I'm finally understanding something else."

"Oh?"

"Maybe Bram's your friend *because* you know you can't tell him the important things. That's as good an excuse as any to keep what's bothering you all tucked up inside. When I think about it that way, lots of things make sense to me. Like why you'd start denying your nightmares and why you'd want to pretend that you don't remember any part of them. Bram wouldn't know what to make of all that unpleasantness, so you figured you wouldn't have any. I bet he hardly ever asks a hard question anyway, and that's what makes you so easy in his company. That sound about right?"

Comfort stared at Newt. She felt the ache of tears at the back of her eyes and a solid lump forming in her throat. She didn't try to speak.

Tuck glanced sideways at his friend. "Never thought much of your carpentry skills, but you hit that nail square. Hard to believe we're only seeing it now." He reached in his pocket and removed a handkerchief. He rose briefly to pass it to Comfort. "What happened the last time you forgot yourself and trusted Bram?"

She squeezed the handkerchief in her fist. That worked as well as pressing it to her eyes. "You know what happened. He announced we were engaged."

"So he did. Seems to me like you need to set that right. First with him and then with Bode. Bram can tell Alexandra the truth himself. That's not for you to do."

"I promised him," she said dully. "Eight weeks."

"Doesn't matter," said Tuck. "You're deceiving people, Comfort. You deceived us. Bode. Alexandra. Everyone at that party. Could be that you're deceiving yourself."

She pressed her lips hard together. If she said something now, there'd be no mistaking the quaver in her voice.

"Could be," Tuck went on more softly than before, "that your head knows better than your heart and maybe you should start listening to it."

Chapter Seven

Sleep did not come easily. She hadn't expected that it would. She tried it with the window open and the window closed, the covers off and on, the pillow pounded flat and pushed plump. There was no position that was comfortable, no activity that was sufficiently tiring. She counted backward from one hundred by threes. She named all the states in order of their admission to the Union. She stared at the clock on her mantelpiece and watched time crawl.

At three o'clock sleep overtook her. At three twenty she was awake again, or nearly so. It wasn't thirst that drove her from the bed. It was Bode. More correctly, it was Bode's kiss. Comfort stood beside her bed with the back of her hand pressed to her lips and imagined she could still feel the warmth of his mouth. Half expecting that he would emerge from the mound of rumpled sheets and quilts that she'd kicked to the foot of the bed, she took a step backward and bumped against the nightstand hard enough to make it wobble.

It was the act of steadying the table and centering the oil lamp that brought her to full wakefulness. She needed a moment to orient herself, and when she did, when she realized why she was standing beside her bed and no longer lying in it, she simply shook her head at the absurdity of her response. It made no sense that she would bolt from Bode in her dream when she had done nothing so sensible in reality.

She released a long, slightly shaky breath that she meant to be self-mocking laughter, and she could only sigh when it didn't touch any of the right notes.

Barefoot, she padded quietly to the bathing room, where she soaked a cloth in cool water and pressed it to her flushed cheeks and forehead. When she was finished, she stared at her reflection in the mirror above the washbasin and wondered what she was supposed to make of it all. "How did things become complicated?" she whispered. Except for an accusing, faintly contemptuous smile, her mirrored self had no answer.

Comfort took her robe from a hook behind the door and found her slippers under the bed. After putting them on, she removed the oil lamp from the night table and carried it to light her way through the house. As much as she would have liked a cup of warm milk, she liked her aloneness more. Entering the kitchen, even at this time of night, would have disturbed one of the servants, and talking to anyone just now was more effort than she wanted to make.

Comfort's intention was not to wander aimlessly through the house like some wraith. She had a destination in mind when she left her room, and she chose her route so she would arrive quickly and with the least chance of being surprised by a servant or her Uncle Newt, who sometimes did haunt the hallways when he couldn't sleep.

Slipping inside the conservatory, she closed the door and leaned against it. The air was pleasantly humid, and she embraced it like a second skin. The heavy scent of rich, dark soil made her nostrils flare as she breathed deeply. The room was crowded with delicate orchids and lush, green foliage, and where her lamp could not penetrate the thickest fronds and ferns, deep and unwelcoming shadows discouraged exploration.

Comfort set her lamp down just inside the door and walked under the umbrella of the darkest shadows without any hesitation in her step. She'd taken the path so many times that her feet knew the way even when the shadows made her eyes doubt the course. Occasionally the feathery fingers of an exotic plant would brush her cheek or the back of her hand. She felt as if she were being greeted by friends.

At the heart of the conservatory was a circle clearing. Benches surrounded a sundial whose pattern had been laid into the green-veined marble floor. Above the clearing was a large glass cupola that, day or night, was a window to the sky.

Comfort chose a bench and sat. She leaned back and tilted her face upward. She never tired of this view, never felt as deserving of her name as when she spied on heaven. It wasn't possible to look up from here and not think of the first time she remembered staring up at the stars. Tuck had been beside her then; Newt hovered nearby. For a long time no one spoke. She'd liked that, liked it still when they sat together and none of them had a need to fill the silence. Those moments had no expectations attached to them, no demands.

What happened earlier when she'd been summoned to the study was different. There, silence was awkward and unforgiving. It yawned as widely as a gulf and required a bridge of such proportions to cross it that none of them could manage that feat of engineering.

Was Tuck right? she wondered. There was no question that she'd allowed herself to be made party to a deception. She accepted that she'd wronged Alexandra and Bode most particularly and had done almost as badly by every other guest that night. It was not as easy to know about the matter of self-deception. What did anyone ever discover by peeling back the layers of that onion except more tears and more onion?

Then there was all that Newt had said. *I bet he hardly ever asks a hard question anyway, and that's what makes you so easy in his company.* Certainly Newt believed that her friendship with Bram was something less than she'd always supposed it to be. How was she to know if he'd truly hit the nail square when every part of her recoiled at the notion?

It was not often that Tucker and Newton stated their expectations so clearly. They didn't ask her to end the fraud that was her engagement. They didn't try to persuade her. They told her to set it right.

Comfort blinked. She'd been staring at the stars for so long that they had begun to pulse, or maybe it was that her eyes were watering from contemplating that onion. She pressed a thumb and forefinger to the corner of her eyebrows and held them there. Calm came upon her slowly, and the urge to weep passed.

She would send a note round to Bram in the morning and call on him after she left the bank. He wouldn't be expecting her visit to have a serious nature, and if it were anything else she meant to discuss, she might have given him a hint. This was different. He could be persuasive in any circumstance, but lying on his back in bed, his leg splinted from ankle to hip, he was likely going to try to engage her pity as well. Knowing that gave her some small advantage. She wasn't going to toss it away by warning him what to expect when she arrived.

Perhaps, depending on how Bram accepted her decision, she would suggest that they tell Alexandra together. It didn't matter if Bram mistook her offer as a gesture of support, or more likely, that she was prepared to share the responsibility equally; being at his side when he told his mother the truth was the surest way she had of knowing that it was done, and done fairly. She also wanted to hear Alexandra explain how they should proceed with a public declaration. Bram's mother knew something about holding herself above personal scandal.

That left Bode. Comfort tried to imagine what she would say to him and could not. Likewise, his reaction to whatever she might eventually say was also outside her imagination. She could tell him what she'd done easily enough. That was not the problem. It was the explanation for it that twisted her tongue.

Does my brother know that you're in love with him?

She wished he'd never put the question to her. She tried to recall if there'd been a hint of amusement in his tone. It seemed that there had. If there was concern, then it had been the pitying kind. Because she'd agreed to support Bram's lie, she'd been trapped into making an admission she would have rather avoided.

What would Bode make of it now, assuming he remembered the exchange at all? She smiled, but the shape of it held more derision than humor. It seemed he remembered everything, and in light of the kiss they'd shared, it was just as likely that he'd ask her about it.

No man had ever kissed her as Bode had. None of the men

who had proposed to her had done more than press the back of her gloved hand to their lips. She had been shown more in the way of physical affection from her cat. Thistle, at least, sometimes nuzzled her under the chin. Bram was more demonstrative, but always in a familial way, a brother to his sister. He bussed her cheek, occasionally her forehead, and was fond of using his forefinger to tap the tip of her nose when she'd amused him. Afraid of what he might glimpse in her face, she was careful never to turn her head into any of his kisses.

She hadn't shown that caution with Bode, but then what he would have seen in her eyes was curiosity, not affection, and certainly not love. Curiosity, she now believed, made for an extraordinarily satisfying kiss, and judging by the dream she'd had, it would be equally satisfying upon repetition.

If she were inclined to repeat it. Which she was not.

Comfort pressed her fingertips to her lips. At least she didn't think so. But then that was the nature of self-deception.

Samuel Travers straightened the covers all around Bram except where the winch, weights, and crank interfered with his efforts. The contraption that kept Bram's leg raised off the bed reminded Sam of a ship's windlass, and he supposed the comparison was close enough. Bram's splinted leg hung in the air as still and heavy as an anchor hoisted up from the sea.

"Careful," Bram said when Sam inserted an extra pillow behind his back. "I swear, Sam, I'll pay you fifty dollars in gold to cut me loose of this thing."

"You don't have fifty dollars. Gold or paper. And I wouldn't do it if you did. I'm more afraid of your mother than I'm bothered by your sour looks."

Bram sighed. He'd heard it before. "Go to the window and see if she's coming."

Sam pretended to misunderstand. "Your mother?"

"No, damn it, Miss Kennedy."

"You're in a mood, aren't you?" Sam crossed the room to the window and stood in a way that gave him the best angle on the street. His view was still limited. "I don't see a carriage."

"She might be walking."

"There's no one on the street. No, wait. There's someone." He shook his head. "Chinese girl. Looks like she's going to the Jenner place with her basket. Probably selling shrimp to the cook."

Bram ordered him back from the window. "Go on. I don't need you any longer."

"Feeling better, are you? Must be those drops." Samuel looked around, made certain everything was in order, and went to the door. "Have a care you don't take too many. They'll wither a man's mind." He left before Bram put his hands on something to throw. He hadn't stepped cleanly into the hallway when he saw Miss Kennedy turning the corner. "You go right in," he told her. "Bram just asked after you."

Comfort paused on the threshold when she saw the hoist attached to Bram's leg. Her eyes widened a fraction as she took it in. "I didn't know," she said. "When did the doctor do this?"

"First thing this morning. Harrison says it's to keep my leg from shortening as the bone knits. I didn't know that could happen, but the way he explained it convinced my mother, and Travers limping in here with that brace on his leg was enough to convince me." He gestured to the system of weights, chains, and pulleys. "It's supposed to keep the bone aligned. I have to trust him about that. What I know is that since he put my leg in traction, I've had less pain."

"I'll have to take you at your word. It looks awful."

"I know." He patted the side of his bed. "Come here. I've been looking forward to seeing you all day. Don't stand on the other side of the room as though you're afraid. It depresses me."

Comfort untied the ribbon under her chin and removed her bonnet. She laid it aside and unbuttoned the black jacket she wore over her daffodil yellow dress.

"You look like a bumblebee," he said. "It's very becoming."

"I don't vaguely understand how that's possible, but I'll accept that you think so." She took off her gloves, laid them beside her bonnet, and crossed to his side. When he put out his hand, she took it in hers and squeezed lightly. "You're warm. Are you supposed to be?"

"I have no idea. I feel fine."

Comfort glanced at the bedside table. In addition to a folded newspaper, a book, a carafe of water, and a lamp, there was a small brown bottle with a black stopper. "Laudanum?"

Bram had followed the direction of her gaze. "Yes, and do not lecture me about its proper use."

"I wasn't going to."

"Good." He released her hand. "Will you sit? Did Travers say he would bring tea?"

"Would you like some?"

"No. I meant for you."

"I don't want anything, thank you."

Bram cocked an eyebrow at her.

"What is it?" she asked.

"I don't know. You sound oddly formal."

"Do I?" She didn't offer an explanation. "What are you doing to amuse yourself?"

"Planning our wedding." Her horrified expression made him chuckle. "*That's* what I've been doing to amuse myself. You rarely disappoint. My mother and Travers are made of sterner stuff. It takes something truly outrageous to move them to a reaction."

"I'm sure you appreciate the challenge."

He smiled. "I do. Tell me what you did today, unless there were numbers involved. If that's the case, make something up."

"I saw Mr. Donald Winstone today. He came to the bank with his mistress on his arm and inquired about setting up an account for her so she can withdraw funds without alerting his wife. Can you imagine?"

"Oh, I can imagine, but I'm not sure I can believe it." His eyes narrowed as he studied her face. "You made it up."

"Well, everything else was about numbers."

"Lord, but you're a breath of fresh air. You have to promise that you'll visit every day from now on. Otherwise my leg will grow long and it's my life that will be shortened."

"Perhaps not every day," she said. "But more often than once a week, if you'll want me, that is."

"Want you? Didn't I just say that I do?"

Comfort took a steadying breath. "I've been thinking, Bram. And I—"

"That will shorten your life."

"What?"

"Thinking."

She didn't smile. "I need to speak to you. It's important."

"Very well. In the event it escaped your notice, I'm not going anywhere."

Comfort realized there was no way she could preface her remarks. He would turn whatever she said back on itself. She thought of something Newton said about Bram not tolerating unpleasantness and knew beyond any doubt that her uncle had spoken the truth. She always allowed Bram to divert her. No longer.

"I can't cooperate with the pretense of an engagement. It's wrong, Bram. You were wrong to make the announcement as though it were fact, and I was wrong to go along with you. I told myself I didn't want to embarrass us or our families, but what would have occurred then is nothing to the embarrassment we face now when the truth becomes known." She paused just long enough to catch her breath. "Do you understand what I'm saying? It's done, Bram. All of it's done."

He rested his head back, briefly closing his eyes. "What if it wasn't a pretense?" he said finally. "What if I made the proposal in earnest?"

Comfort offered no reaction except disappointment.

"I'm not trying to amuse myself," he said.

"Are you certain? It's not always easy to know with you, but it doesn't matter this time. I don't want to marry you."

"You don't mean that."

"I do mean it."

"But you're in love with me."

Before Bode's birthday party, the carelessness with which Bram spoke would have pierced her heart and struck her dumb, if not struck her down. Now she didn't flinch. "I think I might have been," she said slowly, feeling her way. "I'm not sure. If I was, it's not true any longer. And I'm quite certain about that."

"I don't understand."

"Again, it doesn't matter."

"You're wrong."

"We can remain friends," she said. "I'd like to believe that doesn't have to change."

"But if you're not in love with me . . ." His voice trailed off.

He was like a child, she thought; a child who had just discovered an often-neglected pull toy had lost its string. He wanted it fixed so his whims would dictate if it followed him or was left behind. It seemed to Comfort that she had loved him for so long, she'd never asked herself if she liked him.

"I don't want to discuss marriage," she told him. "On that, we have to agree to disagree."

"You promised eight weeks. You gave me your word."

"I know. I thought I could do it. I can't."

"What changed?" He looked from her to his leg and back again. "Is it because of the accident? Because I broke my leg? I can't escort you anywhere. You won't be seen on my arm."

He still had the capacity to take her breath away, but it was no longer accompanied by a stutter in her heartbeat. "Is that how you assess my character? So petty? So small-minded?"

"I thought I could depend on your promise."

"That's no trifling matter to me either. I'm sorry."

Bram shook his head, still trying to understand. "This has something to do with Bode."

Comfort almost reared back at the accusation in his tone. "I don't know what you mean."

"Dr. Harrison saw you with Bode at *Rigoletto*. He said something to you. I know it. You fainted."

"He invited my uncles and me to share your family's box. It had nothing at all to do with me fainting."

"I'm telling you, Comfort, Bode hates the idea of our engagement."

"Then he will be overjoyed. We're *not* engaged."

Frustrated, Bram shoved his fingers through his hair. "If I tell my mother our engagement is ended, she'll believe it's because you don't want to be with a cripple."

"Not if you tell her there never was any engagement. That's what I expect, Bram. I expect you to tell her the truth. I'll sit with you, if you like, and we'll explain it together. She will help us determine what we must do next. I would value her advice."

"We can't end it," Bram said. "We can't."

She frowned. "I don't believe that, but if you do, you'll have to explain."

Bram's lips parted. He was aware of Comfort's frank regard. It silenced him.

"Very well," she said at last. "Shall I ask your mother to join us?"

He shook his head. "I'll tell her myself."

"Will you do right by me, Bram?"

"It pains me that you think you have to ask."

"It pains me also." She put out a hand and touched the back of his. "And you haven't answered my question."

He snatched his hand away. "I'll do right by you. Of course I will."

There was nothing for her to do but accept him at his word. "Do you want me to leave?"

Bram was a long time answering. "No. Stay. A little longer, I think." He looked sideways at the bedside table and reached for the laudanum.

Comfort had the oddest feeling that he wasn't taking the drug for the pain in his leg. She stayed with him until he fell asleep.

John Farwell jumped out of the way as a wagon loaded with casks of liquor lumbered dangerously close to where he was standing. He put out a hand to make sure the gentleman he was escorting to the *Demeter Queen* stayed well out of the dray's path. It was late, nearing dusk on a summer's evening, and the activity on the wharf hadn't slowed appreciably since early morning. John looked side to side and then glanced up before he stepped out again.

"This way," he said. "Before they set those crates down."

The gentleman followed, but his eyes were on the bulging cargo net hoisted high above them. "What are they delivering?"

"Tea probably. That ship just arrived from China. Could be anything."

"Is it part of the Black Crowne fleet?"

The clerk shook his head. John Farwell was a small, tidy man often dwarfed by those around him. While he lacked height, he carried himself with a certain air of self-importance that did not go unnoticed. His demeanor could have made him the subject of ridicule, except that it was widely acknowledged that he *was* important. Smooth operations up and down the wharf depended on him. Only the harbormaster held a position of more responsibility, but not even the harbormaster could create a bottleneck in the bay like John Farwell could with the Black Crowne fleet. It was understood that he acted on Beauregard DeLong's orders, but he carried out those orders with such precision, even enthusiasm, that it was better to give him a wide berth.

"No," he said. "That's *Victoria Belle*. She's out of London. Her master is Gordon Massey, and she's owned by Lord Harold Barclay. You can tell a Barclay ship by its personal standard." He pointed to the blue-and-white flag fluttering above the bow. "That's a griffin. I understand it's a symbol from the owner's coat of arms."

John Farwell put his arm out again, this time to keep the gentleman from stepping into a puddle of beer and broken glass. He directed him around it. "The remains of a brawl," he said.

"That occurs frequently?"

"As frequently as a ship puts down anchor."

"But that must be every day."

"More often than that." The clerk spared a glance for his companion as they walked. "This is your first time here, I imagine."

"That's right."

John nodded. "Folks new to the city are usually surprised by the traffic. Where are you from?"

"Sacramento."

"I've never been. All politics that way."

"Before politics there was gold."

"There certainly was." John Farwell was not particularly curious. If the gentleman he was accompanying to the *Demeter Queen* made his fortune panning or mining, it was a story he'd heard before, or at least some version of it. He cared a great deal more that they were not plunged into the bay by a skittish horse or a runaway wagon, or worse, pressed into service on a vessel that trafficked in human cargo and opium. The lateness of the hour almost assured that the Barbary Coast press gangs would be coming out to prowl the wharf and look for prey.

Weaving in and out of rolling barrels and vendors closing up their carts, John Farwell hurried along, only sparing the occasional glance to make certain his companion stayed in step.

"There she is," he said, coming to an abrupt halt. "The *Demeter Queen*." He pointed to the detailed black figurehead below the bowsprit. "All Black Crowne ships have a figurehead made of ebony wood. Some people see right off that she looks like the black queen on a chessboard. Takes others some time to find the crown that's carved into her hair."

"I believe her hair becomes the crown."

The clerk was impressed that the man could make that out in the failing light, but he didn't pause to remark on it. "This way. Mr. DeLong will be with the *Demeter*'s master." John led him up the gangplank and onto the deck. Looking past the crew members that were orchestrating a massive lift from the cargo hold, John spied Bode and the master standing at the guardrail near the capstan. "There they are. I can make the introductions, but then I must leave. When you've concluded your business, you should ask Mr. DeLong to find you an escort to take you away from the Coast."

"Really? I thought I might want to see for myself what the papers are writing about."

"Then you should have someone who knows the area show you around. The Rangers will pin you right away."

"Pin me?"

"As a mark."

"I see."

John Farwell had his doubts, but he had discharged his warning and bore no further responsibility. If the man didn't use the sense God gave him, then he deserved what happened to him. It wasn't as if Black Crowne would be affected. Beauregard DeLong didn't suffer fools, and he certainly didn't do business with them.

Nathan Douglas, master mariner of the *Demeter Queen*, was the first to see John Farwell approaching. He stopped talking and jerked his bearded chin in the direction of the pair bearing down on them.

Bode glanced over his shoulder. He saw his clerk immediately. It took him a moment to realize John wasn't alone, and a second glance to realize he recognized the man accompanying him. Bode didn't have a chance to excuse himself from Douglas's side before John arrived.

"Yes, Mr. Farwell?"

The clerk stood back at what he judged was a respectful distance. It was natural for him to project the illusion of height by maintaining a correct, if somewhat stiff, carriage. "This is Mr. James R. Crocker of Sacramento. He most particularly wanted to make the acquaintance of the head of Black Crowne Shipping."

"Oh?" Bode held out his hand to Mr. Crocker. "Mr. Farwell should have taken you to meet my mother. I'm Beau DeLong, and I believe we've already met."

James R. Crocker nodded. His slim smile was visible behind his neatly trimmed mustache and beard. "Yes. *Rigoletto*. I didn't know if you would recall. There were several things happening at once, weren't there?"

"Indeed." Bode introduced Nathan Douglas and then excused himself and Mr. Crocker from the circle. Out of the corner of his eye, he saw John Farwell hurry away and realized his clerk was getting off the wharf before nightfall. "Come with me, Mr. Crocker. We can have relative privacy starboard." He led Crocker across the bow to the opposite rail. "How can I help you? There aren't many people that most particularly want to make my acquaintance."

Crocker's smile widened briefly, revealing a small gap between his front teeth. "Those are Mr. Farwell's words, not mine."

"I thought they might be." The night of the opera, Bode had had the impression of a man whose age was near to his own. Now he saw that James R. Crocker was older, more of an age with his mother or Comfort's uncles. There were fine lines around his chestnut-colored eyes, and his beard was salted with wiry white threads. He had a broad, square jaw and a nose whose line was slightly off-center and may have been broken. He wore a short-brimmed hat with a rounded crown that was popular among a certain set of gentlemen. It wasn't what he would have worn to *Rigoletto*. Opening night required a top hat. This was a hat for sporting men. Gamblers.

That explained why he met so many blank stares when he asked after the man. He'd been making inquiries in the wrong circles. He should have asked his brother.

Crocker touched the brim of his hat in a manner that might have been a salute. "I'm here because of what happened at the opera," he said. "I have been concerned about the young woman who fainted. I understand she is Miss Comfort Kennedy, niece of the gentlemen that left with you."

Bode nodded. It was pointless to deny any part of what Crocker had already learned for himself. It hadn't occurred to him that the person he was seeking on Comfort's behalf might be interested in her. "That doesn't exactly explain why you're here, Mr. Crocker. You could be addressing your concerns to Miss Kennedy, or better yet, her uncles."

"I considered that, but I thought it might be deemed too forward. Sometimes coming to the back door is a more effective approach."

"If you're a tinker or a bank robber."

He chuckled. "I'm neither. I was led to believe that her uncles are very protective and that they wouldn't welcome my inquiry. Someone, and I don't recall who it was any longer, told me I might find out what I wanted to know from you."

"Maybe," Bode said, his eyes narrowing slightly. "Depending on what it is you want to know."

"How she fares, that's all. According to acquaintances that do business with Jones Prescott, she hasn't been seen regularly at the bank since the opera. That's been more than a week."

"I don't know about that." And he didn't. He'd been working all day and well into the night. Except to talk to some of the people he remembered standing nearby when Comfort fainted, he'd hardly strayed four blocks in any direction from the office and warehouse. "I haven't seen Miss Kennedy since the day after the opening. She was fine."

"Well, that's gratifying to hear. She collapsed so suddenly. I thought she might have hit her head on the stair railing."

"No. She was already coming around by the time I got her outside."

"That's good to know." He cleared his throat. "Someone told me that Miss Kennedy is your brother's fiancée. Did I understand that right?"

"Yes."

"I thought whoever told me must have got it wrong. I was certain she was with you that evening."

Bode didn't like the direction Crocker was steering the conversation. "She was with her uncles."

Crocker nodded and cleared his throat again. There was still a faint rasp when he spoke. "I understand your brother— Abraham, is it?"

"Bram."

"Yes, Bram. When I learned that he'd broken his leg, I realized that might explain why you were escorting her."

"She was with her uncles," Bode repeated. "I invited all of them to my family's box."

"That was thoughtful." He cupped his hand to his throat and massaged it gently. "Excuse me." Reaching into the pocket in the lining of his jacket, he removed a red-and-white tin. He used his thumbnail to flick it open and took out a lozenge. "Do you want one?"

Bode shook his head.

Crocker put it in his mouth and immediately cheeked it. "You'd be surprised how often people accept the offer," he said, closing the tin and slipping it back inside his jacket. "It's the peppermint, I suppose. People think they're candy."

"So it's not only soprano arias that put a tickle in your throat."

"What?" Confusion brought his eyebrows together. "What are you—" His features cleared as the answer came to him. "You're talking about what I said at the break. I'd forgotten that. No, it isn't only sopranos. I have a . . . a condition . . . I suppose you'd say. That's what the doctors call it. I call it a pain in my neck."

Bode smiled thinly. "Is there anything else, Mr. Crocker?"

"No. No, there isn't. The young lady's fine; that's all I wanted to know. Will you tell her I inquired?"

"Of course." Bode had no idea if he would tell Comfort anything about his encounter with Crocker, but saying as much would have only extended their conversation. "Good evening, Mr. Crocker."

Crocker didn't move.

"What is it?" asked Bode. For the first time, he thought James R. Crocker looked hesitant. "You've decided there *is* something else?"

"Mr. Farwell said I should ask about an escort when I was ready to leave."

"He's right. I'll find someone."

Crocker hesitated. "I thought perhaps you would . . ."

"I haven't finished with Mr. Douglas. I won't be ready to leave for a while." Before Crocker could say that he'd wait, Bode waved one of the crew over and gave him instructions. "Right to his door," he said. "Nowhere else. I want to know he arrived safely." *And I want to know where he's living.* Bode nodded to Crocker. "You're in good hands."

"Thank you, then." He touched his finger to his hat before he turned smartly and followed his escort to the gangway.

It was after ten when Bode awoke. Cursing softly, he rose and drew back the curtains. Light spilled into his bedroom, momentarily blinding him. He put up one hand to shield his eyes and groped with the other one to find his patch. If he'd been less exhausted when he arrived home, he would have opened the curtains before he went to bed. Daybreak would have prevented him from sleeping so long.

He went through all the rituals that followed waking without giving them any thought. Although he managed his routine quickly, he didn't expect to get it done without interruption. There were days when he rose at dawn that John Farwell was pounding on his door inside of twenty minutes.

Bode found John at the front of the office assigning the three clerks he supervised their duties for the day. As he seemed to have it all well in hand, Bode told him that he was going to

Jones Prescott and kept on walking. He felt four pairs of eyes follow his progress out the door and as he passed in front of the window.

Twenty minutes later he was walking under the granite tablature of the bank without glancing up at the cornices or the deeply engraved names. He crossed the lobby to the teller cages and was informed that neither Mr. Jones nor Mr. Prescott was in the bank. Bode hesitated, wondering if he should ask after Comfort. Before he made his decision, Mr. Tweedy offered the information.

"I know the way," Bode said and started for the door.

Comfort nearly dropped the stack of ledgers she was holding when Bode suddenly appeared in the corridor. He slipped a hand under them and lent support until she had them securely in her arms again.

"I thought you'd be at your desk," he said.

Since he moved as lightly as a cat, Comfort thought he would have surprised her in any circumstances. "I'm taking these there," she said, hefting them again. "My uncles aren't here."

"I know. I asked for them."

"Yet here you are."

"Mr. Tweedy told me you were in your office."

Comfort started walking away. "And I will be again."

Bode tempered his amusement in the event she stole a look over her shoulder and threw one of those ledgers at his head. He followed her across the threshold of her office. She set the ledgers on top of a desk that was already crowded with documents, newspapers, and an assortment of odds and ends that she apparently used as paperweights. He just shook his head.

"Is there something I can do for you?" she asked.

He ignored the frost in her voice. "You object to a social call? My business was with your uncles."

"I'm busy, Mr. DeLong."

Bode dropped into a chair on the other side of her desk. "I imagine you are. I heard that you haven't been here for more than a week."

She didn't try to hide her surprise. "Who told you that?"

"Is it true?"

"Yes."

"Then it's not important who told me. Are you well now?"

"I wasn't unwell. I was . . . I was tired." She didn't know how else to explain the melancholia that had overwhelmed her after she'd spoken to Bram. She'd been listless, uninterested, and fatigued to the point that rising from her bed was a hardship. She'd forced herself to leave the house this morning. Suey Tsin's hovering and hand-wringing were wearing. Her uncles' frequent visits to her room clearly communicated the extent of their anxiety. Dr. Winter had been called the second day and left her with a bottle of foul-tasting bromide. The drops only made her sleepy.

"And now?" asked Bode.

"And now I'm not." She forced a smile and inquired pleasantly, if insincerely, about his health.

"I'm well."

"You're wearing the eye patch."

"The swelling's gone, but the bruise is still colorful enough to frighten children. I'll probably wear it another day or so."

Comfort nodded and offered a thin smile because it seemed that she should. Moving behind her desk, she picked up a sheaf of papers that was lying on her chair and set it crosswise on another pile.

Bode's gaze followed her. When she reached her chair, her legs folded under her a bit shakily, and she set her hands on the arms to give her support. Her features were drawn, her normally generous mouth compressed. The color in her face wasn't in her cheeks but in the pale violet shadows under her eyes. She was short-tempered and miserable and doing a poor job of pretending that she wasn't. He wondered about her nightmares, if they were still troubling her and how often she was having them, and then for no reason that he could easily identify, he was struck by the odd thought that she was grieving.

Comfort shuffled some papers on her desk and then neatly squared them. It was difficult to keep from fidgeting under Bode's scrutiny. She had given considerable thought to calling on him since her conversation with Bram, but it had ended there, with thought alone. She began to consider that avoiding him was what she gained by remaining in bed.

The last time she'd been a coward, she'd found rocks where

she could hide. That thought, more than Suey Tsin's distress or her uncles' concern, pushed her out of bed this morning.

Comfort inhaled heavily and pressed three fingers to her temple. She closed her eyes while she massaged the dull ache that threatened to become blinding pain.

"I was going to have a message delivered to your office," she said. "I wanted to arrange a time when I could call on you or you could call on me."

"Then it's convenient that I'm here."

"Perhaps. I don't know." She shrugged. "I may not be able to explain it very well."

Intrigued, Bode merely raised an inquiring eyebrow.

"Have you spoken to Bram since the opera?" she asked.

"No. Does he have something interesting to tell me?"

"We aren't engaged." The words seemed to lie on her lips like toad spit. She pressed her fingers to her mouth and waited for Bode to react. He didn't. He remained maddeningly calm. "You heard me, didn't you? Bram and I aren't engaged."

"I heard you," he said. "Does my mother know?"

"Yes." There was the briefest hesitation. "Bram promised he'd tell her."

"Ah. That it explains it, then."

Comfort had an urge to lay her arms on the desk and bury her head in them. "What did she say to you?"

"She told me the wedding would be a year from now. My birthday, in fact. The anniversary of Bram's announcement."

"She sounded very sure of that?"

He smiled. "This is Alexandra DeLong. Have you known her to ever sound less than sure about anything?"

Comfort hadn't. "It's not true," she said. "I didn't agree to that. Bram and I never discussed a wedding, never talked about a date."

"She seemed to think you had."

"I haven't seen Bram since—" She stopped, counting back. "It's been over a week. The day after I went to your office, I went to see Bram."

"I've spoken to Alexandra since then. I couldn't join her for dinner, but we had luncheon at Morton's. She wanted to know what happened to you at *Rigoletto*."

Comfort didn't know what to say. She simply shook her head.

Bode grew concerned by her lapse into silence. Looking around for something he could give her to drink, he prompted, "You're the one who broke off the engagement?"

"There never was an engagement."

"What?" He thought he could appreciate something to drink.

"No engagement. Not ever. The announcement was a fraud. Your brother never proposed to me."

Bode stared at her, his good eye narrowing. He watched Comfort press back in her chair as if he'd pinned her to it. "You didn't say anything about it that night."

"I know, and I regret it. I was too embarrassed. He surprised all of us with the announcement, including me. I didn't know what to say or do."

"So you went along with him."

"Yes."

"That evening, when I saw you and Bram together on the portico, was that what you were discussing so intently?"

She nodded. "I was angry. He wanted six months from me. He told me that at the end of that time I could break off the engagement in any manner I chose."

"Six months." He wished he had enough confidence in his brother's scruples that he could object to what Comfort was telling him, but he believed her. "Why six months?"

"There was no particular reason that I could see. You know your brother. He thought it. He said it. In his mind it was done." The recollection made Comfort shake her head. "I asked for six weeks. That was as long as I thought he could manage fidelity. Even a false engagement required certain standards of behavior, or at least I believed so."

"He agreed?"

"To not trolling the Barbary Coast for women? Yes, he agreed. Whether or not he could have done it is no longer important. Bram and I decided our engagement would last eight weeks." She turned her head slightly and looked away. There was a pencil lying precariously close to the edge of the desk. She nudged it back with her fingertips. "It doesn't matter what

Bram would or wouldn't have done. I wasn't able to keep my word thirteen days." Bode's silence had her turning back to him. His regard was contemplative. "What is it?"

He shrugged lightly. "I'm wondering how much our kiss might have factored in your decision." Bode watched color rise from under her severely modest neckline and climb all the way to her hairline. "As much as all that."

"Of all the arrogant, self-important, wrongheaded . . ." Comfort threw up her hands as words, specifically adjectives, failed her. She had to draw a deep breath and release it very slowly to clear her head. With considerably more calm, she said, "It had nothing at all to do with ending the farce."

"It was a reasonable question," he said. "You were the one who mentioned fidelity. Of course, you were concerned about Bram's, not your own. You told me you went to see him the day after you visited me. Those events occurred so closely together there's at least some possibility they're related."

"They're related," she said, "but not in the way you think. After you escorted me home, you went to the bank and spoke to my uncles. They heard enough from you to decide that I had to end the arrangement with Bram."

"They knew there was no engagement?"

"Yes. I told them the day after the party. It wasn't something I was comfortable keeping from them."

"Like your nightmares."

She was barely able to keep from flinching. Sometimes talking with Bode was like wandering through nettles. "Yes," she said. "Like my nightmares."

"Did they threaten to tell Bram it was ended if you didn't?"

"No."

"Did they say they would make the truth public if you didn't talk to Bram?"

"No."

"Then they hardly compelled you to do it."

"It felt as if I was compelled."

"I'm sure. You don't like to disappoint them."

Comfort pressed her hand to her temple again and closed her eyes. "Stop it. Whatever it is that you're doing, I beg that you'll stop it."

Bode fell silent. He watched the faint trembling of her lower lip until she sucked it in and bit down on it. A small vertical crease appeared between her eyebrows as she rubbed her temple. She didn't open her eyes. He wondered if she was hoping he would be gone by the time she did.

Comfort never heard him move. It wasn't until she felt the pencil sliding from the smooth twist in her hair that she knew he was standing beside her. His hands, large, warm, rough in their texture and infinitely gentle in their touch, cupped her elbows and lifted her. She laid her forehead against his shoulder as the chair behind her was pushed out of the way. He held her lightly, not an embrace at all, only support. She could have stepped to the side, but then she was turned and the desk was at her back.

She had a moment to wonder why she didn't feel trapped, but no time to arrive at an answer. Bode's fingers had slipped under her chin.

"Look at me," he said. "I want to make it right. Tell me how I can make it right."

Comfort shook her head as she lifted it. "I don't know. It makes it sadder that I don't know." A wash of tears glazed her dark eyes but didn't fall. "I did a foolish thing. Perhaps there's nothing that can be done."

"Do you want to marry Bram?"

She blinked. "What?"

Bode repeated the question.

"What are you saying? That you'd arrange it?"

"I wasn't saying anything. I was asking. Do you want to marry my brother?"

Comfort shifted her weight. She felt his fingers tighten on her elbow. "What are you doing?"

"Waiting for you."

She stared at him. There was a nuance of expectation in his tone that made her suddenly uncertain of his meaning. "No," she said. "I don't want to marry Bram."

"But you're still in love with him."

Comfort didn't know if it was a question or his opinion, and she couldn't see past his remote expression to find the answer. "Do you know, Bram said the very same thing. I told him I wasn't, but he didn't believe me. I wonder if you do."

"I could be persuaded."

She smiled a bit unevenly. "Mmm. It's complicated. According to my uncles, I've been deceiving myself, and I'm learning that finding my way through that is as challenging as negotiating a labyrinth. I thought I was in love with him, so perhaps I was. Perhaps thinking it is enough to make it true. I keep circling that, wondering how anyone knows the fact of love from the fiction of it. I wonder how *I* will know."

"You've been giving it a lot of thought."

"Lately." Her uneven smile turned self-deprecating. "Too late."

"What if it's not?"

Her lips parted in anticipation of what she meant to say, but when there were no words, they remained parted as invitation of what she meant to do.

Chapter Eight

At the moment their lips touched, Comfort's understanding of what a kiss could be was changed. The sudden jolt, that surge of something electric that prickled her skin and made her heart stutter, also lifted her onto the tips of her toes. She faltered, lost her balance, and reached behind her to grab the desk. That was when Bode grounded her, jerking her against him with enough force to absorb the crackling charge.

If it made him unsteady, she couldn't tell. He didn't yield to the press of her body. One hand palmed the nape of her neck, and the other supported her at the small of her back. Her hands climbed his arms to clutch his jacket at the shoulders. The sensation of falling was still with her, but *falling into what?*

She thought she'd initiated the kiss, but perhaps not. He owned it. His mouth plundered hers. He took her lips, her tongue, her breath. The hot suck of his mouth held her fast even as his hold on her eased. Restless, she rose on tiptoe again. Everywhere she was soft, he was not. Her small breasts flattened against his chest, and her heart fluttered like a caged wild bird. She accustomed herself to the slant of his mouth, the rhythm and pulse of his tongue, and although she answered in kind, the kiss still belonged to him.

He claimed her with forays along the ridge of her teeth and the soft, wet underside of her lip. He sucked in her bottom lip, worried it between his teeth, salved it with the sweep of his tongue. Between bites, he savored her. Tasting. Tormenting her with the slow, deliberate savaging of her senses.

His kiss was a drug. It made her breathing quicken and her womb contract. Her breasts swelled. Her fingers tingled. She craved more. Always more.

When he drew back, she felt abandoned, bereft, and then his mouth returned to hers. The slant was different, the shape of his mouth—was that a smile?—changed when it touched her lips. She had no sense that he was amused. What she sensed was hunger.

She responded to that. Her hands moved from his shoulders to his neck. She cradled his head. Her fingertips ruffled and tugged the silky strands of hair at his nape. He said something, but the words were flattened and indistinguishable against her lips, and what she heard and felt was a murmur that chased a shiver all the way down her spine.

Something hit the floor hard. The thump startled her. She would have reared back, but there was no place to go. Another thud. This time she realized it was the stack of ledgers that was falling. She removed one hand from Bode's neck and began searching blindly behind her to find what remained of the stack and pull it away from the edge.

Her fingers had just curled around the spine of one book when Bode's hand closed over her wrist. Instead of helping draw the ledgers in, he directed her hand to nudge them away. They hovered precariously while her fingers scrabbled to catch them. His push was stronger than her pull, and the last three books slid to the floor. Their landing was softened by the ones that had fallen before.

Comfort reared back her head, breaking off the kiss. She had just enough time to suck in a breath. What she meant to say to him was lost as his mouth returned to hers. She heard the whisper and rustle of papers sliding across the desk, the odd skittering sound of rolling pencils, and the flutter of documents as they floated to the floor. Her fingers closed about the crystal paperweight, but he took it from her, afraid perhaps that she meant to bludgeon him with it. She tensed, expecting to hear it crash, but nothing like that happened. She didn't know what he did with it. A moment later, she didn't care.

Bode palmed her hips, lifted her, and set her down on top of the desk. She became the paperweight for those few things that hadn't been cleared away. She laid her hands over his when they came to rest on her knees. His fingers curled around the fabric of her gown anyway, gathering it by inches, raising her hem above the laced tops of her leather boots.

His mouth was humid. Hot. There was a hint of anise on his breath, and the scent of soap lingered on his skin. She had an urge to touch his face, to lay a palm against his cheek, perhaps cup his clean-shaven jaw. It would be like holding the kiss.

Before she could surrender to the temptation, Bode's hands shifted from her knees to her hips. He inched her backward and stepped between her legs. It was the first time she realized her hem was level with her knees.

Startled, Comfort tore her mouth away and turned her head, tucking her chin into her shoulder. His lips touched the exposed cord in her neck. He followed the line to the hollow behind her ear. She put up a hand to push him away, but her fingertips offered no real resistance. He kissed them.

A shiver tripped lightly down her spine. Her breath caught. He teased her earlobe with the tip of his tongue and then whispered something rough and hot against her ear. She didn't know what he said. The warmth of his breath tickling her skin was what mattered.

His mouth brushed her cheek, her temple, and for a moment rested against her forehead. One hand slid deeply into her dark hair, loosening the combs and removing a pencil. She made a grab at them before they clattered to the desk, and her hair unfolded over the back of his hand like a bolt of Japanese silk. He twisted one of the cascading waves around his fingers and tugged, directing her head toward him again and her mouth exactly where he wanted it.

Her mouth, her splendidly formed and inviting mouth, was damp, faintly swollen, and rose petal pink. He could see the tip of her tongue where she pressed it against her teeth. It made his breathing quicken and his nostrils flare. He bent his head and rubbed his lips against hers. Her mouth opened. He pressed his entry, deepening the kiss. They shared a single breath, and when it wasn't enough, he tore away and buried his face in her neck.

She moaned softly as he sipped her skin. The sound of it stirred him. That first taste only whet his appetite. She made him afraid. She always had.

In his eyes she was both temptress and innocent, and for as long as he'd known her, the scales had mostly favored the latter. But they were shifting, shifting quickly, and the balance was precarious at best. She was on the precipice of understanding the change. He could feel it in the advance and retreat of her responses, the way she opened to his mouth and closed to his hands.

She was dangerously curious. Wanting, but not certain what she wanted.

And he couldn't be sure that she wanted it from him.

His little brother cast a very long shadow.

Comfort sensed something was different even before Bode broke off the kiss. She raised her face, following the kiss until it was no longer possible. When he straightened, he rested his chin on the crown of her head so she couldn't meet his eyes.

She drew in a shaky breath and whispered uncertainly, "What is it?" His chin rubbed her scalp, and she knew he was shaking his head. "Tell me."

Bode smiled, but the shape of it was rueful. "It's not you."

"I know it's not."

Her response surprised a back-of-the-throat chuckle from him.

"Well, it's not, is it?" she said. "I'm doing it right."

He raised his head and lifted her chin. "You're doing it very right."

"That's what I thought," she said gravely. She removed her chin from the cup of his hand and placed all of her fingertips against his chest. She applied enough pressure to encourage him to take a step back. As soon as he did, she quickly closed her splayed knees and pushed her dress over them. She didn't jump down from her perch on the desk, but she did curl her hands around the edge to help her shove away when she was ready. Right now, Bode was still standing too close. If she moved, she'd be a barnacle on his hull.

Comfort stared at him, her dark eyebrows lifting a fraction in inquiry.

"Apparently I cannot be persuaded," Bode said.

She frowned slightly, slow to understand his meaning until she recalled their exchange just before she kissed him. She'd told Bode that she did not love his brother and wondered aloud if he believed her. *I could be persuaded*, he had said. And now his answer was *apparently not*.

"Mm." Her gaze fell away, and she looked on either side of her for the combs he'd removed while she gathered her hair and wound it around her hand. She loosely twisted her hair and stabbed it with the combs to secure it. Aware that Bode was studying her again, this time with wry amusement clearly defining the shape of his mouth, she gestured at him to move out of the way. What he did was pull her chair close behind him, palm the paperweight he'd dropped there earlier, and sit down, effectively blocking her from abandoning her roost unless she wanted to land in his lap. Which she did not.

Leaning back, Bode bobbled the paperweight between his hands and stretched his legs under the desk. He saw her eye his shins as if she were gauging the distance between them and the pointed toes of her leather boots, but he judged it was more show than real threat.

Tilting her head to one side, Comfort considered him. "It's difficult to know what to make of you, Beau DeLong."

The infinitesimal lift of one corner of his mouth hinted again at his wry, reserved humor. "Is that right?"

She nodded. "Bram is always so engaged and engaging. You're not at all like that."

"No, I'm not."

"Do you dislike comparisons?"

He shrugged. "It's what people do. How they judge. But I don't know that it's helpful."

"I think it must be human nature to distinguish what sets each of us apart, but there are always more commonalities than there are differences. Certainly that's true for you and Bram."

"Really?" He couldn't recall that anyone had ever said so.

"Of course. There are obvious things like the similarities in your height and frame, your carriage and gestures. You both have a habit of plowing your hair with your fingers, and you arch the same eyebrow. Even the way you sit when formality isn't a requirement is almost identical. While you ease toward leaning but never quite surrendering your spine, Bram, I fear, actually becomes boneless, while you remain alert."

Bode had a vision of himself as she saw him. He was indeed sprawled in the chair, his legs slightly splayed, his shoulders resting comfortably against the leather, his hips inclined forward, but there was a line of tension that was his constant companion, not unwelcome because he believed it was what made him a sentient being. He supposed it was what she meant when she said he never quite surrendered his spine.

"Go on," he said.

"I imagine you're more curious about traits of character."

"That is understating it."

"Very well. You share a wicked sense of humor and uncanny perception. You're both clever, acutely so, confident, convinced of the rightness of whatever you do, and although it reveals itself in different ways, there is generosity in your nature. You both are frequently at odds with your mother, but you appreciate your family even in those circumstances, perhaps most especially then."

"I don't know about that last," Bode said. "But I believe you're right about the rest."

"Oh, I am." Her smile was deliberately smug. "About all of it, actually."

A low, appreciative chuckle rumbled deep in his throat. "Your conceit is rather more attractive than it should be." He wanted to kiss her again. In point of fact, he wanted to do a great deal more than that. It was tempting to think that he could have her. He wondered, though, if he could keep her.

Nothing was so clear to him as his intention to keep her.

"What are you going to do about Bram?" he asked. Like a shadow overtaking light, distress chased away the lightness of feeling he'd glimpsed in her eyes. He regretted the loss.

"I thought I'd already done it," she said. "I was firm regarding my expectations. There could have been no misunderstanding." She compressed her lips, remembering the laudanum.

"What are you thinking?"

"The laudanum that he keeps at his bedside. I wonder . . ." She held up her hands, palms out. "I don't know. Perhaps he never really heard what I was saying."

"Perhaps. But it's more likely that you're excusing him too easily."

"I know," she said, shaking her head. "I've never quite understood how that happens. Does he do something to encourage me to make excuses for him, or am I really so charitable?"

"It's not one or the other," Bode said. "It's both. And you're not alone."

"Oh, I realize that, but it's always easier to see that he's using misdirection when he's not performing the trick for me." Comfort saw Bode's mouth twitch. "I suppose he never catches you unaware."

"He does it regularly. Why do you think he wouldn't?"

She shrugged. "I don't know. I guess I thought you'd be a more skeptical audience."

"I am. But he's good. Very good. And as you pointed out, misdirection is easier to see when you're not the one being misdirected." Bode folded his hands on his chest. "So what will you do?"

"I'll call on him and remind him of our conversation. If he can't, or won't, tell his mother the truth, then it falls to me. I offered before to sit with him while he told her, but he didn't want that, and now, I don't want him. I'll do it on my own."

"Are you certain you want to do that?"

"I'm quite certain I don't, but a letter is a cowardly compromise."

"I wasn't thinking of a letter. I was thinking that you might allow me to explain the situation to her." Bode saw Comfort stiffen, her surprise palpable. "I guess not."

"I couldn't ask you to do that."

"You didn't. I offered."

"Then, no. I can't accept. It will only confuse and complicate."

"Oh, good, because I thought we were already in those waters." He ignored the sour look she gave him. "I have more experience than you delivering unpleasant news to my mother, particularly as it concerns Bram."

"I'm sure that's true, but what is the explanation for your involvement? She'll ask, you know."

"She will. And there's nothing the least complicated about

my answer. I'll tell her that you came to me with the truth about the engagement and asked for my advice."

Comfort's eyebrows lifted. "Asked you for advice?"

"I thought that would be less offensive to you than telling her you nearly ravished me in the venerable offices of Jones Prescott." Bode swiveled his chair out of the way in the event she recovered herself quickly enough to deliver a bruising blow to his shins. She surprised him, though, because when she got over her initial astonishment, she had to press her hand to her mouth to contain her laughter.

It occurred to him that perhaps he should be offended.

"Oh, I'm sorry," she said through her fingers. "But I'm imagining how your mother would greet that news. I think there's every possibility that she might be rendered speechless."

It wasn't difficult to understand why that would amuse her. His mother believed there were correct sentiments for every occasion and not having those at the tip of one's tongue was not only ill-mannered and a sign of poor breeding, but also hinted at an impoverished mind. Alexandra had probably shared her views with Comfort; she certainly had shared those opinions with him.

"You make it very tempting to tell her," Bode said.

Comfort sobered. Her fingers fell away from her lips and curled around the edge of the desk again. "I'll speak to her alone, but thank you for the offer."

"As you like."

Now that Bode's legs were out of the way, Comfort was able to slide off her desk. She didn't ask him to vacate her chair, choosing instead to busy herself picking up the papers and ledgers that he'd swept onto the floor. She was relieved that he didn't lend a hand. It would have made the task awkward somehow. This way, when she finished, she could pretend the warmth in her cheeks was the result of exertion and not from the memories of how each object had come to be where it lay.

She set everything on the desk without attempting to organize it. One of her hands rested on an accounts ledger. "You never mentioned what brought you around to see my uncles."

"No, I didn't."

Comfort told herself to let the matter drop. She was used to confidentiality in banking matters. She pressed for information anyway. "I thought it might have something to do with the drawing I saw."

"What drawing?"

"The one on your table. In your home above the Black Crowne Office. I think you were working on it when I went there. I interrupted you."

"I was, and you did."

She couldn't recall if she'd apologized for it. "Well, I'm sorry for that." Having the desk between them, even if she was opposite her usual place, helped make his presence in her office more in the way of ordinary than outside of it. "It looked as if you were working on the design for a ship."

"An iron paddle steamer."

"I see."

There was a wry tilt to his mouth. "Do you know what that is?"

"From your drawing, I'd say she's two things: a clipper and a riverboat. She has masts and a bowsprit like one and a steam propulsion plant amidships to turn two side paddle wheels like the other."

He was impressed. "I didn't realize you'd gotten such a good look at it."

"I don't think you wanted me to, so I apologize for that. As for remembering it, there are some things that just stay in my mind." She closed her eyes a moment. "I can picture it." She looked at him again. "Though I imagine it's been revised many times since I last saw it."

"Many times."

"There were erasure shavings all over the paper. I had the impression you were revising it almost as fast as you were sketching it."

"I often do. I want to get it right."

"Is there a right way?"

"Probably not. I should have said I want to make it better, the best it can be."

She nodded, understanding. "It's important to do a thing well. When you're done, will you build her?"

"Eventually."

Comfort sat down in a chair usually occupied by visitors. "She deserves to be built."

"You think so?"

"Of course. She's beautiful. She has the majesty of a clipper and the strength of an ironclad. What will you name her?"

"I'm thinking, given your description, I should call her the *Queen Mother.*"

Comfort laughed, delighted by his arid accents. "See? There is your wicked sense of humor. Call her the *Alexandra Queen.*"

Bode found himself staring at her mouth again. Laughter made her lips as tempting as Eve's apple. Reluctantly, he lifted his gaze and met her eyes. *"Alexandra Queen.* Perhaps I will."

"She'll like it. More importantly, she'll be flattered. I would be."

"You'd be a schooner," he said. "Swift. Sleek. A ship that's responsive to a light hand and easy to maneuver."

Comfort's eyes widened fractionally. Her lips parted. She was able to resist placing her hands against her cheeks, which were warming rapidly. There was no need to call more attention to their deepening color. "Forgive my poor breeding and impoverished mind," she said finally, recalling something Alexandra DeLong had told her. "But I'm afraid the proper response eludes me."

"I meant it as a compliment."

"It seemed as if you had."

"But you should probably slap my face."

"I wondered about that." His sudden grin, full of mischief and boyish charm, put all thought of retaliation out of Comfort's mind. "That's Bram's smile," she told him.

"Is it?"

"Yes. The one he uses when he knows he's been naughty and is about to be forgiven anyway."

"I object to 'naughty,' but I am in favor of being forgiven. Am I?"

She sighed heavily. "Yes."

Bode appreciated that she offered surrender against her better judgment. "I wasn't certain I could do it," he confessed. "It was my smile before it was Bram's, you know, but it's been a long time since I've had reason to use it."

"Keeping it in reserve is probably a good strategy."

Bode nodded. He set the paperweight on the desk. His smile faded, and his look became considering once more. "If I hadn't come here this morning, when would you have told me about the engagement?"

The change of subject didn't throw her. She'd known he'd bring her around to it eventually. He was like a dog with a bone. "I don't know," she said. "I fully intended to do it right after I spoke to Bram. I didn't expect to spend so many days away from work—or anything else."

"So you weren't avoiding me."

"I might have been. You are not always a comfortable person to talk to."

"I'm not?"

"No, and don't say it as if you're unaware."

"All right. But doesn't it strike you the least bit odd that you find me comfortable enough to kiss?"

"Comfortable? That is ridiculously inaccurate."

"Convenient, then."

"Hardly."

"Well?"

She fell silent as she searched for the appropriate word. "Compelling," she said at last. "You're compelling."

"Then we're staying with words that begin with C. That's good. I appreciate consistency."

She rolled her eyes at his wordplay but couldn't quite smother her smile. "What do you think explains it?"

"You're curious."

"Really? About what?"

"Kissing, for one thing. Me, for another."

"I think I understand kissing."

"You do now."

She thought he sounded a tad full of himself, but she didn't take issue. Arguing would have had an effect opposite of what she wished, namely that the conversation be steered to a different course. In spite of that, she heard herself ask, "Why do you kiss me back?"

"For the pleasure of it."

"Oh." Comfort found that she was oddly disappointed by

his answer, but then she wondered what sort of response would have satisfied. There was no time to dwell on it. She was suddenly aware of Bode's shifting attention. He was looking beyond her, just above her head, and she realized he was alert to some movement in the corridor. She twisted in her chair to share his view and was in time to see her Uncle Newt step into the hallway from the stairwell. Tuck followed closely on his heels. Bode must have heard them, she decided. His searching look had been in anticipation of their arrival, not because he'd already seen them. Here was further proof that virtually nothing got past his notice.

Bode stood and made himself visible in the open doorway. Newton and Tucker saw him at once and passed their office in favor of greeting him in Comfort's domain. Tucker rounded her desk and put out his hand to Bode while Newton stood behind Comfort and lightly rested his hands on her shoulders.

"I came to ask for a moment of your time," Bode told them as they approached. "And Miss Kennedy was kind enough to allow me to disturb her while I waited."

"How did he get your chair, Comfort?" asked Newt.

"Trickery," she said.

"I prefer to call it misdirection." Bode smiled pleasantly. "I distracted her by rearranging items on her desk."

Tuck and Newt glanced simultaneously at Comfort's desk. It looked no different than it ever did.

"Apparently she's put it back the way she likes it," said Tuck. "Chaotic."

Newt squeezed Comfort's shoulders. "It was good of you not to slam his fingers under a paperweight." He saw Bode wince. "Yes, you were surprisingly fortunate, but then I wonder if she's fully recovered."

Tuck turned to Comfort. "Are you? Should you be home?"

"I'm fine. Really," she added when he continued to regard her doubtfully. She reached up to her shoulder and tapped Newt's hand. "Please take Mr. DeLong to your office and make it a point to discuss something other than me. In fact, ask him about the *Alexandra Queen*."

Comfort was gratified to see them accept her prompting so

readily. Only Bode's sidelong, faintly sardonic glance told her that he wasn't fooled by her misdirection.

Alexandra DeLong sipped her tea with delicate precision and nodded approvingly at her guest. Sunday afternoons were her favorite time for intimate chats, and she'd been looking forward to spending time with Comfort. There was a great deal to discuss, and she favored Comfort's candid recitation of her dilemma. "I know, dear. It's distressing the way men use women. They have every advantage and we have every consequence."

"Then you understand," Comfort said, relieved.

"Heavens, yes. I cannot name another person in San Francisco, perhaps in all of California, who is likely to be as sympathetic of your predicament as I am."

Comfort felt the hitch in her breathing ease. "I hope you will not think me too forward, but I thought that might be true."

"Oh, that's very forward, but I'll let it pass. The circumstances are trying. Bram knows I am unhappy with him."

Comfort felt a crease form between her eyebrows as she drew them together. She touched her fingertips lightly to the area and rubbed. "I'm afraid I don't understand. I made my entire explanation without you giving me any hint that you'd heard it all from Bram. I wasn't aware that he told you anything."

"He did. Of course he did. That's what you asked him to do, isn't it?"

"Yes, but . . ." She fell silent, unsure how to proceed.

"I can't read your mind, Comfort."

"I'm sorry, but I'd been given to understand that since I last spoke to Bram, a wedding date had been set."

"Now, I wonder who could have given you that understanding?"

Comfort said nothing. Alexandra's ironic tone left no doubt that she not only knew the culprit but also was seriously out of patience with him.

"Naturally, I planned to consult you before making the announcement public. I heard you had taken ill, so I thought it better to wait. Bode shouldn't have shared any part of my conversation when nothing was set."

Comfort didn't ask how Alexandra had learned that she was ill. It was inaccurate but the sort of assumption people were bound to make when she remained at home for so long. What she did know was that Alexandra DeLong had an extensive network of confidants and acquaintances that reported to her regularly, vying for favor by being the one to tell her something she didn't already know.

Comfort ventured tentatively, "Then Bode wasn't wrong."

"Wrong? Bode? Goodness, no. It's his most annoying trait. I'm sure he was reasonably accurate repeating what I said. I was thinking a year was sufficiently long for your engagement, given that you and Bram have been friends since your formal introduction to society. In truth, people have expected him to propose for quite some time. You can't imagine how often I've made excuses for him . . . and for you. Frankly, I'm glad the matter's finally been settled, even in this unorthodox fashion."

Comfort set her teacup in its saucer and returned both to the tray that separated her from Alexandra. "I don't think Bram's told you everything, Mrs. DeLong. Or perhaps he wasn't clear." She shied away from saying that Alexandra misunderstood, perhaps deliberately, what her son told her. "I am not marrying Bram."

Alexandra snorted. She managed to make the sound both derisive and dismissive. "He explained he never made a proper proposal, and I fully expect that he'll come around to it by and by, but surely it's a mere formality at this juncture."

It was considerably more than a formality to Comfort, but arguing that point would only put her on a sidetrack. "I don't require a proposal," she said instead. "I don't want to marry Bram."

"What nonsense. You're in love with him."

Someday, Comfort thought, when this was well behind her, she might be able to find the dark humor in her belief that she'd kept her feelings so well guarded. But just now, faced with more proof that she'd deceived no one as thoroughly as she'd deceived herself, amusement, even the self-deprecating kind, wasn't possible.

"I discussed this with Bram," she said. "He knows my true feelings."

"It's your uncles, isn't it? They have reservations. I thought I detected a certain reticence in their attitudes the night of the party. Do you want me to speak to them, Comfort? I'm sure I can persuade them to see that marriage is inevitable."

"It's not inevitable, Mrs. DeLong, and my uncles will support me no matter whom I choose to marry."

"Nonsense. They've objected to all your suitors."

"But they didn't say I couldn't accept a proposal. That was a decision I made on my own, just as I'm doing now."

"You sound unnaturally serious about this," Alexandra said, inclining her head as frown lines deepened around her mouth and eyes. "Very much like Bode."

Comfort could only stare at her hostess. Alexandra was dismissing her; insistent in not accepting that anything she had to say was significant. Comfort knew she was making her points clearly. They were simply having no impact. What she had always believed was Alexandra's iron will seemed to be nothing so much as an unfeeling disregard for the wishes and opinions of others.

"I'm truly sorry," Comfort said. "I appreciate that you're disappointed in my decision, but I have to ask you to accept it. I am willing to entertain whatever advice you can give me about how Bram and I should make the end of our engagement public. We don't have to reveal how it came about, but I believe we should be united on how to put it behind us."

Alexandra set her jaw so tightly a muscle twitched along its sharp line. Her fingertips whitened where they gripped the teacup and saucer. "I've already decided what must be done. You and Bram will go through with it. It's the only reasonable solution."

Comfort couldn't understand it. She had not expected her news to be welcomed, but neither had she expected it to be met with such resistance. "I can't do that."

"You can't abandon my son while he's bedridden."

"He *will* get up from it. It's not his deathbed."

"It may very well be."

Comfort did not have the sense that Alexandra was being

dramatic. She seemed to believe it. Still, Comfort would not give ground. "If that's a concern, then put the laudanum out of his reach."

Alexandra drew in a sharp, audible breath. "I have never thought you cold, Miss Kennedy. Until now." She put down her teacup and picked up a small silver-plated bell, which tinkled out of all proportion to its size when she shook it. "I think you should go. Hitchens will show you out." She stood. Without waiting for Comfort to do the same, she turned her back and left by way of the connecting dining room.

Over dinner, Comfort related her conversation with Alexandra to her uncles. There was no mistaking they were disturbed by it.

"Did you visit Bram? Speak to him?" asked Tucker.

"No. I didn't think I should, not after Mrs. DeLong insisted that I leave."

Newt nodded. "You did the right thing going when you did."

"It wasn't as if I had a choice. At least it seemed there was none. The one good thing to come from my visit was my new appreciation for why Bram acts first and begs forgiveness later. He can't say no to her. I don't think anyone can."

Tuck used his knife to mash a line of peas into his boiled red potatoes. "Bode does. He says no to her regularly."

"Does he?"

Tuck forked a large bite of potatoes and peas into his mouth. He nodded until he swallowed. "I always admired him for it."

"I didn't realize," said Comfort.

"That he stands up to Alexandra or that I admire him?"

"Both." Comfort cut a triangle from her rare beef filet. Blood pooled on her plate. "He's something of an enigma."

Newt and Tuck spoke as one. "Bode?"

Comfort looked up from her plate in surprise, and her glance darted between them. "Well, yes."

Newt just shook his head. "Beau DeLong is the most straightforward, no nonsense, has your back in a fight gentleman I know. I'd include Tuck here, but we all know he's not strictly a gentleman. Bode is."

"I've never heard you say this before."

"Because we don't talk about Bode at this table. It's always been Bram this or Bram that."

"Still is, if you ask me," Tucker said. "And I, for one, could stand to hear a bit more about Bode."

Comfort felt his expectant gaze rest on her and wondered what she could say. Before her face colored with the memory of Bode's mouth on hers, she said, "Did he tell you about the *Alexandra Queen*?"

"Nothing except that it's the name you chose for a future ship in the Black Crowne fleet."

She was disappointed that Bode hadn't told them more. She tried not to imagine what they had talked about in Newt and Tuck's office. Bode had occupied slightly more than a half hour of their time, a lengthy conversation by their standards.

"It's an iron paddle steamer," she said, and she went on to tell them everything she remembered about the design, right down to the location of the donkey boilers fore and aft of the combustion chambers.

"Impressive," Newt said.

Comfort knew better than to suppose he was referring to her memory. Except as it concerned her past, he was used to her uncanny recall. He was talking about Bode's design.

Tuck regarded Comfort with heightened interest. "How big would you say the paddle wheels are?"

She told him the dimensions she'd seen scribbled around Bode's more detailed cross-section drawing.

"That'd be something, wouldn't you say, Newt?"

"It would be," he agreed. "There'd be no lingering in the Doldrums on a ship like that." He asked Comfort, "And you think it would be fit for cargo *and* passengers?"

"I counted thirty-two cabins and a lounge in the fore and aft."

"Berths for the crew? Staterooms?"

"All of that."

Newt removed the napkin from his lap and wiped his mouth. "He's not designing her strictly for the China run. He's thinking New York to London or Paris, and New York to San Francisco." He crumpled the napkin and tossed it on his empty plate. "He's going to compete with the railroads for the cross-country traffic and offer luxury that isn't available on the trains. As for the Atlantic and Pacific crossings, a ship like that will own the sea. He'll be able to move cargo at speeds no one else is reaching right now."

"Like I was saying," said Tuck. "There's nothing not to admire about Beau DeLong."

That wasn't quite what he had said, Comfort recalled, but his sentiment certainly hadn't changed.

"You want to call on him?" Newt asked his partner.

"I think that'd be the prudent thing to do. Of course, if people get wind of a visit, there's liable to be speculation."

"Invite him to the bank," said Comfort.

"He won't bring his drawings. It doesn't sound like he's ready to show them. There's a better chance to see them if we go to him."

Newt rubbed his chin. "Comfort could accompany us. I don't know why, but folks still don't think we discuss business around her. They'll think it has something to do with her engagement."

Comfort still felt compelled to say, "There is *no* engagement."

"Oh, yes. *We* understand that, but until all the other parties are on board, we may as well use it to our advantage."

She sighed, thinking that Alexandra was right about one thing: men had every advantage and women had every consequence.

"You don't want to join us?" asked Tuck.

"No, I do," she said. "I appreciate the opportunity to watch you and Uncle Newt negotiate. I just wish it were not connected in any way to the DeLongs."

"I understand, but I don't know that there's another owner or manager in any industry that would discuss business with you in the room, let alone at the table. Newt's sisters don't think we did right by letting you join the bank, but I don't know what else we could have done, since you're about as necessary as gravy is to biscuits."

"As gravy is to biscuits?" Newt said before Comfort could comment. "That's the best you can do?"

Tuck shrugged. "You try to say something pretty."

"You're as necessary as sunshine is to flowers."

Tuck snorted. "Now you're sayin' we're flowers. If I had my druthers, I druther be a biscuit."

"And I druther be a tea cart, but that's not going to happen."

"A tea cart? Now what kind of fool thing is that to say?"

Realizing this exchange could go on for some time, Comfort quietly excused herself from the table and retired to her room. Newt and Tuck wouldn't miss her until they needed her to settle their argument. She was as necessary as a judge was to lawyers.

Bode saw Bram eyeing the laudanum. He leaned forward and pushed it to the far edge of the nightstand, well outside of his brother's reach.

"That was cruel," Bram said. "Give it to me."

Ignoring him, Bode sat back in his chair, stretched his legs, and hooked his heels on the bed frame. "I am painfully short of patience myself," he said. "It will go better for you if you answer my questions instead of exhausting yourself trying to get around them. Suppose we begin again, and you tell me what's so damn important that you need the pretense of an engagement to make it happen."

Frustrated, Bram's head thudded softly against the smooth walnut headboard. Not once, or twice, but three times he banged it against the wood. "You have it all wrong, Bode, not that I anticipate you'll accept that. You can't be wrong. Not the omniscient Beauregard DeLong. You put things right. You don't make mistakes. You don't stumble or hesitate. You actually expect the seas to part for you, and damned if they don't."

"Careful, Bram, you'll make my head swell to a size that won't easily fit through your door. Then you'll be stuck with me."

Closing his eyes, Bram groaned. "Leave me be. I don't think there's anything I can say that will satisfy you."

"The truth will satisfy."

"I told you the truth. I love Comfort. I want to marry her.

She's turned down five proposals, Bode. Five. I know she's in love with me, but she doesn't trust that it's a feeling I return." He held up his hands in a gesture of helplessness. "So I resorted to manipulating her into accepting an engagement of eight weeks. Until I broke my leg and ended up confined to this room, I was reasonably confident that I'd negotiated enough time to turn her thinking in favor of ending the farce and making it fact."

"You really believe her acceptance was inevitable."

"Yes."

"And your broken leg accounts for your failure."

"A setback," Bram said. "Not a failure. I still have a few weeks left to change her mind."

Bode eyed the weights that kept Bram's leg in traction. "How will you accomplish that from your bed?"

"I can't. Not properly. That's why I need you."

Bode was sure he didn't want to hear this, but walking away now was out of the question. "All right," he said, his gaze sharp on Bram's. "Why do you think you need me?"

"I need someone to be my eyes and ears . . . and speak on my behalf."

"You want me to court her."

"After a fashion, I suppose. You'll tread carefully, of course, because you have to sway her thinking in my favor."

Bode said nothing as he turned this conversation over in his mind. It was as incredible upon review as it had been hearing it the first time. "Do you know her at all, Bram?"

"We've been friends since her come-out."

"I understand that, but I'm asking if you know her?" He watched Bram's fine looks cloud with confusion, and he had his answer. "That's what I thought."

"But I didn't say anything."

"I know that, too." Aware that he was almost as fascinated by Bram's suggestion as he was dismayed by it, Bode could only shake his head.

"So you won't help me?"

"Help you? I'm not sure I even believe you." Blowing out a deep breath, he plowed his fingers through his hair. "I know. That's been your argument all along. I don't know how to get around it."

"Speak to Mother. She knows how I feel about Comfort."

"She knows what you tell her, and maybe she believes half of it. That's always been a question in my mind. In fact, I just left her. She was adamant about wanting to see you and Miss Kennedy married. She told me Miss Kennedy is having doubts. Doubts. That's the word she used."

"What would you have her say?"

"That Miss Kennedy wants nothing at all to do with an engagement, with a marriage, and if you don't tread carefully, Bram, with a friendship."

"Why would you think that?"

Frustrated, his voice approximated a growl. "Because that's what Comfort told her. For God's sake, Bram, it's what she told me, and I believe it's what she told you as well. What I can't account for is why neither you nor Alexandra listen to her."

Bram's mouth twisted in a smirk. When Bode referred to their mother by her Christian name, he was preparing to stand toe to toe with her, and family was no longer a consideration. "I can't speak for Mother," he said, with a slight but detectable emphasis on the relationship, "but I listened to what Comfort had to say. I just didn't believe her. You should be familiar with how that turns out. It's exactly the same for us."

To keep from wiping the smirk from Bram's face, Bode made a steeple of his fingers and rested his chin on the tips. "You're not in trouble, then."

"In trouble? Oh, you've come round to that again. I don't know what sort of trouble I could be in that an engagement would get me out of, so I can't explain how you conceived that idea, but it's just not true. There's nothing occupying my mind except getting Comfort to change hers."

"I hope you're not lying to me, Bram."

"I'm lying right here, Bode. In bed."

There it was, Bode thought, the grin that he kept in reserve and Bram used to punctuate a sentence. It might have been his grin first, but Bram had perfected it. "Newton Prescott and Tucker Jones made an appointment last week to see me at Black Crowne on Wednesday afternoon. Miss Kennedy will accompany them."

"That's good. You can talk to her."

"I'm certain I will talk to her, but not about you. I'm going to throw my hat in the ring, Bram. I thought it was fair to let you know."

"Throw your hat in the ring? Fight me for her, you mean?" He looked down at himself and then at Bode. "How is that fair?"

"I hope it won't come to a fight. I recognize you're at a disadvantage, but I know you're not helpless. You never are."

Bram pushed himself as upright as he was able. "She won't have you, Bode. You scare her. You always have. It can't have escaped your notice that when you walk into a room, she walks out."

"Oh, I've noticed." Bode dropped his feet to the floor and rose from his chair. Favoring his brother with a faint but consciously shrewd smile, he buttoned his jacket. "You're so used to women showing interest in a particular and obvious way that you don't know that some of them reveal it in another."

"Wait!" Bram called after Bode as he started to leave. "What are you saying?"

Bode merely smiled to himself and kept on walking.

It was Tuck who insisted at the last minute that they take the carriage to Black Crowne. His decision had nothing to do with Black Crowne's proximity to the Barbary Coast—after all, it was daylight—or even Comfort's welfare. No, he explained, it was his lumbago that required a little nursing. As a result, all of them climbed into the open carriage in spite of the relatively short distance they had to cover.

Comfort opened her parasol and rested the stem on her shoulder while Newt and Tuck adjusted their hats to shade their eyes from the bright afternoon sunshine. The cloudless sky was azure silk without imperfection. She settled back just as her uncles did, in anticipation of an uneventful journey.

Which was why they were caught unaware and unprepared when the Rangers swarmed.

Chapter Nine

Tuck and Newt put up their fists and fought back as best they could. Instinct sometimes took over when common sense should have made them throw up their hands and immediately surrender. They were woefully outnumbered. The thieves swarmed them like flies on carrion. The Rangers all wore roughly made black woolen jackets with only the uppermost button fastened, short black vests that rode up above their trousers, and black derbies jammed on their heads. Their clothing made them virtually indistinguishable. Newt and Tuck were left to know them by their blows.

One of them favored throwing all his weight into a punch. Another jabbed and feinted. Still another used his head as a battering ram. Newt threw up his forearms, blocking the blows he could and accepting the ones he couldn't. Tucker jammed his shoulder into the chin of one of the assailants and extended the reach of his long arms and lanky frame every chance he had.

Their driver used his whip to good effect until it was torn from his hand and wound around his throat like a garrote. He was thrown to the street still clutching his neck and wasn't steady enough to avoid the carriage wheel when the horse bolted. His scream was louder than the mare's frightened snort, louder even than the cries from people huddled on the sidewalk.

A man stepped away from the curb to drag the injured driver

to safety and was hauled back by his frightened wife. Someone else ventured out but was driven back by the sight of brass knuckles glinting in the sunlight. People shouted for the police. They shouted for help. They raised the alarm but never their fists.

As soon as the first Ranger hauled himself up on the carriage step, Comfort closed her parasol. She used the blunt wooden tip to jab at his chest and belly. It was a moderately successful attack, although it lacked the elegance of a foil thrust and only worked when there was one opponent. When the first attacker was joined by a second, Comfort swung the parasol at their heads. If they ducked, she clobbered them.

Above the shouts from the onlookers, she heard Tuck and Newt yelling at her to jump. To run. To hide.

They never spoke all at once. They were an undisciplined chorus, and what they said came at her in rapid succession, the words separated by half measures, each one an echo of another. All of it indistinguishable.

All of it frantic.

Comfort froze. Her attackers took immediate advantage and snatched the parasol from her nerveless fingers. She stared at them but didn't see. She had an urge to make herself small, and then smaller yet.

She had no weapons when they came for her. Someone was calling after her, calling her name. *What they wanted from her was a mystery. Was there something she was supposed to do? She always wondered if there was something she was supposed to do.*

John Farwell hurled himself through the hatch into Bode's apartment and stumbled forward until he caught himself on the edge of a table. He had a more difficult time catching his breath. "You have to come with me. Now. There's been . . ." He shook his head. "I don't know what there's been."

Bode didn't leap from the stool, but he did set down his pencil. "Calm yourself, John. I only understood every third word."

"The Rangers. I'm hearing they assaulted passengers in a carriage just thirty minutes ago. It happened *outside* the Coast, Mr. DeLong. Two gentlemen and a young woman were in the—" He stopped because Bode was on his feet and heading toward the hatch. "I don't know if it's the bankers and Miss Kennedy. I couldn't learn their names."

Bode threw back the door. "Where did it happen?"

The clerk told him the location. "But I doubt that they're still there. Miss Kennedy—if it *was* Miss Kennedy—she was . . ." He swallowed hard as Bode dropped below the hatch and then resurfaced suddenly.

"She was what? Injured?"

"Taken," he said. "Mr. DeLong, I sincerely hope it wasn't Miss Kennedy, because the Rangers have her now."

Bode didn't ask John Farwell to follow him, but the clerk dogged his footsteps all the way to the police station and was left to pace the floor in front of the sergeant's desk while Bode was shown to the room where Tucker and Newton were being looked after by Dr. Winter.

Tuck pushed the doctor away as soon as Bode entered. "They took her. The Rangers took her. Damn it. I *knew* something was coming. I thought taking the carriage . . ." He put a hand to his head. "I should have made her stay back."

"All right," Bode said, looking them over. Dr. Winter was trying to stitch a cut above Tuck's right eye. Newt had a damp and bloodstained cloth pressed to one corner of his mouth. A button on Tuck's jacket dangled by a thread. Newt had a torn sleeve and his collar was askew. They both sported scraped and swollen knuckles, although in Newt's case it looked as if he might also have broken his right hand. There was no question that they'd put up a fight, but they were ten years past their prime, and the Rangers attacked with the ferocity of hounds from Hell. "Tell me where and when and how the attack happened."

In their anxiety to have it all said at once, Tuck and Newt spoke over each other, sometimes completing the other's thought, sometimes running all their sentences together. Bode had to sift through their explanations for the facts he needed to know.

"What are the police doing?"

"Organizing men to go into the Coast to find her."

Bode didn't comment. The area had alleys too numerous to count. No one except the denizens knew them all. Some streets had innocuous-sounding names like Hinckley, Bartlett, and

Dupont. Others confused their name with their reputation and were called Murder Point and Dead Man's Alley. Below ground in the dank, dark cellars there existed a whole community of felons, wastrels, petty thieves, and prostitutes. They entered and exited their subterranean homes by means of ladders and poles. The odors were vile, the diseases were loathsome, and the chances that any woman could escape unscathed were almost nil. For a young woman of means and more than modest beauty, the chances were . . .

Well, there was no chance. Bode pushed away from the doorframe, where he was resting his shoulder. It was not in his nature to accept what others believed was inevitable. The first thing he did was ask Dr. Winter to leave.

"There might be something we can do," he said, closing the door behind him. "But you have to allow me to act on my own, and you have to trust that I know what I'm doing. When I find her and bring her out, I won't be placing her in your hands. That's what will be different. I can't promise when you'll see her again, but she'll be safe. You need to believe that."

Newt focused on the single word that gave him hope. "You said 'when.' *When* you find her, not if. You can do that?"

Bode had plenty of doubts. He didn't reveal a single one. "Yes."

"You also said 'we,'" Tuck reminded him. "Something *we* can do. If you're acting on your own, what are *we* doing?"

"You're going to have to decide what you're willing to pay for Comfort's return. They'd probably like gold, but they might be willing to accept paper. You'll have to decide what she's worth."

Comfort paced off the space of her dark, nearly airless prison. It was generous enough in length, measuring slightly more than seven feet, for her to lie down if she wished. She did not wish. The floor was packed dirt, relatively smooth, but cool and damp, and nothing had been given to her to make a pallet. The width of the room was considerably less than ideal. The first time she stepped it off, she jammed her wrist against the dirt wall because she came upon it so abruptly. It hardly measured four feet. The height of the room disturbed her most of all.

When she raised her hand above her head and stood on tiptoe, she could press the flat of her palm against the ceiling, a distance she judged to be something less than seven feet. Seven feet, by four feet, by six feet and inches.

Allowing for error in the length of her paces, Comfort thought she might be standing in her grave.

She leaned back against one of the long walls and forced herself to remember how she came to be here. She wasn't a child any longer. She hadn't run to this place to hide, and she hadn't fainted. There'd been a dirty rag thrust in her face and kept there, but for as long as she held her breath, she was fine. She recalled the coarse black hairs on the back of the man's hand as he pressed the rag against her mouth. There'd been the rank smell of unwashed bodies, the odor of a rotten tooth in the breath against her ear. She caught the scent of lye soap in their clothes and the cloying fragrance of pomade. There was a tattoo on someone's forearm, a bird perhaps, a phoenix or a griffin. She saw it when she clawed at his sleeve.

What else? she wondered. What else had she seen before her lungs demanded that she breathe?

Someone's hat had fallen off. She'd glimpsed smooth, shiny hair, more red than blond, but with shades of both. There were beards. Dark. Light. Trimmed. Unkempt. One hairless chin had a dimple squarely in the center.

She thought she'd drawn blood. Scratched a face or a neck. No matter how closely she tried to examine her fingernails, the darkness was absolute. She couldn't be sure that she'd fought hard enough.

Comfort drew a ragged breath, identical to the one she'd drawn with the oily rag over her face. She had no experience with the sweet, heavy fragrance, but she suspected she was inhaling chloroform. Identifying it was her last accomplishment. There was nothing to recall after that.

That was past. Now Comfort concentrated on the present. She extended her arm over her head again and studied the rough edges of the ceiling with her fingertips. There were narrow spaces at regular intervals. By walking slowly and with great care around the room, she was able to identify the cutout in the wooden slats that was the entrance. There were no hinges on her side.

Not so much as a scintilla of light filtered through the slats or around the hatch. She supposed that was because someone had taken the precaution of covering the floor with a carpet. That meant the hatch was hidden from view.

There was a crowd of people overhead that might have seen it otherwise. Their footsteps crisscrossed her ceiling without pause. When she'd had her palm flat to the boards, she could sometimes feel the sag in the slats as someone of more substantial weight pounded across the floor.

There was too much noise above her for Comfort to believe that she had any hope of being heard, but that didn't keep her from trying. She called out for several minutes, trying to time her cries so they came during the brief pauses between bawdy songs and raucous laughter. If anyone heard her, no one came to help. The crowd overhead included women as well as men and numbered too many to have been involved directly in her abduction, but Comfort couldn't imagine there was anyone in that room who didn't know what had happened that afternoon or who would stand against the Rangers to come to her aid.

It was easy to guess that she was being held in a concert saloon somewhere in the Barbary Coast, but whether it was Happy Tim's, Bull Run, the Tulip, or any of a hundred others, she had no idea. Many of the worst dens were in cellars; so the fact that she was being held underground made her think that the establishment above her was at street level. That was only important to know if the opportunity to escape presented itself. Comfort wasn't hopeful that it would.

It made no difference to her situation if she closed her eyes or opened them. Feeling inordinately tired and weak-kneed, she closed them and sagged against the wall. The tune being pounded out on the piano was "Camptown Races." She heard "doo-dah, doo-dah" in her head long after someone began playing another piece. The scuffle that broke out helped remove it from her mind. For the length of the pushing and shoving match, she thought of nothing except that someone might be killed. There was the slender possibility that the police would be summoned, and an even more fragile possibility that they would respond, but what she thought was a likely consequence to the fighting was that she'd end up sharing her confined space with a dead man.

Comfort felt her throat begin to close. She rested one hand against it and forced herself to breathe slowly and deeply. The air didn't stir. It was just damp enough to make her skin clammy, and every time she drew a breath, she tasted it. While no light made its way down to her, the same wasn't true of the smells.

It was a blessing that bad cigars created the heaviest of the odors that assaulted her. Tobacco masked some of the more pungent aromas, chief among them sour beer and urine. The hint of opium smoke took her right back to the tent where she'd lived with Tuck and Newt and whores who answered to any name but their own. Butterfly. Li'l Darling. Mokey. Sweetings. No one was ever an Annie or Emma or Susannah. Whoever they'd been before taking up the life, or being forced into it, they were no longer that person.

Comfort wondered if that was her destiny. She'd been kept alive for a reason. Was that it? There were hundreds of young Chinese girls brought into the city every year to replace the ones who had come before. Suey Tsin had been one of them, held as a sex slave in a crib where she could neither stand nor stretch. Relief from those confines came only when someone spent fifty cents to lie between her legs, or a dollar, and engaged her in some far worse depravity.

Comfort remembered the auctions where girls were paraded across the bar as though it were a stage lined with limelight. Some of them seemed to enjoy the attention and notoriety that making the walk gave them. Most were unsteady on their feet, plied with drink or drugs, so their steps were slow and halting and gave the customers, who were often equally as drunk, more time to appreciate the offerings.

Were there still auctions? She hadn't heard about them for years, but then she was considerably more distant from that hard life than she'd been as a child. Her uncles would be horrified to learn what entertainments she had glimpsed while they were living in the dance hall. The memory of it all made her stomach churn uncomfortably, and the thought that something like it could be her fate brought acid to the back of her throat.

What she did know was that there was traffic in women that

went opposite of the tide. There were stories in the papers, mostly dismissed as rumor and sensational reporting, that women on this side of the Pacific were prized for what they could bring on the Far East shores. Suey Tsin told her it was true, that she'd seen it for herself. Young women, mostly fair-skinned blondes and redheads, were lifted off the streets when certain ships discharged their crews into the Barbary Coast.

Comfort touched her nape and uneasily fingered the short strands of hair that had fallen free of her combs. Perhaps her dark hair wouldn't be prized at all. It was nearly as black as Suey Tsin's. She laid the back of her hand against her cheek. She'd always disliked how fair her skin was, how easily it showed angry or embarrassed color. Now she might have another reason to regret her pale features.

She shook off the thought. It wasn't worth her time lamenting what couldn't be changed when every consideration needed to be given to what could.

Bode heard the first inklings of Comfort's fate from one of the crew from the steamer *Demeter Queen*. Tapper Stewart reported back to him within an hour of being loosed on Pacific Street at nightfall. All of the men from the ship were prowling the alleys and streets that defined the Barbary Coast. With the assistance of the shipmaster, Bode sketched the Coast in detail and then divided the area into sections. Nathan Douglas made the assignments, giving each group of men a list of establishments they should most particularly enter.

No man who sailed for Black Crowne was unfamiliar with the deadfalls, melodeons, gambling palaces, and brothels that made up the Barbary Coast, but there wasn't one among them who'd seen them all. Bode directed them to correct that oversight. He gave them money to purchase drinks but warned them they shouldn't take more than a swallow, and even then they should keep their wits about them because in some of the deadfalls, the drink would blind them.

He asked to see their weapons and was shown a wide assortment of serrated blades, daggers, filleting knives, brass and iron knuckles, garrotes, and in one case, a small and supple leather bag of buckshot that, when held in a capable fist, worked every bit as well as the knuckles. This armament was what passed for calling cards in the Barbary Coast. Bode didn't need to remind them to keep their weapons hidden but also to keep them close.

It was the rhythm of the Barbary Coast's activity that forced Bode to hold back the men until dusk. A widespread foray into the saloons and cheap groggeries during the daylight hours would have attracted suspicion, especially since the *Demeter Queen* was known to be leaving the harbor in the morning. As difficult as it was to wait once their plans were in place, there also existed the hope that Newton and Tucker would be contacted for the payment of ransom. It was what the police wanted them to believe. It made their slow advance on the Coast seem more prudent than cowardly. By nightfall, there was no police presence left. Bode understood their reluctance to remain anywhere on Pacific Street between Montgomery and Stockton. Even traveling in pairs, the police were targets. His men were not; they were marks.

Bode encouraged the crew to make a thorough sweep of each establishment they entered, but at the same time, not appear to linger. He instructed them on what to look for and how they might be able to identify the Rangers from the rest of the riffraff. He described what the Rangers had been wearing at the time of the attack, and because they feared no one in the Coast, the probability was high that they were still wearing the same black hats and jackets. Bode explained that the Rangers would organize themselves into some kind of hierarchy wherever they were gathered. A leader would always emerge in any group, and if Bode's men were fortunate, they'd see this shift of power happen in front of them.

Bode made it clear he wasn't sending them out to find Comfort. She was the proverbial needle in the haystack. What he wanted from them was information, and to get that, they had to listen . . . *everywhere.*

Not long after Tapper Stewart came back to the *Demeter Queen* with what he'd heard, Jimmy Jackson and Dennis Plant arrived slightly breathless with a similar story to report. Another hour passed with no one returning to the ship, but shortly after midnight, two teams of men arrived within minutes of each other. What they'd learned was from different sources and filled in the gaps of the earliest reports. If the information they'd received could be trusted, then it was both better and worse than Bode expected.

Comfort Kennedy was alive, but if her captors had their way, she wouldn't survive until morning.

Exhausted from the lingering effects of the chloroform, her efforts to keep warm, and the futility of continuing to plot her escape, Comfort slipped into sleep. She had no sense of how long she slept, but it was no surprise to her that she woke ravaged by thirst.

She sat up and used what she hoped was a clean part of her dress to swipe at her eyes. Her eyelids felt thick and puffy, and her lashes were matted as if she'd been crying in her sleep. Lifting her head, she pretended she could see the ceiling of her prison and beyond it. Something was different than it had been before she slept, and she was so fuzzy-headed that it required several minutes for her to realize what it was.

Quieter. That's what she finally decided had changed. Not quiet, not by any means, but the ribald cries were less wildly boisterous, the laughter less raucous, and most notably, there was an absence of feminine voices.

No women? That not only struck her as odd; it tripped a shiver that began at the base of her neck and traveled all the way to her toes.

She set her palms hard against the wall behind her as something scraped the floor above. It was the carpet that was being moved, she thought. It thumped and rolled, thumped and rolled. Her heart hammered. It roared so loudly in her ears that she almost didn't realize that the room above her was falling silent. The last piano chords were dying. Fiddle strings twanged hard and then ceased to vibrate. If there was laughter, it was a low rumble. There was shuffling, some footsteps, but the customers were no longer crossing the room from the door to the bar.

Were they gone? Or were they waiting?

She scrambled to her feet as the overhead door was thrown back. She shielded her eyes from the lantern light, though it wasn't particularly bright. After so many hours in darkness, a single candle flame would have been as blinding as the noonday sun.

Stepping as far away from the opening as she could, she was already cornered when a ladder was thrust through the hatch. No one came down. Instead, she was invited to come up. The first invitation was rough, but relatively polite. The second time there was profanity. It was the third summons, which included a threat to throw a fookin' net over her and haul her up like the fookin' baggage she was, that made her leave her corner and take hold of the ladder.

When she looked up, she made out two men standing above her. One of them held the lantern. The other, indeed, held the fookin' net. They both wore black derbies. Twisting her skirts in one hand to lift them, Comfort gripped a rung and began to climb.

Before her head cleared the opening and she could look around, two pairs of hands, neither of them belonging to Lantern or Net, grabbed her under the shoulders from either side and lifted her out with enough momentum that she expected to be tossed to the floor like the day's catch. They didn't do that, preferring to dangle her several feet above the hatch until one of them kicked it closed and they could set her firmly on top of it. Her knees would have buckled if they hadn't maintained their bruising grip on her arms.

The concert saloon had exploded into a cacophony of shouts, cries, fist thumping, and stomping the moment she cleared the hatch. The piano player pounded out dramatic chords, and the fiddler plucked his instrument in earnest. The tables she could see were crowded with men. Since she was in the middle of the saloon, she supposed the ones behind her were crowded as well. Men stood two and three deep along the perimeter. If there was a door, it was either at her back or being blocked. It was the same for the windows.

Someone thrust a glass of stale beer at her mouth. She set her lips mutinously even though she was so parched she wanted to down all of it. She was given no quarter, and the hold on her arms didn't ease. While she tried to twist and avoid the crush of the glass against her lips, fear that she'd be forced to swallow her own teeth made her open her mouth. Someone's fingers yanked on her hair. A comb fell out, but she never heard it hit the floor. The crowd was so loud now that she couldn't distinguish her thoughts from their voices.

The moment her head was pulled back, the glass was tipped and beer poured into her mouth. She gargled and spat and felt some of it slide over her chin, run down her neck, and soak through the ruching of her shell pink bodice. Most of it, though, went down her throat. There was a brief moment of respite before a second tall glass was put to her. She thought of a fledgling eager to take food from its mother. Except for her open mouth, she was not at all like that. She stamped hard on the toes of her captors, kicked sideways at their knees, and more by accident than design, literally bit the hand that fed her when fingers strayed too close to her teeth.

Her efforts were encouraged and applauded by the men who'd come specifically to see this entertainment, but the ones holding her were not so appreciative. After the third glass of beer was emptied, she took an open palm slap to her left cheek and then a backhanded one to her right. She tasted blood and saw stars.

"The bar! The bar! The bar!"

The cry started with a few men at the back of the room who wanted a better view of the proceedings and was eventually taken up by nearly everyone else. Their coarse, drumming chant shook the building. Comfort dug in her heels, but the floor was slippery with spilled liquor and damp sawdust, and there was no purchase to be had. Her show of resistance incited the crowd and angered her captors. She was lifted again, this time only the few inches necessary to make it appear that she was floating. The alcohol was already clouding her senses, making her think she might be floating in fact. Chairs and tables scraped the floor as men scrambled to make way for her.

Her captors also served as her protectors, at least for as long as they had to carry her, and they roughly pushed aside the hands that tried to paw her breasts or finger her gown.

Someone was already standing on the bar when she got there. The man was dressed exactly like the men who held her, but he was clearly the one they were answering to. He carried a silver-knobbed cane that he tapped lightly against the top of the bar, indicating precisely where he meant them to place her. Partly because she was feeling the effects of the alcohol, and partly because she refused to assist their lift, they had some difficulty hoisting her as high as the bar. The man standing on top of it didn't lift a finger to help them.

The chanting was so loud now that Comfort's heart had taken up the rhythm and her head had begun to swim. She faltered a little as she was set in place and found her footing only after the man with the cane casually gave her his elbow. He made the offer with such mannered ease that he might have been escorting her to dinner.

He raised the cane above his head. The silence was immediate and profound.

"You all know me," he said in a voice thick with an Irish brogue. "And if it's not me you're knowin', then it's me reputation. I deal fair, but I deal hard, and I give no man a thing he hasn't earned . . . or stolen."

There was some laughter; a few glasses pounded the tables.

"So what I have for you tonight is a lottery. You buy a ticket, you buy a chance. More tickets, more chances. That's the way it works. Everyt'ing on the up-and-up. There'll be no high bidders takin' it away from you that can't spare a few dollars. If you have a ticket, you have reason to hope."

There were murmurs of approval and a few whistles. Someone shouted, "Hear, hear!" Comfort closed her eyes. She swayed.

The man gave his cane a little wag, and the room quieted again. If he felt Comfort still swaying, he let it pass. "There's more," he told them. "While our lovely bird is entertaining the first lucky winner, we'll be selling tickets for the second go round. Fresh start. Fresh chance. Alas, our lovely bird will not be as fresh as she once was."

"Soiled dove," someone called out.

Comfort repeated the words in a vaguely singsong fashion under her breath. "Soiled dove. Soiled dove." Perhaps it was the name she would take for herself, the one she would answer to when men put down their money and asked for her. How long would it be before she no longer recognized herself?

The man set the cane down firmly, stopping the low tide of laughter before it reached the bar. At his side, Comfort also fell silent. "There'll be a third lottery. A fourth. I'll wager now that her well will go dry before the money does."

"I've got just what it takes to pump a dry well."

This time the man inclined his head, appreciative of the ribald humor. "T'en I hope it doesn't go to waste. My boys will be comin' around to collect your money. Yours and everyone else who wants a chance. We've got tickets stamped blood red for the first drawing, blood red being appropriate to the occasion, to my way of t'inking. Twenty dollars each, my good and not-so-good friends. Twenty dollars could get you the best ride of your life."

Bram woke to the sound of someone scratching at his door. "For God's sake, come in," he called. "Christ, what time is it, Travers?"

"It's not Travers, sir. It is I. Hitchens." The butler held up the lamp so his face was illuminated when he poked his head in the room.

"Well, I see that now. It doesn't change the basic question."

"It's midnight and a bit."

Bram nearly knocked the laudanum off his nightstand as he waved Hitchens in. "Bring the lamp closer. You look like a specter holding it out that way."

Hitchens approached the bed. Without being told, he lighted the lamp at Bram's bedside. A moment later, he reached in the pocket of the jacket he was wearing over his nightshirt and robe and held it up for Bram to see.

"What have you got there?" asked Bram.

"You had a visitor at the door just minutes ago. He asked to see you."

"What? At this hour?" Bram put a hand to his forehead. "You sent him away, didn't you? Tail between his legs?"

"Not quite, sir. He left, I made certain of that, but it seemed telling him to go was not unexpected. He insisted I deliver this."

"You didn't have to keep your promise," Bram said dryly. "It could have waited until morning."

"I thought that myself, but he must have guessed, because the very next thing he said was his intention to wait across the street, and if he didn't see my lamp lighting this room he'd know I lied, and then he'd come back. I think he meant he would wake the household if I didn't come up here."

"I see." He held out his hand. "Then you better let me have it. Take your lamp over to the window while I read. Just so there's no mistake."

"Very good." Hitchens moved to stand at the window, his back to Bram. He could make out very little except his own reflection in the glass. If the visitor was standing across the street where the Chinese girl sometimes did, he couldn't see him. He estimated the passing of several minutes and thought that Bram must be rereading the note. It wasn't more than a single sheet of paper folded into quarters. There could only have been a few paragraphs.

He turned when Bram called to him, instantly alert to the fact that something was deeply wrong. "Yes, sir. What can I do?" Bram was pulling at his leg, trying to free it from traction. Hitchens hurried over, set the lamp down, and yanked Bram's hands away from the splints. "No! Stop. You can't do that. You'll hurt yourself."

"Damn it. Let go." Hitchens's grip was surprisingly strong. "Let. Go."

Hitchens hung on. "I'll fetch your mother."

Bram sagged against the bed. He eyed Hitchens with deep hostility. "I just bet you would, too."

"Certainly. I don't threaten."

"I need Travers. Bring him here. Don't wake anyone else, and don't tell Travers anything except that I want him. You can go then, and I expect that you won't be speaking to *anyone* about this. I need to know you're clear on that."

"I understand," he said gravely.

Bram waved him off, gritting his teeth when the butler took his leave in precise, even steps, demonstrating that while Bram could order him about, there were limits to the speed at which things would happen.

A quarter of an hour passed before Samuel Travers limped into the room. Bram didn't waste any time with explaining the situation to his valet. He said, "Get my brother."

Sam's cheeks puffed as he blew out a lungful of air. "And tell him what? That you can't sleep?"

Bram kept the note fisted. Sharp edges of the crumpled paper dug into his palm while he considered the words that would get Bode's attention. "Tell him that I'm not only lying in bed. Tell him I need him. Do you have that?"

"You're not in bed and you need him. I've got—"

"No. That's not it. I'm not only lying in bed. You must say that. Exactly."

"You're not only lying in bed."

"And I need him."

"And you need him. Is that all?"

"You know where he lives?"

"Certainly."

"At this time of night, you'll need my key to get into the office. It's in the top drawer of my bureau."

"I know where it is," Travers said. "I didn't know that you did."

Bram ignored the barb. "Just hurry, old man. Don't bother coming back if he's not with you."

After Comfort was escorted down the length of the bar and back again, she was whisked away by the pair of strongmen and half led, half carried to the concert saloon's second story. A door in the middle of the hallway opened, and she was shown through it. The men backed away and closed it, but she didn't hear them leave. The only woman she'd seen all evening was waiting for her by the room's sole window. As soon as the door shut, the woman dropped the shabby curtains in place and turned to her.

"Suey Tsin," Comfort said, as if there was nothing at all odd about seeing her maid in this place. Her stomach lurched suddenly. She was dizzy and the room was tilting. She closed her eyes and pressed her thumb and forefinger against them until she saw small points of light. It was a long moment before she dared look again, and this time she saw the truth. "Not Suey Tsin."

The Chinese woman didn't speak. She pointed to the bed, where a gauzy batiste gown lay draped over the foot. Through a series of gestures, she indicated what Comfort was meant to do with it.

Comfort understood the gestures well enough, but she wasn't so drunk that she was going to comply. She gave the woman a start when she pushed past her and headed for the window, but she wasn't strong or steady enough to keep the woman from yanking her back. Comfort stumbled over her own feet and sprawled backward on the bed. She thought she would be sick. Apparently the woman thought so, too, because she produced a chamber pot from under the bed and held it out for Comfort to use.

Comfort recoiled and turned her head away. The odors emanating from the pot were so noxious that she buried her face into a pillow and swallowed the bile that rose in her throat. She waved the woman away and didn't sit up until she heard the pot being pushed under the bed again.

She didn't know how she'd mistaken the woman for Suey Tsin. The similarities started and ended with the fact that they were Chinese. The woman was half again as wide as her maid, and her shoulders sloped forward as though her back was fixed in a position of obeisance. There was no compassion in her sloe-eyed watchfulness. The expression there wasn't inscrutable, merely implacable.

The woman picked up the gown from the foot of the bed and pushed it at Comfort. She communicated her expectations through the same series of gestures, but this time she pointed to the door and imitated the strongmen on the other side. Comfort understood that she was being threatened. She could dress herself or be dressed. She reluctantly chose the former.

Her fingers were slow and clumsy. She could sense the woman's impatience, but except for the gesturing meant to hurry her, no help was offered. The woman snatched and flung at the door each article of clothing as Comfort removed it. Comfort had only her stockings, shoes, and chemise left to take off when a tremendous roar from below shook the floor. She dropped back on the bed as her stomach lurched. The building shuddered with the thunderous clapping and foot stomping. Glass rattled in the window beside the bed.

Comfort stared at her companion and saw she was unmoved. Downstairs, the stomping and shouting stopped, the frenzied applause died, and the walls, floor, and window ceased to vibrate. Caught in the eye of the storm, it was Comfort who trembled.

She bent over and tried to remove her boots. Her fingers were shaking so badly she couldn't manage the laces. Tears blurred her vision. She turned her hands over helplessly and heard the woman's annoyed grunt. When she looked up, the woman was heading for the door.

"Wait!" she called after her. "I'll do it. I can do it." She was ignored. She bent quickly and scrabbled at the laces. The door opened anyway. Comfort applied herself more diligently to the task. She didn't dare look away from her feet, but she heard the men speaking and sensed the woman was gesticulating again. "See! See! I have it!" She held up her hand, one shoe dangling from her fingertips. It was perverse, she thought hazily, that she should feel any sense of accomplishment. She was going to be raped, and here she was raising one of her shoes over her head like a trophy.

The woman stepped out of the doorway back into the room. The door closed behind her. Comfort saw she was carrying a small glass. More beer? The shoe was taken out of her hand and the glass pressed into it. The woman placed her palm under Comfort's hand and pushed up, encouraging her to drink.

She drank. The woman kept the glass against her mouth until she drained it. The liquid was as thick as syrup, sweet at first, but with a bitter aftertaste that lay unpleasantly on her tongue. She swallowed several times trying to get rid of the taste in her mouth. When the glass was taken away, she asked for water. The woman shook her head, tossed the glass into the pile of discarded clothes, and knelt in front of Comfort to remove her other shoe.

As soon as the woman was in position, Comfort kicked. At least that was her intention. There was no force behind it. It was as if her leg had been shackled to the floor. It came up slowly, with great effort, and was so heavy that it would have fallen back if the woman hadn't cupped the heel in her hands. She tried again, this time with the foot that was already shoeless. The woman simply batted her foot out of the way, no more annoyed than if she were flicking off a pesky fly.

Comfort didn't stir as her stockings were rolled down her calves, nor did she flinch when the woman produced a small knife and cut away her chemise. She made no attempt to cover her nakedness. She watched her ivory chemise, now stained yellow along the neckline with spilled beer, delicately float and flutter before it came to rest on top of everything else she'd worn.

Soiled Dove.

She remembered it would be her name now. It's what they'd called her downstairs. She would answer to it just as she'd always answered to Comfort. No one knew her real name. That was a secret, even from her.

Comfort closed her eyes as the woman slipped the batiste gown over her head. It lay soft against her shoulders and smelled faintly of rosewater. She allowed the woman to raise her arms to accommodate the garment, because they were simply too heavy to raise herself. The light material drifted over her breasts and stomach and gathered softly around her hips.

There was no gesturing for her to lie down, so she didn't. She sat on the edge of the bed while the woman gathered the piled clothes and lifted them close to her chest. The door opened and closed, and then she was alone.

She sighed. She was tired but not sleepy. She felt enervated. Her pulse beat slowly, and she imagined her blood was as thick as the syrup she'd been forced to drink. That was probably good. It would be better for her if she couldn't move, couldn't fight. Perhaps, if she survived, she would regret not fighting, but for the moment, at least, it seemed that not fighting might be the key to surviving.

Except for the bed, the malodorous pot underneath it, and the lantern hanging beside the door, the room was empty. It had but a single function, and when she heard footsteps on the stairs, she understood it would soon be put to that use.

The man who entered the room was not what she expected, though she'd tried to shy away from thinking about that. He was neat and trim, shorter than she was, and his clothes looked relatively clean. He smelled rather powerfully of spirits, but he walked toward her in a straight line, suggesting he'd spilled rather more on himself than he'd drunk.

He hesitated a moment after the door was closed, looking around the room; in fact, looking everywhere but directly at her. Comfort still had wits enough about her to find that behavior odd. She smiled, although she didn't think she meant to. The smile flickered uncertainly across her face before she felt it freeze in a ghastly parody of welcome and warmth.

He did an even more surprising thing when his eyes finally alighted on hers. He removed his hat, inclined his head, and

introduced himself as properly as any gentleman might who
hadn't just bought the winning ticket in the lottery to molest her.

"John Farwell," he said.

Comfort frowned. The name was tantalizingly familiar, but
the face was not. She pressed two fingertips to one corner of
her mouth to prop up her faltering smile. Her skin felt as elastic
as rising dough. She began to knead it.

"John Farwell, Miss Kennedy." He approached the bed.
"Mr. DeLong sent me. Mr. *Beauregard* DeLong." He added
this last in the event she mistook the man who orchestrated her
rescue for her fiancé. "We haven't a great deal of time. Do you
understand? They're selling more tickets. I have twenty minutes, and the Rangers thought that was very generous."

Comfort attempted to nod. Her head simply flopped forward
and stayed there.

"Miss Kennedy?" John Farwell took an uneasy breath.
Thinking back to what Bode had told them about Miss Ken-
nedy, he was loath to touch her. "You do understand, don't you?
When the time comes, we must move quickly."

Comfort's head lifted a fraction before her chin dropped
back to her chest.

"Oh, dear." He removed his jacket and flung it around her
shoulders. When she made no attempt to put it on, he helped
her into it. "Really, Miss Kennedy, you have to look at me." He
snapped his fingers in front of her face. Her eyes were open,
but she didn't blink or acknowledge him in any way.

John went to the door and removed the lantern from the
hook. He crossed to the window, drew back the curtains just
enough to set the lantern on the sill, and then went to the bed
and sat down beside Comfort.

"It will be helpful if you can make some noises, though I
suppose I can manage for the both of us if I must." He began to
bounce on the bed. The frame rattled. Cornhusks stuffed the
mattress, and they crackled and rustled with every bounce. Comfort also bounced, but not by conscious choice. Her movements
were a consequence of his enthusiastic springing. He interspersed
harsh grunts with high-pitched squeals and moans. Except for
softly groaning each time her stomach lurched or her head jerked
painfully, she didn't add to the spirited cacophony.

He couldn't use her name, so he called her "baggage" and "bitch" and added the vilest words he knew. They didn't come naturally to his lips, but he believed he gave a good accounting, because the men on the other side occasionally called out coarse encouragement.

He was breathing hard by the time the riot started downstairs. As far as he was concerned, it hadn't happened soon enough. Comfort was as limp as laundry ready for the line. He was barely able to haul her back on the bed once she began to slide forward. Her hair swung like a heavy curtain against her cheek. She swiped at it once, twice, and then let it be.

"Now, Miss Kennedy, it has to be now." Farwell stood and pulled Comfort behind him. He knew it would be difficult for her to stand, but he hadn't anticipated that in her stupor she wouldn't be able to help him at all. He gave her his back and brought her arms over his shoulders, and supporting her in this fashion, he dragged her to the window. When he tried to raise the sash, he discovered it was nailed shut. Cursing, he yanked one of the curtains down and wrapped it around his arm.

He was rearing back with his elbow, trying to keep Comfort from falling to the floor and the lantern from tipping and the shattering glass from blinding him, when fighting broke out in the hallway. The door shivered in its frame as someone was hurled against it. He winced at the soft thud of body blows and shied closer to the window as someone grunted, fending off a punch. Downstairs, the fighting was as ferocious and considerably louder. He repositioned Comfort when she started to slide down his back again. They were already supposed to have made their escape. There was help on the other side of that window. He had to trust that was still true.

Securing Comfort's wrists as best he could with one hand, he raised his elbow a second time and prepared to strike the glass. Simultaneous to smashing the window, the door behind him crashed open.

Bode hurried to the window before John Farwell could hurl himself and Comfort out of it. He appreciated the man's commitment to seeing his assignment through, but getting himself killed was not part of it.

The clerk nearly fell through the window anyway when a

strong pair of hands landed on his upper arms. He tucked his head between his shoulders like a turtle and tried to jerk away. The hands that frightened him also saved his life.

"It's Bode, John." He slipped one arm around Comfort's waist and drew her away from his clerk. He kept his other hand on John's arm and pulled him back from the window.

"Mr. DeLong." John straightened, bewildered. The battle that was still raging under their feet made it difficult to think clearly. "I didn't expect . . . that is, you weren't . . ."

"Plans change," said Bode. "At least mine do." He turned Comfort so she faced him. She was smiling, and he was fairly certain it had nothing to do with him. He wet his thumb and swiped at the flecks of dried blood just under her lip. Her mouth drooped. She was as pliable as wet clay. Bode lifted her chin and looked into her eyes. "Hold up that lantern so I can better see her face."

John Farwell did as he was told. "They drugged her, Mr. DeLong. The three beers they made her drink before she came up here wouldn't make her numb and dumb."

Bode agreed. Her pupils were dilated. Only a sliver of dark chocolate iris was visible in each eye. "All right. It'll have to be this way." He picked her up and slung her over his shoulder. She didn't fuss at the indignity of it, and Bode didn't count himself lucky for it. "This way, John. There's an exit at the back. We saw it when an old Chinese woman used it to slip outside." He saw the clerk glance uneasily at the doorway. "All done in, John. Both of them. Let's go. My men can't keep fighting forever, no matter how much they're enjoying themselves."

When Comfort awoke, she was deliciously warm and strangely restless. She stretched, turned, and snuggled closer to the source of all that heat. Her body conformed to the shape of the pillow she was hugging. Her knees came up, and her hands slipped neatly between the pillowcase and the mattress. She pressed her face into soft folds of linen. Her nose twitched; the fragrance provoked a pleasant memory. Her mouth softened and parted. She breathed in a sigh. It was like filling her lungs with contentment.

It didn't last nearly long enough. The edgy feeling returned.

Her skin felt tight and tingly, and the muscles in her legs jumped and jerked unexpectedly. Her nipples had become hard, little buds that she ached to flatten against her palms. She licked her lips. They were extraordinarily sensitive to the sweep of her tongue. The lightest touch tickled her and sent a lovely shiver down her back.

She stirred again and rubbed against the pillow. The friction momentarily eased the tenderness in her breasts, but it also created a blossom of heat between her thighs. She tightly pressed her legs together and waited for it to subside.

It didn't, not until she felt the pillow shift and brush against her just so.

"Better?"

Comfort opened her eyes and stared into Bode's face. That single word, delivered as it was in a voice that was part growl, part chuckle, and all heat, simply took her breath away.

Chapter Ten

"You're here," she whispered. Comfort slid one of her hands out from under him and laid it against his cheek. "I thought you were a pillow."

"That's not the worst thing you could have said."

She flicked a few copper strands of hair back from his temple. "What's the worst thing?" She waited, stroking his cheek, wondering if he could make himself that vulnerable.

"You could have said you thought I was Bram."

"No, I couldn't." She touched her thumb to the corner of his faint smile. A memory stirred. He'd done something like that to her. "I don't mistake one of you for the other . . . Bode." His slim smile widened a fraction, and she willed him to believe her. "I never have."

"Mm." Bode caught her wrist as her fingers drifted to his neck. She didn't resist. Her fingertips brushed his skin as lightly as feathers. "What do you remember about yesterday?"

"Most of it, I think. Except how you got me out of that horrible place." Her own smile was a trifle rueful. "And everything after that."

"I see."

She thought he looked vaguely troubled. "I'm sorry," she said softly, "but I don't want to be sensible. You make it safe for me not to be sensible."

"I'm not sure that's—"

She stopped him. "And there'd be so many questions you'd have to answer, beginning with are Newt and Tuck well?"

"They are. They're at home, and they know you're with me."

Relieved, she closed her eyes briefly. Her heart wasn't squeezed so tightly as it had been. "And then you'd have to tell me why we're on a ship." She paused. "We are, aren't we?"

"Yes."

"You see? After that, you'd have to explain why we're sharing a bed and continue working backward from there. There'd be questions one after the other and perhaps answers I don't want to hear right now. All of it would simply get in the way of what I want."

He thought he shouldn't ask, and then he did. "And that's what, exactly?"

"Exactly this." She leaned into him, her mouth changing shape from rueful to slightly wicked. Her lips covered his. It was all the encouragement he needed.

Bode rolled Comfort onto her back and pressed her into the mattress. His mouth was hard, hot, and hungry. He still had one of her wrists in his hand, and now he took the other. He leveled them on either side of her head and ground his lips against hers. She whimpered. He eased the pressure. She opened her mouth wide and took him back. Her tongue speared his mouth.

Restless, she dug her heels into the mattress and arched her back. Except for her wrists, he didn't restrict her movement. The press of her tight, lithe body teased him in every way that satisfied. Her small, perfect breasts rubbed his chest, and he could feel the hard points of her nipples through her nightgown and his shirt. Breaking off the kiss, ignoring her guttural cry of displeasure, he bent his head and took one of those sweetly maddening little buds into his mouth.

"Ah!" Comfort squirmed, pushing ineffectually against the hands holding her down. She closed her eyes. His tongue made her gown damp. The sensation was exquisite. Her nipple was so tender, so achingly tender, that he could only hold it between his lips. The suck of his mouth radiated so much heat that bursting into flame would have been a welcome diversion. The sound that left her throat was something between a gasp and a giggle.

Bode lifted his head and gave her a narrow look from under heavily lidded eyes, trying to gauge whether or not he had actually wrested laughter from her.

Pinned back by his blue-violet glance, Comfort said the first thing that came to her mind. "You're not wearing your eye patch."

"That's what you have to say to me?"

She bit her lower lip, feeling the full impact of his dangerous look. "Um . . . it's very nice. Not your eye, although that's lovely as well. I meant that what you're doing is very nice. Or what you were doing."

"Mm. I can do better than very nice."

"Oh. Can you?" She released a short burst of air to prepare herself. "You won't mind, then, if I spontaneously combust?"

He arched an eyebrow. "Not only won't I mind," he said, bending to her breast again, "I'll be flattered."

"Ooh!" Every muscle in her body contracted as his teeth closed lightly over her nipple and tugged. It happened again when he captured her other breast in exactly the same manner.

When he released her wrists, her hands flew to his head. Her fingers twisted his hair, threaded together, and kept him exactly where he wanted to be.

Neither of them paid the least attention to the oil lamp fixed to the shelf above the bed until it guttered. Shadows flickered wildly on the wall for a few moments before the flame was extinguished. Their room was thrown into darkness, not as absolute as Comfort had experienced in the cellar of the concert saloon but near enough that she tensed and clutched Bode's shoulders.

He gently removed her hands and propped himself on an elbow. "Give it a minute," he said. "And then tell me if you want me to light the lamp."

She did as he asked. He lifted one of her hands and placed the palm over his heart. He held it there. She felt the steady beat, much calmer than her own. She kept her eyes on his face, and gradually she began to make out his precisely carved features. Moonlight cast his face in silver-blue relief. He'd been twenty-three when she'd first seen him, younger than she was now, but oh, so much older than that. She remembered how he stood at the back of the salon during her coming-out party, remote and unapproachable in his blue custom-made regimental uniform. The party must have seemed so silly to him. A young girl's introduction to society; his introduction to war. She didn't know how he bore it. She'd hated it, too, right up until the moment Bram asked her to dance.

If she'd been less of a coward, she'd have hinted to Bram that she wanted to dance with his brother. Perhaps she should have marched right up to Beau DeLong and asked him about his orders and when he expected to leave. Adults spoke to him at length, probably about all the things she wanted to know, but she never did. He'd been forbidding; worse, he'd been indifferent.

She understood her reaction better now. Bode had grown into his features; they were cut from a cloth that made him look older than his years at twenty-three and suited him perfectly at thirty-two. He would look much the same at forty-two and a decade beyond that. He didn't worry about matters he couldn't change, and he didn't wear regrets like a hair shirt. What if he'd never been indifferent to her, only wary?

"Bode," she said, liking the way it shaped her lips and made her tongue rest just behind her teeth at the roof of her mouth.

"Mm?"

"Just . . . Bode."

"Do you want the lamp?"

"No. Moonlight becomes you." She laughed because she'd startled him into raising both eyebrows. "It does, you know. The color of your eyes is extraordinary. More blue-silver than blue-violet just now. I've always wondered if you can see things beyond what is natural."

"I don't think so."

"Oh. It seemed as if you might be able to."

"I see you," he said. "And it's always been my perception that you're otherworldly."

Comfort was rather more pleased by that than not. "You're going to kiss me again, aren't you?"

"Yes."

"I don't think I can wait much longer. The Chinese woman . . . she gave me something to drink. It made me very tired, but it also . . ." She squirmed, uncomfortable in her skin again. "It would be better if you did it quickly."

"I understand." He bent his head and nudged her lips with his. He released her hand and slid his to the inner curve of her waist. It rested there while he teased and tasted her lips, but as he deepened the kiss, he moved it to cradle her breast. His thumb made a pass across the beaded nipple. She whimpered softly; the sound of it was her pleasure and her surrender.

Bode wanted both. Blood pooled in his groin. His fingers gathered her shift in bunches, and he pushed his knee between her legs. Her response was immediate. Her hips rocked against him. He was achingly hard. The warm weight of her pelvis rubbing against his erection made him bite off a groan. She was going to make him spend as quickly as a schoolboy getting his first glimpse of the sweet curve of a woman's naked back.

Bode gripped Comfort at the hips and put her away from him. She still tried to move against him, but what she wanted was her own release, not his. He slipped one hand under her shift and cupped her mons. Her hips jerked. She reached for his shoulders. Her fingers fluttered just above his collarbone and then slid down his chest.

He waited until she stilled. Her breathing changed from ragged to steady. He would make it ragged again, would insist on it, but wanted her to anticipate the moment.

The heel of his hand rubbed her mons. His fingers slid between the cleft. She was damp. Her flesh was soft and warm and pliant. His touch was light, and she was quick to respond and easily maneuvered. He slipped one finger inside her, then two. He pressed another kiss to her mouth, and this time his tongue moved languidly, as slowly and deliberately as his fingers did between her thighs. She made the sweetest sounds of yearning at the back of her throat.

His thumb brushed the cowl of her clitoris. Touching that tiny nub of flesh fairly made her skin hum. She pressed herself to him, wanting him close, then closer still. Her fingers curled in the loose fabric of his shirt. The movement of his hand was gentle. It was also relentless.

Bode lifted his head. Comfort's eyes weren't closed in helpless bliss. They were open, open wide, and watching him. Sentient and responsive, those dark eyes were unrecognizable as the vacant and impassive ones they'd been hours earlier.

They held his gaze, focused on it, really, as if he were the steady center of a world that was shifting around her.

Moonshine bathed her face, lending her features a transparent wash of light and silver-blue color that might have made her seem ethereal if he weren't touching her so intimately that he could feel her pulse and her heat and her wetness.

He listened to the rise in her breathing as she sipped the air in tiny increments. The soft pitch of each breath changed, rising like a musical scale. Her fingers loosed his shirt, and her hands disappeared under the blankets. She did a surprising thing then, covering his hand with both of hers and holding him exactly as she wanted. Her single-minded attention to her own pleasure moved him to a rough, vaguely diabolical chuckle.

"There?" he asked, turning the pad of his thumb just so.

She bit her lip in earnest and nodded quickly.

"You have to say so," he said.

"There. Yes, there."

"And here?" He spread his fingers so they pushed against the damp walls of her vagina.

She squeezed his hand. When nothing happened, she understood he expected her to answer that as well. "Yes. Just there. Like that."

"Just. Like. That."

And just like that, every thread of tension that had been holding her together broke at once. She gripped Bode's hand, afraid she would lose herself in the release of so much pleasure. Her back lifted. Her neck arched. Her heels dug deeply into the mattress. Every part of her quivered. She'd witnessed buildings collapse with less provocation. She thought it was possible that she'd do the same.

She did, of course; however, the aftermath wasn't destruction, but a delicious languor that turned her bones to warm candle wax and made her glad she hadn't come out of her skin.

Bode saw that she'd finally closed her eyes. Her lips were parted. He touched his mouth to hers and kissed her softly. Her hands slipped away from his, and he withdrew from between her thighs. She murmured something against his mouth that might have been a protest.

"We're not done," he whispered.

She nodded faintly, opening her eyes when he raised his head. "There's you."

"Yes."

"All right." Without being directed, Comfort swept aside the blankets. Her shift was already bunched at her thighs, but when she raised her knees, the hem gathered around her hips. She concentrated on arranging the material comfortably under her, lifting her hips and settling her bottom. When she'd finished, she glanced at him, prepared to say that she was ready, but the expression on his face was so full of astonishment that she quickly dropped her knees, pushed at her gown, and yanked the covers back over her for good measure. Less confident, but still curious, she asked, "Should I have let you do it?"

Bode's eyebrows remained as high as they had been, but the rest of his face relaxed. "No. Oh, no. What you did was fine."

She shook her head. "No, it wasn't. I surprised you."

"Surprised" was perhaps too mild of a descriptor, but he wasn't going to tell her that. "Well, yes, but in a very good way. And I'm over it."

Comfort reached out from under the covers and touched his eyebrows with her thumb and forefinger. She gave them a gentle nudge downward. When they were positioned properly, she withdrew her hand and studied her work. "At least now you look as if you might be."

"I am," he said. "I certainly am." He had questions, but as she'd pointed out earlier, there'd be one after the other and perhaps answers he didn't want to hear. Whatever he thought he needed to know could wait. "Again," he said. And when she didn't move, he added, "Please."

Comfort didn't throw back the blankets this time, but after considering his request and watching the centers of his eyes grow wider and darker, she did rearrange her shift and raise her knees. She found his hand and tentatively squeezed it, as much because she simply needed to touch him as to let him know she was ready.

He brushed his lips against hers and then sat up and knelt between her knees. Raising the tail of his shirt with one hand, he took her by the wrist with the other and set her fingers against his erection. Her eyes widened, but he'd never been disappointed by counting on her curiosity. Her fingers circled his cock, squeezed lightly, hesitantly, and then she slid her fist along the hot, pulsing length of it.

He had an urge to tuck her eyebrows back into place. Instead, he chose to be flattered.

Bode leaned forward, supporting himself on his forearms, and covered her with his body. He pressed his hips against her, and with only this for encouragement, she helped him find his way.

His first thrust was cautious. Whatever he'd seen her do, no matter how forward and experienced she seemed at times, he was guided by the belief that the truth was somehow different, and that what she required was care, not carnality.

Comfort felt an immense pressure in her chest, greater even than the one between her thighs. She pushed at Bode's shoulders and turned her head when she thought he meant to kiss her. What he did was whisper in her ear.

"Breathe."

She sucked in a lungful of air. Her chest expanded. The pressure eased. She was suddenly aware that he was in her more deeply than he'd been in the moment before. Clever man. Clever, considerate man.

She took the time he gave her to accommodate his entry, and then she nodded once. He moved slowly at first, just that little bit to help her understand his intentions. She felt the rocking motion of the ship and concentrated on that. The rhythm of his stroking was much the same. Rise and fall. Rise and fall.

In time, she no longer thought about it. She simply felt it.

Her hips rose to meet his thrusts. Nerve endings that had only just ceased to vibrate were jangled back to life.

Bode's face was a study in pleasure denied. His features, shown in sharp relief by virtue of skin pulled taut across his bones, were those of an ascetic. His mouth was set in a grim line, and twin vertical lines creased the space between his eyebrows.

Comfort slipped her hands between their bodies and searched until she found an opening under his shirt. She pushed her fingertips into the smooth mat of hair that covered his chest and pressed the cup of her palm against his heart. The beat was strong. It pounded against her hand. She kept her palm in place as she would cup it over a seashell, and what she felt became a sound, and the sound was like the roar of the ocean in her ears.

But then again, it might have been Bode.

His shout made her eyes go wide, and she bit her lip to keep her from gaping. She was not unfamiliar with grunts of men finding their release, but she hadn't expected his to be quite so loud or expressive. Had he really cried out "Brother of Cod"?

"Mother of God," he rasped against her cheek. His body shuddered once, twice, and then was still. He lay heavily on top of her, but when he tried to heave himself away, her arms circled him. Her fingers walked the length of his spine. He didn't think it was possible, but his cock stirred, his hips twitched, and he shivered again.

"I think you better stop," he said.

"All right." Comfort's fingers stilled. His mouth was only a hairbreadth from her cheek. Her skin was warmed by his soft expulsion of air, and the weight of him covered her like a snug blanket. It hardly mattered that her breathing was a trifle labored.

It mattered to Bode. He pushed himself up, made a thorough job of kissing Comfort, and rolled away, sprawling on his back with such abandon that he took most of the sheet and all of the quilt with him. Out of the corner of his eye, he saw her once again arranging her shift so she was modestly covered. His sigh was sincerely meant.

Comfort took one corner of the blue-and-green star-patterned quilt and tugged hard. She knew he let her have it, because she couldn't have wrested it from him otherwise. Turning on her side, she edged closer to him and tucked some of the quilt around her back.

Bode patted his shoulder, indicating there was a place there for her head. She levered herself up just enough to nestle her cheek against his smooth linen shirt.

"There's a washroom over there, on the other side of that forward door," he told her. "If you'd like to use it."

"I would. In a moment. Not just yet." She was aware of the wetness between her thighs. She tried not to move. "Do you think I'm bleeding?" She cringed after hearing the blunt question. "I'm sorry. I shouldn't say—"

"No," he said. "You should *always* say."

"And have everyone know that I'm coarse and common? When Newt and Tuck needed to put a roof over my head, we all lived in the back of the Snow Palace with Bottle Betty and her girls. My uncles tried to keep me from seeing and hearing things, but you already know they were only modestly successful. Opium was traded in the alley behind the place, and Chin Fong, the master who taught me the cat stance and a great deal more besides, was employed to regularly clear out the opium eaters who tried to squat under Bottle Betty's tent."

As brief as her explanation was, Bode thought it explained a great deal. "If you're concerned that childhood curiosity made you coarse and common, and you are convinced it must be hidden, then perhaps you should confine your more outrageous comments to the limits of my hearing."

"I think I already do that," she said quietly, finally. "It's you, Bode. You provoke me to say astonishing things."

"Well, that's something, then."

Comfort wasn't sure what he meant by that, and she let it pass. "So," she said, persevering with what was uppermost in her mind. "Do you think I'm bleeding?"

"I don't know. Do you want me to look?"

That was too bold, even for her rather unconventional sensibilities. She brought up her knees and tucked her shift around her, pressing her thighs as closely together as she was able. He wasn't going to thread her needle again so easily.

Laughter rumbled deeply in his chest. He pressed her head back to his shoulder. "I didn't mean I was going to examine you," he said. "I was going to look at myself."

"Oh." She hadn't thought of that, and now that she considered what he was telling her, she changed her mind about leaving the bed. "Maybe I will get up."

Bode would have liked to have lain with her a little longer, but he didn't try to stop her. She seemed to know he was watching as she rose from the bed and crossed to the washroom. She kept tugging at her shift as if it already didn't fall well below her knees, and her steps across the stateroom floor were hurried. He gave her what he thought was a decent amount of time to compose herself before he followed.

Comfort was staring in the mirror above the washstand. She looked as if she might have been doing that since she'd closed the door behind her. The washbasin was dry, and the linens hanging on the rod hadn't been touched. The room was small, but it was able to accommodate a commode, a washbasin, a copper hip bath, and a tall, narrow cabinet that held more linens, soaps, and items for shaving and teeth cleaning. What it did not easily accommodate was two people.

Bode stepped behind Comfort and circled her loosely with his arms. He nudged the crown of her hair with his lips. His breath stirred silky, ebony strands. "What are you thinking?"

"Nothing, really. Wondering if it shows, I suppose."

"If it shows," he repeated slowly.

"Didn't you wonder after your first time?"

"Oh," he said. "Oh, that."

She looked at him in the mirror. "What did you think I meant?"

"Well . . . you came in here to see if you were . . ." The vaguely sheepish expression he saw reflected back was unfamiliar. Perhaps he should be the one wondering if he'd been changed. Something was different. Something showed.

"Were you as young as Bram?" she asked.

He'd never been as young Bram, but he knew what she meant. "I couldn't say," he told her. "I don't know how old Bram was the first time he was with a woman, and right now I'm trying to recover from the notion that you do."

She set her arms over his and leaned back into him. "He liked to shock me, or liked to think he could. It was a game for him, not only with me, but with everyone."

"But mostly with you."

"Yes. I think that's true." Her smile held a hint of amusement as she watched Bode mull that over. "It didn't matter what he said to me. I thought it was because he believed I'd remain his friend, but I'm coming to understand that he knew all along that I was in love with him. He took advantage, I suppose you'd say."

"I would say." Bode felt as if she'd taken him to the very edge of a precipice. He wasn't certain if he would jump or wait for her to push him. Talk of Bram could put him in that quandary.

"He was twelve, by the way."

As easily as that, she'd pulled him away from the verge. "Twelve." He raised his eyebrows a fraction. "Even adding a couple of years to that, supposing that he wanted to truly shock you, I will tell you honestly that I wasn't as precocious as my little brother."

"But you won't tell me how old you were."

"No. Some things about one's first encounter should remain a secret."

"But this was my first time."

"Then it is a good thing I was there."

Laughing, she turned in his arms, stood on tiptoes, and placed her hands on his cheeks. She pressed a warm, hard kiss to his mouth that set him back on his heels.

Bode steadied himself, then her. He bent his head and touched her forehead with his own. "A very good thing."

"Mm." Comfort tugged on Bode's sleeve. "I still have to attend to . . . attend to certain . . ."

"Ablutions," he said. "Yes, I'm aware. I'll wait."

She gave him a little push and pointed to the door. He backed up and leaned against it. "Bode."

"All right. I'm leaving. But that's only because I know what you can do with those dainty bare feet." He turned the handle behind him and gave her the privacy she wanted.

Moonlight had given way to dawn by the time they were both in bed again. Bode sat with his back against the headboard, the quilt drawn over his lap. Comfort eschewed the blanket in favor of sitting cross-legged with her shift stretched tautly over her knees. She'd found a brush in the washroom cabinet and was applying it to her hair in long, even strokes.

Bode watched her. The rise and fall of her arm, the twist of her delicate wrist, the wave and ripple of her silky hair, all of it fascinated him. Still.

The first time he'd seen her, she had been twirling a heavy tendril of hair around her finger. She'd lifted it above the nape of her neck and stabbed it so viciously into her chignon with a pearl-studded comb that he'd actually winced. Moments later, she was going through the motions again, twisting, lifting, stabbing. When her hand went to her nape again, he realized she was tugging at her hair, making it fall so she could occupy herself in this small way.

She was bored. It was hard to imagine that she could be bored at her own coming-out. *He* was bored, but it wasn't his party. He hadn't wanted to go. Alexandra had insisted. He looked too fine in his uniform to keep it in his wardrobe until he was called up. She was proud of him, proud of his decision to serve when he easily could have avoided it. And unlike his father, he had chosen what she deemed was the side of the angels. The Crownes had been abolitionists long before it was a popular cause, and California had been admitted as a free state, so she believed that serving the Union was a mandate from God, not a choice.

That was how he had come to be at Comfort Kennedy's coming-out. He was Alexandra's showpiece, her public apology for her husband taking leave of his senses and deciding to support the Confederates' fight.

He knew Mr. Jones and Mr. Prescott by reputation, if not on sight, but he'd never met their niece. The seven years' difference in their ages yawned as wide as the bay, and he wasn't interested in giggly, simpering girls.

At the point of their introduction, he learned that she was neither of those things. She had grave, dark eyes and solemn features. She smiled politely, if not comfortably, and gave him her gloved hand. He bent over it, not touching it to his lips, and moved on through the receiving line. When he glanced back, she was stabbing the comb into her hair again. He wondered what his mother would make of it when she arrived.

Alexandra and his brother were late. He recalled now that Bram had chosen the point of their departure to decide that his jacket was too ill fitting to wear for an entire evening. Bode knew better. Bram didn't want to arrive beside him in uniform. He was afraid his own light would shine less brightly, and try as he might, he couldn't convince Alexandra to allow him to enlist.

One son in the Union ranks was an apologia; two sons were a vulgar excess of contrition.

So he stood at the rear of the salon, drinking very good brandy while an orchestra played and young ladies danced. Comfort Kennedy was taken onto the floor many times, first by her uncles and then by a steady procession of gentlemen, some as young as she, others considerably long in the tooth.

His eyes followed her taking each turn around the floor. She laughed perhaps a trifle too gaily and smiled too brightly. He thought she was miserable; at least as miserable as he.

And between dances he noticed her trying to vanish to the far end of the room, where she could stand beside her uncles and pretend she was genuinely happy they'd planned this event for her.

Twirling. Lifting. Stabbing.

Sometimes he would catch her staring at him. It was always when he was engaged in conversation, and he could never sustain her glance. There was no end to the guests who wanted to know his opinion of the war and what a Californian might do when the fight was in the East. Young girls, the giggly, simpering kind, came up to him, too. They circled him and made comments about his uniform, how handsome he looked, and how brave he must be. He supposed Alexandra would have been proud. He wasn't. He didn't ask any of them to dance.

He wanted to ask her. No one else. She held his attention with her fathomless dark eyes and her small, reserved smile. She had a slender neck and the poise to hold her head at an angle that showed it to its best advantage. He doubted she had practiced it; that tilt of her head was naturally hers.

Her gown was pale pink silk. It shone with the opalescence of mother-of-pearl every time she passed under the light of the chandeliers. He carefully drank his brandy and considered her from far away. Her skin would have the same opalescence, he decided. The difficulty would be getting her out of that dress, and for now that could only be accomplished in his mind.

It was as good a use of his time as any, and he passed the next half hour in contemplation of the dress, her skin, and how to separate one from the other, stopping only when Bram entered the salon and went straightaway to her side.

He saw her laugh, saw her throw back her head and laugh, and although he couldn't hear her, he imagined the sound of it was as rich as cream and as smooth as the brandy he was drinking. He was certain he'd never have her. It was the only time he'd actually envied his brother.

"You lost your combs," he said, returning to the present.

"It's all right. I can never keep them in my hair anyway."

"Pencils work better?"

She smiled. "Sometimes. I forgot that you've seen them in my hair." The brush strokes slowed. "Why am I here, Bode? Why am I not at home?"

"For your safety. What happened . . ." He shook his head and raised his palms. "It's not clear yet why it happened."

She accepted that. For now. "What ship is this?"

"*Demeter Queen*."

"This is the master's cabin?"

"The stateroom. Sometimes Mr. Douglas uses it, but if there's a passenger who wants to pay for the best quarters, this is where he stays."

"Mm. Are we paying?"

"I'm going to send a bill to your uncles."

Comfort stopped brushing and rolled the smooth wooden handle between her palms. "They're really all right?"

Bode described their scrapes and stitches as best he remembered and told her they returned to their home once they knew she was safe.

She looked pointedly at Bode's knuckles. All of them were rough looking; a few were swollen. While he'd cleaned up, she could still make out the angry red lines running perpendicular to the creases. "You have quite a few scrapes and bruises yourself. How did you get those?"

"There was a scuffle."

"I remember a brawl."

"That was downstairs. The scuffle was outside your door."

She stared at him. "There were *two* men outside my door, Bode. Both of them as big as Jonah's whale."

"Not quite. And they were slow."

"I couldn't get away from them."

"I know. But I heard you acquitted yourself favorably."

"How do you know that? You weren't in that saloon."

"There were almost a hundred men packed in there, so how can you be sure?"

"I just would have known." She shrugged. "I always have."

Her answer surprised him. Was it true? "You're right," he said after a moment. "I wasn't there. Not when they brought you up from the cellar, and not when they hoisted you onto the bar. I know my limits; so do the men who work for me. I couldn't have been in that room."

"I'm glad you weren't. I wouldn't have wanted you to see me." She hesitated. "I think that begs the question, who did?"

"Are you certain you want to know?"

"No, but I think I need to hear it anyway."

"Very well." He pushed a hand through his hair and told her. "Every man I could spare from this ship and a few from the other Crowne merchant in the harbor, the *Astarte Queen*. They numbered forty-seven. There were four clerks and seven of the men who work mostly at the warehouse. That's . . ." He paused, adding it up.

"Fifty-eight," she said before he could. "More than half the men were yours."

"It was the only way we could hope to win."

"The brawl."

He shook his head. "No, the men could have won the brawl with a third of that number. We had to win the lottery."

Comfort put a hand to her mouth and spoke from behind it. "That man. John Farwell. He's your clerk."

"Hm. You remember."

"I do." Her hand fell back to her lap. "I wish I didn't, but I do. Oh, Lord. He saw me in that awful thing that Chinese dragon made me wear."

"He swears he closed his eyes."

Comfort closed hers. "He sat beside me on the bed and made it . . . he made it *bounce*." Her eyes flew open. "He made noises. Grunts and moans and . . ." She snatched a pillow from the head of the bed and buried her face it.

Bode reached for her, alarmed when her shoulders began to shake. "Comfort? It's all right. John won't ever—" He stopped, his mouth flattened, and he leaned back. "I'm sure it was amusing," he said dryly.

Comfort lowered the pillow. Her eyes were luminous with unshed tears, and her cheeks were rosy. She hiccupped once, surprising herself, and then sobered. "It wasn't amusing," she said earnestly. "Not then. None of it was. It was awful. But now, I'm fine. More than fine, and Mr. Farwell, well, he was heroic." In spite of her best intentions, another bubble of laughter surfaced. She hiccupped again. "I think he meant to throw us both out the window, though. I'm not sure why."

"Escorting—not tossing—you out the window was the original plan. Several of us had been waiting there to help you. We needed the distraction of the brawl to get the ladder close enough to the building without being noticed. When we saw the Chinese woman slip outside and light her opium pipe, the plan changed. My men dealt with your dragon, and I went upstairs to find you."

"Have I thanked you? I don't think I have."

"It's not—"

She put out her hand. "Thank you," she said solemnly. And because he seemed to have no idea how to answer her, Comfort leaned forward on her knees and kissed him. Bode always knew how to answer that, and by the time he was done, she was more than a little out of breath.

She hiccupped and then blinked owlishly. A trifle embarrassed, she pressed her fingers against her lips. Her shoulders and head jerked with the violence of the next one. This time she merely rolled her eyes.

Bode swung out of bed. "Hold your breath while I get you something to drink."

Neither of those remedies had ever worked for her, but she was willing to try them again. She took a large gulp of air and clamped her lips around it while Bode padded off to the washroom behind her. She never heard him turn back, so when large hands suddenly seized her shoulders and a deeply rough voice growled her name close to her ear, she nearly came out of her skin.

She also had the presence of mind to use the brush to clobber her assailant on the head.

"Ow!" Bode let go and jumped back before she managed a second swing. He rubbed his head. "Why did you do that?"

She turned around on the bed to face him and reared up on her knees. She shook the brush at him. "Because you scared me. Why did you do that?"

"Because I wanted to scare you." Bode took her dismayed expression to mean that she clearly did not understand his intent. His slight smile mocked her. "Your hiccups. Remember? I believe they're gone."

Comfort took inventory. "Mm. So they are. You're very clever."

"I'm wounded." He snatched the brush out of her hand, tossed it over his shoulder, and bore her back on the bed.

Comfort didn't protest; she didn't want to. He spread kisses across her face while she finger-searched his scalp for a bump. Not finding one didn't change her mind about accepting the consequences. She very much enjoyed Bode's sense of justice.

He got her out of her shift this time. She helped him out of his shirt. For warmth they mostly stayed under the sheet, but sometimes their own heat was all they could bear. Hesitancy was absent from their exchanges. He knew when she wanted her breasts touched and when it was too much. He made certain it was only *almost* too much. She understood that there was a sensitive spot at the base of his spine that made him shiver if she touched it exactly right. She made sure she did.

He could get her to move closer by running his hand along her thigh from knee to hip, but not when he caressed her in the other direction. The soft underside of her elbows was like velvet. He could kiss her there. She was too ticklish to let his fingertips brush that sweet curve.

She could make him go absolutely still by walking her fingers down the arrow of crisp hair below his navel to his groin, but not when she slid them through the mat of hair on his chest. He grew restless then, but in a very good way.

Her throat had a special fascination for him. He liked to press his mouth against the hollow. She liked it, too. She would arch her long, slender neck and let him feast. He sipped her skin, bruising her just a little with the suck of his mouth. She'd see the marks later when she looked in the mirror. It would be something that would show.

His eyes intrigued her. She liked to watch them while her hands moved over him. When did the balance of color favor violet over blue, and when did the pupils become so large and bottomless that she imagined she could see her reflection in them? She saw one thing when she used her knuckle to trace the line of his jaw from just behind his ear to his chin. She saw another when she cupped the sac under his cock.

"A light touch," she whispered. "Responsive. Easy to manipulate."

Bode might have choked on his laughter if his earnest groan hadn't pushed it out of the way. "Maneuver," he said when he could manage it. "Maneuver, not manipulate."

She kneaded his balls. "Are you certain?"

He wasn't. He was clearly under a siren's spell, and the siren knew it. She was smiling at him, full of her new power, full of herself. That gave him the impetus he needed. He startled her by grasping her wrist, hauling her hand up to his chest, and turning her onto her back. He pinned her with his hands and then his body. She squirmed, but that was better than when she was still, and he told her so.

Comfort stopped trying to avoid his kiss and welcomed it instead. It was long and deep and warm, and when it ended, he was inside her, moving steadily, evenly, drawing out each thrust as though he were drawing in a slow breath. He gave her time; he gave them both time.

She thought she knew what to expect: the sense of climbing, the desire to grasp for something just outside her reach. It was like that again, but different, too. She understood she wasn't alone, that he was taking her there, and that he would be in the same place at the end, spent but satisfied.

And when their breathing quieted and what they heard was the rush of water against the ship's hull, they were lulled into sleep without speaking a word between them.

Comfort's nose twitched. She warily opened one eye in time to see Bode pulling back a steaming mug of coffee. She thought he intended to pass it to her, but he merely raised it to his own lips.

"Cruel man." The words were muffled by the pillow she dragged over her face. "Go away."

"There's some for you," he said. "Biscuits and honey, too. But you have to get up. It's almost noon, and Mr. Douglas would like to see you. You can't avoid him or the rest of the men indefinitely."

She raised the pillow a few inches. "I'd like to know why not."

He took the pillow away from her and tossed it to the foot of the bed. "Because you owe them your life."

Comfort flushed. She knew that, and she was ashamed that he'd had to say it aloud. "I'm sorry." She pushed herself up with one hand and clutched the sheet to her chest with the other. "You're right. Of course I want to thank them. I'm just not sure how one does that exactly."

"One says, 'Thank you.'"

"Naturally you'd think it was that simple."

Bode sat on the edge of the bed. "It's only difficult if you decide it is." He offered his mug to her. "Decide that it's not."

Comfort took the stoneware mug, sipped, and handed it back. "I'll get up."

He nodded and stood. "There's a chest full of your belongings over there." He pointed to the leather-bound trunk sitting beside a cherrywood armoire. "You can decide what you want to put in the wardrobe later. Your uncles had Suey Tsin pack it for you."

"I don't understand. How did they know I would need it?"

"I told them you would."

"But when? They weren't around last night."

"I told them before."

"Before?"

"Before you were rescued."

She tried to take that in. "You were that certain you would be able to do it?"

Bode shrugged and gave her a small, modestly self-assured smile as he raised the mug to his lips. "It's only difficult if you decide it is." Anticipating that she might lunge for the pillow and throw it at him, he retreated to the table. Comfort muttered something under her breath that he didn't catch and thought he probably shouldn't anyway. She didn't have much difficulty saying things clearly when she meant him to hear.

He sat down on the bench that was fixed to the wall behind the table. Angling into one corner, he brought up a leg, knee bent, and stretched the other out. He held the mug in both hands and watched Comfort manage the sheet a bit too deftly for his tastes. He had hardly any good view of the curve at the small of her back before she disappeared into the washroom. Since she hadn't taken anything from the trunk with her, he was hopeful that a second opportunity would present itself.

When she emerged some ten minutes later looking fresh, brushed, and rested, she was wearing the sheet tucked and knotted just above her breasts with one tail draped over her shoulder. It had as many folds as Aphrodite's gown and looked as if it might be as inviolate.

"I'm hungry," she said, approaching the table. "I'll change afterward."

Did she think he required an explanation? Complaining wasn't among any of the first hundred things he thought of when he saw her. He nudged a chair out for her with the toe of his shoe. "I sliced a biscuit for you. I didn't know if you'd want honey, or if you did, how much." He pointed to the plate in front of him where his own biscuit dripped with so much golden honey that it looked trapped like a leaf in amber.

Her eyes widened a little. "Thank you, then, for letting me do it myself." She arranged the sheet so she could sit comfortably. She thought Bode looked as if he was holding his breath waiting for the knot to slip. She patted the back of his hand as she sat. "I made a decent hitch. It's not going to come undone."

"You're telling me not to hope."

Comfort pulled the plate with the sliced biscuit on it toward her. "I'm telling you the knot is going to stay precisely where it is. Whether you continue to hope for a different outcome is up to you." She picked up the honey pot and used the stick to drizzle some over the face of both biscuit halves. She heard Bode chuckle and smiled to herself as she lifted a biscuit to her mouth. She tasted honey first, and then the rich, flaky dough of the biscuit melted on her tongue. "Exquisite."

"Mr. Henry will be pleased to hear it," Bode told her. He poured a mug of coffee for her and set the cup beside her plate. "He's in charge of the galley on the *Demeter Queen*."

"Was he at the saloon?"

"Yes. Outside, though. With the ladder."

Comfort nodded. With credible calm, she said, "Then I have reason to thank him twice." She took a second bite of biscuit before she set it down and picked up the mug. "Tell me how you won the lottery."

Bode raised his knee again and rested his mug on top of it. "At the outset, I thought there might be a demand for ransom, and I told Newton and Tucker they would have to put together money sufficient to meet it. None of us could guess what the Rangers would ask for, and your uncles couldn't set a limit on what they were willing to pay, so I finally set the figure myself at ten thousand, but told them to be prepared to pay more."

Comfort gaped at him.

"When no demand came in those early hours after you were abducted, I sent the crew out at dusk. The first rumors the men heard were about an auction. They knew that it involved a white woman, not a China girl or a Negress. No one was certain it was you, but the speed with which the event was being organized made all of us think it must be. The men learned the location quickly enough, but there was no information about you being held in the same place. We had to wait. All of the plans involved Mr. Farwell making the winning bid. No one knew it would be a lottery until the announcement was made. John carried in money sufficient for his bid."

"Surely not ten thousand dollars."

"No. No single person could have taken in that much money and kept the Rangers in the crowd from seeing it. It was divided among the men. When they realized it was a lottery, they all bought tickets."

Comfort swallowed. "So any one of them could have won."

"*Anyone* could have won, but Newton told me later that given the number of my men in the crowd and the amount of money they had to spend, the odds were almost seventeen to one in favor of someone from Black Crowne holding the winning ticket."

It still made her shudder. What if it had been the one?

"Think of something else," Bode said, guessing that the thing that occupied her mind was the same as what occupied his. There was no question that she was sitting beside him now because they'd gotten lucky.

"All right," she said, nodding slowly. "Tell me how I came to be in bed with you."

"That's easier to explain. You insisted."

Chapter Eleven

Comfort decided she would always be suspicious of Bode's answer, so the only sensible thing to do was not dwell on it. She had no memory of asking—demanding, according to him—that he stay with her. It might have been easier to accept if he'd led her to believe she wanted him there because she was afraid to be left alone. That would have been difficult to hear, but she'd have understood it better than being told she clung to him like a Barbary Coast whore to a sailor with five dollars in his pocket.

Of course, he'd said, "like a limpet to a rock," but she knew what he meant. He reminded her that she'd been drugged, as if that was supposed to ease her mind. That was why she concluded the better course was to remain suspicious. Otherwise, she had to accept that the responsibility for all that followed sat squarely on her shoulders. It was a considerable burden.

After she ate, she dressed in the apple green walking dress that Suey Tsin had carefully packed for her, fixed her hair in a simple plait that she tied off with a matching grosgrain ribbon, and presented herself to Bode for inspection before she met the shipmaster and crew.

"Very nice." He watched the way her hand fluttered to the nape of her neck. If she'd wound her hair in a chignon, there would already be several curling tendrils slipping out of it. "You don't have to be nervous."

"I know I don't have to be," she said, annoyed. "I just am. Bode, the last time these men saw me, I was—" She stopped. She didn't want to think about it, let alone say it aloud. When he opened his mouth to speak, she shook her head, holding him off. "It's all right. I'm ready to go."

He took her arm. "You'll meet Mr. Douglas first. The men will come by as they're able after that. You can stand between Nathan and me and greet them."

"A receiving line. I can do that."

There'd never been a question in Bode's mind.

Nathan Douglas made Comfort feel at ease almost at once. He reminded her a little of Uncle Newton, with his broad brow and silver-flecked black hair. His eyes were blue, not green, but they were kind, and they looked at her directly. If he was recalling anything he'd seen from the evening before, it wasn't showing on his face. He didn't regard her with pity, or worse, embarrassment. He took her hand, bowed his head over it, and then enthusiastically welcomed her aboard the *Demeter Queen*.

"She's the goddess of the harvest, Demeter is. And that's what this queen carries, plenty of bounty. We've got rum and other fine spirits, machine parts, steel, and finished hard and soft goods, all of it going to Hong Kong or Shanghai."

Comfort's head snapped around to Bode. "We're going to China?"

"No. *Demeter Queen* is. The *Artemis Queen* was supposed to have reached San Francisco by now, but we know from a report by a master on one of the Barclay merchants that the *Artemis* came across high seas and took on some water and damage that put her behind schedule. She's limping in, but as long as she's true to her course, we'll meet her in a week, three at the most. *Demeter* will pull alongside and we'll board her."

He saw that Comfort was still skeptical. It seemed to be in her nature today, because she hadn't believed what he'd told her about not allowing him to leave her bed either. He crossed his heart. "You're not being shanghaied. It will be fine."

"Does boarding her involve walking a plank between two rolling ships?"

Mr. Douglas inserted himself into the discussion. "Now, Miss Kennedy, I'm going to keep the *Demeter* riding the water as smoothly as a lily pad floating on a pond."

For his benefit, she smiled. "May I depend on it, Mr. Douglas?"

Following Bode's example, the shipmaster crossed his heart.

Comfort appreciated the gesture. The simplicity of it calmed her and made her introduction to the crew less difficult than she'd imagined it would be. *It's only difficult if you decide it is.* She had just finished thanking Mr. Tapper Stewart when those words came back to her. They prompted her to firmly press her elbow into Bode's side.

"What was that for?" he asked out of the side of his mouth as Tapper moved on.

"For being right."

"Then I suppose I'll have to get used to it."

"Unlikely." She turned politely to the next man who stepped up to meet her and thanked him warmly.

And so it went.

There was a long bench upholstered in dark emerald velvet beneath a bank of windows in the stateroom. Comfort pushed several plush pillows with gold tassels into one corner of the bench and sat down with her back against them. She opened the book Mr. Douglas had given her, an impossibly romantic adventure of treachery and revenge that she'd read several times but never tired of, and ran her fingers across the frontispiece. The illustration showed Edmond Dantès surrounded by his newfound treasure, in deep contemplation of how to make it best serve his purpose.

She was well into the first chapter when Bode returned. She motioned him over and flipped back to the frontispiece, holding up the illustration for him to see.

"Yes?" he asked after looking it over.

"It made me think of you."

He studied it again but could see no similarities between him and the soon-to-be Count of Monte Cristo. "Do you believe I'm that wealthy?"

"Are you?"

"No."

"Well, that isn't it regardless. I thought you might have looked like this, sitting on piles of my uncles' money and plotting my rescue and our revenge." His shout of laughter made her flinch. With some dignity, she said, "I guess not."

Although the bench was long enough that they could have sat at either end and extended their legs toward the middle and still not tapped toes, Bode nevertheless made her draw up her knees so he could sit where her feet had been. He plucked the book from her hands and put it on the other side of him.

"Your uncles brought the money to the ship in three large black leather valises. No chests. And we didn't take it out until we were ready to distribute it. As for your rescue, that was already plotted, and this is the first I'm hearing about revenge."

"Isn't there going to be any?"

"We recovered you and almost all of the money during the brawl. There's a certain amount of revenge in that, don't you think?"

"Yes, I suppose, especially about the money since that's what the Rangers wanted all along." She expected Bode to nod his head or say something that encouraged her to think along those lines. What he did was wince. It was barely perceptible, but not for a moment did she think she'd imagined it. "That's right, isn't it? They wanted money."

"Yes, they wanted money."

Comfort regarded him through eyes that had narrowed. "But?"

"Hm?"

Now he was being evasive. She wondered how he was able to meet her eyes so candidly and still be cagey. "Tell me," she said. "There's something else. What is it?"

Bode set a hand on her knee. He used his other hand to run four furrows through his hair. "It's almost unheard of for the Rangers to be active outside of the Barbary Coast, and while they can commit crimes with impunity on Pacific Street, they typically don't begin their reign of terror until nightfall. So, you see, they went out of their way, well beyond their usual sphere of influence, and in broad daylight, to attack your carriage. They wanted money, yes, but you were their specific target. Their only target. Ransom should have been enough; there must have been a reason they didn't ask for it."

He gave Comfort's knee a gentle squeeze. She was frowning deeply, more confused than concerned. She needed to understand before she could begin to worry.

"I can't be certain, Comfort, but I believe the Rangers were acting on someone else's behalf. Carrying out orders, if you will. It explains why they were willing to go outside of the Coast. Someone was making good on a threat, but he couldn't do it alone. He used the Rangers. They would have been paid well for abducting you, and that money would likely have changed hands the moment they closed the cellar door on you."

"But the lottery. They were trying to raise money."

"I don't think the lottery was meant to make money for them. That was someone else's idea. The Rangers deal in auctions, and no auction in the Barbary Coast could have reasonably been expected to bring more than a few hundred dollars."

"Your men had one hundred times that."

"No one knew that. If there'd been an auction, Mr. Farwell could have probably won you for as little as seventy dollars. But the lottery, and the number of times they would have run it that night, would have raised thousands as word spread and men with all of twenty dollars to their name came calling. The crew didn't spend every dollar on the first round of tickets." He paused, pained to have to say it. "They couldn't."

Comfort thought she understood. "I suppose if none of them had their ticket pulled in the first round, they needed to have money for the second."

Bode nodded faintly. Just the possibility that that could have been the outcome made his stomach clench.

Comfort realized she was able to put it behind her more easily than he was. He looked as if he'd been gut-punched. She caught his eye. "You said someone was carrying out a threat. Do you have any idea who that is?"

"No. Not one."

"Do you know who was being threatened? If you're right, and I was used to make a point that threats would be carried out, then it must be very personal. It's a short list of people that would be affected by my abduction."

"I know."

"You must have considered it. You've speculated about everything else."

"I have, but I'd rather not say."

She rubbed her temple. The seeds of a headache were being sown. "That doesn't make sense."

Unmoved, Bode shrugged.

"It's not my uncles," she said. "If that's what you're thinking and don't want to say, you can put it from your mind. It's a ridiculous idea. They don't have the sort of enemies that would resort to heinous threats, and if they did, they would do whatever was necessary to keep me safe, even if that meant paying a blackmailer. When you asked them for money, did they hesitate?"

"No, there was no hesitation."

"See?"

Bode stood and went to the small drinks cabinet that Mr. Douglas always kept well stocked. He poured himself two fingers of scotch.

Comfort recognized the delaying tactic for what it was. She let him go. Even if pressuring him didn't go against her grain, responding to it went deep against his.

"They were together," Bode said.

"What?"

"Newton and Tucker. They were together when I asked for the money."

She stared at him blankly. "So?"

"What if only one of them was threatened?"

"I don't see how that's possible. They're partners. They share an office. They do almost everything together. They always have." Comfort couldn't imagine it. "Goodness, Bode, sometimes they finish each other's sentences."

He went on doggedly. "If only one of them was threatened, and didn't tell the other, he couldn't very well decline to give me the money without having to explain himself."

"You don't know them. It wouldn't matter if the threat were meant for only one or both of them; somehow it involved me, and that would have changed everything. I'm telling you, either of them would do anything to protect me."

"What if the threat wasn't believed?"

She put up her hands in surrender. "This has become ridiculous. For someone who didn't want to share his speculations, you're working very hard to convince me they're right."

"You mentioned your uncles. I didn't. And I'm not trying to convince you of anything. I'm still speculating, only this time out loud. Every possibility should be considered, even the ones that seem far-fetched. Ridiculous ideas can always be put to the side, but not entertaining them is reckless. Sometimes they're the genesis of a better idea."

Quite suddenly, Comfort found herself recalling his drawing for the iron paddle steamer. It took her a moment to realize it was what he said that had sparked that memory, one notion igniting another. How many times had he reworked those plans, scratching out or erasing the ridiculous in favor of the better idea? It was in his nature to think in that fashion. Why would he try to look for answers to this problem in any other way?

"Very well," she said at last. "My uncles aren't *always* together. Uncle Newton has a friend that he visits from time to time."

"I take it the friend is female."

"Mrs. Terry. She's not his mistress. His visits are occasional, not regular. She's a widow, a customer of the bank. She makes an appointment to see him, and sometimes they leave together. They're discreet."

"Yet you know about it."

"Discreet is not the same as secretive. Uncle Newt never tried to pretend it was anything but what it was. My uncles enjoy the company of women. I've always understood that. They're simply cautious about attaching themselves to a particular female."

"Except you."

Her smile was rueful. "Yes, you can say that. I think they could never decide what would become of me if one of them married. They've been together since the war with Mexico. If Uncle Newt married, it would have been as if he were divorcing Uncle Tuck. Who would then take responsibility for raising me?"

"I don't suppose they thought they could invite the new wife to live with you and them under one roof."

"I don't know. It was never a discussion they had within my hearing."

Bode accepted that was true, and very unlike his mother and father, who'd had candid discussions at operatic levels that could not be ignored. When it came to their marriage and his father's proclivity for stepping outside of it, Alexandra and Branford were neither discreet nor secretive for the benefit of their children.

"What about Tucker Jones?"

"There's no woman friend now. He is even more wary of attachment than Newt. I think he favors a paid arrangement." She added quickly, "Not anywhere in the Barbary Coast. There's a house on Pine Street west of Powell that—"

Bode nodded, interrupting. "Maggie Drummond's establishment."

Comfort stamped down hard on the irritation she felt because Bode offered the madam's name. If her uncle could frequent the place, surely Bode had the same right. Certainly he had the same needs. "I suppose that's the one," she said. She knew it was. Margaret Drummond was a loyal customer of Jones Prescott, and had been since the days before the bank had a proper storefront. By investing at Tuck's direction, Mrs. Drummond now enjoyed considerable wealth, and while the public might know the nature of her business, they did not know the state of her finances.

Bode sipped his drink and considered what she'd told him. "It doesn't seem likely that Mrs. Terry or Maggie Drummond would be blackmailing either one of them."

"I never thought they were. I only told you about them to point out that my uncles don't do everything together. I thought it was the sort of thing you'd want to know."

"It is. Who's to say where it will lead?"

Comfort was tempted to raise her hand and tell him that she could say where it would lead: nowhere. "Bram's infinitely more likely to be blackmailed because of a woman than either of my uncles."

Bode lowered his glass slowly. "Why do you say that?"

"Because he has so little regard for them that he frequents the dives and cribs in the Coast. A man with even faint affection for women doesn't go there for his pleasure."

"You know that about him?"

"I didn't in the beginning. I was sixteen, Bode. Bram was overwhelming. I came to understand how he felt about women over time. Years. I can't tell you when I fully realized it. One day, I just knew."

"But you fell in love with him."

"That *did* happen in the beginning. There's no explaining it."

"No, I don't suppose there is." He looked down at his glass. There was a swallow of scotch left in it, just enough for him to see his dim reflection, but in the eye of his mind he was almost ten years younger, wearing Union blue and watching a woman younger still lift a thick tendril of jet hair from the nape of her neck and stab it with a comb.

Glancing up, he found Comfort watching him. Her eyes were curious, her mouth tender. "No," he said again. His throat thickened. He cleared it and finished his drink. "There never is."

Comfort turned on the bench and dropped her legs over the side. Her fingers curled around the edge of the velvet seat. "I'm not in love with him now, Bode. I thought you understood. I know I said I fell in love with Bram at the beginning, but that's because what I felt was what I imagined love felt like. I had no comparison. How was I supposed to know? And later, when I came to know Bram better, how was I to understand that what I still believed I felt for him was merely a habit, like putting on my right shoe before my left or fiddling with my hair when I'm nervous?"

She stood and pressed her hands together. "I believe what I said about Bram having little regard for women. What I didn't tell you, because frankly, it's rather lowering, is that he doesn't think of me as one."

Bode stared at her. She could have been the inspiration for any of the ebony figureheads at the bow of a Black Crowne ship. He itched to loosen the plait of hair that rested against her spine and let it fall in dark waves around her shoulders. She didn't shy away from his study, didn't hint that it troubled her.

Her bearing remained regal, fitting for a *Queen*. Her small chin was raised, her gaze direct. His eyes followed the long, slender line of her body, the concave curve of her waist, the provocative outward curving of her breasts and hips. The apple green walking dress was the only anomaly. She should have been naked.

"If what you say is true," he said at last, "my brother is an idiot."

Comfort's smile was a bit uneven. "Thank you . . . I think."

Bode set down his glass and approached her. "It's hard to believe he couldn't see what is so evidently true."

"As I said, it's rather lowering, but there you have it."

Bode slipped his palms under her elbows. "He says he's in love with you."

"He told you that?"

"Yes."

"He's lying." She held his gaze. "He's lying to you or trying to convince himself. He's never said as much to me."

"Never?"

"No. Not even when I was telling him we had to end the farce. I thought he might say it to convince me otherwise, but he never did. I suspect he knew I wouldn't believe him."

"He tried very hard to convince me," said Bode. "Maybe he did, a little. I said some things to him that I probably should have kept to myself."

Comfort didn't ask him what they were. "Don't all brothers do that?"

"Probably. Cain and Abel come to mind."

"Bode."

He smiled crookedly. "All right. That was perhaps too dramatic of an example." Because the line of Comfort's mouth was still set in a scold, Bode felt obliged to kiss it. His hands went to the small of her back and pulled her up so she was pressed to his chest. Her fingertips fluttered against the sleeves of his jacket before they settled on his arms. She fit him as neatly as a glove.

Their mouths met and clung. The kiss that he'd meant to be a period on their conversation became sweetly languorous. Neither of them felt any urgency to end it quickly or alter the tempo to make it something other than what it was.

They drew back simultaneously but only so far as their mouths were concerned. Their bodies remained flush. Her dark eyes were searching; his were grave.

"What is it?" she asked.

He shook his head. He couldn't tell her yet. He couldn't anticipate her reaction, and he needed to have more certainty than he did now. She wasn't a plan that he could revise and redesign. He had one chance to make it right. "I was wondering if you'd like to take a turn with me on deck."

Comfort didn't believe he had been wondering that at all, but she didn't challenge him. "I'd like that," she said and slipped her arm in his.

Alexandra removed her hat and handed it to Hitchens. "See that Madsen gets it. I'll be with Bram."

"Of course." He held out his arm and she draped her mantle over it. "I'll make sure she gets both."

Alexandra was already moving across the entry hall to the stairs and gave the butler only an absent nod. It wasn't until she reached the newel post that she paused and turned to look back at him. "Hitchens?"

"Yes, Mrs. DeLong?"

"Have you seen Travers today?"

"I haven't, ma'am. I thought you might have sent him out on an errand."

"Me? Why would I do that?"

Every crease in the butler's brow deepened. "I couldn't say why, but I spoke to Master Bram just an hour ago and asked him if he knew where Travers was. He said he didn't. He indicated that you would know."

"Did he? Thank you, Hitchens. Have tea sent up." She turned away and began mounting the stairs.

Bram had copies of the *San Francisco Call* and the *Chronicle* strewn about his bed. Some pages lay crumpled on the floor, evidence that they could not hold his interest or were no longer of any use to him. Alexandra curled her lip disapprovingly as she eyed the state of his room.

She shut the door firmly with the express intent of making

him look up from behind the paper he was holding. When he didn't, she crossed to the bed and rattled the pages between her fingertips.

Bram set the paper on his lap, but he only glanced at her before looking down again. "Yes, Mother?"

She cupped his chin and jerked it up. "Show me," she said. "I want to see your eyes."

The effects of laudanum softened the features he meant to set defiantly. "Happy?"

Alexandra snatched her hand away, but she did not back up. Bram's pupils were dilated so wide she could barely make out the pale blue irises. His expression was as vague and unfocused as his tongue was sharp. She glanced at the nightstand. Except for the oil lamp and a book he'd never opened, it was empty. "Where is it?"

"You're referring to . . . ?"

His insolence set her teeth on edge. "The laudanum, Abraham. Where is it?"

"Abraham? You *are* out of sorts, aren't you?"

"It's fair to warn you that I've already had a trying day. I would consider it a favor for you not to try my patience further."

"Well, since I'd be doing you a favor . . ." He shrugged. "Please, Mother, won't you sit down?"

"Tell me where the laudanum is, Bram. Have you finished the last of it? Is that why Travers isn't here?"

He sighed and pressed his fingers to either side of his head at his temples. Why was the laudanum effective against every pain but the one she caused between his ears? "There's none of the laudanum left that Dr. Harrison gave me. I used the last of it an hour ago." He had three small brown bottles tucked between his splints and the cloth bindings, but they weren't from the doctor. This morning, when Travers still didn't return, he sent the man Hitchens directed as his valet's replacement into Chinatown to make the purchase. To his way of thinking, Travers's continued absence was going to work in his favor. The new man—and he couldn't remember his name—had already proved he was more accommodating than Bode's spy had ever been.

"I'm finished with it, Mother," he said. "Unless you'd return the favor I've done for you and purchase some for me yourself."

Alexandra arched an eyebrow at him and let that suffice as her answer. She kicked aside some of the papers littering the carpet and made an elegant sweep of her gown before she sat. "Where is Travers?"

"I don't know. Did you ask Hitchens?"

"I did. He seemed to think I would know. Apparently you gave him that impression."

"I can't account for what he thinks he heard." He disregarded her quelling look. "I don't know where Travers is, Mother. I haven't see him since he tucked me in."

She regarded him narrowly for a long moment before she sighed. "Have you read the story?" she asked, waving at the papers all around him.

"What story is that?"

"The one about the attack on a carriage by the Rangers. It happened yesterday afternoon."

"I read that. It was more of an incidental account, not the usual denunciation against the Rangers they typically print. Why do you ask?"

"None of the papers reported the names of the victims, but it was all anyone could speak of at Clara Rapp's luncheon. I was there to assist with the church charity work, remember?"

He didn't, but he nodded anyway.

"The carriage belonged to Tucker Jones and Newton Prescott. Miss Kennedy, the same Miss Kennedy who is your fiancée, was with them."

Bram grabbed at the papers, looking for the story. He needed to demonstrate that much interest to his mother even though he could have recited the articles in the *Call* and the *Chronicle* almost verbatim. He found one of the pages partially tucked under the leg that wasn't injured. He smoothed it over his lap as best he could and pretended to read it. "How do your lady friends know who it was if no names are mentioned?"

"There were witnesses. It must have been horrible. The paper doesn't say so, but Clara says she heard that Miss Kennedy was taken by the Rangers."

"What?" Bram sat up straighter. He forced himself to focus.

Alexandra would expect that. "What do you mean she was taken?"

"Just that. Abducted. By the Rangers, Bram. The Rangers. The same men, no doubt, that attacked your brother."

"What makes you say that? Bode said he was felled by barrels and crates at the warehouse."

"You know that was a story for the benefit of our guests. And me. He will never convince me it wasn't the Rangers."

Bram didn't care about that. "What about Comfort? Has she been found?"

"I can't say. I was told that none of them were at the bank today. That could mean anything. They might all be safe at home, resting. I don't think I would have the fortitude to leave this house so quickly if something like that happened to me. Your brother didn't have the same sense to stay away after he was assaulted."

Bram wanted to ask a question that had nothing to do with Bode, but tea arrived and it was several minutes before he was able to prompt his mother to continue.

"Everyone at the luncheon expected me to be upset, and I was, but not as much as I might have been if Miss Kennedy had not recently been so inconveniently obstinate."

Bram blinked. It was a harsh view, even for Alexandra. "No matter how inconvenient she's been of late, she didn't deserve what happened."

"Of course she didn't. Did I make it seem as though I thought so? I don't believe that at all." She added another lump of sugar to her tea and sipped. "I told you it's been a trying day. I sent my card around to their home, inquiring after their health, but there's been no reply. Really, I don't know if I can trust what I heard this afternoon. There were so many versions. Different details about everything. I want to believe that it's all been exaggerated."

"What did they say about Newton and Tucker?"

"Someone said they were knocked to the ground and one of them—Newton, I believe I was told—was run over by the carriage."

Bram sagged back against the headboard.

"It's awful," Alexandra said. "Terrible."

He thought she sounded sincere, but sometimes it was difficult to tell. "Have you spoken to Bode? He's bound to know more than the women at your luncheon."

"I certainly made the attempt. He is as trying in his own way as you are. I believe he's avoiding me. I had the driver take me to the office for the express purpose of speaking to him. I could not escape the feeling that Mr. Farwell was putting me off."

"Putting *you* off?" He lifted his eyebrows, astonished.

"That was my reaction. Officious little man. Bode should show him the door."

"Why didn't you?"

"Because I allow your brother to make those decisions. That is our arrangement, and if I overstep, he will leave."

Bram saw Alexandra's fingertips whiten where they held the teacup. He knew she disliked the deal Bode struck with her, but the flash of fear he saw in her eyes surprised him. He'd never considered that she might be afraid. "Bode was probably with the harbormaster or touring one of the ships."

"If that were the case, Farwell could have sent one of the other clerks after him, or gone himself. I don't think he was on the wharf."

"Well, what did John say?"

"He said Bode left clear instructions that he wasn't to be disturbed. By *anyone*. He added the last to make certain I wouldn't mistake the intent. As if I were just anyone." Her hand had a small tremor in it that made the teacup rattle in its saucer.

Bram stretched his arm as far as he was able and very gently steadied the saucer. "Perhaps you should hold some righteous anger in reserve. John doesn't act on his own. Those were Bode's orders."

Alexandra waved Bram back and set her tea down. "I have no shortage of anger."

"Did you go to his apartment?"

"I can't manage those outrageous steps in a gown. They're quite intentional on his part, and he doesn't mind that I know it. I stood at the bottom and called to him, but if he was there, he refused to answer."

"Perhaps tomorrow."

"You're not suggesting that I go back?"

"No. I believe he'll come here when Farwell tells him you stopped by. If he were in his apartments, Mother, he would have come down to see you. You can't seriously believe otherwise. He must have been out, probably with investors. He's always been guarded in business."

Bram saw that she was calmed, at least for now. It was interesting to him that she would leave his room in a less agitated state than she'd entered, while he would lie there as inert as a sponge, soaking up every one of her anxieties and making each his own.

Bode and Comfort ate dinner with Mr. Douglas in his cabin. Comfort was aware that the *Demeter Queen*'s cook wanted to impress her, and she was flattered and grateful for his effort. The halibut was baked to perfect flakiness in a tomato sauce with onion, cloves, and sugar. It was served with small white potatoes and green beans with almond slivers. Mr. Douglas opened a bottle of white wine to drink with their meal. Afterward, there was angel cake and strawberries.

"May I meet Mr. Henry?" she asked when she'd finished forking the last crumb of angel cake into her mouth. "He wasn't on deck this afternoon. I was in awe of his biscuits then. Now I am seriously thinking of asking him if he'd take a position in a landlubber's kitchen."

Mr. Douglas chuckled. "If I weren't certain that he'd turn you down, I'd lock him in the galley, but give me a moment, and I'll arrange that introduction." He excused himself from the table and stepped into the passageway.

Bode took advantage of his absence to reach across the table and take Comfort's hand. He brushed his thumb over her knuckles. "You should know now that there won't be anything like this on the *Artemis Queen*."

"There won't? But she's your flagship."

"She's also nearing the end of a journey already delayed. Her stores will be low, and Mr. Gilroy, her chief cook, will have used most everything in his galley by the time we board her. There won't be tomatoes, potatoes, or green beans. We'll have what's been smoked and pickled and fermented. And you shouldn't judge Mr. Gilroy's culinary skills by what appears on your table once we're there."

"I don't suppose we could take some provisions from this ship?" she asked, teasing more than hopeful.

"We could, but we won't."

It was the answer she expected to hear. During their turn on deck, she'd witnessed his attention to every detail of the ship and how the crew worked her. She imagined that he had the paddle steamer laid out in his mind, and as they walked, he was making a small change here, a larger one there. She saw the *Demeter Queen* through his eyes and began to understand what drove him to seize on her strength and make something stronger, to capture her speed, and to build something that would outrun the wind. She didn't mind that her presence at his side was incidental; she appreciated his concentration to a single undertaking. There would come a time when they were alone again, and she would be the undertaking that focused all of his concentration. The thought of it made her shiver then and now.

Comfort's gaze dropped from Bode's sly, knowing one to where his thumb passed back and forth across her hand. The gesture was more intimate than she could have imagined. She regretted that Mr. Douglas would return at any moment.

Bode removed his hand just before the shipmaster stepped into the cabin. Comfort slid hers to her lap and positioned it in the folds of her gown as carefully as a jeweler setting a ruby in a velvet bed.

The man who followed Mr. Douglas into the room filled the doorway first. He had to duck his head to enter, and Comfort supposed that had he been anything but clean-shaven, he would have had to dip his head even farther. This giant's skin fairly radiated a blue-black sheen that, by contrast, made the whites of his eyes glow as though lighted from within. For all the strength inherent in his large hands and muscular forearms, he was clearly nervous about making her acquaintance. He shifted his weight from foot to foot and couldn't quite meet her eye.

Comfort knew she was at her best when she could make other people feel at ease. It was when she became the very essence of her name.

"It's a pleasure to meet you, Mr. Henry. I am grateful you would remove yourself from your duties to allow me to thank you."

His head bobbed once. "Welcome, Missa DeLong. You very welcome."

Comfort was so intrigued by the soft lilt of an accent that what he said to her didn't immediately register. It was catching the quick exchange of glances between Mr. Douglas and Bode that directed her attention to what was said. "Miss Kennedy," she corrected him.

"Ah, yes. Miss Kennedy," he said, carefully pronouncing her name. "Not Missa DeLong. Forgot."

She smiled, but she felt herself flushing. She didn't dare look away from him. "It's all right," she said graciously. "May I ask where you're from, Mr. Henry? Your accent . . . it's quite musical, but I can't make it out."

"Tobago."

"Oh. You are the first person I've ever met from there. And you're here now. I'm sure there's a story."

"Plenty story, Missa DeLong." He heard what he said this time and quickly corrected himself. "Sorry. Miss Kennedy. Story is Mista DeLong make me free. Now I cook for him. Now he give me money." He smiled broadly, without guile. "Maybe he give me more because I please his missa so well."

Chuckling, Bode waved him off. "Go on. I don't know why I thought you wouldn't seize the opportunity to ask for money. You, Mr. Henry, are as dependable as the tides."

Mr. Henry smiled broadly, revealing a gold tooth where his right canine used to be. He nodded at everyone just once before he backed out of the room and closed the door.

Mr. Douglas held up a second bottle of wine and cocked an eyebrow at Bode. When Bode nodded, he opened it and poured some in each glass.

Comfort raised her glass but didn't drink. She rolled the stem between her fingers and watched Bode across the table. "What did Mr. Henry mean when he said you made him free?"

"I tell him all the time that God made him free, but he's as persistent along that course as he is in asking for more money."

Comfort had no intention of accepting that answer, but before she could prompt Bode, Mr. Douglas helped her out.

"Mr. Henry was a house slave on a Georgia plantation. The best I've been able to get from him is that he was tricked into leaving Tobago for work and good wages in Philadelphia. Or New York. He's never been clear about where he was supposed to have been going. The men who misled him and a good number of his friends posed as missionaries. They all ended up somewhere in Georgia, probably first coming ashore near Savannah. Mr. DeLong encountered our Mr. Henry during Sherman's march."

Comfort had politely inclined her head to Mr. Douglas while he spoke, but now her attention returned to Bode. She wasn't used to seeing him looking awkward in his own skin. He was self-conscious and mildly embarrassed, and he clearly wished himself elsewhere. She was charmed.

"What's the rest, Bode?"

He took a swallow of wine. "We made overnight headquarters in a plantation house that the owners fled in advance of our arrival. The slaves were still there. There was no place for them to go. Some were glad to see us. Most were afraid. The ones that didn't hide helped us. Mr. Henry prepared dinner for the general and his officers that evening, and it fell to me to send the general's compliments to the cook."

He shrugged lightly, a mostly helpless gesture, and shook his head. "I still don't know what I said to encourage it, but Mr. Henry attached himself to me. When we left the next morning, he came along. The other officers thought it was amusing until I tried to persuade Mr. Henry to stop following, then they were nearly apoplectic that I was going to send away the best cook they'd ever had. Someone, not me, got him to enlist. He was an Army cook until Lee's surrender, and when I mustered out, he followed me home. I'm not sure he ever had an official discharge, but then not many did at the end."

Comfort sipped her wine and regarded him past the crystal curve of her glass. There was still something left unexplained. Bode said that Mr. Henry followed him home, but home, for however briefly, would have been the mansion on Nob Hill.

"How is it that he's working on the *Demeter Queen* and not in your mother's kitchen?"

Bode's smile was tight and wry. "It seems Alexandra's abolitionist views hinge on theory, not practice. Not so dissimilar from Leland Stanford's hypocrisy of publicly denouncing the Chinese immigration when he was governor while employing them by the hundreds to build the Central Pacific. He paid them wages that made them virtual slaves. My mother and Stanford are merely different sides of the same coin."

Comfort wished Mr. Douglas were not in the room. She would have asked Bode if his mother's intolerance for Mr. Henry contributed to Bode's reasons for not living on Nob Hill.

Nathan Douglas stroked his beard. "Mr. Henry was allowed to choose the ship he wanted to work on. One of my men had just finished polishing the figurehead. Mr. Henry said she brought his mother to mind. That's how we got him."

Bode and Mr. Douglas finished the second bottle of wine while Comfort allowed her glass to be refilled just once. She didn't drink most of it, but she wasn't ready to excuse herself from the conversation. Even when it turned to maritime matters, she hardly cared that she didn't understand most of it. She was reminded of all the times she sat between Newton and Tucker while they discussed capital, trusts, debt, interest, and amortization. As a child, that conversation quite literally had taken place over her head. When she listened to Bode and Mr. Douglas discussing propeller pitch, bilge pumps, and trailing astern a taffrail log, it was still true, at least in the figurative sense.

It was only when she saw Mr. Douglas eye his pipe and tobacco tin with something akin to longing that she pleaded exhaustion and asked to be excused. Bode would have accompanied her back to the stateroom, but she insisted that he stay. It wasn't entirely selfless on her part. She wanted to be by herself while she prepared for bed, and she needed time alone to weigh the benefit to cost ratio of him joining her.

Comfort was sitting much as she had been earlier when Bode came upon her, wedged in one corner of the window bench with her legs extended in front of her. This time, however, she wore a white cotton shift and sat in a pool of light from an oil lamp while she read. The book lay open in her lap, and she appeared to be making good progress, because it looked as if a quarter of the pages had already been turned.

She looked up when he didn't move away from the door once he was inside. He was leaning against it, his hands behind him, not bothered in the least that she caught him out staring. Resisting the urge to fiddle with her hair, she wrinkled her nose at him instead.

"You brought the captain's pipe smoke with you," she said.

"I'm afraid I did. There's no way to avoid it short of leaving, and I don't mind it. My father smoked fat Cuban cigars. Those, I minded."

"It's all right. It's rather pleasant, a little sweet. I couldn't have stayed in the room, though. I'm still finding my sea legs. I hope my departure was not too abrupt and obvious."

"No. Not at all." He pushed away from the door, removed his jacket, and slung it over a chair. "You haven't mentioned sea legs before. Are you feeling well? Some people take days to accustom themselves to the rolling."

"It comes and goes. Mostly it passes quickly."

"If you can read, then it passes very quickly. There are passengers who would throw themselves against one of the rails just thinking about it."

"Mm." She was on the point of raising a question, but he started for the washroom and she let it go. He seemed remarkably steady on his feet, so she supposed there hadn't been a third bottle of wine uncorked in her absence. That was good; she wanted him to have a clear head.

When Bode emerged, his hair was damp and spiky. He'd removed his vest, collar, and bib. The shirt was open at the throat, and a towel lay around his neck. He held an end in each hand, tugging first one way and then the other.

"I thought you might be asleep by the time I returned." He'd been hoping, actually. He was careful not to glance in the direction of the bed. "I suppose we should talk."

"It's why I'm still awake."

"Would you like to go first or shall I?"

"I will. I doubt that anything I'm going to say will surprise you." She closed the book over her finger. "I don't think we should share the stateroom any longer. I'm willing to move to another cabin tonight if you like. I'll pack my trunk again in the morning. It will be no trouble."

"You can have the bed," Bode said. "I'll sleep on the floor."

She hadn't expected him to acquiesce quite so easily, and she recognized her own contrariness when she was hurt by it. Shaking her head, she pressed on. "No, that's not good enough. You probably think I don't trust you, but I don't trust myself. I'm not confident that you're far enough away if you're still in this room. One of us needs to be somewhere else, and since I've already proven that I can attach myself to you like a Barbary Coast whore to a sailor with five dollars in his pocket, I think it should be me."

It was rare, but not unheard of, for Bode to lose his footing. There had been the stumble during the fight with the Rangers, and later that same evening Comfort had tangled his feet during their waltz. Those recent examples came to mind quickly. There were other occasions, he was certain of it, but none that he could recall when he had been away from shore. He was reliably sure-footed here, always oriented to the wind, his position, and the motion of the ship.

Except now. Right now he felt as if his sea legs were failing. In his mind, he was lurching for the table. In reality, he only pivoted forty-five degrees and hitched a hip on it.

"I think you'd better explain that last remark," he said. He was clutching each end of the towel a little more tightly than before, but his voice carried none of that tension.

"You were very clear that I wouldn't allow you to leave me alone." She put out a hand, staving him off when he would have interrupted. "I know that's not what you said, but it's what I heard. And really, comparing me to a limpet and you to a rock flatters you rather more than it does me. I told myself I wouldn't dwell on it, but I am doing so. So there you have it. I'd like you to arrange for me to be able to sleep somewhere else."

Bode nodded slowly. He stopped working the towel back and forth and crossed his arms over his chest instead. "This is really about what Mr. Henry said, isn't it? He called you Mrs. DeLong."

"That's part of it, but so is the other. I behave differently when I'm around you. Out of character and contrary to the way my uncles raised me. They would be disappointed in me, but no more than I am disappointed in myself." She set the book aside. "Perhaps if I *were* Mrs. DeLong . . ." She looked away, embarrassed that she'd said it aloud. It was difficult not to think about it since meeting Mr. Henry.

"But you are," Bode said. "It's why I thought we should talk. Mr. Douglas performed the ceremony as soon as we reached open water."

Chapter Twelve

Comfort was quiet for so long that Bode wasn't certain she meant to speak at all. When she finally did, he wished the quiet had lasted longer.

"This changes everything," she said, preternaturally calm.

"Yes," he said. "It does."

"You'll have to leave."

"I don't understand."

"I'm not sure how I can make it clearer, but let me try again. You must find other accommodations. I'm staying here."

"I understood what you said," Bode told her. "I don't understand why."

"Then perhaps you're the one who should have been clearer." She picked up her book, riffled the pages to find her place, and pretended to read. A pretense of reading was all that was possible, because she couldn't make out a single word for the red haze clouding her vision.

"Comfort."

She ignored him.

Bode closed his eyes and rubbed the bridge of his nose with a thumb and forefinger. When he opened his eyes again, she hadn't moved. He wondered if she had breathed. Her concentration was absolute, but it wasn't on the book. She was committed to ignoring him.

He dropped his hands to his side, lightly resting them on the table. "Please look at me." She didn't, but he saw an almost imperceptible tightening of her fingers on the book and knew she heard him. He didn't ask her a second time to look at him. He went on as if she had. "Only minutes ago you started to say that if you *were* Mrs. DeLong . . . How did you mean to finish that sentence? That if you were my wife, things would be different? That you would no longer be disappointed in yourself? That sharing a bed would be right and proper?"

Bode stretched, reached for his jacket lying over the chair at the head of the table, and dragged it toward him. From an inside pocket, he pulled out a piece of paper that had been folded into thirds. "This is our marriage document. The ceremony was also recorded in the ship's log. It's a legal and binding contract between us, but I will destroy it if that's what you want. I'll remove the page from the log. I'll have the witnesses killed."

Bode let his offer lie there for a long time, and then, when he was on the verge of speaking again, he decided to let it lie a bit longer. He was rewarded for his patience. Comfort didn't so much as glance in his direction, but she did speak.

"How many witnesses?"

"The entire crew was there."

"And you'd have them all killed."

"Yes."

"Mr. Henry?"

"Yes. I might begin with Mr. Henry."

"Because he called me Missa DeLong."

"That's right."

Comfort closed the book and looked up at him. Her features were gravely set, her dark eyes only luminous when she angled her head and they reflected the light from the lamp. "It wasn't a new idea, Bode. Mr. Henry merely said it aloud. Can I assume you told everyone not to mention the ceremony?"

"Yes. This morning, I asked you what you remembered about last night. When I realized you had no recall of anything between leaving the saloon and waking up, I asked Mr. Douglas to tell the men not to say anything."

"But you planned to tell me."

It would have been hard to mistake her skepticism for anything but what it was. Bode absently turned the marriage paper over his hands. "Yes."

"When?"

"I already said that. I was going to tell you tonight."

Her eyes narrowed. "You were hoping I'd be asleep when you returned. You said as much when you came in."

Bode couldn't remember what he'd said, but he had certainly thought it. "If you'd been sleeping, I would have told you in the morning."

"Before or after I displayed my limpet-like qualities?"

"Don't say that, Comfort."

"I didn't. You did." She clutched the book hard against her midriff. Bode was eyeing her warily, but she had too much respect for books in general, and Edmond Dantès in particular, to throw it at him. "You are more like your brother than even I suspected." She saw him flinch and realized she didn't have to throw the book to hit her target. "That paper you're holding means nothing, Bode. My engagement to Bram was more real, and it was a sham. At least he had the decency to make the announcement when I was fully conscious. It didn't seem as if I had any choice except to go along, but I know that's not true. As unpalatable as it was, I *had* a choice. You didn't give me that." Her short laugh was bitter. "How many men were required to prop me up? Did I speak any vows? Did you?" She held up her left hand and examined it briefly. "There's no ring. I hadn't thought it possible for that paper to mean less than nothing, but without a ring, perhaps it does."

Bode waited. If she wanted to say more, he would let her. He owed her that. Her hurt was palpable. It came at him in cold, unrelenting waves that he didn't try to avoid. He let the silence yawn again, until finally, quietly, he said, "There's a ring."

She stared at him blankly. Color receded from her face.

"You took it off before you went to bed. It's where you left it. On the shelf above the bed, behind the lamp." He made no move to get it, and neither did she. "My offer still stands, Comfort." He held up the document in his hand. "I'll destroy it. Better yet, I'll let you destroy it. You can also remove the captain's log."

"And kill the crew? That's for me to do as well?"

"If you like."

The enormity of it all suddenly overwhelmed her. Comfort thrust the book away and turned her face to the wall. Tears welled. She dashed them with her fingertips, and when that proved inadequate to keep them from spilling over, she used the sleeve of her nightgown to swipe at her cheeks.

"Here." Bode stood just behind her and offered his handkerchief.

Comfort didn't look back. She just held up her hand and let him press the handkerchief into her palm. Her fingers crumpled it into a ball that she held against each damp eye in turn.

"I don't like crying," she said.

"I know."

"I hardly ever do." It was difficult to move words past the hard, aching lump in her throat. Swallowing only lodged it more deeply. Her voice rasped in a way that made her skin prickle. "But sometimes at night, when I dream, I do."

Even though she couldn't see him, he nodded.

Comfort took a jerky breath. "Do you have the paper?"

"Yes. Right here."

"May I see it?"

"Of course." He wasn't surprised when she still didn't turn away from the wall. She swiped at her eyes again before she tucked the handkerchief under the gathered sleeve of her nightgown. When she reached over her shoulder, he slipped the document between her fingers.

Comfort held it in both hands. Her thumbs passed back and forth over the paper while she stared at it. She felt Bode's presence at her back, but he was quiet. If he wanted her to hurry, or if he was regretting giving it to her, he gave no indication either way.

There was a fine tremor in her fingers as she carefully unfolded the document. The record of her marriage had been made in plain language and neat script.

Be it known by all peoples that on
12 July in the year of our Lord 1870, at
38°3' North and 123°45' West,
Beauregard Crowne DeLong
and Comfort Elizabeth Kennedy
were joined in matrimony by the
Master Mariner of the Black Crowne Merchant
Demeter Queen, Mr. Nathan Douglas,
and duly witnessed by her crew.

Below this announcement on the left was Mr. Douglas's copperplate signature. Under the master's name were two more signatures, one by James Jackson and the other a simple X with MR. HENRY neatly printed in parentheses beside it.

On the right side was Bode's bold scrawl, and just beneath, her own signature, written in a fine, precise hand that she could not mistake for anyone's but her own.

Comfort slowly released the breath she'd been holding. "I signed this," she said.

It wasn't a question, but it seemed to Bode that she wanted confirmation anyway. "Yes, you did."

"It doesn't look as if my hand was shaking."

"If it was, you hid it well. You took considerable care with your signature."

Now she glanced up at him over her shoulder. Her slim smile was rueful. "I don't usually. This is my practice hand. From childhood. You know, the one you use when you're learning to write, when you want every letter to be perfectly formed."

Bode took a step back from the bench as Comfort turned around. She dropped her legs over the side, awkwardly tugging on her nightgown with one hand because she held their marriage record in the other.

"I think I must have been very drunk," she said. "What do they say? Three sheets to the wind?"

"That's what they say." He tore the towel from around his neck, tossed it on the bench, and hunkered down in front of her. "I had to sling you over my shoulder to get you out of the saloon. You couldn't walk, couldn't stand. Do you remember that?"

She shook her head. He might well have been talking about someone else, but in her heart she knew he was telling the truth. "I remember Mr. Farwell smashing the window. He was going to push me out."

Bode's smile was wry. "I think he might have leaped first." He sobered. "We had a wagon waiting. Mr. Henry stowed the ladder. I stowed you. You hardly stirred on the way back to the ship. I thought I was going to have to put you over my shoulder again, but by the time we reached the *Demeter*, you told me you were able to walk. You weren't steady—I had to keep a hand under your elbow—but you managed to board the ship without falling into the drink, and once we were on deck, you stopped weaving altogether."

"How could you tell? The ship was rocking."

"I know the difference. You had your balance back. The men started arriving, and I took you down to the stateroom. You sat just where you're sitting now, and you let me wash your hands and face, and get you out of John Farwell's jacket and the—"

"And that awful shift," she said, closing her eyes a moment. "I let you take it off me."

"You're remembering?"

"No." She regarded him with sad, solemn eyes. "But I must have let you do it, because I wasn't wearing it this morning. I never thought about that before."

She was fingering the paper. He wanted to stop her and take her hand. He didn't; he was still feeling his way. "I tried to leave. I wanted to go on deck, help the men, thank them for what they'd done. Only a few of them had seen you come aboard. I wanted to let them know you were recovering."

"And I wouldn't let you leave?"

This time it was a question. "You wouldn't let me get to the door." He watched her shoulders rise and fall, but her sigh was inaudible. "I made a decision, Comfort. I suppose we can debate how much it was influenced by what I wanted and how much you were pushing me in that direction."

"Because I was clinging to you like a wet shirt."

His brief, slim smile was wry. That sounded better than what either of them had said before. He wished he'd thought of it. "Something like that. If it matters, I didn't want to leave you either."

It mattered. She pressed her lips together and willed her tears back.

Now Bode did reach for her. He put his hand over the one that was holding the evidence of their ceremony. "I *wanted* to marry you, Comfort. I saw an opportunity, and I took it."

"You took advantage."

"Yes. I told myself something different. I wanted to believe you were as aware as you seemed to be, and that what you agreed to was an act of conscience and consciousness, but I knew otherwise. Deep down, I knew. It was a carefully reasoned proposal. I told you that if I was going to stay with you, it had to be as your husband. I explained that the men hadn't rescued you just so I could win the lottery." Bode watched an uneasy smile flicker across her lips. "I said your reputation would be ruined, and Newton and Tucker would be disappointed in both of us if you didn't marry me."

"You said all of that?"

"Very quickly, but yes, all of it."

"Did you say you loved me?"

"No."

She nodded faintly. Although appreciative of his honesty, she still couldn't look at him. "It's probably better tha—"

"That's why I'm saying it now," he said, stopping her. "I love you. I should have told you last night."

The lump was back in Comfort's throat, and there was an ache behind her eyes. She remembered Bode's handkerchief was tucked under her sleeve, but she didn't want to use it. She would *not* cry. She sniffed instead. "I wouldn't remember," she said on a thread of sound.

He frowned. "What?"

Comfort fanned her free hand in front of her mouth, trying to catch her breath. "If you'd told me last night, I wouldn't remember it now. And now, I'll remember it always."

Bode had no warning, no way to prepare himself. He was

still on his haunches when Comfort launched herself off the bench and into his arms. He toppled backward and she followed. He didn't have a long way to go to the floor, but he still landed hard. He thought she might have laughed, or it might have been a hiccup, and neither of those things mattered because she was placing small, darting kisses at the corners of his mouth, his jaw, his hairline, and his temple.

He kissed her back. The salty residue of tears clung to her cheeks. He caught her face in his hands and held her still. "Look at me," he said. She did, with eyes so dark they might have been black, and so deep they might have been touching her soul. "I love you."

She bit her lip and nodded.

"Tell me you believe me."

"I believe you."

He studied her face. "All right." His fingers slipped into her hair. He undid her braid and brought her hair forward in two handfuls. He tugged. She bent her head and kissed him again. The heavy curtain of hair threw her face into shadow. He had a glimpse of her parted lips before she whispered in his ear.

His back-of-throat chuckle made her shiver and her nipples tighten. The document she'd been holding was wedged between them. He insinuated his fingers between his shirt and her shift, took the paper out of her hand, and flicked it to one side. He rolled and turned Comfort on her back, and then he began working his way down her body, starting with the hollow just below her ear.

He spent some time there, teasing her with the tip of his tongue until he heard her breathing quicken. He followed the sensitive cord in her neck to her throat. He pulled on the ribbon that closed her neckline and spread the material so he could see her collarbones. His fingers traced the line of one; his mouth followed the other. The gown slipped off her left shoulder. He attended to that sweet curve before he slid lower. His mouth dipped between her breasts.

Her breath hitched. She closed her eyes in anticipation of his mouth closing over one of her breasts. It seemed an eternity before he made his choice. She cried out softly when his mouth settled on her left breast and his thumb and forefinger rolled the right nipple.

Her movements were edgy, restless. He was plucking all the right strings. Her breasts swelled. Her belly was filled with heat. And between her legs she was moist.

He did that to her with his mouth and his hands and his whisper that was like honey over sand.

She helped him raise her nightgown so his lips could trail over her belly and his tongue could dart around her navel like a whippet. He slid even lower, pushing up her knees, opening them, and then moving between her thighs to kiss her in a most intimate, unexpected way.

His tongue flicked her clitoris. She thought she should pull away. What she did was lift her hips and make an offering of her body. She knew that she was lost, that she would let him do anything, and that the inherent contradiction was that there was nothing selfless in her giving, no sacrifice. She was taking all the pleasure for herself.

There was nothing under her fingers except the hard deck, and she desperately wanted something to hold. She grabbed her knees. Her nails made tiny crescents in her flesh. He jerked her legs so her calves lay over his shoulders and against his back. Her hands fell away and found his head. Her fingers made runnels in his hair. It was still faintly damp. The texture was silky, cool to the touch.

She would have thrown her head back, but there was no give to the floor. It maddened her, this restriction, and it excited her as well. There was only the steady climb, no retreating. Her heels beat a soft tattoo against his back, and she flung her arms sideways. Heat uncoiled in her belly, her womb contracted, and a pink flush spread over her skin from her breasts all the way to her hairline.

"Bode!" She was seized by pleasure so intense that her breath caught, and what she thought she shouted was in reality only a constricted gasp.

She lay very still and let him be responsible for the parts of her that she could no longer move. He eased out from under her legs, closed her knees gently, and reluctantly reintroduced the notion of modesty by tugging on the hem of her nightgown until it flirted with her thighs. He closed the gap in her neckline, thought better of it, and folded it back so her throat and the twin points of her collarbones were visible. Her arms were still flung outward at three and nine o'clock and looked as if they might be boneless. He pulled them in and folded them one at a time over her chest, then sat up on his knees and examined his handiwork.

"I'm not dead," she said.

Bode wasn't convinced. "Perhaps if you opened your eyes."

She raised her eyelids a fraction and looked at him from under her lashes. "What did you do to me?"

"It has a name. Do you want to know?"

"I know what it's called. I want to know what you did to me."

He chuckled. "Will you be all right?"

"Mm-hmm."

Bode got to his feet, grabbed the towel from where he'd tossed it on the bench, and disappeared into the washroom. When he came out, he was shirtless but wearing a pair of loosely tied silkaline drawers that rode low on his hips. Comfort was exactly as he'd left her. He stood over her, shaking his head. For a moment, just before her mouth tilted up at the corners like a cat that'd tasted the cream, he thought she might have been sleeping. He bent and extended his hand. "C'mon. Up."

Her eyelids fluttered. She looked at him and then at his hand. She raised her arm in a graceful arc and showed him the backs of her fingers as though she meant him to carry them to his lips. He gripped her wrist and pulled her to her feet in one fluid motion. Before she recovered from her surprise, he lowered his shoulder to her waist and slung her over it.

"Bode! What are you—" She stopped because it was obvious he was carrying her to the bed. When they reached it, she begged, "Wait! Wait, just a moment! Turn around. There's something I—no, the other way—I want to get the—" She lifted her head and shoulders as best she could and reached for the shelf above the bed. She rested the fingertips of one hand on the ledge and nudged the oil lamp with her other hand. The ring was exactly where he said it would be.

She slipped it on. "All right," she told him. "I'm ready."

Bode turned and flipped her head over bucket onto the bed.

Before she had time to catch her breath or admire the ring, he was bearing down on her. He removed the ring as a temptation by taking her wrists in one hand and holding them above her head. Accepting the invitation of her parted lips, he kissed her deeply and for a very long time.

Comfort sucked in a deep breath as he drew back. She was aware that the hem of her nightgown was no longer a modest covering and the gap in the neckline was now wide enough to reveal a breast. More important than either of these things was the rigid stem of heat pressing against her belly.

Bode let go of her hands and knelt between her thighs. He lifted her hips, angled his, and pushed himself into her. It wasn't the force of his entry, but the relative novelty of it, that made her go still. She needed a moment, just a moment to . . . yes, there. Her hips twitched. Her vagina contracted around his cock. She smiled when that small intimacy caused him to close his eyes. She made herself relax everywhere but there. Her hands lifted to his shoulders and rested. She raised her legs and tucked them behind his thighs.

"All right," she whispered. "I'm ready."

Bode wanted to believe that mattered to him, but he wouldn't have wagered on it. She was tight and wet and squeezing him with tiny contractions that made him want to grind his hips against her. He eased back and then plunged. And he did it again. He felt her legs tighten and her fingertips press harder against his shoulders. The tips of her nails scraped his skin.

He was in her so completely that he touched her womb. Every stroke was deliberate; every stroke was deep. Each time he thought it would be enough, but until he hovered on the brink, it never was. His pulse quickened. The rhythm of his thrusts changed to rapid and shallow, except for the last. Every contraction was a shiver of intense pleasure. His skin could barely contain it. He buried his face in her neck as he spilled his seed.

Groaning, Bode pushed away and rolled onto his back. He started to reach for his drawers, but Comfort brushed aside his hand and dealt with his modesty in much the same manner that he'd dealt with hers. That left him to put a forearm over his eyes and wait for his heartbeat to slow.

Comfort turned on her side and propped herself on an elbow. She looked down the length of him to his bare feet. They were long and narrow, finely boned, with perfectly articulated toes and broad nails. "Goodness, but you have pretty feet."

Grunting softly, he curled his toes as if he were making fists.

"That's why you didn't want to take off your shoes, isn't it? The afternoon I visited you and walked on your back, I asked you to take off your shoes and you wouldn't. I thought you were being fastidious or difficult, but you didn't want me to see your feet." She imagined that behind his arm he was rolling his eyes. "I suppose I'm not the first woman to remark how elegant they are."

Bode cleared his throat uncomfortably.

"You're right," she said. "I don't want to know." She fell quiet, smiling to herself as she placed her hand, the one with the platinum band, on Bode's chest.

"You're looking at the ring, aren't you?" Bode said.

She glanced at him. He hadn't lifted the arm over his eyes even a fraction of an inch. "I am. How did you know?"

"You're wiggling your fingers."

Laughing softly, she let them lie still. "Tell me about our wedding. Where did Mr. Douglas perform the ceremony?"

"On the forward deck. More or less in the same place where you met the crew this afternoon."

She wished she could say it had been familiar to her, but when she'd stood between Bode and Mr. Douglas as each member of the crew filed past, she had no sense that she'd stood there before. "What did we say to each other?"

"Very little except for the exchange of 'I do.' It wasn't a religious ceremony."

"Oh. Did I sound sure of myself?"

Now he lifted his arm a fraction and looked at her askance. "Yes."

"Good," she said, satisfied.

Bode dropped his arm back into place. "In the event you're wondering, I was equally confident."

"I wasn't wondering. You must have been; you had the ring."

That made him smile. "I did."

At the risk of being teased, she stole an admiring glance at it again. The slim, polished platinum band was inlaid with sapphire and diamond chips. No matter how she turned her hand, the effect was sparkling. "How long have you had it?"

"It belonged to my father's mother. It passed directly to me when she died. That was eight years ago." Bode felt the steady drum of her fingertips on his chest. He didn't have to raise his arm to know that her mouth would be compressed or that she'd be giving him an arch look. "Oh, you meant how long have I been carrying it around with me." He chuckled when she emphasized that point by lightly stabbing him several times with her index finger. He caught her with his free hand and threaded his fingers through hers. That quieted her, and then the only drumbeat was his heart.

"I put it in my pocket a few days ago after I spoke to Bram."

"You did?"

He nodded. "I'd planned to talk to Newt and Tuck after our appointment, show them the ring, and ask if they thought you'd like it."

"But you knew I was going to be with them. How would you have arranged a private talk?"

"I was relying on Mr. Farwell to create a distraction that would require your attention for as long as I needed to speak to your uncles."

Comfort recalled the clerk's enthusiastic bouncing and dramatic moaning. "I don't think your trust would have been misplaced," she said dryly.

Bode finally removed his forearm. Comfort's face hovered nearby. He met her eyes and returned her wry smile. "John excels at diversion, particularly when it comes to confusion in the harbor. He can tie up commerce for half a dozen vessels while Black Crowne ships are slipping in and out of their berths."

"Mm. Why do I think you're the real architect of that chaos?"

"Careful. You're confusing me with my brother."

"I'm not. Bram creates chaos because he's thoughtless. If it happens around you, it's because it's been planned."

"It's flattering that you think so, but no one—"

Comfort stopped him by placing a finger against his lips.

"I've seen you attend to detail yet never lose sight of the whole. It's been my experience that people are generally good at one or the other, but you are able to seize both at once. It's impressive, and I want you to allow me to be impressed." She withdrew her hand and laid it once more on his chest. "I saw your gift in your design for that remarkable ship. You know the ship is the reason my uncles arranged the meeting, don't you?"

He was still absorbing what she'd said and didn't respond immediately. He'd been taken to task before, but not for a long time, and never by anyone trying to compliment him. *I want you to allow me to be impressed.* God, he thought, but he needed her.

"I suspected," he said at last, "but they weren't clear. I imagine they didn't want word to get out. I know their reputation for secrecy. I guessed that you'd told them more about the ship than I did."

"Was I wrong to do that? They were very interested."

"I didn't ask you not to say anything. I don't know what I would have shown them. I wasn't ready, but I also didn't want to turn down the opportunity to talk to them. The ship's changed a great deal since you saw it."

"You mentioned that when you came to my office."

"It's not a paddle steamer any longer," he said. "That's how much it's changed."

"What is it?"

"It still has an iron hull, and the steam propulsion plants, but I eliminated the paddle wheels in favor of a three-bladed brass propeller. I'm fiddling with the shape and pitch of the blades. A propeller, especially if I can refine the design of the blades just right, will work more efficiently than paddles. It will make a ship easier to handle in rough seas, and it's less exposed in collisions."

"Will the ship have sails?"

"For now, yes. No master would be willing to take out a merchant ship without sails to rely on. The crew, too, is fearful the mechanics of the steam plant will fail them. When nature denies them a good wind or calm seas, they might curse the heavens, but they accept it. When a flywheel fails to turn or a boiler ruptures, they want to find the inventor and flay him alive."

"Then, yes, it should definitely have sails."

"Don't want to see me flayed?" When she shook her head, he showed her his crooked grin. "Thank you for that."

"Will you be looking for financing?"

"Yes."

"Then you'll still talk to Newt and Tucker?"

"Perhaps. There are complications. I didn't marry you to get access to Jones Prescott money."

Comfort didn't miss the thread of tension in his voice when he said the last, and she wondered at it. "I never thought you did. Not once. I can't say the same about the other men who wanted to marry me. Jackson McCain, for instance. He remarked on the value of almost everything he touched. Teddy Dobbins? He proposed something more like a merger than a marriage."

"And the others?"

"I just didn't like them very much." She raised her knee and rested it on his thigh. She rubbed her foot against his leg. "Did you ever propose to anyone else?"

"No."

"Bram told me once that you would never marry. He said you were already wedded to Black Crowne, that you're driven to make money."

"Did he? That's an interesting perspective, coming from him."

Comfort was uncertain what that meant, but Bode didn't seem to be inclined to explain. "I think he misunderstood what he saw. You're passionate about what you do. That design, for instance, for the propeller. It's as much a work of art as a feat of engineering."

Bode stroked her arm. "Thank you," he said. He turned his head and touched his lips to her brow. "But there's truth in what Bram said as well. Not about being wedded to Black Crowne, but about making money. The business doesn't survive without it."

"I know. I've worked alongside Newt and Tuck almost all of my life. I have more respect for what it takes to make money than Bram does." She waited to see if Bode would say something, but he remained oddly quiet. "Why did you move out,

Bode? I thought about it again this evening when I heard Mr. Henry's story."

"Mm. Tolerance is not one of Alexandra's virtues." He stared at the ceiling and felt his chest swell with his indrawn breath. He let it out slowly. "I think you know that, though. I remember telling you that Suey Tsin could have waited for you in Alexandra's kitchen while you visited. You knew better."

"Your mother's not reluctant to express her opinion," she said carefully. "On the matter of the Chinese, she's hardly alone."

"Yes, well, I find that Alexandra's opinions occupy too many chairs at the dinner table and too many rooms of the house. Living under her roof is tantamount to living under her thumb. There's no peace." He found her hand again and held it. "No comfort."

Bode caught her glance when she lifted her head, and without a word passing between them, he let her know he meant it in every sense. When she returned her head to his shoulder, the pressure in his chest eased.

"Bode?"

"Hmm?" She had been quiet so long he thought she'd begun to drift off.

"I need to know if you still think Newt or Tuck had something to do with my abduction."

Bode frowned. "I thought we agreed to consider every possibility."

"I just thought by now that you'd have ruled each of them out."

"By now? We only discussed it this afternoon."

"It's neither one of them, Bode."

"It probably isn't."

There was nothing reassuring about his answer, but she was certain she didn't want him to placate her with telling her what she wanted to hear. She turned away abruptly and sat up. She felt Bode's fingers graze the small of her back. She rose from the bed anyway.

Their marriage document was lying on the floor where Bode had flung it earlier. She picked it up and laid it on the table on her way to the washroom. She spent a few minutes there composing herself and attending to her needs. When she emerged, Bode was sitting on the edge of the bed waiting to change places with her.

While he was in the washroom, she extinguished the lamp at the bench where she'd been reading and turned back the one on the shelf above the bed. She pulled back the quilt and sheet and crawled into bed, and when he joined her, she didn't edge toward him.

"You're angry." He didn't try to touch her.

"I'm out of sorts."

The distinction seemed important to her, but it was lost on him. Short of telling her that he was no longer entertaining any suspicions about either Tuck or Newt, he didn't know if there was anything he could do. He lightly punched the pillow under his head until it conformed to the shape he wanted. He rested his head on it and stared at the shoulder and rigid back that she presented to him.

"I'm sorry," he said, because it seemed as if he should. It wasn't a lie, and it wasn't meant to placate her. He was sorry that he couldn't tell her what she wanted to hear, sorry that he hadn't kept the inner workings of his mind to himself. Just like the plans for his propeller ship, they weren't ready to be shared with others.

"I'll be fine, Bode. I merely need time."

"Do you need it over there?"

A trace of a smile touched her lips. He made it sound as if she were on the other side of the room when the reality was that less than a foot separated them. She understood that they were each feeling their way. If she wanted his honesty, then perhaps she needed to be less prickly when she got it. Still, her reaction shouldn't dictate what he decided to share with her. They'd never be able to sustain a marriage with so many eggshells lying at their feet.

Comfort didn't turn over, but she did inch backward. That small overture brought him closer, and they closed the gap. He made a cradle for her bottom and supported the backs of her thighs with his. His arm slipped around her waist, and she laid hers over it. She felt his breath stir her hair. His lips lightly touched her head. Her shoulder lost its inflexible curve, and she yielded her back to him. Her heart settled into its natural rhythm, and she closed her eyes.

Comfort.

In moments, they were both asleep.

She couldn't make herself small enough. That's why she squeezed her eyes shut. She could be smaller then. She might even disappear altogether. She bit down on her lower lip hard enough to taste blood. The pain didn't bother her. She barely noticed it. The taste of her own blood is what kept her alert. She needed to be alert. Men were coming closer. Above all the other voices in her head, she could still make out theirs.

"There's something over here. Under these rocks. See the way they're arranged? It ain't natural."

"Leave it be."

"Could be they hid something before the fightin' started."

The rocks shifted over her head. Sunlight touched her face. She didn't open her eyes.

"Christ. It's a kid. Goddamn it, I can't do another kid."

"You got to. Someone's got to. I figure I'm up two or three on you. Maybe four if you count that woman and the baby like they was separate."

"Ain't you got sense enough not to remind me? You wanna see me puke? This ain't what I signed on for."

Comfort stirred. It seemed that she would break the surface to wakefulness, but she only skimmed it. She dove deep again.

She gave a start. The two men were now three. When this newcomer spoke, his voice was like sandpaper against her skin. It set her teeth on edge. She stopped flattening her hands against her ears and hugged herself.

"Thank you," he said. "I thought I'd lost my glove. I am cursed with an annoying inclination to lose one."

"It's a kid glove," the first man said. "Somehow that makes it worse."

The third man to come upon her bent and peered into her rock shelter. "Christ. She has it." He reached into the opening in the rocks and took his glove back. After a few moments spent fiddling with it, he raised a hand to his mouth and yawned. When he spoke, his voice didn't prickle her skin quite so much. He sounded bored. "Leave her be," he said.

"But you said no survivors," the second man said.

"And now I'm saying leave her be. Do you have a problem with that?"

"No, sir."

"Seems like you do."

"No, sir. Not really."

"That's what I thought," said the third man. He stared at the glove and finally stripped it off while the others waited for him to speak.

She waited, too. It would be important, what he said.

"Leave her," he said at last. "And leave her this."

She didn't have time to prepare to catch it. He tossed it as an afterthought, and it landed in the cradle of her dress between her knees. She stared at it, had one clear image of the afterthought before she was plunged into darkness.

And then the voices began calling to her again.

"Comfort. Wake up." Bode placed one hand on her shoulder, cautiously at first, then with more pressure. "Comfort!" He thought she might sit up abruptly or try to shake him off. What he didn't anticipate was that she would scream.

He reacted without thinking and put his hand over her mouth. She bit him. He yanked his hand back and pressed the web of flesh between his thumb and forefinger against his lips, nursing it. He tasted blood.

Comfort screamed again, and this time he didn't try to interfere. The sound of it raised the hair at the back of his neck. It wasn't a cry a fear, but one of pain. It tore at him to listen to it. Without warning, she turned on her side and drew her knees up to her chest and bent her head toward them. She clasped her legs tightly. Her eyes weren't merely closed; they were squeezed shut. She didn't scream again, but her wounded whimper was harder to bear.

Someone pounded on the stateroom door, distracting Bode. He was almost grateful for the interruption. Because he didn't want to yell and startle Comfort into screaming again, he levered himself over her to reach the edge of the bed and rolled out. The quilt was lying on the floor where she'd kicked. He scooped it up and covered her before he went to the door.

He opened it a few inches. Tapper Stewart stood in the passageway, rocking heel to toe and looking as if he wished he were anywhere else. The space between his heavy black eyebrows had vanished with the intensity of his frown.

"Just finished my watch, Mr. DeLong. Thought I heard the lady." He raised himself up a little higher on the balls of his feet and tried to get a look over Bode's shoulder. "Is she all right?"

"A bad dream," Bode told him. "She's fine now."

"Anything I can get for her? Some tea? It's no problem."

Bode started to say that Comfort didn't want anything, but then he remembered that she would wake thirsty. "Tea would be very good, Tapper. The pot, please. Not only a cup. Thank you." He stepped aside just enough for Tapper to glimpse the outline of Comfort's huddled body under the quilt.

"Won't be but a few minutes," Tapper said. His fiercely drawn features finally relaxed. He bobbed his head once, and then he was off.

Bode closed the door and returned to the bed. He adjusted the wick on the oil lamp and allowed the dim pool of light surrounding Comfort to widen and brighten. He immediately saw her eyes were open.

"You're awake?" He had to ask because her stare was so vacant that he wasn't sure.

She blinked, nodded.

"Tapper's bringing tea. I can get you a glass of water or some sherry."

"Water," she said. It hurt to talk.

Bode nodded, disappeared into the washroom, and returned in short order with a glass. "Will you sit up?"

Comfort didn't try to answer. She simply raised her head and held out her hand. When Bode put the glass against her palm, she seized it and drew it quickly to her lips. She barely swallowed, emptying the glass in a single pour.

"More?" he asked, taking it from her when she gasped. She nodded, and Bode brought another. Comfort finished the second glass with only a little less enthusiasm, but when he asked if she wanted more, she declined the offer and said she could wait for Tapper to bring tea. Bode set the empty glass on the table and came back to bed. She'd uncurled but moved so close to the edge that there was nowhere for him to sit.

Bode dragged a chair away from the table, spun it around, and sat. He laid his forearms across the back and rested his chin on top. "What finally awakened you?"

"I'm not sure, but I heard you and Mr. Stewart. I couldn't make out what either of you was saying." She pressed her fingertips to the hollow of her throat and massaged. The ache was on the inside, but it helped just to do something. "It was kind of you to ask him to bring tea, but what did he want?"

"He wanted to be sure you were all right. Tapper was leaving watch on his way to his quarters. He heard you screaming." Bode's grin was humorless. "He probably thought I was hurting you."

Comfort closed her eyes. "Oh God," she whispered. "I'm so sorry, Bode."

"It's all right. You didn't do anything wrong." He decided against telling her about the injury to his hand. If she saw the teeth marks tomorrow, he'd explain. Otherwise, she didn't have to know.

"But Mr. Stewart . . ."

"I told him it was a dream, and he'll see that you're fine when he returns."

Comfort levered herself up to a partial recline and glanced sideways to where her nightstand would be if she were in her own bed.

"What is it?" asked Bode. "What are you looking for?"

"Hm? Oh, nothing. It's not important."

Clearly it was. "Tell me."

Comfort still hesitated. If his voice had been less gentle,

she would have refused, but he spoke with rather more encouragement than command. "I was looking for my tin. At home, it would be at my bedside." Self-conscious, her eyes darted away. "I like to hold it sometimes."

Bode understood. She meant that she liked to hold it after a nightmare woke her. "One of the crew might have—" He stopped because she was shaking her head. "No, I don't suppose it would be the same, would it?"

"No."

"Will you tell me about your dream this time?" he asked.

She had become accustomed to saying no to that question, and the word hovered on the tip of her tongue. She withheld it just long enough to change her mind. Bode was her husband; he should know.

Comfort sat up and edged backward until she could rest against the headboard. "It was different. I can't explain it, but the glove was part of it this time."

"You mean the glove that you thought you saw?"

"Yes." She smiled crookedly. "I know. It's confusing. The same men find me hiding in the rocks, and they're joined by a third. The third man is the one who tells them to let me be. His voice . . ." She shivered involuntarily and dragged the quilt up to the level of her breasts. "His voice is rough. Raspy, I suppose you'd say. I can't see his face, but his voice is like a signature to me, and when I hear it, my skin prickles. He takes a tin out of his pocket, opens it, and drops something into his mouth. That didn't happen this time. The other men told him they'd found a kid glove, not a kid, and he took it from me and then tossed it back. Usually it's the tin he tosses. That's how I came to be clutching Dr. Eli Kennedy's Comfort Lozenges when Newt and Tuck found me."

Bode was quiet, taking it in. He wanted to ask her to repeat it, and this time tell him everything she remembered, but that could wait until later. He could hear the strain that speaking put on her voice. "Why do you scream?" he asked.

"They put the rocks back. Close me in. I'm afraid of the dark. They leave me, and I know they can hear me screaming."

Bode had learned about the saloon cellar from some of the

men. Small. Dark. Virtually airless. It was her nightmare all over again.

Comfort saw a muscle jump in Bode's jaw. His expression was grim. "What is it?" she asked.

He started to shrug and thought better of it. "The cellar," he said. He heard the harsh rasp in his voice and wondered if she could distinguish it from the one she heard in her dream. "I was thinking about you in that cellar."

"Mm." He looked as if he was also thinking about revenge. She didn't know what to say to him. She wasn't capable of talking him out of it. Not yet. Perhaps never.

Bode lifted his head, straightened his back, and braced his arms momentarily as he blew out a short breath. Tapper Stewart couldn't arrive soon enough as far as he was concerned.

"Why do you suppose I dreamed about the glove?" Comfort asked. "I don't understand that at all."

Bode didn't either. "I wish I could explain it."

"I was so confused." She suddenly recalled something she'd heard the third man say in her dream. "The third man, the one who told them to leave me?"

"Yes?"

"What he said was odd." She closed her eyes, concentrating. "After he thanked the other men for finding his glove, he said, 'I am cursed with an annoying inclination to lose one.'"

Bode didn't understand, and his expression revealed as much.

"That gentleman at the opera house," Comfort explained. "He said something very much like that to you. 'I am cursed with an annoying tickle in my throat.' Don't you find it strange that I would more or less hear those words again in my dream?"

Bode found everything about her vivid dreaming strange, but he refrained from saying so. "It seems as if you're melding the experience at the opera house with what happened after the attack."

"I wonder if I've done it before, perhaps without knowing. What if my dream has changed in small ways over the years and no longer bears any resemblance to the truth of that day?"

"Is that important?"

"I don't know. It's not as if I've ever seen the faces of the men who were talking over me, but now that you ask, I think that I really have allowed myself to believe that I would know them again in any circumstance." She shook her head. "I *am* self-deluding."

"That's hardly true."

She snorted. "That's not the view from my porch."

Chuckling, Bode rose from the chair to answer Tapper's knock. He accepted the wooden tray while Comfort called to Tapper from the bed and apologized for worrying him. They had a brief exchange, and Bode waited until Tapper bid Comfort easy sleep before he turned away and used his heel to close the door. He set the tray on the table and poured a cup of tea for Comfort. Tapper had been thoughtful enough to add a second cup to the tray, but Bode didn't take any. He carried the cup to her and made sure it was prepared the way she liked it before he returned to straddling his chair.

"I was curious about the gentleman at the opera house," Bode said. "After you and I talked about him, I spoke to your uncles. They gave me permission to make some inquiries." Not surprisingly, he saw Comfort's eyebrows arch. "I know. No one asked for your permission."

Comfort didn't anticipate there would be an apology. She wasn't disappointed. "Well? Did you?"

"Yes. And I couldn't find anyone who knew him."

Comfort blew softly on her hot tea. The surface rippled. "Perhaps he was only visiting the city."

"That's what I thought, but I've since learned he's renting rooms at the Carter House near Union Square."

"But you said you couldn't find anyone who knew him."

"That's true. I never did. Mr. James R. Crocker found me."

Chapter Thirteen

"Naturally, I've heard of the Pinkerton National Detective Agency," Alexandra said, once her guest was seated. "This is my first occasion to have need of their services."

The detective inclined his head to indicate that he understood. "Then I imagine you are experiencing a trying time, and I'm very sorry for it. I find it is often best for our clients to simply state the problem and allow me to ask questions that will provide the detail I need. If that is satisfactory to you, then we should begin."

Alexandra nodded. She approved of this straightforward approach. Making the decision to meet with someone from the agency had been difficult in its own right. She had no liking for involving outsiders in the affairs of her family, and she required some guidance as to how to proceed.

She purposely chose her husband's library for the meeting. While this room was the site of countless infidelities, Alexandra still believed the spirit of Branford's intellect and scholarship favorably influenced all business conducted here. Until he made the unfortunate, and she would add, wildly romantic, gesture to support a cause as ill conceived as the secession of the Southern states, she had trusted his judgment as it related to Black Crowne.

The Pinkerton man sat opposite her in a Queen Anne chair that was easily the least comfortable chair in the room. It seemed to her that he had chosen it purposefully, underscoring that this was a business meeting, not a social call. She appreciated that he was direct and self-assured, yet also respectful. Had he demonstrated the least inclination for toadying up to her, she would have had Hitchens escort him out.

The fact that he was of an age with her supported her confidence that he was experienced. He did not smile continuously as men sometimes did when they were trying to please her. His expression was more carefully guarded than that, but when he tilted his head and offered a slim, encouraging smile from behind his neatly trimmed mustache, she noticed there was a small gap between his front teeth. For reasons she couldn't begin to understand, that put her at her ease.

"All right," Alexandra said. "I shall start by telling you that there is little distinction in my mind between matters of business and matters of family. They are inexorably linked. Whether your view is the same, I don't know, but I require strict confidentiality regardless."

"Of course."

"My immediate concern is for my older son, Beauregard. He is the head of Black Crowne and has been since my husband's death. While he often consults me and values my opinion, I have entrusted him with the day-to-day management of the operations. Until recently, I have not been displeased."

"I hope you will forgive me, Mrs. DeLong, but perhaps engaging your lawyer would better suit than hiring a detective agency." He cleared his throat. "Pinkerton men don't settle disputes; we often enforce the settlement."

Alexandra found the slight rasp in his voice pleasant, but she noticed that he raised one hand to his collar as if his throat were bothering him. She offered him refreshment earlier and he refused. She offered again.

His hand dropped back to his lap. "No, thank you. Go on."

"I haven't asked for your help with a dispute. Rather, I want your help finding my son." She folded her hands together. Her knuckles whitened. "For all intents and purposes, he's disappeared."

"Disappeared," he repeated calmly. "Has he done this before?"

Alexandra supposed that from his vantage point it was a reasonable question, but she could barely contain her annoyance. "He has *not*," she said firmly. "This is out of character."

"When did you last speak to him or have some sort of correspondence?"

"He was here eight days ago. I spoke to him briefly, and he spent some time with, his younger brother." She explained Bram's bedridden condition. "I did not see him leave."

"I hope you will allow me to speak to . . . Bram, is it?"

"Abraham. Yes, of course you may. He says Bode gave him no indication that he meant to travel or would be unreachable, but Bram might reveal something different to you. It is entirely possible that he is lying, although whether his intent is to protect me, his brother, or himself, I cannot possibly know."

"What inquiries have you already made?" the detective asked. "Friends? Relatives? Business associates?"

Alexandra told him about her encounter with John Farwell. "When I didn't hear from Bode the following day, I sent a second message. Several days later, I sent a third. Mr. Farwell insists that my son has received the notes. He will not say more than that. He is not at all helpful. Bram seems to think that Mr. Farwell's behavior can be laid at Bode's door, but I am not happy with that explanation. Mr. Farwell must be made to give over information about my son or be held accountable for his disappearance."

"Do you suspect this Farwell of foul play?"

"Until my son is standing unharmed in front of me, I am not ruling it out. I am hiring you, of course, to do exactly that. Find my son. I will give you a list of business associates. Bode rarely speaks of friends, so neither can I. Bram might have information. We have no relatives here in California. My late husband and I have family in Boston. Bode and his cousins occasionally correspond."

"Your son is unmarried?"

"Yes. This is not about a woman." The detective did not given any indication that he was skeptical, but Alexandra felt compelled to explain, "If we were discussing my younger son, I would tell you that it is certainly a possibility you should consider. I have complete confidence in my answer as it pertains to Bode. He is ruthlessly devoted to Black Crowne. That is something all his competitors will tell you."

"Very well." He asked one question after another regarding Bode's living arrangements, his activities outside of work, and the management of Black Crowne in his absence—if indeed he was truly absent. "I must tell you, Mrs. DeLong, that I haven't heard anything that convinces me your son has disappeared, and I say that to ease your mind, not to distress you further. I will pursue every one of the leads you have given me, but you must prepare yourself for the possibility that Mr. Beauregard DeLong's absence is because he's deliberately ignoring you."

Although Alexandra's nostrils tightened with her sharply indrawn breath, she maintained her composure. "Do not concern yourself that I will kill the messenger. If it turns out that all my fears can be explained because Bode has suddenly decided he must have secrets from me, I will deal with him. And no, it will not be pleasant for either of us."

Alexandra raised an inquiring eyebrow. "Is there anything else?"

"No. Not right now." He cleared his throat again. "I would like speak to Mr. Abraham DeLong if that's convenient."

"It's convenient for me. I cannot say that Bram will find it so. He is unapologetically disagreeable. Bed confinement does not suit his temperament in the least."

"I understand." He stood as Alexandra came to her feet.

"I'll have Hitchens escort you." She tapped her temple suddenly. "Ask my son about Samuel Travers. He was Bode's valet before he was Bram's man."

"Perhaps I should talk to Mr. Travers."

"I'd like nothing better, but none of us know what's become of him either."

Making the transfer to the *Artemis Queen* did not involve crossing a gangplank set between the two ships. Instead, Comfort, Bode, and their belongings were lowered in a boat over the side of the *Demeter* and rowed sixty yards to the sister ship. Bode insisted the other crew was going to use a cargo net to hoist her aboard, but when they got alongside the *Artemis*, it was the boat that was raised, and Comfort's arrival was uneventful, not the tangle of skirts, netting, and immodestly displayed limbs that she had been imagining.

When Bode stepped on deck beside her, she pressed her elbow into his side and kept it there while he introduced her to Mr. Benjamin Kerr, the master of the *Artemis*.

They were welcomed aboard as if there were nothing at all unusual about their arrival. Mr. Kerr did not ask for any explanation beyond what had been communicated to him by the *Demeter*'s semaphore flags, but Bode offered a brief one before they were shown to their quarters. Because the stateroom was occupied by a passenger who had paid very well for that accommodation, Bode and Comfort accepted quarters that were considerably less spacious than what they'd enjoyed on the *Demeter*.

Comfort looked around the room in a single glance. The bed fixed to the wall was narrow. There was no separate room for bathing, only a commode that held a basin on top and a chamber pot below. There was no wardrobe or table. No window bench because there was no window. The sailor who escorted them to their cabin lighted the lantern that hung by the door before he helped the two men that followed carry in Comfort's trunk and Bode's large valises.

Comfort thanked them. She thought they did a remarkably good job of avoiding looking Bode in the eye on their way out. "It will be like living in a teacup," she told Bode. "Really, I don't mind."

He raised an eyebrow at her. "I mind for you." He took in their new quarters much as she had, in a single glance. Her teacup analogy was accurate.

Comfort faced him and took his hands in hers. She gave them a small shake. "Consider this, Bode. If this cabin is the best Mr. Kerr can show us, it means that all of the adequately appointed rooms are occupied by people who paid. Put another way, we are victims of your successful commerce." She saw that he was unconvinced and was likely regretting that he had turned down the master's offer to vacate his own quarters in favor of them. "It isn't forever," she reminded him. "We'll be home within the week. I've lived in a tent before. This is much better." Standing on tiptoe, she kissed him on the cheek before she let him go. "You know it, too. You must. You marched with Sherman."

"You're right." It was only on Comfort's behalf that he took issue with their quarters, but she managed to make him believe she found them tolerable. "There is a lounge for the passengers, and you are welcome to use it as freely as you like. I'll take you there now, if you wish. I need to speak to Mr. Kerr."

Comfort knew Bode was less interested in a conversation with the shipmaster than he was in inspecting the damage to the *Artemis Queen*. It had taken them longer to cross paths with the *Artemis* than either Bode or Mr. Douglas had anticipated, and Bode wanted to know the reason why.

"I'd like to visit the lounge," she said. "You'll come for me when you're done, won't you?"

"Certainly." He gave her his arm. "We'll spend time on deck afterward. There's no reason for us to hurry back here." Her arch look momentarily arrested him. "On the other hand," he said, returning her look, "perhaps there is."

The moment Bram heard footsteps approaching his room, he corked the bottle of laudanum in his hand and slipped it into his hiding place between the splints. Occasionally the precaution was unnecessary, but he'd noticed that in the past week he was being visited more frequently by either his mother or a steady parade of servants sent by his mother. He realized Alexandra remained suspicious of his laudanum use and was trying to catch him out. Thus far, he'd been alert enough to keep anyone from seeing him with a bottle, and the servant who purchased the drug for him in Chinatown had not yet betrayed his trust.

He settled back against the headboard, picked up the folded copy of the *San Francisco Call* from the bedside table, and dropped it in his lap. He was not surprised to see that it was Hitchens at the door; however, the man standing just to one side of the butler surprised the hell out of him.

Hitchens announced the visitor, asked Bram if there was anything he needed, and then took his leave.

Bram flung the newspaper onto the floor. "What are you doing here?"

James R. Crocker smiled thinly. He approached the bed and looked over the weights and pulleys attached to Bram's splinted leg. "What happens if I knock this out of the way?"

"I can't stop you, so if you came here with that in mind, then have at it."

Crocker eyed Bram's raised leg for a long, contemplative moment before he turned his attention to Bram. "It's tempting," he said, pulling the nearby chair even closer to the bed. He sat. His knees bumped the mattress. "I'm still not convinced it's broken. Regardless, it's been a good strategy. Whether by intention or happenstance, you've made yourself difficult to reach."

"What do you want?"

Crocker lifted an eyebrow. "You're not in a position to make a single demand. Consider your tone, and consider whether or not you want the use of your other leg." He cleared his throat and absently touched his collar. "Your mother's hired Pinkerton to find your brother. Please tell me you appreciate the irony."

"I'm beginning to."

"At first I thought it would be a simple matter to put someone on the household staff here, but every person I sent to inquire about a position was turned away. The only outside visitors to get past the front door were your brother, your fiancée, and your doctor. This is not a welcoming home, Bram."

"What do you mean about the visitors? Are you saying I've had others?"

"You didn't know?" Crocker's smile was derisive. "You aren't master here at all, are you? Alexandra controls everything."

"Mrs. DeLong," Bram said. "Call her Mrs. DeLong."

Crocker chuckled. The sound was vaguely hoarse. He reached into his jacket and withdrew a red-and-white tin of lozenges. He opened it and, out of habit, offered one to Bram. When Bram waved the tin aside, Crocker merely shrugged. He flicked a lozenge into his mouth and cheeked it. "So here I am," he said, putting the tin away. "Granted access at last because your brother's disappeared. Or so your mother thinks."

"He's avoiding her."

"She doesn't like that idea. I can tell."

Bram pressed one hand to his forehead. He was regretting the last dose of laudanum. He couldn't think clearly. In spite

of the danger that James R. Crocker presented to him, Bram
wanted nothing so much as to close his eyes and go to sleep.
"Bode's working on something. A new ship design, I think. He
hasn't said much about it to me and apparently has said even
less to Mother. He doesn't want to be disturbed." He pushed
his hand through his hair. "How is it that you were assigned to
this? The agency could have sent anyone. Why you?"

He shrugged. "Good fortune favors the prepared. I happened to be there when your mother's inquiry arrived, and
since I've already met your brother, I was the obvious choice."

"You met Bode? When?"

"Twice, actually. The first time was at the opera house. I
attended the opening night performance of *Rigoletto* because
I'd heard you'd be there. I also heard you'd invested in the
production. You understand I had reason to hope that it would
be a successful venture for you."

Bram merely stared at him from slumberous, heavy-lidded
eyes.

"My companion pointed out your family's box," Crocker
said. "You weren't there. I learned from someone else that the
person occupying it was your brother. We had an . . . an
encounter, I think you'd say . . . during the break. Quite by
accident." He patted his jacket over the place where the tin of
lozenges was pocketed. "I dropped my tin, and your brother
returned it. An uneventful moment by anyone's measure, except
that the young lady on his arm fainted dead away. I discovered
afterward that she was your fiancée." He smiled thinly, revealing the gap in his front teeth and no humor. "It turned out to
be . . . providential."

Bram stirred uncomfortably. He looked away.

"Nothing to say?" asked Crocker. "Perhaps later. The second time I met your brother was intentional. I went to Black
Crowne and asked after him under the pretense of doing business. The introduction was made on the *Demeter Queen*. He
recognized me immediately from the opera house. I believe I
was flattered. After all, he had his hands full that night." He
chuckled quietly at his own joke. "Full of your fiancée."

"I understood," Bram said without inflection. "Very
amusing."

Crocker made a small whistling sound as he sucked hard on the lozenge. After a moment he tucked it back against his cheek. "I wouldn't have pursued a meeting with your brother if I could have learned anything substantial about Miss Kennedy. I thought I knew her routine, and then she suddenly veered from it, staying at home for an entire week by my reckoning. You were helpful there, of course, as you should have been."

Crocker watched Bram's eyes dart away again. "You don't like to remember that, do you? But I find that threat of pain or death prompts people to act in ways that might otherwise be abhorrent to them. You have nothing to regret. It could have been your mother, Bram. It could have been you. I think everyone but your fiancée and her uncles would agree you made the only choice you could have."

Bram clenched his teeth hard enough to make his jaw ache.

"It isn't your fault that the money didn't follow. I may have overstepped, and I take responsibility for that. Naturally, you are responsible for everything else. It's your debt, Bram. I think I've proven I'll do whatever it takes to collect it. That's what people expect when they hire me. Your associates in Sacramento sent me here because they know my reputation for results. They don't care how I do it; they want what they're owed. You'll want to consider how you're going to make this right. I require nothing at all from you about your mother's comings and goings. Thanks to your brother, I can reach her anytime I like."

Crocker's last statement sharpened Bram's dulling senses. "Do you know where Bode is?"

Crocker pointed to himself. "Do *I* know?" He chuckled. "It's a compliment that you think I might."

Bram rephrased his question. "Did you have something to do with Bode's disappearance?"

"According to you, he hasn't disappeared." He saw Bram's fists clench. The ineffectual threat made him smile. "And between you and me, I don't have much incentive to find him."

"What about Miss Kennedy?"

Crocker didn't answer immediately. He made a show of checking his pocket watch. "Twenty minutes," he said. "I made a wager with myself before I stepped in here. I didn't think you'd ask about her welfare quite so soon, but I'm wondering if you don't feel quite as guilty as I would in your place."

It was almost laughable to hear James R. Crocker speak of guilt. The man had no conscience. "There was nothing in the papers following the first report of the attack. My mother received a note from Miss Kennedy's uncles indicating that she was recovering and resting at home. She wanted no visitors." The note had also said that as far as they were concerned, the engagement was ended and that Comfort wished to have nothing further to do with the DeLong family. Bram didn't share any part of that. It was still to his advantage to allow Crocker to believe he and Comfort were engaged.

Crocker nodded slowly. "That's what I've heard also. No one's seen her, but that isn't unexpected. She had a harrowing experience."

"You made certain of that."

"I did? Didn't I say that you were responsible, Bram?"

"I have the note you delivered the night she was abducted. Your threats were very clear."

"I didn't deliver anything like that."

"You tried to see me that night. You left a message for me when Hitchens wouldn't let you in."

"I've never been to your front door before. Ask Hitchens. Don't you think he would have said something to your mother when I arrived to meet with her?"

"I told him not to say anything about that night. To anyone. Ever."

"Then ask him privately. I wasn't here."

Bram frowned. "So it was someone you sent instead. It doesn't matter. You made it plain what you were going to do with her."

"Mm. If that's so, you made it plain you weren't going to do anything about it. I didn't receive anything from you, did I?"

"I don't have the money. I told you before that you would have to wait for it until Comfort and I were married."

"Those terms were accepted on the condition of a prompt exchange of vows. You can't truly have believed anyone would wait a year. I received the message you sent about setting a date. You can't pay what you owe now; why would anyone suppose you could manage the interest at the end of a year? You really don't understand the men you're dealing with."

"She's good for it," Bram said defensively. "Her uncles are good for it."

Crocker removed another lozenge from the tin and dropped it in his mouth. "Everyone knows they have money. Whether you'd be allowed access to it is something else entirely. Everyone was intrigued by the idea of Miss Kennedy as collateral on your debt, but I wonder now if that wasn't a mistake. When you could have raised money to prevent her abduction, you didn't. Instead of applying to your brother for help, you surrendered her instead, essentially counting on her family to pay what you owed."

"They must have paid at least part of it."

"Why do you say that?"

"Because she's home. You wouldn't have let her go if they hadn't paid something toward her release."

Crocker regarded Bram with more suspicion. "Is it opium?" he asked. "Is that what you're using? Or cocaine?" He gently sniffed the air. "No trace of smoke. I'll wager it's laudanum you've been spooning down your throat. That would account for it."

"Account for what?"

"The fact that your thinking is as cloudy as an opium den. In your right mind, you'd know I wouldn't accept a partial payment. We're long past that point. It was all or nothing. You have no idea how much could have been raised that night. As I said, I overstepped, but I think it gives you a taste of things to come."

"But you let her go."

He fell silent as he debated what, or if, he should tell Bram. He decided that Bram's reaction would not be so blunted by laudanum that he couldn't learn something from it. "No. Not exactly. The Rangers failed to control their house. She got away."

Bram blinked owlishly, then he threw back his head and laughed. By the time he reined himself in, there were tears at the corners of his eyes. "Of course she did. My God, but she's one of a kind."

Crocker grunted.

Bram wiped his eyes with one corner of the sheet. He sobered with difficulty, swallowing more laughter as it stirred in his chest. In Bram's experience, there was only so much Crocker would tolerate, and the limit had been reached.

Crocker waited for the full implication of Comfort's escape to hit Bram. He saw the moment clearly. Bram's jaw sagged. Crocker nodded. "Did you think I wasn't serious when I said your mother would be next? You really should stop taking the laudanum. Your judgment is never impressive, Bram, but it barely exists now."

"How do you suppose threatening to harm my mother will get you your money? There *is* no money. Now that I'm bedridden, I can't even take my small stake and turn it around at the tables."

Crocker didn't bother to point out that it was exactly that thinking that got Bram into trouble in the first place. "Your brother will pay for your mother."

"He won't." Bram hesitated. He'd held out as long as he reasonably could. Bode and his mother couldn't blame him for telling the truth. Wasn't that what Bode was always asking him to do? "He can't, and not because he's a cold-blooded bastard. How many ways can I say there's no money? What we have is debt. The house. The ships. The bank owns us. It has since my father mortgaged everything and bet it on the Confederacy to win the war. You think my judgment is less than impressive? Ask Bode about my father's. My brother has had his sights on repairing the family fortune since the end of the war. He can't see anything outside of that. He doesn't take a salary beyond what is required to keep him alive. He gives my mother and me an allowance. It is generous by any standard except for the one we were used to. He stopped advancing money better than a year ago. He's never wavered. When he thinks Mother is going to pressure him for funds, he stays away. She'd never tell you about that, but there's a better than even chance that's why he's ignoring her now."

Crocker was thoughtful as he scratched his beard just under his chin. He wondered if he could believe Bram. "This isn't common knowledge."

"God, no. It would ruin us. And if you let it get about, you'll never see your money. Black Crowne will collapse. The creditors will take everything first."

"How do I know that you're telling me the truth?"

Bram shrugged. "You're the detective, but I'd advise caution in the event you decide to ask questions. You might raise suspicion, and in this city that would become fact before nightfall. The creditors would start sniffing around, and you'd still have nothing."

"Who holds the lien against this house?" When Bram said nothing, Crocker sighed. He stood slowly, as though reluctant, and put a hand on Bram's broken leg just above the knee. "You think I can't make you feel pain past the laudanum? I'm warning you, I can. Tell me who holds the lien."

Bram watched Crocker insinuate his hand between the bandages. The man's fingertips were warm against his skin. There was the slightest downward pressure as Crocker straightened his elbow and began to push. "Croft Federal," Bram said. He felt the pressure ease immediately.

"Who would be the best person to speak to?"

Bram closed his eyes this time. He didn't try to hold out. "Mr. David Bancroft," he whispered. "You can talk to David Bancroft."

Crocker nodded, satisfied. "One last thing. Your mother said I should ask you about Samuel Travers. Who the hell is he?"

They were still a day out when Bode happened upon Comfort sitting on a large coil of rope on the foredeck. Her concentration was fixed on the tails of two ropes that she held in her hands. She didn't notice him standing beside her until he nudged the toe of her boot with his.

"I thought you were going to the lounge after breakfast," he said when she looked up.

Comfort dropped one of the ropes so she could use a hand to shade her eyes from the sun. "I was there for a little while. I couldn't think of a thing to say when the women began discussing whether shaped undergarments were more flattering than shifts. It was all very serious and utterly boring. I would rather have been playing cards with the gentlemen. I'm very good at card games."

Bode thought of Newt and Tuck and Comfort's early

education at their hands. "I'll bet you are." He pointed to the length of rope she was still holding. "Are you trying to make a bend?"

"Mm. Trying. I've been shown twice how to make a hunter's bend, and I still can't do it."

"So many times? And you still can't do it? That's hard to believe." He motioned her to make room for him, and when she did, he sat beside her and held out his hand for the ropes. He demonstrated how to twist them together, and then he let her try, guiding her hands when she hesitated. She joined the two ropes on her next attempt. "Very good. Now this one." He showed her a double carrick bend that was only a little more elaborate than what she'd been trying. "We'll make a sailor out of you yet," he said, handing over the finished bend so she could study it for herself.

"I'm coming to it rather late," she said a trifle wistfully. "We'll wake up tomorrow morning in the bay."

"Do you want me to delay our arrival? I'm sure there's something on board that I can sabotage."

"After you worked so hard to repair the boiler? I don't think so. Anyway, I'm anxious to see Newt and Tuck, and I've been thinking about what you told me about Mr. Crocker. I want to meet him."

Except to give her a sideways glance, Bode didn't react. "When did you decide that?"

"This morning. I had a lot of time to consider it once the conversation turned to undergarments." She tried to work the ropes in her hands, but her fingers weren't as steady as they'd been moments before. "I want to know why I fainted, Bode."

"I don't think Mr. Crocker's going to be able to explain that."

"I don't either, but it would be interesting to find out if I can control it."

"Interesting," he said. "Yes, you'd think that."

"If it were you, you'd want to know."

He couldn't deny it. "We'll see."

Her eyebrows lifted slightly, and her fingers stilled. "I wasn't asking permission."

Bode said nothing.

"Bode?"

"I heard you. I'm trying to decide what I think about it."

"I want you to go with me," she said. "I'm hoping you will."

He clearly heard what she didn't say. She would arrange a meeting with Mr. Crocker with or without him. "Newt once offered me twenty dollars to be your keeper, and I refused."

"You should have taken the money and kept the ring."

He was tempted to kiss the sass right out of her smile. Later, he thought. He would wait until they were alone. They would both enjoy that. "All right," he said. "But I want to arrange the meeting."

"Of course."

"Of course," he repeated. "You don't care about that at all, do you?"

"Not a bit." She wove one rope through the loop she'd made in the other and pulled tight. Grinning widely, she raised the double carrick to show him. "Hah! Now, point out someone I can hang from a yardarm."

This time he gave in to temptation. He took the carrick bend out of her hand as though to examine it, and as quickly as either one of them could have said, "Bear away before the wind," he used one of the ropes to make a bowline around her wrist.

Comfort stared from him, to her wrist, and back to the darkening centers of his blue-violet eyes. She felt a delicious shiver travel down her spine. "You're going to tie me to a yardarm?"

Bode couldn't hear any concern in her voice. In fact, she sounded a bit hopeful. He stood, drawing her to her feet by means of the bowline. She didn't resist. Stepping close enough to keep anyone from seeing that she was bound to him, Bode bent his head and whispered in her ear, "Let's start with a bedpost and see how that goes."

The stool under John Farwell thudded to the floor as he leaped to his feet and grabbed the young runner who'd just come up from the wharf. "You're sure? The *Artemis Queen*?"

"She's here. I saw her comin' in and came straightaway, just like you asked. They'll be opening up the gangway by the time you get there."

Farwell found a quarter, tossed it to the boy, and told him

to leave. He went in the back, where the other clerks were doing inventory, and alerted them that he was leaving to meet the ship. He didn't ask any of them to come along.

Comfort saw John Farwell first. She stepped closer to Bode. This was her first encounter with the man since the concert saloon, and she was not quite as prepared to face him as she'd hoped to be.

Bode sensed her unease first and then found the source of it. "Think of something else," he said. "If it helps, think of all the ways we found to use that rope."

Comfort immediately stopped thinking about Mr. Farwell bouncing on the bed beside her and remembered Bode removing the lantern from the hook just inside their cabin and fastening her wrists there instead. She hadn't objected except to inquire about the bedpost. His answer was practical: during the walk back to their quarters, he'd realized their berth didn't have one. She would have smiled because, really, he was so excellent at revising a plan, but then he took a step back and studied her, grazing every part of her with his eyes as thoroughly as if he'd used his hands, and what might have been a smile was only the narrow parting of her mouth around a sharply indrawn breath.

She was wet by the time he blew out the lantern and plunged their tiny cabin into complete darkness. She was too excited to be afraid of anything except that he wouldn't touch her soon enough. The waiting was an agony. When she softly cried out, it was because he'd finally begun to lift her underskirt.

He pressed her back against the wall; his breath was hot on her neck. He worried her earlobe with his teeth and touched his tongue to the shell pink whorl. He used his body to keep her pinned while he fumbled with her drawers and the front of his trousers and, frustrated with the difficulty of keeping her flat to the wall, tugged at the fastenings to her bustle. When he finally yanked it out from under her skirt, she heard him grunt softly in triumph.

The next time he made a sound like that, it was because he was deep inside her, and her legs were clamped hard against his hips, and she was clenching him intimately with muscles that were sleek and slippery. It didn't matter that her wrists were bound. She had him in ways that mattered more.

Bode touched Comfort's elbow and gave it a gentle squeeze. "Perhaps you should think of something else," he suggested quietly. "You're looking unnaturally flushed."

Comfort raised a hand to her cheek. She could feel heat against her fingertips. "It's because of you," she said, her glance accusing.

He showed her his secretive, selfish smile, the one that made her breath hitch. "I know. And it makes me very, very happy."

There wasn't time for her to reply or even tread lightly on his toes. The passengers were moving toward the gangway, and Bode steered her in that direction.

John Farwell culled them from the crowd as quickly as a miner plucking gold nuggets from a sifting pan. There was no opportunity for awkwardness on Comfort's part, because Mr. Farwell had a list in his head of all the things that must be accomplished without delay. He began by asking about their individual arrangements, barely blinked when Bode announced their marriage, and launched into a somewhat confusing recitation of what had transpired in their absence.

Comfort was grateful when Bode held up his hand and silenced the clerk. "All in good time, John. You need to take care of Mr. Kerr and the *Artemis Queen* first. I've already made arrangements for the delivery of our belongings. I want to hear everything, but not all of it before I've reached the office."

"Yes, sir. There are just a couple of things you should—" He cut himself off because Bode shot him a warning glance over the top of Comfort's head. "Yes, sir. I'll talk to Mr. Kerr right now." Reversing his direction, he headed back to the ship.

"Thank you," Comfort said softly. "He was making my head swim."

"I know. He means well. He had a lot of responsibility these last weeks, more than he's taken on before. If he did well . . ." Bode fell silent, thinking.

"Yes?"

"If he did well, I might be able to spend more time doing what I want and not what I have to."

"Designing, you mean?"

"That's part of it. Testing. Construction. Sailing. All of that."

"Then I hope Mr. Farwell has done exceedingly well."

The Black Crowne Office came into sight as they turned the corner. Bode deliberately slowed. He usually felt a quickening in his steps as he approached. The sign above the entrance was nearly as long as the building was wide, and the affectation of the fancy English script rarely failed to amuse him. This time, though, he barely noticed the sign. His attention was focused higher than that. He was staring at the windows on the second floor, the ones that looked out on the street from his home.

He stopped walking altogether and took Comfort by the arm. He turned to her. "I should have said something before. Maybe I would have if I'd even thought of it, but I didn't, so here we are. I don't know how to make it right on short notice. A hotel, perhaps. Or your uncles' home. It would only be temporary until I can find a more suitable place."

Comfort tried to recall if she'd ever seen Bode ill at ease. He spoke as rapidly as John Farwell and, from her perspective, made about as much sense. "Please," she said. "You're making my head swim."

"We don't have to live here if you don't want to."

She blinked, surprised. "Why wouldn't I want to? You're my husband, and this is your home." She raised one hand to the back of her neck and fiddled with several loose strands of hair. "Unless you don't want me there. It's your private stateroom. I understand that you might not—" She stopped because his face was no longer shadowed by concern. He was grinning at her and looking about as irrepressible as a ten-year-old boy with a ball and a stick. Shaking her head, she let him lead on.

Bode bid good morning to the clerks working in the storeroom as he ushered Comfort to the stairs. He gestured to her to go first and enjoyed the view from behind.

Comfort pushed at the hatch when she reached the top, but it didn't budge. "I think it must be stuck," she told him.

Bode climbed higher and carefully maneuvered himself beside her on the narrow stairs. The hatch didn't move for him either. "I don't understand. Something must have fallen over on it." He pushed again, harder this time, and felt the door give a little. "Can you go down a few steps? I don't want to knock you out of the way while I'm pushing."

Comfort didn't move immediately. They were balanced precariously on the same step twenty feet above the floor of the storage room, as close to each other as was possible without embracing, and Comfort was struck by the fact that she was safe. Perfectly safe.

"I love you," she said.

He slowly lowered his arm from over his head while he stared at her. "Does your timing strike you at all as peculiar?"

She made a small, helpless gesture with her shoulders. "I didn't know how to be sure. After Bram . . ." A vertical crease appeared between her eyebrows. "I needed to know that what I feel for you is true."

"You're certain of it?"

"I am."

"And you understand it would be reckless to kiss you just now."

She nodded.

Bode didn't think she looked disappointed, but it was what he felt. He'd given some thought to what he would do when she finally said those words, and in every one of the scenes that unfolded in his mind, he'd kissed her so thoroughly that they had no breath between them.

"Hold on," he said, lowering his head. Recklessness was exactly what was required. He held on to the rope railing with one hand, put the other at her back, and covered her mouth with his. Astonishment made laughter bubble to her lips. The vibration tickled him. He found himself smiling, then chuckling, and in the end it wasn't the kiss that made them breathless, but something as memorable, and perhaps even better.

When he lifted his head, he stared down into eyes that were bright and lively with mischief and the promise of more to come. He was tempted to be reckless again, but the harsh scraping noise over their heads diverted his attention and hers.

They both stared at the hatch as the door began to open. Bode moved instinctively to shield Comfort. He nudged her gently, encouraging her to take a step down. When she did, he took a step up.

Samuel Travers bent over the opening and stared down at Bode. "I guess John didn't get around to telling you about the secret knock. Good thing I recognized your voice." He glanced past Bode to Comfort. "And yours, too, Miss Kennedy. Always did think you had a pretty voice. There's music in it."

Comfort recovered before Bode. "You're very kind, Mr. Travers. Thank you. May we come up now?"

Bode said, "Secret knock?"

Sam let the door fall back and waved Bode up. He stayed close to lend a hand to Comfort.

"What secret knock?" Bode asked again as he and Sam lifted Comfort through the hatch.

"Three sharp raps, then two, then one."

"Good to know. But why do we need a secret knock?" He heard Comfort laugh softly as he plowed his fingers through his hair. He probably looked every bit as confused as he felt. She, on the other hand, was already moving away, staking her claim on territory that had always been his. Before he could stop her, she was bending over his drawing table to study the pitch and curve of his three-blade brass propeller. He put out a hand to stave off Sam's explanation and asked a more salient question. "What the hell are you doing here?"

Samuel's eyes made a significant roll in Comfort's direction. "Language."

Comfort glanced up. "It's all right, Mr. Travers. I've been at sea for better than two weeks. I can make hitches and bends and swear like a sailor."

"You see?" Bode said. "What are you doing here?"

Sam closed the door. He didn't bother shoving the bookcase back on top. Now that Bode was here, the precaution was unnecessary. "Your brother sent me the same night you left, although I didn't know then that you'd gone anywhere. I only knew you weren't here. He gave me a key to get in the office and a message to deliver to you. He was clear that if I didn't bring you back with me, I shouldn't come back at all. I've been here ever since."

"You've been living here." It wasn't really a question. Bode just needed to say it again to put it solidly in his mind.

"That's what I meant when I said I've been here ever since."

Bode made a noise at the back of his throat. "How did you convince John to let you stay?"

Sam pointed to the brace on his leg. "It didn't take much

convincing. He's a good man. Wasn't going to throw me out. I was already nicely settled in before he found me. What with you being gone, he didn't have any reason to come up here. My thumping around gave me away." He shrugged. "I would have had to show my face sooner or later. You didn't have much in the way of food."

"I wasn't expecting visitors."

Sam grunted softly. "You didn't have enough to feed the mice, but I've taken care of that. I made a list of things I needed and your clerks brought them. And don't worry that I put it on your bill. I paid for it all myself."

"Jesus, Sam, I don't care about that."

"Well, you should. I know you don't have two nickels to call your own, and it just makes sense that I should—" He stopped because Bode's head had snapped around to look at Comfort. She was no longer studying the drawings. She'd pushed herself up from the table and was staring at him.

"You heard what he said?" Bode asked her.

She nodded faintly, the rest of her very still. "Is it true?"

"Yes."

"All right." She paused, turning her thoughts and feelings inward, taking measure of herself. After a moment, she said, "No. Nothing's changed. I don't think you married me for my money, and I don't care if you *don't* have two nickels."

Samuel Travers slapped his good leg and thumped his bad one. "I'll be damned. You're married. That's where you've been. John Farwell wouldn't give you up for anything. Not to me, not to your mother, not to anyone else who came around looking for you, and all this time you've been on your honeymoon. I suppose that's about the best news these old ears have heard in a long, long time. A honeymoon. Aren't you the deep one? Well, congratulations." He limped to the drawing table and thrust out his hand to Comfort. "Hope you'll accept my best wishes, Miss Ken—er, Mrs. DeLong."

Comfort took his hand and laughed when he pumped it enthusiastically. "Your best wishes are very welcome."

"I hope you'll excuse my forwardness, ma'am, but I need to say—" Bode's soft groan interrupted him. He glanced over his shoulder.

"Maybe you should hope that *I'll* excuse you," Bode said.

Ignoring him, Samuel Travers turned back to Comfort. "I need to say that I never warmed to the idea of you marrying Bram. Bode here is the right man. Always has been. I didn't know if he'd ever get around to convincing you. I figure he's been thinking about it these, oh, maybe eight, nine years now. It's something you should appreciate, how steady he's been in his affections. Watching you and Bram together all this time, well, that takes its own kind of toll on a person's soul, and I don't suppose it was any different for Bode, but he's patient and constant, and he knows how to persevere."

He smiled broadly. "And hasn't he done just that? It makes a body proud, I can tell you."

"And you certainly have." Bode's mouth twisted wryly. He spoke to Sam, but his eyes were on Comfort's. "Told her, I mean. Told her everything."

Samuel was unapologetic. "Seems like there's been some secret keeping. Best to air it all before the honeymoon's passed."

"You know that from experience, do you?"

Comfort gently chided Bode. "Leave him be. You'll get to be on the other side of this when we sit with my uncles. They're bound to say something I'll wish they hadn't. You'll enjoy that."

He conceded the point. "Give my wife back her hand, Sam, and have a seat. Is there anything to drink?"

Sam released Comfort's hand and stepped toward the table. "I didn't drink all your spirits if that's what you're asking."

"It's not even noon. I wasn't asking for whiskey. Is there tea?"

"Lemonade in the icebox."

"That's sounds good. Comfort? Would you like a glass of lemonade?"

"I would. No, you sit with Mr. Travers. I'll get it."

"Icebox is in the pantry," Travers told her. "That's the first door on your left."

She thanked him and went about finding glasses while Bode sat at the table. She heard Sam congratulate Bode, his wishes perhaps even more heartfelt than the ones he extended to her. Smiling to herself, she set out three glasses.

"So what did my brother need me for that was so important?" asked Bode.

"I don't know. He never told me."

"But you said he had a message."

"Sure. But it didn't explain why he wanted you at his bedside."

"Do you have it?"

Samuel Travers tapped his temple. "Right here. Haven't forgotten a word. I'm supposed to say that Bram's not only lying in bed and that he needs you."

Except for the slow downturn of his mouth, Bode was still. "Tell me again," he said finally.

"Bram said, 'Tell Bode I'm not only lying in bed. Tell him I need him.' Do you know what that first part means? He was particular that I get it right."

Bode nodded. "I had some questions for Bram and I didn't trust his answers. I told him I hoped he wasn't lying to me. He made a joke of it. Said he was lying in bed. What he was telling you, what he wanted me to know, was that, yes, I was right. He's been lying all along."

Chapter Fourteen

"He's in trouble," Bode said quietly. "I knew it, but I let him put just that much doubt in my mind." He closed the gap between his thumb and forefinger and stared at the infinitesimal distance between the two. "Just that much. Did he say anything else, Sam? Anything at all?"

Samuel shook his head. "Nothing. Whatever trouble he got himself into, it must have happened before he broke his leg. Except for you and Miss Kennedy, I mean, Mrs.—"

"It's all right, Mr. Travers." Comfort set a glass of lemonade in front of him. "You don't have to keep correcting yourself. We know who you mean."

He nodded. "Well, then, like I was saying, the two of you, Dr. Harrison, and his mother were the only visitors he had. The help was in and out, but he couldn't get up to much trouble with them. Pardon my frankness, but he doesn't carry on with the maid like your father did."

Bode didn't even wince. "No one else? What about his friends? He never wants for company."

"They came around, most of them anyway, but your mother told Hitchens and anyone else who answered the door to send them away."

Bode absently thanked Comfort for the glass she put in his

hand. His attention was all for Sam Travers. "Why would she do that?"

"Couldn't say except to make a guess."

"Well?" Bode prompted when Sam took a long drink and said nothing afterward.

"I have to believe she thought she was keeping him out of trouble. Your brother and his friends will make a wager on how many times the *Chronicle* uses the word 'depraved' on the front page. He once told me that he put down money on the number of Chinese immigrants that walked off a Barclay ship and the number that had to be carried. His friends don't have to work very hard to provoke him to make a bet, and I'd say he's more often the one needling them. Did you know he invested in *Rigoletto*?"

"No."

"Mr. Jefferson, your mother's friend, encouraged him to do that."

"Where does he get the money?"

"Don't know. I always supposed he uses the allowance you give him. And he wins sometimes, so there's money there. He reinvests it, I guess you'd say."

"I would *not* say."

Comfort pulled out a chair and joined them at the table. She wrapped her hands around her cool glass. "Bram borrows money." When both men turned to look at her, she nodded faintly. "I'm afraid so."

"He told you?" asked Bode.

"No. He wouldn't. I think I mentioned once that Bram and I didn't discuss money. He never hinted that Black Crowne was in financial trouble." She gave Bode a pointed look as she raised her glass and sipped. "I probably shouldn't be telling you this—I'm sure I was never meant to know—but Bram once took out a substantial loan from Jones Prescott. He arranged it privately with Uncle Tuck. I wouldn't have known except I was closing out the books last year, and I found the entry. Usually Tuck would have handled the closing, and I wouldn't have seen it, but he took ill for several days and Newt asked me to begin the work."

"How much is substantial?"

"Twenty thousand."

Bode swore softly. "Tucker Jones lent my brother twenty thousand?"

"The bank lent the money," said Comfort. "Uncle Tuck approved the loan."

"Thank you for clarifying." Frustrated, Bode shoved his hand through his hair. "That makes all the difference."

Comfort bristled. "I'm sure Uncle Tuck didn't know Bram was going to use the money to gamble. Bram repaid it quickly. That must have alerted Uncle Tuck, because I'm unaware of any other loans that he arranged for Bram. It could be that Bram never asked for another."

"At Jones Prescott," said Bode. "But if it worked with someone as shrewd as Tucker Jones, then he's probably done it elsewhere."

Comfort nodded. "That's why I thought I should say something."

"God, what a mess."

Samuel Travers leaned back in his chair. "Shouldn't you be talking to Bram about this?"

"I guess I have to." Bode wanted to press the glass to his forehead. He took a drink instead. "Tell me again when it was that Bram sent you out to find me."

Travers was silent as he reflected back. "A bit more than two weeks back. It was a Wednesday. Well, Thursday actually. It was after midnight. No one was in the office. Not that I expected anyone would be, but I was surprised not to find you at home."

"What could have happened that late that would make Bram send for me?"

Sam shrugged. "The house was quiet. Hitchens is the one who woke me. Bram asked him to."

Bode stared at his glass, trying to make sense of what he was hearing. "How would Bram have summoned Hitchens? And why wouldn't Bram ring for you directly? I thought his bell pull was rigged so he could reach it from his bed."

"It is. I guess I assumed he didn't want to wake anyone else."

"Have you ever known him to be that considerate?" He put up one hand to keep Samuel from answering what was essentially a rhetorical question. "So Hitchens went to Bram first. Is that what we're all thinking?"

Sam Travers said, "Maybe your mother sent Hitchens to Bram's room."

"Or maybe someone came to the door," said Comfort. "Hitchens would answer that, wouldn't he?"

"Yes," Sam told her. "He always does."

"Still," Comfort said, "it was terribly late. What would bring someone to the house that—" She didn't finish; she didn't have to. Out of the corner of her eye, she saw Bode's fingers tighten around his glass. He clenched his jaw. She said, "You think it had to do with me."

Bode nodded.

Sam looked from Comfort to Bode and back again. "How's that again?" When Comfort and Bode exchanged looks without answering, he said, "It's like I was set adrift these last weeks. Could be someone needs to say something, because that Farwell's been like a sphinx."

Smiling faintly, Comfort reached for Bode's hand. "You can tell him. We can't really discuss it around him otherwise. Go on," she said when he hesitated. "I can bear to hear it if you can stand to tell it."

Slipping his hand out from under hers, Bode turned his attention back to Travers. Beginning with the attack on Comfort's carriage, Bode told all of it. By the time he was finished, Samuel Travers had his elbows on the table and his head propped up in his hands. He looked like a man bowed at last by the weight on his shoulders.

"It's not your fault," Bode said. "You couldn't have known he was so deep in debt he was being threatened. None of us could have suspected that someone would use Comfort to force Bram's hand."

Comfort turned her glass slowly. Wet circles stained the tabletop. "You have to go see your brother, Bode. We don't even know if he's all right. Mr. Travers doesn't know anything that's happened at the house since he left."

Sam stared at the table. "Mrs. DeLong's been real anxious to talk to Bode. I know that much." He glanced up and saw that Bode and Comfort were both waiting for him to go on. "She was here that Thursday afternoon, the day after the Rangers attacked the carriage. I know it because she stood at the bottom of the steps and called up for you. That's why I shoved the bookcase over the hatch. I didn't trust her not to make the climb. She sounded that determined. Later, when I finally talked to Mr. Farwell, I learned he told her that you didn't want to be disturbed. He and I worked out the secret knock in case she sent someone from the house to fetch you. She did, but they didn't try to get in, and so no one knows I've been hiding out here."

Sighing deeply, he finally raised his head. "Maybe I should have gone back, in spite of Bram telling me different. I guess I wanted to show him he needed to think before he issued orders like he was a potentator . . . a postenator . . . a—"

"A potentate?" Comfort asked gently.

"That's right. One of those."

Bode looked at Comfort. "The first thing we need to do is get you back to your uncles. They had one job to do while we were gone, and that was to make certain everyone thought you were at home. If I can't be here with you, then I want you there."

"All right. But what is it that you're going to be doing?"

"Killing Bram and calming Alexandra."

"Bode."

He shrugged. "I'll come for you later, or we might even stay with Newt and Tuck for a while. I'll know better what we should do once I've heard what Bram has to say."

"I'll go," she said, "because I want to see my uncles, but you shouldn't plan on abandoning me there. I won't stay without you. And you should expect that at this hour of the day they'll be at the bank, not at home."

"You're right. Sam will escort you to the bank." Bode pushed back his chair and stood. He went to his drawing table, scribbled a few lines on a pad, and then tore the paper loose. He handed it to Travers. "Can you get someone to gather those things for her?"

Sam looked at the list. "I can do this myself. I know just where to go."

"There's money in a coffee tin in the pantry. Take what you think you'll need. Can you negotiate the stairs?"

"I can. I'm not as limber as I once was, but I still do for myself." He got up. "Won't take but an hour or so."

Comfort waited until he was gone before she went toe to toe with Bode. "Why didn't Bram's name come up when we were discussing threats and motives on the *Demeter*? You asked me questions about Newt and Tuck and never once offered Bram's name as a suspect. I know you, Bode. You've been thinking about him all along. Why wouldn't you tell me that?"

Bode didn't flinch, but he found it was more difficult to square off against Comfort when she was hurt than when she was angry. "I wanted to be wrong," he said quietly. "And if I was right, I needed to be sure. He's still my brother, Comfort. Nothing he's done changes that. After I see him today, I may never speak to him again, but it doesn't alter the fact that we'll always be brothers. If there were other people who could have been responsible for what happened to you, I owed Bram the benefit of the doubt until all doubt was erased."

He saw Comfort draw in her lower lip just enough to still its trembling. Tears welled but didn't spill. "I wanted to believe I was protecting you from his betrayal, but like everything else where Bram is concerned, it's more complicated than that. I knew that if Bram was responsible, then I was the one who made the attack on your carriage possible."

She blinked and swiped impatiently at her eyes. "You? You didn't mention that when you were telling Mr. Travers what happened."

"Because I wanted to say it to you first. I told Bram that I was going to meet with you and your uncles. I told him when. I told him where. Without that information, the Rangers couldn't have attacked your carriage."

"That afternoon," Comfort said. "They couldn't have attacked *that afternoon*. I've accustomed myself to the idea that it was inevitable. Someone wanted to make Bram pay by using me. It would have happened sooner or later. I was the security on his debt."

"Do you understand that Bram gave someone the informa-tion that was needed to carry out the threat? No one else knew about our appointment."

"But it was Bram who did that, not you. You probably thought nothing of it when you told him about our meeting."

"I was angry with him. I stuck the knife in when I reminded him that he couldn't get out of bed, and I twisted it by telling him I was going to see you."

"Still, that's hardly Cain and Abel."

"I told him I was going to marry you."

"You did?"

"Not precisely in those words. I told him I wouldn't try to convince you to marry him. I said something about throwing my hat in the ring."

"Oh, well, that *was* rather Cain and Abel of you."

Bode's attention was caught by the sly and wry twist of her mouth. He felt the corners of his mouth lift. She grounded him. "All right," he said. "I'm done trying to martyr myself."

"Good. It doesn't suit." He surprised her by laying a hard, brief kiss on her lips. "What was that for?"

"For me," he said, unapologetic. "That was for me."

She gave him a small push that would have had no effect at all if he didn't want to be moved. "What was on that list you gave to Mr. Travers?"

He started to tell her but was interrupted by thumping and scraping noises on the stairs. "That's your trunk they're trying to bring up. Let me stop them until we know if we'll be staying with your uncles."

Comfort removed herself to the bedroom to look around while Bode dealt with the men. As soon as he was finished with them, he went to get her. He stood in the doorway, leaned against the jamb, and watched her as she smoothed the coverlet on the bed and refolded the quilt at the foot of it. She was a study in the economy of movement, every line graceful, no twist or turn without purpose. Nothing wasted. He recalled how she'd set him back on his heels the one time they had waltzed together, the lithe, catlike motion that would have put him on the floor if she hadn't saved him from himself.

"Can you put me down?" he asked suddenly.

Startled, she glanced up. "Put you down? Like an old nag, you mean?"

"No. The way you did when we danced. Can you do that again?"

"Now?"

"Yes." He glanced around. There wasn't enough clear space for a proper demonstration. "Not here, but in the other room."

"I suppose. You're expecting it, so it would be more difficult, but I think I could." She hugged the quilt to her chest. "Why would you want me to?"

"Humor me." He saw she was still doubtful. "Please?"

She laid the quilt on the bed and followed him out of the room. "I wish you'd explain what you want," she said, holding her ground when he turned to face her. "More importantly, why you want it. Do you think I'm still in danger, Bode? Is that it?" She began to circle him slowly, finding her balance and shifting her weight imperceptibly from heel to toe on her forward foot. "I hope you appreciate that these petticoats and all this drapery are an encumbrance." Her arms lifted in an elegant arc, drawing his eyes to them. "And I did very little in the way of practicing while we were gone. Tell me, do you want me to draw back on the thrust or—"

The moment Comfort saw his thoughts turn inward in contemplation of the answer to her question, she struck. Grabbing fistfuls of her skirts, she yanked them up around her knees and pivoted. Her kick followed so swiftly that it seemed to be part of the same motion. Her foot landed solidly against Bode's abdomen, driving the breath from his lungs. Although he responded swiftly, Comfort had every advantage, and by the time he made a grab at her, momentum was already spinning her out of his reach. She danced away as nimbly as a water sprite.

His arms were still outstretched when she struck again. Her first kick knocked the arm nearest to her out of the way and cleared the path for her to plant her heel solidly against his hip. He staggered sideways but didn't fall and came at her as a boxer would, feinting, bobbing, and weaving. Comfort raised her skirts even higher, showing off a pair of lacy drawers that closely followed the line of her hips and thighs. She anticipated that his glance would drop, and he didn't disappoint. She kicked again, and this time put her foot firmly against his groin, applying only enough pressure to let him know how much worse it could have been.

Even if Bode's instinct hadn't been to double over to protect himself from a second strike, Comfort retracted her leg too fast for him to grab it. Once again, she danced out of the way and continued to circle him. Her dark eyes fairly gleamed. She was a watchful predator, seeing all of him in a single glance.

The next time she struck, it was with the heel of her hand, and she brought it down solidly between his shoulder blades before he straightened. Bode lurched forward and was able to keep from falling by grabbing one of the chairs at the table. It wobbled noisily and then tipped backward on its rear legs. Now Comfort attacked the chair, not Bode, and when it crashed to the floor, he dropped to his knees, threw up his hands, and offered surrender.

Standing outside of his reach, Comfort watched him warily, suspecting a trick. Bode looked less like a man defeated than one enjoying himself. There was nothing contrite about the smile he flashed at her. His amusement made her want to pick up the chair and clobber him with it. She lifted a single eyebrow and conveyed that sentiment without saying a word.

Bode sobered, but even on his knees he couldn't manage penitence. "Will you allow me to get up?"

Comfort didn't answer immediately. She straightened her overskirt, paying particular attention to the ruffled trim, and then smoothed the front of her bodice. "Perhaps if you tell me the point of that exercise."

"I needed to be reminded that you're not without defenses."

She simply shook her head, her mouth flattening. It required some effort not to roll her eyes. She picked up the chair and slid it back into place while Bode jumped to his feet. She sensed him behind her but didn't try to evade his embrace when his arms circled her. Leaning back against his chest, she set her arms over his.

"I'm not afraid," she said quietly. "I don't want you to be afraid for me."

"If only it were that simple."

"I know. I feel the same for you."

"Me?"

Comfort turned her head and gave him a significant look. "As I recall, you were no more able to hold your own against the Rangers than Newt or Tuck or me." She paused a beat. "Or the pack of young ruffians that finished what the Rangers began."

He made a slight grimace. "Present company excepted, I do all right when the odds are a little closer to even."

"I'm sure you do." She turned in his arms and lifted her

mouth to kiss his wounded smile. When she drew back, she asked, "Did you ever reckon with the boys?"

"No. I thought I'd be able to find at least one of them, but they disappeared like shadows at high noon."

She nodded, not surprised. "What about the Rangers?"

Bode's eyes darted sideways.

"Bode?"

"The men standing guard outside your room at the concert saloon?"

"Yes? What about them?"

"I'm fairly certain they were two of my attackers. You understand, there wasn't any time to exchange pleasantries, but I like to think I got some of my own back."

Remembering the breadth and brawn of the pair who all but carried her up the saloon's stairs, Comfort couldn't quite contain a shiver. She'd been helpless, but Bode had summarily dispatched them. Feeling the need to move and shake off her unease, she separated herself from Bode and collected the glasses on the table. "I've been thinking about the attack," she said. "The one against you, not me."

"So have I."

"You have?"

"For a quite a while." He watched her set the glasses in the sink and waited until she turned to face him before he cocked an inquiring eyebrow. "Do you want to tell me?"

"It's occurred to me that the attack on you wasn't random. I've been wondering if the Rangers were waiting for you."

"You're thinking that Bram was responsible."

"Yes. I'm sorry, Bode, but yes."

He exhaled softly. "It's all right. I suspected him almost at once."

"The night of the party?"

Bode nodded. "When I learned about your engagement, I began to think that Bram's announcement wasn't the whim of a moment. He only wanted to convince you that it was. We expect him to act on impulse, so it wasn't hard for him to make us believe that he'd done it again, but I believe he had the attack and the announcement planned. You said it earlier. You were the collateral on Bram's debt. He made you his security that evening."

"How much do you think he owes, Bode?"

"It's hard to say."

"More than a thousand?"

Bode's short chuckle was humorless. "Conservatively? With interest on the debt, I'd say roughly a hundred thousand now."

Comfort dropped like a stone on the window bench. She stared at him. "Surely not."

Bode pulled out the stool under his drawing table and sat, hooking one heel on a rung. "How much are you worth, Comfort? You. Tucker. Newton. What's an estimate of your family's holdings?"

"Between three and a half and four million."

He whistled softly. "I really didn't know, but it makes my point for me. Bram wouldn't understand your astonishment at the size of his debt. What he owes isn't a small percent of your total assets. Once you were married, he'd have expected to be able to put his hands on that money very quickly."

Comfort's eyes dropped to her lap, her brow furrowing as she considered what she could do. She pleated her overskirt between her fingers and then smoothed it out again.

"Don't say it," Bode said, watching her. "I know what you're getting ready to propose. Don't."

Her head snapped up. "But I could pay the debt. I could sell some stocks and bonds and—"

"No." Bode sliced the air with his hand. "I've done what you're suggesting. It only fixes the immediate problem, not the one at the root of it all. I love my brother, Comfort, but I'm no longer willing to save him from himself. Not financially, not even if I could." He ran a hand through his hair, a gesture that spoke to weariness and frustration. "I can't stop you from doing it, and I know you mean well, but it's wrong. If you help him this time, you can expect that his debt will be half again as much in the future. My mother sold heirloom jewelry the last time. I imagine that's why she's been so adamant that you and Bram marry. She's looking for someone else to manage the burden of his debt."

"She knows?"

"She knows Bram. I'm guessing that she suspects everything else. It was no different with my father. Alexandra's nature is to protect her family. She can't help herself."

Comfort could appreciate Alexandra's urge to make things right. "She doesn't have as much to do with Black Crowne as people think, does she?"

"No."

"But you allow everyone to believe differently."

He shrugged. "It not important to me, and it's a matter of pride for her. She and I have an arrangement regarding the business. I agreed to manage it, and she agreed not to interfere. We lost five ships during the war, Comfort. Three to capture that were never recovered and two others to damage so extensive that they were not worth saving. Black Crowne used to dominate the most important Atlantic shipping lanes. That changed when my father redirected our ships to be used for assisting other vessels running the blockades, not for trade. My father mortgaged everything. He used his influence to get credit and then extensions on the credit. My mother appealed to him to reconsider, but there was no reasoning with him, because he believed in the cause he was supporting. We only managed to save those ships that were on Pacific trade routes and didn't arrive in time to go with the fleet that my father put together. Alexandra thinks he was reckless. I prefer to think he was passionate. Sometimes there's not much difference between the two."

Comfort had no trouble recalling the power and majesty of the ship depicted in the painting in Alexandra DeLong's parlor. She also remembered how Bode had described his artist father. "He was a romantic," she said.

"Yes. Romantic. The collision of passion and recklessness."

Her smile was faint, gently chiding. "You're a romantic, Bode. Passionate and principled. I'm not sure that reckless has anything to do with it."

He wanted to thank her for that, wanted to kiss her in fact, but her comment passed without acknowledgment of any kind because of the thump and drag on the stairs. Bode pushed away from the table before Comfort could rise, and he went to the hatch.

"Ahoy!" Sam called up as the door opened. He clutched the rope railing tightly with one hand and held up the bundle he was carrying in the other. "Got everything you wanted."

"Good. Do you need help?" Bode didn't know why he bothered asking. Sam's reply was a snort and a sneer. "I'll just hold the door," he said.

Sam handed over the bundle when he reached the top and made it through the opening without assistance. He grinned at Comfort. "You're going to want some help if this is where you and Master Bode are going to live, and even if it's not, you're going to need someone to manage your household."

"Are you applying for the job, Mr. Travers?" asked Comfort.

"Could be that I am." He smoothed his jacket and stood at attention, presenting himself for inspection.

"Well, I am very interested." She stood and took the bundle that Bode held out to her without looking at it or him. "I will have to check your references, of course."

"Of course."

Now Comfort glanced at Bode. He was trying to look as if he were merely resigned to the inevitable, but she glimpsed approval and something like relief in his eyes. She smiled at Samuel Travers. "Welcome aboard."

"Thank you, ma'am." He pointed to the wrapped bundle in her arms. "I think you'll find everything's to your liking."

Comfort finally looked at what she held. The shape of what she'd been handed was conical with the tip of the cone pointed toward the floor. She loosened the knot in the string that kept the fabric cover in place and then tugged the string free. She laid back the material and saw she was holding clothing that had been neatly folded and placed into a Chinese straw hat. She didn't have to ask the purpose. "Excuse me, gentlemen."

Comfort could hear Bode and Sam talking as she changed clothes in the bedroom. She couldn't make out what they were saying, but it was reasonable to suppose they were discussing getting her safely to the bank. When she finished dressing in the tunic, pants, and slippers, she scraped back her hair and plaited it, tying it off with a black band that Sam had provided for just that purpose. She set the dou lì on her head and slipped the black silk strap under her chin.

Comfort tried to match Suey Tsin's small, careful steps and slightly bowed head when she walked back into the other room.

She only looked up when neither man spoke. Sam Travers gaped at her, but Bode was studying her critically.

"What are you looking for?" she asked. "*I* thought I was Suey Tsin."

"So did I until you thrust your chin out and dressed me down."

"Oh." She dutifully lowered her eyes, tucked her chin, and folded her hands in front of her.

"Much better," Bode said. "And don't worry that I'll expect it when you're not wearing that hat. I know who I married."

Sam chuckled as Comfort raised her head just long enough to give Bode a smug and saucy smile.

Bode took Comfort's hands and held them. He welcomed her looking at him now. "Sam and one of my clerks will follow you to the bank. Escorting you would seem odd, and I don't want anything to draw attention to you." He glanced over his shoulder at Sam. "Did you get the market basket?"

"Downstairs waiting for her."

"Good." He turned back to Comfort. "You'll have something to carry. You should arouse no comment or suspicion as long as you keep reminding yourself that you're Suey Tsin. Go straight to the bank. If Newt and Tuck aren't there, wait for them. I imagine your maid's been to Jones Prescott before."

"Yes. Not often, but the tellers know her. She'd be allowed to go upstairs without question. Everyone will assume her visit has something to do with me."

"That's what I'm counting on. You'll leave with your uncles in a carriage. Once you're at home, stay there until I come for you. I have to speak to John Farwell first, then to Bram and Alexandra, but I'll see you tonight."

She nodded. "You'll be careful?"

"I don't think anyone but my mother's particularly interested in me." He saw immediately that she wasn't satisfied with his answer. "Yes, I'll be careful."

She took off the dou lì and used it to shield their parting kiss from Sam. She thought she heard his light laughter, but she and Bode ignored it. They separated after Sam was through the hatch. Bode took the hat from her and set it properly on her head.

"Tonight," he promised.

Comfort hurried off before she thought better of it.

Tucker Jones leaned forward in his chair and rubbed the back of his neck. He'd been feeling unsettled and edgy since he woke. Newton hadn't helped by being alert to every one of his fidgets and commenting on it. Now was no exception.

"Is that a prickle?" asked Newt. "Looks as if it might be."

"It's a pain in my neck," Tuck said. "Same as you."

"Never known you to be bothered quite so much." He checked his pocket watch. "It's not even noon."

Tucker swept aside the documents on his desk. "Too early for a drink?"

"Probably too early to get drunk, but there's nothing wrong with a drink." He stood. "Don't trouble yourself. I'll get it." He rounded both desks and headed for the Hildesheim safe. He removed two glasses and a bottle of whiskey and set them on top of the safe. "Will one finger do the trick?" He looked back at Tucker for the answer. His partner was holding up two fingers. Nodding, Newt gave each glass a generous pour and carried them back. He handed Tucker one and returned to his side of the desk with the other. "I miss her, too," he said. "Hate it that I can't go down the hall and count how many pencils she has in her hair. I usually win that bet."

Tucker's smile was rueful, even a little wistful. He didn't feel much like the soldier who had been at the battle for Monterrey or even the one who'd stood at his post drinking tequila while Newt negotiated terms with a fiery Mexican *puta* at the bar. "When do you suppose we stopped being the ones who found her and started being the ones who fathered her?"

Newton knew exactly what Tuck meant, and he didn't have to think about his reply. "For me it was the first time I braided her hair. Knew it right off. She put a slippery blue ribbon in my hand and just sort of expected that I would know what to do with it. She was real patient, too. Stood there as stoic as a Spartan and waited me out. I was all thumbs, and that ribbon wriggled in my hands like a worm on a hook. Still, she looked pretty when I was done. I remember that like it was yesterday. What about you?"

Tucker considered his answer before he spoke. "We were living in the mining camp? Remember?"

Newt nodded. "Too well."

"We were barely scratching out a living for ourselves at that point, and we had this extra mouth to feed, only it didn't occur to me that it was an extra mouth. Having her there gave me a purpose, you know, and I sort of realized that I was doing it for her. It felt right. I wanted to do it for her, like I would my own. Guess I knew then that she was my own."

"Seems like it wasn't so long ago."

"I know, and it's been twenty years."

"Did you ever think we should've done more to find out if she had any family?"

"Nope. Never once. Always thought we did enough. We're her family."

Newt sipped his drink. "It's the same for me. I never did want anyone else to braid her hair. Not even you."

Laughter rumbled from deep in Tucker's chest. He just shook his head. "Some tough old soldiers we turned out to be. Guess we'd be the talk of every man in B Company if they knew." He put a hand to the back of his neck again and rubbed. He felt Newt's eyes on him. "What?"

"You're doing it again. It's a prickle."

"It's a damn sight more than that." He rolled his shoulders. It was impossible for him to get comfortable in his own skin.

"What does it mean?" asked Newt.

"You know what I know. Something's coming our way."

"Good fortune? Bad? Can't you tell?"

"It'll be what we make of it. That's always how it is. Twenty years ago we happened upon a massacre and found a daughter. You tell me. Good fortune or bad?"

Newt didn't answer. His attention was directed to the soft footfalls in the hallway. He hadn't heard anyone on the stairs. He swiveled in his chair and faced the open door as Suey Tsin stepped into view. Setting down his drink, he started to rise. A deepening frown pushed his dark eyebrows together. "What's happened?" he asked. "Are you all right?" He could see that she was trembling slightly. Across from him, Tuck was also getting to his feet. "Suey Tsin. Look at me. What are you doing here?"

Comfort barely glanced at Newt before she threw herself at him. She felt him rock back on his heels and bump the desk. She simply held on. There was an infinitesimal pause, and then his arms came around her. She smiled. It had taken him no longer than a single beat of his heart to recognize her. She pressed her face into his neck and clutched him, giving up the embrace only so she could make Tuck part of it.

"It's you," Newt said, his throat thick. "It's her, Tuck. It's our girl."

Comfort could hardly draw a breath for the fierceness of Newt's hug, but the light-headed, giddy feeling that accompanied it kept her right where she was. Tucker's hug was only marginally less enthusiastic. When they finally released her, she stepped backward and lowered herself into the nearest chair. She tilted her head up and looked them over, wondering if her smile was as drunkenly happy as theirs appeared to be.

"Can we go home?" she asked. "I really want to go home."

Bode usually made it a point to knock when he visited Alexandra or his brother. It was his way of reminding them he didn't live there any longer. He did it more for his mother's benefit than Bram's, because Bram had never cared, and Alexandra had cared too much. He was already halfway up the stairs when Hitchens appeared in the entrance hall.

"Mr. DeLong! Sir! Can I take your—"

Bode paused only long enough to direct the butler. "Tell my mother I'm here. I'll be with Bram if she'd like to come up."

Bram couldn't say what woke him so abruptly. He blinked several times, disoriented but aware that his heart was racing. He wondered if he'd had a nightmare, but nothing came to him. He couldn't even recall when he fell asleep. He'd been roused for breakfast but ate very little of it. He'd allowed his new valet to tend to him, bathing him and seeing to his needs, and then he'd sent the man to Chinatown. Was he back? Was that what had wakened him?

Bram pushed himself up on his elbows. His vision was finally clear enough to see that someone was standing in the doorway. "Bode." His voice was pleasant if still a bit groggy. "You're back."

Bode shut the door hard, jerking Bram to attention. His brother's focus only lasted for a moment. Bode watched Bram's shoulders slump. The rest of him followed suit until he was as inert and shapeless as warm candle wax on the white linens.

"You look like hell, Bram." He walked over to the bed, glanced around for the laudanum, and then began a careful search between the mattress and the headboard and under the sheets. Bram didn't protest until Bode began patting him down, which was how Bode knew he was getting close. He found two small bottles tucked away in Bram's splint. He pocketed them. The droopy look of alarm on his brother's face would have been comical if it weren't so damned pathetic.

Swearing softly, Bode grabbed Bram by the collar of his shirt and twisted hard. Bram clawed at Bode's wrists, but Bode held on. "Get yourself together, Bram. You find your wits, or I swear I'll yank you right out of this bed and make you look for them."

Bram choked out something that Bode didn't understand. He loosened his grip a fraction. Bram gasped and kept trying to break Bode's hold. "You're choking me," he ground out.

"Good. That's what I want to do."

"Jesus! Bode!" Bram felt himself being lifted off the bed. He held on to Bode's wrists. "Put me down. My leg. You're—"

"Killing you? How would you know? You can't feel a damn thing."

"I can! I swear I—"

Bode shoved Bram hard against the headboard and let go. The bed frame shuddered. The back of Bram's head bounced off the dark wood, and then he was still, dazed but conscious. Disgusted, Bode stepped back. He wanted to break something, and at the moment, Bram's head was the easy target. Turning his back on Bram, he went to the window and opened the drapes. It was satisfying to hear his brother's pained groan as late afternoon sunlight flooded the room.

"Are you awake yet?" Bode asked, turning around to face Bram again. "Ready to answer questions?"

"God, Bode. What the hell—"

"My questions, Bram. You don't get to have any." He took a threatening step toward the bed and stopped when Bram nodded quickly. "Good. I spoke to Samuel Travers this morning. I know what you told him, and I know what it meant. Now I want to hear the rest from you. So help me, Bram, it had better be the truth. Why did you send Sam out to get me that night?"

"Jesus, Bode, someone delivered a message to me about Comfort. Mother told me that afternoon that Comfort had been taken away by the Rangers. I didn't hear another thing about it until I got the message. It was a ransom demand. They wanted money. You know I don't have any. The threat was explicit. The note was clear. They wanted me to know exactly what Comfort's fate would be if I didn't meet their demand."

"Do you still have the note?"

Bram shook his head.

Bode's eyes narrowed faintly. "Why send for me? You know I don't have any money. Why didn't you send for Newt or Tuck?"

"It was too late for that."

"Too late? Didn't you say it was a ransom note? How could it have been too late to ask them for money?" When Bram merely stared at him, Bode said, "You can't help yourself, can you?" He went to the foot of the bed and studied the apparatus that held Bram's leg at the correct elevation and tension. He set his hand on the crank and began to slowly turn it. Bram flailed wildly and shouted for him to stop. After one full turn, he did. "Try again, Bram."

"No one asked for ransom," he said quickly. "The note only told me what was going to happen to her."

"I see. And what was that?"

"The Rangers were going to put her on the block. Sell her off to the highest bidder."

"Why would they do that, Bram?" He rested his hand lightly on the crank and waited.

"They wanted to prove they could."

It was a partial answer at best. "Most people would take a threat from the Rangers seriously the first time they heard it. You didn't, though, did you?"

"I *did*," he insisted. "I did. But I thought I could hold them off."

"Because you were engaged to Comfort."

"That's right. They knew I'd be good for what I owed them. They *knew* it."

"Apparently not. Apparently they didn't trust you."

"I didn't know. I thought they accepted the arrangement." Bram pressed a hand to his forehead and massaged it. Sweat beaded on his brow. It was so damnably difficult to concentrate. "Can you at least take your hand off the crank?"

"Take it off? I was considering giving it another turn. You gave her up, Bram. You told someone where she could be found. That's how the Rangers were able to take her on the way to my office. You did that to her."

Bram groaned softly and closed his eyes. "God, Bode. No. It wasn't like that. You have to believe me."

"Actually, I don't." He looked his brother over. Bram's eyes were still closed, and he looked childlike, as if squeezing them shut made him invisible to others. Bode stepped away from the machine so he wouldn't be tempted to turn the crank for no reason other than spite. He sat in the chair at Bram's bedside and nudged the mattress with his foot so Bram would know he'd moved and open his eyes.

Bram turned his head and looked at Bode. His eyes were damp. "I thought you could get her back. That's why I sent for you. You always think of something. Nothing was supposed to happen to Comfort. It should have been a ransom. That's all. I love her, Bode. I would never do anything to hurt her."

"Except make her your fiancée," Bode said dryly. "And then dangle her like shark bait. Do you even know what happened to her?"

"I know she got away."

"How do you know that?"

"I've heard from her since that night. Her uncles wrote to me on her behalf." He stared at the ceiling. "She ended our engagement. They said she doesn't want anything to do with me. With any of us, really. None of the DeLongs." Bram glanced at Bode again. "Where were you that night? Why didn't you come?"

Bode didn't answer. There wasn't anything he was going to tell Bram that he didn't have to. "I spoke to John Farwell this afternoon. He had as many interesting things to tell me as Sam."

Bram rubbed his eyes until he saw color swirling behind his eyelids. He couldn't think properly. He needed more laudanum to clear the fog from his brain. "I don't care about Farwell. Where's Sam been? He never came back."

"You told him not to, not without me."

"Did I? Maybe I did. I don't remember." He took his hand away from his eyes. His sigh was shaky. "So where was he?"

"It doesn't matter. He was finally able to deliver your message, and here I am."

"I don't need you now."

"You don't? Did you pay off your debt? That's what all of this is about, isn't it?"

"I worked something out."

"I'd like to hear about that. How much do you owe?"

"It's been taken care of."

"You did that on your own? From your bed?"

"Yes."

Bode couldn't tell if Bram was tiring or needed the laudanum so badly that he couldn't string two thoughts together. Perhaps it was both. His face was flushed and his forehead glistened. Bram's hands rested on his chest. There was a slight tremor in his fingertips.

"Look at me, Bram," Bode said. "I need you to concentrate."

"Then give me back the laudanum."

Bode shook his head. "I want to know about the Pinkertons. Farwell told me a detective from the agency was asking after me. Did you hire them to find me?"

"No. Mother did."

That lifted Bode's eyebrows. After listening to what his clerk had to say, he'd been certain it was Bram who was connected to the detective. "John said Alexandra was there the day after I left and sent someone from the house to find me a few days after that."

"Why are you surprised? She was worried about you. Where

did you go, Bode? You brought the Pinks down on your own head. You could have just told her what you were doing and where you went, and she would have left you alone."

"It was business. John told her that. It should have been enough. It satisfied the detective."

"I'm sure it did," Bram said tiredly. "I tried to tell her that Farwell was acting at your direction, but she couldn't let it be. I didn't know about the Pinks until after she hired them."

"I'll set that right with her." He glanced toward the door. "I thought she'd be here by now. I told Hitchens to tell her I was here."

"She's out. One of her charities."

Bode realized he hadn't given the butler any time to explain that. "It's probably just as well. It'll be better if I speak to her alone."

Bram frowned. "What do you have to say to her that I can't hear?"

"I was thinking it was better for all of us if she didn't see me turn the crank."

"You're going to turn it again?"

"I might, if you don't tell me more about the Pinks."

"I told you. She hired them. I didn't."

"Who came to talk to her? I want a name."

"God, Bode. I don't remember. I only talked to him the once."

He watched Bram closely. The soporific effects of the laudanum made his features difficult to read. He decided to say the name John Farwell had given him and see if there was any reaction. "What about James R. Crocker?"

Bram's frown became more pronounced. "That might have been it." He closed his eyes. "If you already knew, why did you need to hear it from me? You're giving me a headache, Bode."

"Did Mr. Crocker tell you that I met him before, Bram? Twice. Once at the opera house and later on the *Demeter Queen*. I thought you might have had something to do with that."

"Is there anything you're not going to lay at my door? Jesus, Bode. Go away."

Bode wasn't moved by Bram's weary whine. "It always struck me as odd that he came to the ship for the purpose of inquiring about Comfort's welfare. He saw her faint at the opera. He didn't identify himself as a Pinkerton agent when he introduced himself."

"So? It doesn't sound as if he was there on agency business."

"He's from Sacramento."

"And?" Bram rubbed his face hard, trying to stay alert.

"A little over six months ago I sent you to Sacramento. You only had to talk to some people, but I'm thinking that's when you got yourself in trouble." When Bram didn't say anything, Bode went on. "You don't owe the Rangers, Bram. They wouldn't let you get in as deep as I think you are. I think you owe men considerably more influential than thugs from the Barbary Coast. Men who could ruin us. If you've really paid off your debt, I need to know who you sacrificed this time."

Bram's laughter was more a jerky heaving of his chest and shoulders than an actual sound. "Can't you guess, Bode?" he said when he could speak. "You know everything else. I sacrificed you."

Chapter Fifteen

Comfort sat on the sofa in her uncles' study and turned the red-and-white tin over and over. Neither Newt nor Tucker asked her to stop. She hadn't requested the tin, but Suey Tsin had shyly produced it almost at once, offering it in place of a welcoming embrace. Comfort had gravely accepted the tin as well as Suey Tsin's apology for not packing it. At the conclusion of that small ceremony there was an exchange of brief, faintly watery smiles, this time between Newton and Tuck.

Comfort still wore the tunic, trousers, and slippers that Sam had given her. The cat curled next to her on the sofa, the largest part of him hidden under the dou lì. Occasionally Thistle poked his nose out from under the hat and demanded some attention, but mostly he was content to have the heat and scent of his mistress close by.

It hadn't occurred to Comfort to change clothes. Not that either of her uncles would have let her out of their sight long enough for her to put on something else. They had so many questions on the ride back that a great deal of her story came out in fits and starts, disjointed by more questions and told in a manner that had no straightforward timeline.

Once they were home and settled in the study, Comfort began again, this time at her own pace and with fewer interruptions. They ate very little of the luncheon that was served while she was still relating her story, but once she was done, Newt and Tuck indulged the appetite that had suddenly and fiercely returned to them.

Now they sat leaning back in their chairs, legs stretched before them, their hands folded and resting on hard, slightly swollen bellies. They had the look of men exhausted by their good fortune. It made Comfort smile to see them replete and relaxed. With no conscious thought given to the activity, she stopped turning over the tin.

"When will Bode get here?" asked Tuck.

"He said it would be this evening. He had to talk to Mr. Farwell and then to Bram and his mother. There're still things we don't understand."

"I wonder what Bode thinks he'll get from his brother," Newt said. "Except lies. Seems like Bram's good at that." He lifted a finger and pointed to Tuck. "What were you thinking, lending that boy twenty thousand dollars?"

Tucker shrugged. "He told me it was for an investment with Clinton Maddox's railroad. He knew quite a bit about the business plan. I learned the rest for myself before I gave him the money. It was a sound investment with the possibility of a good return. I thought he deserved a chance."

Newt snorted. "He deserved a thrashing."

"He paid the loan back," Tuck pointed out. "We didn't lose a dime."

Comfort could tell that Newt wanted to needle Tucker a little bit longer. She stopped him by asking, "Did you know that the DeLongs have almost no money?"

"Almost no money?" asked Newt. "Did Bode tell you that?"

"Actually, he said they had none."

"Well, that's all right, then. Better that you know the truth. There's a creditor attached to every one of the family's assets, and Croft Federal holds it all."

"How do you know that?"

"Branford told us," Tuck said. "He came to us for money. Newt and I could see things were going badly for him. The one time Branford DeLong stood for anything, he stood with the side that couldn't win. We saw how the war turned after Gettysburg. We couldn't lend him anything. He was trying to rob

Peter to pay Paul. He'd already lost a couple of ships. It didn't look as if Black Crowne could survive the war."

Newt nodded and tapped his thumbs together. "When Branford was killed, we figured it was the end of Black Crowne. 'Course we never thought that Bode might step into the breach, or that once he did, that he'd be able to keep his head above water. He knew about sailing and trade because he'd been around the business all his life. But there was college first, and then there was the war. Neither one of us thought he knew enough about Black Crowne to keep it afloat." He winced. "Forgive the pun."

"But he has, hasn't he? Kept it afloat, I mean."

"More or less," Newt said. "Staying with the theme, he's treading water. That's a remarkable accomplishment in its own right. It taught me not to underestimate him."

Tuck knuckled his chin. "That drawing you saw, the one of the iron paddle steamer?"

"Yes?" asked Comfort. "What about it?"

"Newt and I thought it might just be what Bode needed to turn things around. We know a little about his situation from Bancroft. He gives his mother and brother money that he could be using to better manage the debt. I imagine he keeps a tight rein on them, but it's still a strain. This ship of his could help him get out ahead. We thought we'd like to help him with that. It wouldn't hurt us either."

"It's not a paddle steamer any longer," she said. "It will still have an iron hull, but he's designing a three-bladed brass propeller to power her."

Tuck and Newt exchanged glances. It was Newt who spoke. "Better yet. That's the future. He understands what it will take to compete."

"Then you're still interested?"

"Of course." He frowned at Comfort's less than relieved expression. "What is it? I thought that would please you."

"What?" She realized she was turning the tin again. "Oh. It does. It pleases me a great deal."

"But?" asked Tuck.

She shrugged lightly. "I don't know if Bode will take your money. He might have before, but now that we're married, I don't know. It seems to be important to him that I know he didn't marry me because of my connection to the bank or the money I have in my own right."

"Well, that's easy to fix," Newt said. "We'll fire you and then cut you off."

Comfort might have believed him if Newt had ever been able to keep a straight face. He always let her know he was teasing. Tucker liked to make her wonder for at least a few seconds longer. "Mm. There's a solution I hadn't thought of. It would be interesting to hear what Bode had to say about it."

"Better not tell him," Tuck said. "If he's confused about why you think he married you, he might just be fool enough to accept those terms. Lord, but I've been counting on him not being an idiot."

"He's not that," Comfort told him. "Never that. He loves me. Sam Travers seems to think Bode's had feelings for me for a long time. Can you imagine?"

"As a matter of fact, I can." Newt's cheeks puffed like two small balloons as he blew out a long breath. "I'd say it was the coming-out party that did him in." He looked at Tuck for confirmation, and when his partner nodded, he went on. "Yep. The come-out. He couldn't take his eyes off you. Can't say that he knew a damn thing about love back then, but he sure looked like he was interested in knockin' on its door."

Comfort blushed. "That can't be right. I was sixteen. He was . . . well, he was—"

"He was a man," Tuck said flatly. "A soldier facing nothing but uncertainty. I can't say that I was sorry when he stayed on the other side of the room. It was probably the first and last time I was grateful to Bram DeLong for making an entrance."

"I knew he was there, but the rest . . ." She raised her hands a bit helplessly. "I didn't know about the rest."

"A man's entitled to keep a few things to himself, I reckon."

Agreeing, Newt grunted softly. He drew in his legs and sat forward in his chair. "Are you going to leave with him tonight?"

"If he goes, yes. My home's with him now."

"I don't disagree, but that's no place for you to live."

"Once you get past the entrance, it's surprisingly welcoming."

"Black Crowne practically sits in the Barbary Coast."

"That's an exaggeration, Uncle Newt. And don't forget that you and Tuck thought it was safe enough to let me accompany you there."

Newton frowned deeply. "Are you arguing for or against living in that place? Because reminding Tuck and me about letting you come along that day isn't the way to convince us that it's safe."

"He's my husband," said Comfort. "I want to be where he is."

"Well, there's no reason you both can't settle here for a time. We've got so many rooms that if I don't visit them once a month, I forget they're there. You and Bode can have a whole suite to yourselves. Take your meals there, if you like. We won't get underfoot."

Comfort's fingers tightened on the tin. "Please don't press me for an answer now. Let me talk to Bode. I think he might agree with you."

Tuck intervened when he saw Newt didn't want to give up just yet. "Leave off, Newt. Bode will do right by her. He has already. She's here now, isn't she? That's his doing, no one else's."

Newt heaved himself back in his chair. He was quiet for a long moment, settling himself down. He finally nodded.

Tuck directed his faint, knowing smile at Comfort. Newt just needed time. He glanced at the tin and then at her again. "Nightmares?"

"Once. A day or so after we boarded the *Demeter Queen*. Not since."

"That's good. I thought that maybe the way you were holding on to Dr. Kennedy's lozenges meant there had been more."

She shook her head. "I think I had the nightmare because Bode and I argued about you."

Tuck pointed to himself. "Me?"

"Both of you." She saw Newt sit up straighter. "He was trying to understand why I was abducted. Looking at all the possibilities, you know."

"And our names came up?"

"Yes." She started to say that she was the one who mentioned them first, but she didn't have the chance. Newt was laughing and reaching into his pocket at the same time. "You said it, Tuck. Damn me for not believing you." He extended his hand and dangled a twenty out to his partner.

Tuck took it, thanked him, and put it in his vest pocket.

Comfort came close to throwing the tin. It was owing to the fact that she couldn't decide who deserved it more that she kept it in her hand. "You are both ridiculous. Aren't either of you insulted?"

"I told Newt that Bode would have to eliminate us as suspects before he'd let you come back here. That was good thinking on his part. I figured when we saw you at the bank, he'd decided it wasn't one of us."

"You didn't suspect each other, did you?"

"Now that would have just been plain foolish," said Newt. "Bode doesn't know us the way we know each other. Sounds like you tried to set him straight, so we appreciate that."

Comfort simply shook her head. She'd never understand the way their minds worked. She set the tin down beside the dou lì and let Thistle paw at it. "Tell me about the bank. What have you been doing while I've been gone?"

Comfort was enjoying a hot bath when Bode arrived. She heard Newt and Tuck greeting him like the prodigal son and wondered if they were contemplating killing the fatted calf for dinner. She thought Bode would come straightaway to her room, but the voices receded, and she realized her uncles were stealing him away. If she didn't join them soon and carefully pour their drinks, they would all be three sheets to the wind.

Suey Tsin helped her dress and fixed her hair. She hadn't realized how much she missed the luxury of this attention, and judging from Suey Tsin's expression, her maid had missed it as well. "We'll work something out," she said. "I promise. I won't leave you again, not if you want to stay with me."

Suey Tsin's fingers stilled in Comfort's hair. "Mista Bode say okay?"

"He will. I let him have Mr. Travers. He can't deny me you." She saw that Suey Tsin didn't understand, and she didn't try to explain. She reached over her shoulder and found Suey Tsin's small hand. She squeezed it gently. For now, it was enough.

Comfort expected to find them gathered in the study. When she didn't, she stopped one of the maids and was directed to the conservatory. She heard their low, distinctly male voices the moment she opened the door. They weren't immediately in sight. She followed the familiar path through the palms and ferns to the clearing at the center of the room. Each man was seated on his own bench, a drink in hand. They stood as one when she came upon them.

Comfort waved them back. Bode invited her to sit beside him, but she shook her head and took a seat on the last empty bench in the six o'clock position. Newt was directly opposite her at twelve, Tuck on her right at three, and Bode on her left at nine. She had the sense that they had only been passing time until she arrived. Now they were ready to talk.

"It's hard to know what to make of anything that Bram says," Bode told them. "The laudanum doesn't help. In the short time I've been gone, I can see what a difference the use of it's made. Alexandra wasn't at home, and I didn't want to wait for her, so I'll go back and see her later. I wanted you to know what Bram told me."

He set his drink aside while he ticked off the important points on his fingers, most of which Comfort already knew. Newt and Tuck listened without comment or question as Bode outlined his brother's betrayal. "He says he's taken care of the debt, but that only means he's pushed it onto someone else. I didn't think he'd admit it, and I suppose that's where the drug worked in my favor. He either couldn't control his tongue or his conceit, but he told me where the men he owes would be looking for their pound of flesh."

Newt's fingertips whitened on his glass. "Not Comfort. Not again."

"No. Not this time. I'm the one they're after."

Tuck pointed at Bode's chest. "You?"

Comfort's stomach turned over. The marble bench under her fingers suddenly felt warmer than she did. "What does that mean, Bode?"

"It means they're going to call in Black Crowne's debt, take over the business, and sell off assets to recover what Bram owes."

"Bram told you that?"

Bode didn't look at her. He stared at his folded hands and

recalled how the crank turned slowly under his palm. Bram's arrogance was short-lived, but he hadn't caved as quickly as Bode hoped. His ability to tolerate the pain spoke more to his fear of the man sent to collect the debt than it did to the laudanum still dulling his senses. "Eventually," he said, making a steeple of his fingers. "He told me eventually."

"Oh, Bode," Comfort whispered. "What can we do?"

"Tomorrow I'm going to visit Mr. Bancroft at Croft Federal to see if I can stop him from calling in all the loans."

Comfort saw Newt and Tuck share a glance, but neither spoke. Bode had picked up his glass and was studying it as he rolled it between his palms. He missed the exchange. Comfort didn't ask them what they were thinking.

"Did Bram tell you how much he owes?"

"It's a little more than I thought." Newton whistled softly when Bode told him the amount. Tuck was more stoic, showing no reaction. "He said he was trying to win enough money to contribute something toward Black Crowne's debt. That's not true, but he's always at his most sincere when he's lying through his teeth."

"You didn't knock them out, did you?" asked Comfort.

"You knocked them out, didn't you?" asked Newt.

Bode heard the questions posed simultaneously. The answer to both was the same. He shook his head. "Tempted, but no."

"Do you think Bram's said anything about this to Alexandra?" asked Tuck.

"No. I told Comfort that I think it's likely she knows that Bram's in trouble, but the depth and details of it are only what she's been able to imagine. Bram didn't want to tell me any of it. He's that afraid of Crocker. I'm fairly confident that it's still a secret from my mother."

There was so much silence around him that Bode looked up. They were all staring at him, nearly identical frowns pulling at their mouths. "What is it?"

They all spoke at once. "Crocker?"

Bode didn't realize he'd said it aloud. He hadn't meant to, but the name was a low, persistent drumbeat at the back of his mind. It was inevitable that it would roll forward like thunder. He took a swallow of his drink. "James R. Crocker," he said. "You all recall the name?"

Comfort certainly did. She saw her uncles were also nodding. "That's the gentleman from the opera house. The one
who dropped the glove." She sighed. "The tin. What does he
have to do with Bram?"

"He's the collector. When Bram stopped paying toward his
gambling debt, the men he owed hired Crocker to get their
money. I'm certain Bram wouldn't have given me Crocker's
name if I hadn't already been suspicious of him."

"So it's this Crocker fellow who is responsible for Comfort's
abduction," said Tuck.

Bode couldn't let his brother off so easily. "With some help
from Bram."

"Bram knew what would happen to me if he didn't pay?"
asked Comfort.

The set of Bode's mouth was grim. "He'd been threatened,
yes. Not with the details of what they would do, not then. He
says he thought he could hold them off. I don't believe that. I'd
told him about our meeting, remember? He let Crocker know
exactly where you'd be. He thought you'd be held for ransom,
Newt and Tuck would pay, and you'd be safely returned. Crocker's plans were different. He wanted to make a point."

The pressure on Comfort's chest was enormous as she considered the breadth of Bram's betrayal. She could only draw a
shallow breath.

Newt knocked back what remained of his drink. "Good
thing you left his teeth, Bode, because it'll be a pleasure for
me to take them out."

Tuck put out a restraining hand even though he was too far
away to reach Newt. "Give it a chance to sit awhile," he said
calmly. "There's no reason to jump at the first thing that crosses
your mind." He watched Newt's puffed-out chest slowly deflate.
When Tuck was confident that his friend wasn't going to storm
out of the house and take his fight to a cripple's bed, he withdrew his hand and returned his attention to Bode. "You understand that it's hard to sit here and not want to do something.
He's your brother, so you have to weigh that, but Newt and I
don't have to give it much thought. We like you just fine, Bode,
and we don't hold what Bram's done against you, but this won't

be over for us until we've settled with him. There's money debt and then there's the other kind. Bram owes us the other kind."

"Please," Comfort said, shaking her head. "Please don't say that."

Bode cocked an eyebrow at her. "You wanted revenge. It's what you said back on the *Demeter*."

"I know, but I was talking about the Rangers. Uncle Tuck's talking about your brother."

"And not saying anything I haven't been thinking. It's only complicated by the fact that I believe it's my responsibility, not their privilege."

Newt leaned forward and rested his forearms on his knees. He looked intently at Comfort. "You could have been killed. It doesn't matter what Bram thought would or wouldn't happen. He made sure the Rangers could find you. He might as well have planned the attack."

Comfort could see that Newt meant to give no quarter, and then she saw it was the same for Tuck. She turned to Bode, and her heart broke for him. His beautiful blue-violet eyes were bleak with anger, sorrow, and hurt that cut bone deep. It was all she could do not to look away, but it was in that moment she forgave her friend Bram DeLong for what he had done to her and came to understand that she would never forgive him for what he had done to Bode.

"Tell me about Mr. Crocker," she said. There was nothing to be gained by dwelling on what Bram had done. What James R. Crocker was setting in motion lay before them. "He's not above the law. Surely there's something we can do about him."

"Above the law," Bode said, cynicism edging his tone. "I'm not so sure. It seems Mr. Crocker is a Pinkerton man."

"No," Newt said, shaking his head fiercely. "No, that can't be right."

Tucker ignored Newt's outburst. "What makes you think Crocker's one of them?"

"As luck, coincidence, or careful planning would have it, Alexandra hired the Pinkerton Agency to find me, and—"

Newt's eyes practically bulged. "Are you going to tell me that Crocker is the one who showed up at her door?"

A very slim smile touched Bode's lips. "Not now that you've said it for me."

Newt apologized to Comfort in advance of letting loose a string of inventive curses. He didn't so much wind down as sputter to a halt.

Tuck looked at him sideways. "You done now?"

Newt merely grunted.

Tuck set his attention on Bode again. "Just because the man says he's from Pinkerton doesn't make it so."

"Bram didn't dispute it when I brought up Crocker's association with the agency. It makes sense that the men Bram owes would hire a Pinkerton man to collect the debt. My experience with the Pinks is that they're better enforcers and bodyguards than they are detectives. I didn't anticipate my mother would be so frantic about my absence that she'd make use of their services. My father and some of the other shipowners would hire Pinkerton agents when word got around that the men working the wharf were organizing."

"Organizing what?" asked Comfort.

"Themselves. Mostly they got together to talk about wages, and that never set well with the owners. Pinkertons were good for getting into the meetings and turning the talk around. If they couldn't make it work from the inside, there were more direct means."

"Broken hands," Newt said.

"Broken heads," Tuck said.

Comfort put out a hand. "I understand." The troubled smile she turned on Bode was also a bit rueful. "They prefer to use clear examples."

"I'll keep that in mind."

Comfort set her hands firmly in her lap. "So what's to be done about Mr. Crocker? Can we appeal to the men that hired him? Tell them to rein him in? Tuck and Newt have some influence."

"That's a risk since we don't know yet who hired Crocker. Bram didn't get into trouble here. Six months ago I asked him to go to Sacramento for me on business. It was Alexandra's idea, one of the few that I could agree to without reservation. Whether Bram was successful or not wasn't a large concern.

I didn't think past the business to how he might conduct it. He had meetings with the governor, a couple of legislators, and some railroad men. The temptation to join them for cards or at the races would have been enormous."

Tucker struck a thoughtful pose. "Pretty fast company."

"Powerful, too," said Newt.

Bode agreed. "That's what I'm thinking. There's no safe harbor there. Any or all of them could be involved. The governor's used Pinkerton men for protection. The Pinks also kept peace among the Chinese immigrants for the railroads. If there's going to be any justice where Crocker's concerned, it'll be because we mete it out."

"I'm prepared to do that," Newt said. "You, Tuck?"

"The same."

Comfort had heard enough. She felt as if she might be sick. "You're all talking as if this is what we do every day. I'm not aware that any of you have the experience to confront someone like Crocker."

Newt was offended. "I beg your pardon," he said gravely. "But your Uncle Tuck and I confronted Santa Anna at Buena Vista."

"You, Uncle Tuck, and a few thousand other soldiers, including Old Rough and Ready."

"Yes, well, Santa Anna had thousands more and we sent him back to Mexico City."

Comfort looked to Bode for help and saw immediately she'd get none. "I suppose you have a similar story."

Bode didn't draw on his war experience. He reminded her of what was relevant. "We've already gotten the best of Crocker once, Comfort, and we didn't know who we were fighting then. The lottery was certainly his idea. If he'd been in the saloon that night, he would have recognized John Farwell. It's fortunate for us that he wasn't. He likes to manage things from a distance."

"The Rangers will never confirm that he hired them," she said.

"They might," said Tuck. "If they knew Crocker was a Pink. I think it's safe to suppose he kept that from them. The Rangers have no use for the Pinks."

Comfort could see Bode was considering that, wondering if there was an advantage to turning the Rangers against Crocker. "You can't control the Rangers," she reminded all of them. "You can set them on a course, but believing that you're in command after that is foolish."

Newt looked from Tuck to Bode. "She's right."

Comfort thought that would be the end of it, but then she glimpsed a look passing among them, guarded and restrained, and she realized that they were thinking about what she'd said but differently than how she meant it. "I was trying to caution the three of you."

"So you have," said Tuck. "And we're grateful."

Comfort fell silent, waiting. When none of them spoke, she tilted her head to one side and lifted an eyebrow. "I'm to be excluded, then. Very well." She stood and addressed Bode. "Should I assume that we will be staying here for the present?"

"I think that's for the best, don't you? Newt and Tuck say we're welcome."

"Then I'm sure we are. Excuse me. I want to speak to Mrs. Hilliard about dinner." She turned, skirted the bench, and quickly put herself on the path to exit the conservatory. As swift as her retreat was, she was still within hearing distance when Newt said, "She's got her hackles up, gentlemen. Could be we'll need to hire a taster for the soup course."

Standing outside Comfort's bedroom, Bode wondered what he could expect from her when he entered. She was polite at dinner, deliberately so. Newt and Tuck didn't comment, but he didn't believe that they'd failed to notice. All of them had survived the soup, so it seemed that if she meant to kill them, it would be done with kindness. He'd had to leave immediately afterward in order to speak to Alexandra. Comfort hadn't asked to join him, and he hadn't invited her. It was a strained parting, and it left him feeling unsettled and wanting to make amends even though from his perspective he'd done nothing wrong.

He wasn't convinced it was safe for Comfort to leave her uncles' home, but that was only part of the reason he didn't want her with him. Being fairly certain how his mother would react to what he had to say concerned him almost as much. Alexandra's habit of rushing to protect Bram meant that she would look for and find someone to blame. Comfort was the likeliest scapegoat whether or not she was in Alexandra's sights. Better that she was not.

Comfort was sitting cross-legged on the bed when Bode eased into the room. "You don't have to tiptoe," she said, not looking up. "I'm awake." She examined her fingers where she'd been pushing at the cuticles with an orange stick. Satisfied with her effort, she set the stick between her tin and the oil lamp on the nightstand and picked up a glass of water. Trying to judge his mood, she watched him as she sipped.

Bode removed his jacket and laid it over a chair. "I stopped by my place and asked Sam to come back with me. Your uncles said it would be all right. We brought your trunk and my bags. It's all downstairs. Sam didn't have much except for what John gave him. Your butler . . . Mr. Barker?"

"Barkin."

"Yes. Barkin. He's showing Sam where he can stay. I told Sam I wouldn't need him this evening."

"Good." She emptied the glass and put it back beside the carafe. "The dressing room's through the door on your left. I didn't know that you'd bring anything from your apartment. Tuck gave me some nightclothes for you. It's all in there. Suey Tsin brought fresh towels."

"Thank you." Bode didn't try to engage her in conversation. He went straight to the dressing room, pausing on the threshold when he saw the ball-and-claw-footed tub had been filled with water. Slim fingers of steam rose from the glassy surface. A nightshirt draped the back of a chair, and neatly folded linens rested on the seat. He glanced over his shoulder and found Comfort watching him. "For me?"

She nodded. A slightly crooked smile edged her lips, and for the first time since leaving the conservatory, the smile wasn't forced. It touched her eyes as she waved him on. "Go. The water will get cold."

Bode didn't require more encouragement. He quickly stripped off, sank halfway up to his chest in the fresh, hot water, and immediately closed his eyes. His arms rested on either side of the smoothly curved rims of the tub. Except to raise two fingers in greeting, he didn't trouble himself to stir when Comfort approached. Her hand brushed the back of his, and then she moved the towels from the chair to the floor and sat.

"In the event you don't realize it," she said, "this bath is by way of an apology."

He opened one eye, his expression wary. "Hackles down?"

"More or less."

Satisfied that she wasn't going to push him under, Bode closed his eye and slipped lower into the tub. He rested the back of his head against the rim. "How did you know when I'd get here?"

"Suey Tsin was watching for you. We started the bath as soon as she saw you. She didn't mention Mr. Travers was with you." Comfort edged the chair closer to the tub. "Was it awful?"

The question puzzled him for a moment until he realized she was talking about his conversation with Alexandra. "By the time I arrived, Hitchens had already told her that I'd visited earlier. Whatever relief she felt on hearing that was forgotten by the time I returned. She was unhappy that I hadn't waited for her this afternoon and angry with me for disappearing in the first place. She didn't want to hear about Bram, but I made her listen. I was right that she suspected gambling debts. I think she was genuinely shocked by the amount."

"She supported the engagement," Comfort reminded him quietly. "She must have had some idea that what he owed was considerable."

"Perhaps I should have said that she didn't admit to it. I didn't press her, Comfort. I know from experience that nothing comes of it. She would only say that she was in favor of seeing the engagement through to becoming a marriage because it was the proper thing to do. She mentioned your leveling influence on Bram and that you would do well by him, but she never once hinted that she was looking at you and your family to assume responsibility for his debt."

Comfort nodded. "I think it would have been astonishing if she had. It's one thing for her to acknowledge that Bram has failings of character, but quite another for her to admit that she's supported them. What did she say about the part Bram played in my abduction?"

"She didn't believe it."

"Oh."

"And when you told her we're married?"

"I didn't." He opened his eyes and regarded Comfort steadily. "I never told Bram that we were married either."

She frowned slightly. "I didn't realize."

"Both of them think that you were here all the time that I was gone. They don't know where I was, and they don't know the details of how you were able to get away from the Rangers. Bram knows more, of course, but if he discusses it with Alexandra, he has to admit his involvement. If Mother broaches the subject with him, she risks hearing things she'd rather not know. I don't think they'll talk about it."

"What about Mr. Crocker?"

"Bram clearly understands what the man is capable of, and Alexandra knows now that he is trying to collect Bram's debt. She holds me responsible for Crocker getting into her home and getting so close to Bram." Bode responded to Comfort's confusion with a wry chuckle. "If I hadn't disappeared, she wouldn't have hired the Pinkertons. She's angry with me for putting Bram in danger and reminded me that he can't defend himself."

"I'm sorry, Bode."

He shrugged. "It wasn't unexpected."

"It's oddly complimentary that she doesn't feel compelled to be so fiercely protective of you. When you left without a word to her, she did whatever she could to find you, but when she has to choose which one of her cubs to shield, she'll always choose Bram. That's because she realizes you can take care of yourself."

"I know. I came to understand a long time ago that it's infinitely better to be the son she pokes in the chest rather than the son she coddles."

Comfort moved from the chair to kneel on the folded towels beside the tub. "Sit up and I'll wash your back."

"Feeling the urge to coddle me?"

"I am, and you shouldn't get used to it." His low chuckle made the water ripple. Ignoring him, she dipped a washcloth in the water and lathered it with soap. "Lean forward."

"Yes, ma'am." Bode closed his eyes as she pressed the

washcloth to his back. Every wiry thread of tension tugging at his shoulders began to snap or soften. His skin tingled with the sensation. An electric spark skittered down his spine. Groaning softly, he let his head fall forward.

Comfort lightly scrubbed the exposed line of his neck. Under her fingers, she could feel him begin to relax. It only bothered her a little that she still meant to question him. "Will I have an opportunity to meet Mr. Crocker?"

Bode laughed. "You have no shame." He reached back and pointed to a spot on his shoulder. "Right there, please."

She pushed his hand out of the way and applied the washcloth with rather more industry than was required. After a few moments of scrubbing, she eased off and leaned over so she could whisper in his ear. "Well?" she asked. "Will I?"

"Not if I can help it," he said. "I don't know what he'd do."

Bode's answer wasn't unexpected. "It seems that he's no longer interested in me."

"And if that's true, I'd like to keep it that way."

"Can he really do what Bram said? Take over Black Crowne and sell off the assets piece by piece?"

"You know he can. He'll have the backing of the men who hired him. That's what will move David Bancroft to sell off the mortgages and loans."

"He has to notify you of the intent."

"Yes, but my only recourse is to come up with the money myself. Bancroft knows I can't do that. Thanks to Bram, so does Crocker."

"When do you think it will happen?"

"According to Bram, Crocker's already set things in motion with the bank. He and Bancroft are just waiting for me to reappear. If someone hasn't informed Crocker already, then Bancroft will tell him after we meet tomorrow morning."

"Did your mother know anything about this?"

"No. None of it. She's frightened."

"I don't understand why anyone is waiting for you to show yourself. Your mother is still the owner of Black Crowne, isn't she? If Crocker's already spoken to Mr. Bancroft, then why didn't Bancroft tell your mother that he was going to sell the mortgage and call in the loans?"

"Perhaps because Crocker asked him not to, or it might be that Bancroft knows she defers to me in matters regarding the business." Bode felt Comfort's hesitation in the slowing circle of her hand across his back. "You have another idea?"

"Not really . . ."

He turned his head to look at her. "You do. Tell me."

"I wondered if it's because she's a woman. She told me once that men have all the advantages and women bear all the consequences. I think she acts as she does at times so that she might have the advantage."

"Are you suggesting something?"

"Invite her to join you when you go to see Mr. Bancroft."

"That complicates the arrangement I have with her."

"The one where you take the responsibility for the business and she takes the money from it?"

Bode's grin was wry. "That's the one."

Comfort held out the soap and washcloth to him. "It's just something to think about." She stood. Her nightgown was damp where she had leaned against the tub. She plucked it away from her breasts and gave the fabric a little shake. When she saw Bode's attention shift from the soap to her, it was difficult to suppress her amusement. "Don't be long," she said.

And while her retreat was hasty, the look she cast over her shoulder lingered long after she disappeared.

Bode couldn't say what woke him. He only knew that it wasn't Comfort. She was sleeping so deeply beside him that he could hear her breathing. Except for a sliver of moonlight coming through a slender part in the curtains, the room was dark. He pushed himself up on an elbow and looked around. He could make out the chair beside the fireplace and the small writing desk near the window. Closer to the bed he saw the outline of the extinguished oil lamp, the water carafe and glass, and the shadowed line of the orange stick on the night table. Some light was reflected in the mirror above the vanity and revealed the clutter of small pots of cream, perfume atomizers, and combs.

Bode's eyes traveled to the foot of the bed, where an extra quilt lay teetering on the edge in a rumpled mound. He stretched his leg, pushed, and it slid out of view. He stared at the door, listening. When a long minute passed and he heard nothing, he lowered his elbow, and finally his head.

Comfort was turned on her side away from him. He edged close and matched her position. Once they were spooned, he slipped an arm around her waist. She didn't stir.

His nostrils caught the subtle fragrance of mint in her hair. He brushed the back of her head with his mouth, pressing the lightest of kisses against her. Only a few hours had passed since she'd done the same to him. Every time she touched him with her lips, it was as if a bumblebee alighted. He could almost feel the vibration of delicate wings. He never knew if she'd sip his skin like nectar or sting him just a little with her teeth. He anticipated both and found acute pleasure in either.

She'd moved slowly over his chest, teasing and tormenting him on her way across his abdomen, past his navel, and then following the coppery arrow of hair all the way to his groin. Every part of him contracted now as he remembered how she'd taken him in her mouth. He could still feel her there, hot and humid, her tongue sweeping around his erection, the suck of her mouth drawing him in. He'd had to revise his opinion of what constituted carnal torture, because whatever she'd done before hadn't been that. Not really.

He smiled his guarded, secretive smile and touched it to Comfort's hair again. It was her smile anyway, the one she owned because she knew how to ease it out of him. He closed his eyes and saw her again as she had been so many years ago at her coming-out, her fingers fluttering against her nape, twisting and tugging on the loose strands, anchoring them back into place with her comb. He wondered if she'd glimpsed his smile on that occasion. It had been hers even then.

Bode sat up suddenly. Squinting, he stared at the nightstand, looking for the one thing he hadn't seen earlier: the red-and-white tin. It was gone. He gently searched out Comfort's hands and made certain she wasn't holding it. When he couldn't find it, he patted the area around her. He finally risked waking her by leaning far over her so he could see the floor beside the table. He couldn't make out the familiar shape anywhere.

"What are you doing?" she asked sleepily, batting him away.

Bode didn't answer. He rolled out of bed on his side and went around to hers. Kneeling, he slipped a hand under the table and began searching. A moment later, he did the same under the bed.

Comfort moved closer to the edge of the mattress and watched him from under heavily lidded eyes. "Bode?"

"Hmm?"

"Did you lose something?"

"I don't know." The sweep of his hand brought him nothing. He lay on the floor and peered under the bed. Except for Comfort's slippers, which he lifted and shook out, there was nothing there. He sat up and raised himself to his haunches. He was eye to sleepy eye with Comfort. "Did you do something with your tin?"

"No. It's right there." She glanced at the bedside table. "There." She raised a hand and patted the tabletop. Her fingers found the cuticle stick and nudged the lamp. They did not touch the tin. Comfort's sleep-worn expression faded in advance of her troubled one. "I put it there. I had it earlier today, but I put it back. It was there when I—"

"I know. I saw it when I came in."

"What happened to it?"

"I don't know. It's what I'm looking for."

She pushed herself up and opened the drawer in the table. She took out a box of matches. Bode lifted the glass globe so she could light the lamp. They both blinked rapidly against the burst of fire from the match head. He replaced the globe, and she blew out the match.

Bode stood, raised the lamp, and looked around. Comfort also surveyed the room. After a few minutes spent in this fruitless activity, he returned the lamp to the table and glanced at the clock. It was twenty minutes after three.

Comfort had followed his eyes to the clock. It made no sense to her that he was awake. Certainly the missing tin wasn't responsible for that. "What woke you?"

"I don't know. Something . . . a sound, I think." He walked to the window, knelt on the bench, and parted the curtains. It was raining lightly. The nightscape darkened as the fingernail moon slipped behind a cloud. "It might have been the rain."

He let the curtains fall back into place and walked to the door. He was still several feet away when he stopped in his tracks.

"What is it?" asked Comfort.

"I'm not sure." He lifted one bare foot and touched the bottom of it. His sole was damp. "Will you bring the lamp?"

She threw back the covers and quickly joined him, holding the light where he directed. He pointed to the hardwood floor beyond the edge of the rug. Beads of water trapped the lamplight. "Are those footprints?" she asked.

"Yes." He turned and studied the patterned area rug, but evidence that someone had crossed it in shoes wet with rain was impossible to see. It didn't matter. The best evidence that someone had been in their room was the missing tin. Bode went to the door, opened it, and stepped into the hallway. He held out his hand for the lamp.

Comfort shook her head. "I'm going with you."

He didn't absolutely need the lamp. The hallway had several gaslights that he could have turned up. She realized it as well but stood there anyway, feet firmly planted until he decided to move. Once he did, she'd follow. "Very well," he said quietly. "But stay behind me."

"As long as you stay ahead of me." She pretended she didn't hear his exasperated sigh and held the lamp out to the side so it would benefit both of them.

Droplets of water were scattered at odd intervals on the floor as though they'd been shaken off the sleeve of a jacket or the hemmed edge of a trouser leg. There was only the occasional stamp of a shoe. The prints they saw were heading in the direction they were coming from. There were none that revealed the return trip. Bode realized the rug had absorbed the last bit of water from the shoes. They could learn where the person had entered the house but not how he left.

Or even if he had.

Bode traced the intruder's steps all the way to an open window in the conservatory. He removed the rod that kept the window in the raised position and closed it. "I think it's safe to assume he came in this way. I doubt anyone could have heard him."

"Do you think he's gone?"

He chose honesty over false reassurance. "I can't answer that until we search the house. We need to rouse the staff and your uncles. Get everyone to start looking."

She nodded. "I'll wake Newt and Tuck. You can—" She stopped because he was shaking his head.

"We'll go together," he said. "I'm not letting you out of my sight."

Comfort didn't argue. She touched the sleeve of his nightshirt. "Do you think it was Crocker?"

"Possibly." He pinched the bridge of his nose, thinking. "Probably. Him, or someone working for him. Rangers. Maybe Pinks." He could see that she was prepared to ask more questions. "I don't know the purpose behind it, and I don't know why he'd lift your tin except that he carries the same kind of lozenges. That's what you wanted to know, isn't it?"

"Yes." She released his sleeve. "We should go."

"Now you're reading *my* mind."

In ten minutes the house was filled with activity. Bode organized the servants to search in pairs, and every pair had a specific part of the house to walk through. Newt and Tuck carried guns they cleaned regularly since the war with Mexico but hadn't fired in more than a decade, and the cook had her meat cleaver, but everyone else was unarmed. With people tiptoeing around the house and then jumping at shadows, Bode would have preferred that Newt and Tuck and Mrs. Hilliard had never picked up their weapons. He kept Comfort at his side with Suey Tsin and Samuel Travers hovering nearby.

The search went on for more than a half hour. When the clock in the entrance hall struck four, everyone moved to the front parlor to report that they'd found nothing and no one. Tuck dismissed the servants. They were reluctant to return to their quarters until Newt barked at them. They scattered like rabbits after that.

Tuck set his gun on the mantelpiece and quietly urged Newt to do the same. Newt didn't realize he was holding his .44 caliber Walker Colt aloft until Tucker stared pointedly at it. He slowly lowered his arm, and his grimace transformed into something approximating sheepishness. He put his weapon on an end table and dropped on the sofa.

"I don't know about the rest of you," Newt said, "but I could use a drink."

Comfort started to move to the sideboard, but Tuck put out his hand and forestalled her. "I'll get it," he said. "Anyone else?"

Bode declined. So did Comfort.

Tuck nodded. "We've done everything we can for now. There's no point in the two of you staying here and watching Newt and me drink our nerves steady. Go on back to bed."

Comfort saw that Bode was trying to gauge Tuck's sincerity. She took him by the arm. "He means it," she said. "He wants us to go." She released him long enough to kiss her uncles good night and then led him out the door. "They'll have one drink, and then they'll take turns standing guard until morning. It's what they did when we lived in the mining camp. It's how they looked out for me. Some things don't change."

Bode glanced back just before he closed the door. "Thank God."

Chapter Sixteen

Tuck waited until he heard Comfort and Bode on the stairs before he spoke. "Did we do right by not telling them where we went after dinner? Could be that what we did provoked someone."

"You mean Crocker," Newt said. "I thought of that. Figured we'd talk about it and then decide if we should tell Bode tonight or let him find out in the morning like we planned."

Tuck perched on the wide arm of an overstuffed chair. He took a swallow of his drink. "I'm inclined that it will go better if Bode learns we made an offer on Black Crowne from Mr. Bancroft. Bode's not likely to be grateful for our interference. Mostly he'll see us as the lesser of two evils. He might not accept what we're offering. The man's prideful."

"I suppose we have to hope that doesn't get in the way of his good sense. We don't exactly employ men like Crocker when there's a debt outstanding."

"Maybe we should. Bram DeLong makes a powerful case for it. Or am I the only one tempted to go after the leg that's not broken?"

"Thought about it myself, and I wouldn't be surprised if Bode did." Smiling narrowly, Tuck raised his drink in a mocking salute. "Do you suppose Bancroft might have told Crocker that he got a better offer? Try to sweeten the pot?"

"After we asked him to keep it confidential?" Newt snorted derisively. "Sure he might've. I always figured there was less honor among bankers than among thieves. There'd be plenty of folks that'd fail to make a distinction between the two."

Tucker didn't disagree. He glanced toward the window. Rain drummed steadily against the glass, streaking it like acid etchings. "What do you make of Comfort's tin disappearing?"

"Don't know. That's a puzzle. It'll probably turn up when she's on her way to looking for something else."

"I've been thinking that she did all right without it while she was with Bode, but did you notice this afternoon when he wasn't around how she kept twisting it in her hands? I'm surprised she ever put it down, and I can't recall that she's ever misplaced it."

Newt couldn't remember that happening either. "Well, Bode's with her. That should help if she gets all pins and needles about not having it."

Tuck nodded. "So. Are we going to tell Bode or—" He stopped, his attention arrested by something he heard outside the window. He caught Newt's eye. "Did you hear that?"

"Hear what?"

Tuck set his drink down and got to his feet. He motioned to Newt to stay where he was. He took his Walker Colt from the mantel on his way to the window. If someone was out there looking in, he wanted it known that he had a gun.

Newt inched forward on the sofa. He put his tumbler on the table and let his hand hover over his military revolver. "I hear thunder," Newt said quietly.

"I hear it, too. This was different." He approached the window from the side and tried to peer out. Most of what he could see at first was a reflection of the room. He stood perfectly still and tried to look beyond it. There was a disturbance in the rhododendrons. The rain beat the oblong, leathery leaves hard enough to make them scrape against the granite sill and the lowest panes of glass.

Tuck waited. The bush shifted suddenly; the leaves rattled against the side of the house like bony fingers. Tuck jumped back as the ginger kitchen cat leapt out of the bush and onto the sill. The tom let out a cry that alerted every feline on Nob Hill that he was on the prowl.

"Damnation!" Tuck lowered his gun. He tapped the window with the nose of the gun and startled the cat. "Serves you right," he said when the cat hurtled off the sill and over the bush. "I could've shot you."

Newt let his gun stay where it lay and picked up his drink. He didn't try to pretend he wasn't amused when Tucker turned around. "Seems like you've got another reason to want to kill that cat."

Tucker merely grunted. He returned his gun to the mantel and took up his perch on the chair. He picked up his drink and knocked back what remained in the glass. "At least I know my hearing's as sharp as it ever was."

Newt chuckled softly, not caring whether Tuck heard him or not.

Comfort released Bode's arm when they reached the top of the stairs and turned toward their bedroom. "I was thinking earlier today how nice it is to have all the men I love together. I hope it lasts longer this time."

"Lasts longer? What do you mean?"

"It's just that we were together in the conservatory and again at dinner, but afterward . . ." She waited for him to open the door and continued once he followed her inside. "Afterward everyone disappeared."

Bode frowned. "We did?"

"Well, yes. You went back to your mother's, and Newt and Tuck went . . ." She shrugged. "I don't know where they went. To the bank, I suppose. They said it was business."

"They didn't mention it to me."

"This is what comes of having secrets. The right hand doesn't know what the left is doing."

Bode went around to his side of the bed and snapped covers out of their disarray before he climbed in. "What is it that you think we're keeping from you?"

"If I knew that, I wouldn't have to ask, now would I?"

Bode grinned at her. "You probably think that made sense." He watched her mouth snap shut and appreciated the view as she gave him her back and carried the lamp into the dressing

room. "You know I was teasing, don't you?" He winced when
the door shut hard behind her. Perhaps she didn't know. "It isn't
a fully formed plan," he called to her. "Nothing that involves the
Rangers can be. We have different ideas about how to use them."

Bode thought Comfort would have some comment about
not using them at all, but there was only silence from the other
side of the door. "Comfort?" He started to rise, but then the
door opened and a shaft of light came from the dressing room.
He propped himself on an elbow, waiting for her to step out.
"You're not really mad, are you?"

Comfort appeared in the doorway. She held the lamp in
front of her with both hands as though she was preparing to
serve it. The flame flickered, creating an ebb and flow to the
tide of warm light bathing her face. It was only when she turned
her head to the side that the man standing at her back was as
clearly illuminated.

James R. Crocker pushed Comfort forward with the barrel
of his gun. He watched Bode over her shoulder. When Bode
threw off the bedclothes, Crocker shook his head.

"Stay where you are," he rasped.

At the sound of his voice, Comfort felt her flesh prickle.
Even with his weapon pressing against her spine, she'd been
steady on her feet. These first words, though, made her knees
go weak. She closed her eyes and concentrated on what he said,
not how he said it, but when he cleared his throat, it was like
fingernails scraping a slate, and she shivered.

"What are you doing here, Crocker?"

"Came to strike a deal with you," he said hoarsely.

Bode had lots of questions, but the one at the top of his list
he was able to answer for himself. Crocker hadn't been found
during the search because this bedroom was the one place no
one had looked again. Neither he nor Comfort had considered
that Crocker might have fled to the dressing room. They'd left
him behind when they followed his damp tracks, and he stayed
there until the search was over.

"We're not discussing any deal while you're using Comfort
as a shield." To Bode's surprise, Crocker thrust his chin to the
side and indicated that Comfort could step in that direction. She
didn't move immediately, but Bode knew better than to suppose

she was hesitant. It spoke to her grit that she was still standing. She was trying to make certain her feet stayed under her.

"Don't go far," Crocker said.

Comfort went sideways, sliding more than stepping to achieve a foot and a half of separation from Crocker.

"That's enough." His gun showed clearly in the lamplight. He held it steadily, keeping it aimed just below Bode's chest to account for the kick that would bring his hand up if he fired. "There are people back in Sacramento expecting me to return with your brother's full payment. Like I told Bram, they're not real particular about how I accomplish that."

"They might change their mind if they knew that you arranged Comfort's abduction. The lottery could make them think twice about using you again. I don't know, of course, but perhaps it's not the sort of event they'd want to have associated with them."

"You're making a powerful leap there, Bode, since I don't know anything about an abduction except what I read in the papers. This is the first I'm hearing about a lottery. The last time I saw Miss Kennedy—it's still Miss Kennedy, isn't it?" He looked from Bode to Comfort and back to the bed again. When neither of them spoke, he raised an eyebrow and shook his head as though disappointed in them. "Does your brother know you're sleeping with his fiancée?"

Bode didn't answer. Instead, he asked, "Can I sit up?"

Crocker cleared his throat and nodded.

Bode pushed himself to a sitting position but didn't rest against the headboard. He was mostly clear of the bedcovers. He carefully pedaled his feet so the quilt shifted sideways. "Put the gun down, Crocker. I can't believe there is any benefit to shooting me, and you lose every advantage if you hurt Comfort. If you mean to deal in good faith, then you should show some." He waited, his gaze as steady as Crocker's gun. He believed it was getting heavy enough for Crocker to consider lowering it.

Crocker brought the weapon down slowly. He didn't tuck it behind him but kept it against his side so he could bring it up smoothly if he had to. "I'm here about the arrangement I had with Bancroft over at Federal."

Bode didn't blink. "Shouldn't you take it up with him? For

God's sake, Crocker, it's the middle of the night, and you're talking like I'm supposed to understand what you mean. I don't even know how you found me here."

"I've been watching your office. Your mother hired me to find you. Sam Travers, too."

"Sam? Really?"

He massaged his throat. "She seemed to think that if I found Travers, I'd find you. I finally caught sight of him this afternoon leaving your office with that Chinese girl who works here. Followed them to the bank and then went back to Black Crowne to see if you'd appear. Had to cool my heels for a while, but I'll be damned if you didn't step out of the building and head directly to your mama's house. I know she was gone when you got there, but you spent so much time inside that I have to assume you spoke to your brother. I can only imagine what he told you, but I'm certain not a quarter of it was the truth. You surprised me by coming here when you left. Now that I'm seeing the lay of the land, so to speak, I'm beginning to understand a few things I didn't before."

"Have you spoken to Alexandra?"

"Didn't see the need. You went back there. She knows you're home. Where were you?"

"You never figured that out?"

"I confess I didn't try very hard. I wasn't nearly as concerned for your well-being as your mother was. She thought that little man that escorted me to the *Demeter Queen* had something to do with your disappearance." The notion still amused him. He chuckled. "She doesn't like him very much."

Crocker's eyes suddenly swiveled sideways. He crooked a finger at Comfort. "Over here," he said. "Do you think I don't know that you've been inching away?" He cleared his throat again. "Do you have any more lozenges? That tin on your night table was empty, same as mine."

Comfort didn't speak. She didn't think she could. It was enough that she held the lamp steady. She answered him by shaking her head.

Crocker regarded her curiously. "Are you afraid of me?"

"Leave her alone, Crocker," Bode said. "Talk to me."

Crocker was in no hurry to comply. He studied Comfort for

a long moment, stroking his beard, a small smile playing about his mouth. The narrow gap between his front teeth was visible. He turned back just as Bode was sliding one leg over the side of the bed. He used the gun to gesture him back.

"It'd be better if you stayed where you are while we discuss this," he said.

"Then get to the point."

"You're the one with all the questions. Think about how much you want to get out of the bed before you ask another one." He lowered the gun again. "I had an understanding with Bancroft that a certain group of men were willing to assume Black Crowne's debt. Because of what's happened, I have to believe that Bram told you about that."

"What's happened?"

"There's been another offer."

Bode's brows lifted. "Another offer? Who?"

Crocker's eyes narrowed. He ran his index finger down the slightly off-center line of his nose before he rubbed under his nostrils. He glanced at Comfort. "Is he lying? Keep in mind I heard what you were saying when you returned to the room."

Comfort cast her mind to try to recall her conversation. She came up blank. She shrugged at Crocker.

"You told him Jones and Prescott left the house sometime after he did. Business, you said. Is that right?"

She nodded.

"Bank business."

Bode drew Crocker's attention back to him. "They didn't tell her anything. That's why she was upset."

"Did you ask them to take over Black Crowne?"

"I did not."

"I don't believe you."

"Then don't ask. Is that what you're telling me they did? They made an offer for my family's business?"

"Exactly. Bancroft came to me, thinking he could squeeze more juice from the orange. I told him that's not going to happen. You need to convince her uncles to take back their offer."

"Why would you want me to do that? You'll still get your money. I'll be able to pay back what Bram owes."

He laughed without humor. "That would have been good

enough months ago. They're all agreed that it's too little, too late. They can realize a much greater return on his debt by selling off Black Crowne, and I admit, there's something deeply satisfying about doing it this way. It can't be helped that you and Alexandra will also suffer for it, but then you did very little to stop Bram from his excesses. You sent him to Sacramento, didn't you?"

Bode nodded slowly.

"That's what he said. I didn't know if it was true. He managed to get himself into four kinds of trouble up there. The boy just doesn't know when it's time to step away from the table." He raised the gun slightly. "Now, about Jones and Prescott. I'd be most appreciative of your help with my little problem there."

"I'm sure you would, but why would I do anything for you?"

Crocker turned his gun on Comfort. "You wouldn't," he said. "But I think you would do it for her. And so will they. Am I wrong?"

"No."

"Then let's go downstairs. They're still up, I believe. I never heard them in the hall." He waved Comfort to step forward and go around him, and then he pointed at Bode and told him to do the same. "Be very careful, Bode. I have friends waiting for me. Men who know something about taking orders." He glanced at the clock. "I really should let them know I'm all right. Otherwise they'll storm the gates. These men don't take prisoners."

Bode came around the foot of the bed. "If they take orders, I can assume they're not Rangers. I guess you learned your lesson there."

Crocker ignored that. "Go on. Through the door, down the stairs. I believe they'll be in the front parlor. I know where it is, so don't think you can lead me somewhere else."

"Allow Comfort to put on her robe. She's cold. You can see that she's shivering."

"She's not cold. She's scared." He looked Bode over, trying to gauge how far he could trust him. Comfort's fear gave him confidence. "Go on, get her robe. Make it fast."

Bode hurried into the dressing room. He stepped into a pair of trousers, hastily tucked in the tails of his nightshirt, and grabbed Comfort's robe. He reappeared in less than half a minute, but he could see that Crocker was impatient with the delay. He held up the robe. "Let me take the lamp," he told Comfort.

Crocker shook his head. "No. Just put the robe around her. I want her to hold the lamp."

Bode did as he was directed, taking the opportunity to squeeze Comfort's shoulders as he settled the robe on her. He wanted to reassure her in other ways, touch his lips to her temple, whisper in her ear, but Crocker was already gesturing with the gun and Bode didn't want to tempt him to aim it at Comfort again.

"The two of you walk in front of me," Crocker told them. "Go on."

They startled the cat when they stepped into the hallway. Thistle wound in and out of Comfort's legs, meowing softly in anticipation of being scooped up. When he wasn't, he threw himself in front of her and rolled on his back. Afraid that Crocker would kick Thistle out of the way, Comfort nudged him along with her toe until he got up suddenly and all but flew down the stairs.

"I hate cats," Crocker said under his breath. "Keep it out of my way."

"I don't think that will be a problem," Bode said. "He doesn't care for you either." Bode thought he might feel the barrel of Crocker's gun shoved hard against his back, even hoped that would be the outcome, but Crocker wisely kept his distance on the stairs.

When they reached the entrance hall, Crocker told Comfort to remain at his side and gestured to Bode to open the front door. Bode blinked against the flash of lightning that rent the night sky. He stepped up to the threshold. Raindrops as sharp as needles glanced off his face and shoulders.

"There's no one here," he said.

"Give them a moment."

Bode put out a foot to halt the entry of a wet ball of orange fur that might have been a cat. Frustrated, the cat yowled. His cry brought Thistle running. Bode grabbed Comfort's cat before he pounced and slammed the door shut on the other animal. This set up another round of piercing cries. Thistle's claws dug into Bode's shoulder.

"What the hell?" Tucker peered down the long hall from

outside the study. "Bode. Leave the cat be. He doesn't like to go out. Send him here."

It took Bode a moment to understand that Tucker couldn't see Comfort and Crocker. They were hidden from view by the angle of the staircase. It didn't appear that Tucker had armed himself. And why would he? He'd come out to see about the cat.

Bode disengaged Thistle's claws from his shirt, bent, and pitched the cat lightly in Tucker's direction. Out of the corner of his eye, he saw Crocker motion him to go forward. He started down the hall. Once he was past Crocker, he rolled his eyes in that direction, hoping to make Tucker take a second look. Tuck's attention, however, remained on Thistle. Bode was tempted to echo Crocker's sentiment. Just now, he hated cats.

Tuck stooped and scratched Thistle between the ears. "The ginger's been making a racket all evening, lookin' for a female or lookin' for a fight. Wouldn't keep him around except Mrs. Hilliard thinks he's the best mouser we've ever had in the kitchen. I never thought too much about it, but you should see the pair he brought in tonight."

The hesitation before Bode's next step was outwardly imperceptible. Bode, though, felt as if he'd been made to stop dead in his tracks. Tuck's words had an impact, but not only his words. Crocker had expected to find Tuck and Newt in the front parlor. So had Bode. When he and Comfort left her uncles, they had showed no inclination to leave it. It was, after all, a better location to see anyone approaching the house from the front. The study had almost no view except of the neighboring property, and like his father's library, it tended to be a quiet place where sound neither escaped nor intruded. Yet here Tuck stood. There had to be a reason for it.

Tuck straightened and caught Bode's eye, and no look at all passed between them. It was the complete lack of expression that communicated caution.

Bode knew the moment that Crocker pushed Comfort into Tucker's line of sight, because the older man's eyes swiveled in that direction, and although he had been expecting something like it, his loose-limbed frame went rigid. It made Bode wonder if Crocker had poked Comfort with the gun again.

"Go on," Crocker ordered, nudging Comfort forward. "Everyone. Inside. We need to conclude this business." He glanced briefly at the front door but kept moving Comfort ahead of him.

Tucker slowly backed into the study. Bode started to follow but was ordered to wait until Comfort caught up to him. They entered as a pair with Crocker close enough behind them to make his shots count if he fired.

Crocker stepped sideways, staying closer to Comfort than Bode. He waved Bode off, told Tucker to halt, and quickly took in his surroundings. His attention alighted on Newt sitting behind the wide walnut desk. "Let me see your hands."

Newt raised them, palms out, fingers spread wide. "Nothing here."

"Stand up."

Newt did as he was told. "I'd be obliged if you'd point your gun somewhere else. I'd take it real kindly if you'd point it at me or my partner, say, instead of at my niece."

"I like it where it is. Come around the desk so I can see all of you. Slowly. No need to be a jack-in-the-box just now. Jones. You sit on the sofa. Bode, you put yourself right beside him." He cleared his throat. "Miss Kennedy, you stay just where you are. How you holding up?"

Comfort wondered if he truly expected an answer. She followed Newt as he moved around the desk and hitched a hip on the back edge. He folded his arms across his chest and looked for all the world as if there were nothing at all unusual about conducting business in the middle of the night and at the point of a gun. She wanted to be encouraged by the faint smile she glimpsed hovering about his lips, but Crocker's voice had unleashed an army of tiny spiders that were marching up and down her spine.

James R. Crocker did not like improvisation. He'd carefully thought through what he would do once Beauregard DeLong reappeared, but he'd never considered the possibility that Bode would find sanctuary with Jones and Prescott. There'd been no hint from Bram that he and Bode were rivals for the affections of Miss Kennedy. It made Crocker wonder if Bram had ever thought of his brother as a serious threat. Clearly, a winner had emerged.

Crocker glanced at the lamp Comfort was holding. There was enough light in the study without it, but he liked having her hands occupied. Her quiet concerned him, and her pale, stoic features told him nothing about what she was thinking, or if she was thinking at all. Would she faint? Would she fight? Either would cause a disruption he didn't need.

Her trembling caused the lamplight to flicker and her diamond to flash. It was the ring that caught Crocker's eye. When he looked at Bode, it was with new appreciation for the situation he was confronting.

"You married her," he said. His words were accompanied by a low chuckle that was as gritty as sand. "I'll be damned."

"One hopes," Bode said.

Crocker merely grinned, amused. "You DeLong boys really have no shame. I begin to understand this alliance. Bram said you'd do whatever it took to save Black Crowne. Even I didn't suppose that could mean you'd marry his fiancée." He looked at Newt and Tuck for confirmation. "You did insist that he marry her, I hope, before you agreed to make an offer for his business."

No one responded. Crocker took it in stride. "Where're my men?"

"Your men?" asked Bode. "That's the second time you've referred to them that way. Men who take orders, you said."

"My *friends*." He stared pointedly at Newt.

Newt shrugged. "I'm not sure why you need any friends save for the one you have in your hand. That's a Walker Colt, isn't it?"

"It is."

"Thought it might be. Tucker and I each have one like it." He held up his hands again to show they were empty. "Not on us. Not now. But we're familiar with it."

"That so."

Newt nodded. "Military issue. Colt sent a thousand of them to the Texas Rangers for the Mexican War. You recollect that, Tuck?"

"I do," said Tuck. "Stamped them all. B Co. #41. Were you part of that company, Crocker? Seems like you might have been."

Before Crocker could respond, Newt inserted another opinion. "Just as likely that he stole it."

Tuck shook his head. "Don't think so. There're better guns around now. Bet you twenty that's a sentimental piece he's holding."

"Twenty it is." Newt raised an inquiring eyebrow at Crocker. "Sentiment or stolen? Twenty dollars hangs in the balance."

Crocker stared at them, disbelief etched deeply on his face.

Bode's sardonic chuckle came from the back of his throat. There was no hint that it was forced or that it left the taste of acid on his tongue. "They're serious, Crocker. If you want to do business with Jones Prescott, you have to accept there will be certain peculiarities in the rhythm of negotiations. I don't suppose a gun changes that."

"Christ," Crocker said hoarsely. He cleared his throat and stretched his neck above the collar of his shirt. Out of habit he reached for his tin of lozenges. His hand hung awkwardly in the air as he remembered the tin he'd brought with him as well as the one he'd stolen were both empty. He patted down the bulge in his pocket anyway while he jerked his chin at Bode. "Tell them what I want."

"I think they understand."

"Tell them anyway."

Bode shrugged. "All right. But you're confusing peculiar with stupid."

"That's a fact," said Tuck, looking sideways at Bode. "You do what he says. The gun's a distraction, but Newt and I will try to pay real close attention."

"Mr. Crocker wants you and Newt to withdraw the offer you made Mr. Bancroft for Black Crowne. The men he represents aren't willing to offer more."

"No surprise there," Newt said. "Most of what comes out of Sacramento is shortsighted." He addressed Crocker. "How's this supposed to work exactly? We tell you that we'll square things with Bancroft, and you go on your way?"

"More or less."

"Which is it?" asked Tuck. "More? Or less?"

"I'll need more than your assurance."

"Thought you might. It's insurance, then."

"That's right."

"Newt and I require specifics. Bode, too, I imagine, since Black Crowne is his family's business."

Crocker angled his head in Comfort's direction. "I'll be escorting my insurance out of here."

Tuck looked at Comfort. "What do you think about that, Comfort? You want to go with Mr. James R. Crocker?"

She gave a small, fiercely negative shake of her head.

"I didn't think so." His attention returned to Crocker. "She doesn't want to go with you. Perhaps you should reconsider."

"Wish I could."

Bode stood suddenly. "Take me." He ignored Crocker motioning him to sit again. "I'll go with you." He willed Comfort to look at him and gave her a glimpse of his guarded smile. "And I won't be half the trouble."

"She's no trouble at all. I don't see how you can be half of that."

"No trouble now," said Bode.

"I'll take my chances."

Bode offered a careless shrug. "You probably think that gun improves your odds of getting her to do what you want. I'm telling you, it doesn't. What I can't figure is why you don't know that."

Newt knuckled the underside of his chin thoughtfully. "Have to say that Bode's got a point. It's hard to believe the Rangers didn't tell you what a scrapper she is. Tuck and I didn't do too badly against them when we were attacked, but Comfort here held her own better than either one of us."

Crocker arched an eyebrow. Behind his mustache, his slim smile was mocking. "Right up until the moment they stole her away."

"There were five or six of them," Newt said, unperturbed.

"And not a gun among them," said Crocker. "These Rangers like weapons that get them in close. I've always preferred some distance."

Tuck clapped one hand on his knee. "I knew it. *These* Rangers, you said. You *were* with the Texas Rangers." He pointed to the Walker Colt. "Sentiment trumps practicality. That's twenty you owe me, Newt, but don't trouble yourself to get it now. Double or nothing, James R. Crocker's a deserter."

"I was thinking a thief," said Newt. "But you could be right. Deserter fits. Still, I'll take the bet." He jerked his chin at Crocker, who was simultaneously clearing his throat and tugging on the collar of his shirt. "Now see that right there, Crocker, the way you slip a finger inside your collar and pull at it? If I did that, everyone here would know my collar was too stiff or too tight on account of me having a neck like a bull, but we can all see that isn't the case with you. Not that you have a scrawny neck. Looks normal size to me. You, Tuck?"

"Normal size."

Newton nodded. "Maybe stretched a little, though. I've been thinking about that. Sometimes when you give your shirt a good yank, I can make out the rope scar. You must've wiggled pretty good on the noose to get burned that deeply. Damaged your voice box, too. That's why you sound like you're swallowing glass when you talk, in spite of you always clearing your throat."

"And," Tuck said, "why you keep reaching for the inside pocket of your jacket. There's something in there you want. A tin, maybe? Could be you have a taste for Dr. Eli Kennedy's Comfort Lozenges. The peppermint ones in the red-and-white tin like you dropped at the opera house."

"It's empty," Bode said quietly. "That's why he took Comfort's."

"Guess that makes him a thief," Tuck said. He regarded Crocker through narrowing eyes. "You've always been one, I imagine. A thing like that goes bone deep. Unless you tell me they strung you up for deserting, it looks like I owe my partner forty."

Crocker didn't say anything.

Newt watched the man swallow hard. "You must have a powerful urge right about now to give your collar another jerk. If you were a deserter all those years ago, I guess you've got some kind of notion what it was like for the men fighting with you. I can't help but notice no one's arrived to back you up. Seems you're the one that's been deserted this time. Always strikes me funny how things have a way of evening out."

Crocker slowly reached into his pocket and took out the tins. At a glance he could see which one had belonged to Comfort.

He slipped the more brightly colored one back inside his jacket and held on to the other. "It seems like there's been a lot of fuss made over a little thing like this."

Tuck said, "She treasures it. You might want to give it back to her." He glanced at Comfort. "Go on, Comfort. Put the lamp down so Mr. Crocker can give you back your tin."

Crocker opened his mouth to tell her stay where she was, but she was already turning to set the oil lamp on a nearby table. When she was done, she faced him, not defiantly, not fearfully, but virtually without expression. Her hands hung limply at her sides, and her dark eyes were wide and vacant. She seemed oblivious to the gun he leveled at her. Neither did she look at the tin.

He frowned slightly. "Is she touched?"

Bode leaned forward as if he meant to step in Comfort's direction. He was waved back immediately. "You know what the Rangers did to her, Crocker. Drugged her. Put her in a hole. Took her out to amuse themselves and sold tickets to amuse everyone. That was your idea whether you admit it or not. I know these Rangers better than you, and I know something about the way they do business. You're a stranger to the Barbary Coast. You should have let them do things their way. It wouldn't have been so obvious they were working for someone else."

"Is that right?"

"Yes. You should have talked to Bram. When he hired the Rangers to keep me from arriving at my own birthday party, he knew enough to leave the details to them. They like to stay in the Coast, and they do their best work at night." He smiled without humor. "And they damn sure never used a lottery."

Crocker said nothing for a long time. He stared at Bode with something like grim admiration for his adversary. "They couldn't control their own kind," he said at last. "I was led to believe that was never a problem."

"It isn't usually."

"I suppose I asked too much of them. I told Bram I overstepped." He glanced briefly at Comfort. She hadn't moved. She continued to regard him blankly. "They said they lost her in the brawl. I should have been there, but I stayed away on the off chance she would recognize me. Perhaps that was another error of judgment. Things might have gone differently if I'd been around. They were too rough with her, I gather. She has a delicate constitution."

"Delicate," Bode said. "Yes. She's certainly that."

"I'll make sure that no harm comes to her," Crocker said. "Provided you do as I've asked. I'm sympathetic to her condition, but it doesn't alter my terms. I need you to convince Jones and Prescott here that they have to withdraw their offer. I don't think they believe I'm serious."

"We believe you," Newt said. "Tell him, Tuck."

"We believe you," Tuck said dutifully. "We just think you need to consider if you're going about this the right way."

"So it would be a kindness to kill her now, is that what you're saying?"

Comfort's skin prickled again as a chill slipped under her skin and burrowed like a weevil, deep into her marrow. Her attention was caught, but this time in a new way. It was no longer only the sound of his voice that scraped her nerves raw. What he said was important to her, not because he said it, but because she'd heard him say it before. She waited to see what her uncles would do.

Neither Newt nor Tuck said anything. They didn't shrug. They didn't move.

"That's why I thought," said Crocker. He glanced at the tin in his palm, turning it over and over while everyone waited for him to speak.

Comfort waited, too. It would be important, what he said.

"You want me to leave her," he said at last. He smiled derisively. "And leave her this." He tossed the red-and-white tin at Comfort.

Twenty years ago she'd been unprepared to catch the thing he tossed in her direction like an afterthought. Back then it landed in the cradle of her dress, and she'd only had one clear image of it before darkness trapped her as much as the rocks. This time, though, she knew it was coming; knew it before he did, because her dreams had been a safe harbor for her memories after all.

She deftly plucked the tin out of the air with one hand. The robe slipped off her shoulders. She crouched as though to catch it, but the move was a feint, and before Crocker could register what she meant to do, she attacked.

Twisting her body around, she brought up her back leg in a high fold, her knee higher than her raised foot. She struck hard at his gun hand with the ball of her foot, snapping her leg back to keep him from grabbing it. The Colt flew out of his hand and thumped hard on the floor. He ducked and tried to reach it, but his fingers were numb from the blow, and he couldn't feel the gun when his fingers grazed it. He threw up his other hand to block another kick, one she delivered with the heel of her foot this time. It caught him on the shoulder, knocking him sideways. He recovered quickly and sprang up. He shook himself off and stepped over the gun so it was protected between his feet, out of easy reach for anyone trying to get it. It only occurred to him as Comfort tossed the tin sideways at Bode that no one was coming to her aid.

He held his ground when she danced closer to him, but when he drew back his fist, she struck him hard between his ribs with the heel of her hand. The blow drove the breath from his lungs and rocked him backward. He staggered, working his arms like windmills to regain his balance. A chair fell sideways. One of the end tables teetered.

He put up two fists and successfully blocked her next blow. She countered with the other hand and yelled something he didn't understand at the same time she struck him on the chin. His head snapped back so sharply that he thought she'd separated it from his spine. Dazed, he continued retreating. The gun lay in the open. He waited for her to stoop to get it, his hands fisted and raised again as he prepared to deliver a knockout, roundhouse punch that would render her senseless. She stepped over the Colt instead, so confident in what she could do to him now that she didn't even kick it out of the way.

That enraged him. He snarled at her. She came at him anyway, her dark eyes no longer vacant, but feral. There was no anger in her that he could see, only ferocity. She meant to kill him if she could.

Fury focused him, keeping the periphery of his vision dark. She was all he could see, and the need to make her cower, to make her fear him again, was all that was on his mind as he leapt at her. He telegraphed his intent a full second before he jumped.

Comfort heard the voices clearly, all of them faintly hoarse, urgent, all of them calling her name. Was there something she was supposed to do? It always seemed as if there was something she should do.

She pivoted sideways and met Crocker's leap with her elbow, jabbing it solidly into his ribs. His momentum still drove her down, and she had to bend under his weight or risk dislocating her collarbone. She vibrated with the force of his leap, absorbed the energy of it, and just when she thought he might take her down, she was able to twist her shoulder and roll him off her. He sprawled facedown on the floor, his chin rippling the carpet until he stopped his long skid forward. He flopped awkwardly for a moment, his body as ungainly as a fish out of water. When he was finally still, he also had the gun back in his hand.

Comfort was quick, but this time Bode was quicker. He hadn't counted Crocker out just because he was finally down. He stomped on Crocker's wrist with his heel and held it there even after Crocker's fingers unfolded around the gun. Comfort started to reach for it, but Bode shook his head. "Let Tucker get it," he said. "You hold this." Over Crocker's prone body, Bode passed her the red-and-white tin.

Comfort took it and brought it close to her chest. "He's the one, Bode."

"The one?"

"The one who gave this to me." She stepped back as Tucker dropped to his haunches and took the gun from Crocker. "Did you hear me, Uncle Tuck? He was there before you found me." She looked past Bode to Newton. "He's the one who led the raid, the one responsible for the murders. He was supposed to be our guide, but he left us. And when he came back, there were more men. They answered to him. I heard them. I know they did."

Newt nodded slowly. "Not hard for me to believe at all."

"Well, how about that?" Tuck said.

Crocker turned his head. There was a carpet burn the size of a quarter on his chin. His voice was weak because he was still fighting for breath. "What's she saying?"

Bode ground his heel harder against Crocker's wrist. "Twenty years back," he said. "A wagon train on the other side of the Sierra Nevada."

Newt stood, drawing Crocker's attention, and pushed the desk four feet to the right to reveal the pair trussed in drapery cord like lambs for the slaughter. Their mouths were stuffed with the lacy antimacassars from the arms of the sofa, but making certain they couldn't talk was merely a precaution. They were unconscious, one with a bleeding scalp wound, the other with no visible injury. "Guess that ginger cat's good for something after all." Newt made certain Crocker had a good look at his cavalry before he came to stand beside Tuck and took up where Bode left off. "I have to believe you recall a wagon train you attacked and plundered. Left everyone for dead or dying. Only our little girl survived."

Tuck said, "You probably didn't expect that. Who could have?"

Comfort stared down at Crocker. "You told them to leave me," she said on a thread of sound. "I was hiding in a shelter of rocks. You tossed your tin inside and told them to leave me." She drew a shaky breath. "They replaced the rocks. I couldn't get out. You let them bury me alive, and you left."

Bode held out a hand to her. Her fingers tightened on the tin before they relaxed, but then she freed one hand and put it in his. He smiled gently and brought her around, careful to keep her out of reach of Crocker's free hand, the one he wasn't crushing under his foot.

"Who'd have thought after so long that she'd know you?" asked Bode.

"She doesn't know me," he growled. "She's dreaming if she thinks she knows me."

Newt, Tuck, Bode, and Comfort all stared down at him. It was Comfort who finally broke the silence, the shadow of a rueful smile slowly changing the shape of her mouth.

"It's fitting," she said softly, "that you should speak of dreams."

Epilogue

Bode slipped an arm around Comfort's waist the moment he became aware that she was stirring in her sleep. He knew the difference between the lazy feline stretch that meant she was seeking his warmth and the first fitful movements that were the portent of a nightmare. He responded to either of these moments in nearly identical ways, drawing her close, cradling her bottom against his groin, rubbing his chin gently against her hair. He had learned that if it was warmth and ease that she wanted, he could safely close his eyes and drift back to sleep, but if it was a dream that prompted her restlessness, then it was better for both of them that he stayed awake.

He stayed awake, waiting. She stirred again and whimpered. Bode nudged her hair. She'd washed it this evening with soap infused with peppermint oil. His nostrils flared as he breathed in the cool, clean scent of her. He whispered her name; she quieted. Not trusting that the moment had passed, he stared beyond her head to the fireplace, where gold and orange flames crackled and occasionally an ember popped.

His gaze shifted to the dressing room door as it was nudged opened and Thistle emerged. The cat padded silently toward the bed, crouched, and leapt. Bode batted him away when he began a precise, delicate walk up Comfort's leg, but he allowed the cat to advance again when Thistle decided to test his balance on his own leg.

"Mind that you watch her elbow," he whispered to the cat. "She'll knock you out." He thought that Thistle seemed unconcerned. The cat kneaded the flesh of his upper thigh and buttock, circled the area twice, and finally curled on Bode's hip. "You're not long for that perch."

Bode felt Comfort stiffen. That afforded him enough time to move his chin out of the way. The arm she had under her pillow went rigid, and she banged her knuckles hard against the headboard. The bed shuddered. Thistle stood, arched, and jumped over the arm Comfort flung backward, elbow sharp and high. Bode sat up, caught Comfort's arm, and watched the cat flee back to the dressing room.

"Coward," he muttered under his breath. He released Comfort's arm, stroked her shoulder, and quietly said her name.

Her eyes fluttered open. She blinked once and then squinted against the firelight. Bode moved away and gave her room to turn over. When she did, he slid back under the covers and propped himself on an elbow, facing her.

She pressed an index finger against his chest. "Did you call me 'coward'?"

"The cat."

"Oh. He was in here?"

"Briefly. You scared him away."

Comfort folded her finger back and lightly knuckled the underside of Bode's chin. "But not you." She smiled. "I'm glad of that."

He glanced at the carafe of water and glass on the bedside table. "Are you thirsty?"

She nodded. When Bode started to rise, she stopped him. "I can get it." She pushed herself up into a sitting position, folded her legs tailor fashion, and poured water into the glass. She drained the first glass quickly but only sipped the second one. "It's been months since I dreamed about the raid on the wagon train. That's good, isn't it? I think it must be good."

He smiled. "I'm sure it is."

Comfort was visited by nightmares off and on for several weeks after Crocker had been laid out on the study carpet.

Although Newt and Tuck made sure the Pinkerton man and his followers were escorted to the county jail before dawn broke, no one, least of all Comfort, held out any real hope that they wouldn't be freed. Bode visited the jail every day for almost three weeks to test the alertness of the guards and discover all the ways the jail was vulnerable to an attack. During that time, Newt and Tuck applied legal, political, and financial pressure to the city council to thwart similar influencing efforts out of Sacramento. The Pinkerton Agency insisted that Crocker was working within the scope of an investigation but would not offer any details to the newspapers.

Lack of information fed speculation for a time, but in the end the public grew weary of smoke without fire and turned their attention to a scandal involving a brothel owner named Maggie Drummond and her lawsuit against David Bancroft of Croft Federal. She alleged he failed to make payments on a line of credit that she'd extended to him over a period of eighteen months. He insisted he'd never frequented her establishment. While the city reveled in the classic she said/he said debate, Crocker and the pair who'd followed him remained behind bars, no longer the subject of gossip and rumor.

The morning after Comfort's last nightmare, Bode didn't visit the jail. He also didn't make an appearance that afternoon. In his absence, a mob stormed the county jail at nightfall, overpowered the police, and made off with all the prisoners through a back door that opened into a narrow alley. The authorities initially blamed the Rangers, but that theory didn't hold up under scrutiny. Not all of the prisoners had ties to the gang, and there were witnesses who reported the prisoners weren't freed as much as they were carried off. The police revised their thinking and looked to the crimps and runners who swarmed the wharf like pirates and engaged in the practice of shanghaiing.

When not one of the prisoners reappeared anywhere in the city in the following two months, it was assumed they'd been pressed into service on one of the ships making a China run. The harbormaster's records indicated that four ships sailed before daybreak: *King's Ransom* of the Barclay Line; Mannering's *Sea Pearl*; the British merchant *Loch Err*; and Black Crowne's flagship, *Artemis Queen*.

The harbormaster stood by his records and his recollection of the night's events, giving a particularly detailed account of how Mr. John Farwell had managed to cause nothing less than chaos when he insisted on a departure schedule that was at odds with what had been agreed upon. Farwell was so damnably adamant that sides were drawn, and the crews of every vessel began shouting curses and threats and waving weapons with the expressed intention of commandeering one another's ships. The harbormaster settled the dispute by holding out a torch and threatening to burn every ship to a hulk unless the masters took control of their men. To punish Farwell, he did a second inspection of the *Artemis Queen* on the pretense that she wasn't yet seaworthy and that releasing her to the open water would risk the life of every man aboard. Farwell had nothing to do but swear and sputter on the pier as the other three merchants were released.

It was the harbormaster's opinion that John Farwell was guilty of being a horse's ass, but he could be acquitted of pressing the city's prisoners into service on Black Crowne ships. Two inspections had revealed nothing.

The direction of Bode's thoughts raised his slight smile, one that didn't go unnoticed by Comfort.

"What are you thinking?" she asked.

A chuckle rumbled at the back of his throat. "That John Farwell is a very good man."

She lowered her glass. "You're thinking about John Farwell? Here? In our bed?"

"Sure. As far as I know, he's the only other man to ever share a bed with my wife."

Comfort dipped three fingers in her glass and flicked water at him. "You weren't my husband then."

"That's all you're going to say?"

She set the glass aside, leaned forward, and kissed him full on the mouth. "That's all I'm going to say."

"Cheeky." Bode caught her by the elbows when she would have drawn away. "Let me see if I can taste that sass." What he tasted was her laughter, and that was satisfying in its own right. She was smiling, contented and a little pleased with herself, when he raised the covers and helped her nestle in beside him. They faced each other, he with an elbow raising his head, she with one arm pushed under her pillow. Comfort drew up her knees, and Bode stretched out. Her back was to the firelight so that her face was in shadow, while his features were cast in a bronze glow. She found his hand and threaded her fingers through his.

"I'm not certain why I had the dream tonight," she said. "I was very happy with how this evening turned out. It doesn't make any sense."

One of Bode's eyebrows kicked up. "Alexandra can provoke a nightmare even in people who aren't susceptible to them. You need look no further than my mother's visit for the catalyst."

"She was on her best behavior, Bode. And really, wouldn't it have been more reasonable for me to have had the dream last night when I was anticipating entertaining her?"

"You hardly slept last night," he reminded her. "I know. I was there. You didn't have time to dream."

Comfort squeezed his fingers. "I'm sorry. I tossed and turned a lot, didn't I?" She raised his hand to her mouth and kissed his knuckles when he nodded. "You know," she said thoughtfully, "the next time we invite her to dinner, perhaps we could ask Bram to come as well."

"I don't think so."

"All right." She didn't press. She waited for the tension that she felt in his handclasp to fade. He'd resisted, too, when she first suggested having his mother to dinner. Newt and Tuck offered no objections, but Bode had plenty, although what he mostly said was no. It wasn't that he never saw his mother, only that he visited her as a matter of business. Ever since Jones Prescott assumed the debt for Black Crowne, Bode had been exercising complete control over his mother's spending. Bram no longer received an allowance. Bode invited his brother to work for Black Crowne, but as soon as Bram's leg healed enough for him to be up and around on crutches, he took a position working for the law firm of Wheeler and Sutton, making a clerk's wages, and moved into the apartment above the Black Crowne office once it was clear that Comfort and Bode would not return. He paid rent. Bode remained skeptical of Bram's turn, prepared to learn at any moment that his brother was only playing at assuming duty and a conscience. Perhaps if Newt and Tucker weren't exacting their revenge by letting Bram know at every turn that they were watching him, he would have already begun his descent into gaming and whoring, but Comfort didn't think so.

"I won't bring it up at again," she said.

"Yes, you will." His brief smile removed any accusation from his words. "But you'll choose the moment very well. And I might say yes . . . eventually."

Not only was it the best she could hope for right now, Comfort decided, it was probably for the best. "Alexandra said something this evening that I wasn't certain I understood."

"Oh? What was that?"

"I think you know, Bode. She said it to you."

He sensed a trap and proceeded cautiously. "Perhaps you better just tell me what it was."

She chuckled appreciatively. "I don't know why I thought I could catch more with a net than a pole. Very well. She said it was right and proper what you had done. I had stepped out of the room, so I didn't hear everything that came before, but I heard her mention Mr. Crocker."

"Oh, that. You and my mother go fishing with the same net. She believes I had something to do with that incident at the jail."

"Does she? So do my uncles. So do I, actually."

"Really?"

She searched his face, but he was giving nothing away. He looked vaguely amused. "Really."

"Mm." He slipped his fingers from hers and touched her cheek with his knuckle. "You know, if you've been thinking about that this evening, it could explain your nightmare."

He was right. Crocker had been hovering at the back of her mind even before she overheard Alexandra's remark to Bode. Alexandra's mere presence had prompted the first inklings. Had Bode suspected that might happen? Probably. "It's more than a little disconcerting that you know me so well."

"For me, too."

That made her smile. He traced the shape of it with his fingertip before he tapped her lightly on the chin.

"Put him out of your mind, Comfort."

Still uncertain, she nodded anyway.

"He's not coming back. Not to San Francisco. Not to California. Not ever."

Comfort knew it as an absolute truth. Bode's features were no longer shuttered. His candor made him vulnerable, but he returned her steady regard without flinching. "All right," she said.

"Good." He leaned down and kissed her on the forehead. "Sleep."

She slipped her arms around his neck and lifted her face. Her lips brushed his chin. "Not just yet," she said. "In a little while, yes, but not just now."

Her mouth was gentle on his, almost tentative, as though she had never kissed him before, searching out the right way to slant her head and avoid bumping his nose. He kissed her back almost as awkwardly. Soft laughter bubbled up between them.

"I think we would have kissed like that," she whispered. "The first time, I mean, when I was sixteen and you were going off to war. I've thought about it."

"Have you?"

"Mm. Why didn't you ask me to dance?"

"You were sixteen and I was going off to war."

"That's what my uncles said."

"They were probably relieved."

Her smile was a shade rueful. "They said that, too."

Bode fingered the hair at her nape. "You looked as if you wanted to be anywhere but where you were. Do you remember that?"

She nodded, sighing softly. "It's just as well. If you had approached me, I would have run the other way."

"More likely you would have stabbed me with one of the combs you had in your hair."

"Do you think so?" she asked, pleased.

"I do."

He made love to her then, first to the girl she'd been at their introduction, and later to the woman she'd become. By turns he was cautious and caring, deliberate and dangerous. She met him halfway, easy in his arms, playing out the hand he dealt.

She loved him back, her heart full and open, unafraid that she'd come to this pass where she could want him so badly that she ached with it. Long before she understood his intent, he had been waiting for her, watching over her, always just there at the periphery no matter how often she turned her head. He filled her vision now, and that was exactly as it should be.

She looked in his eyes and imagined she saw what was reflected in her own. They were as furtive as thieves in the night, the two of them, trading secretive, knowing glances while they bartered touch for pleasure and guarding their voices to exchange words whispered in passion for laughter.

Afterward, when she rested her head on his shoulder, Bode felt her expel a soft breath. He thought she might say something, but she yawned sleepily instead and closed her eyes. That was all right, then. He idly stroked the arm she slid across his chest and listened to her breathing quiet. He kissed the crown of her head, a slip of a smile touching his lips, and in the stillness of the room it wasn't long before he drifted off to sleep, unapologetically stealing Comfort.

Keep reading for a special preview of
Jo Goodman's next historical romance

Wyoming Territory
October 1888

Kellen Coltrane glanced up from his reading to acknowledge the stranger. The interruption annoyed him, but he didn't allow that to show. It was impossible for him not to hear his mother's gentle admonishment at times like this: "There is no reason you cannot remove your nose from a book long enough to be civil." That's why a smile was tugging at the corners of his mouth when he met the eyes of the dead man.

Not that the stranger was dead yet. Just that he soon would be. The man's gaunt face was nearly drained of color, and in spite of the chill in the passenger coach, his skin had the damp sheen of a sickly sweat.

Then there was the blood. It was not immediately evident. The dying man was making some effort to hide his condition, perhaps even from himself, but his posture was listing now, the knees no longer locked to attention. The hand he had pushed inside his coat to cover the wound was insufficient to staunch the flow of blood. A dark crimson bloom had begun to appear on his shirt above the button closures of his vest and coat.

Kellen looked around quickly and saw the man had attracted no particular notice. This passenger car hadn't been overcrowded since Omaha and was down to five other souls since the stop in Cheyenne. There were cars forward where passengers were still seated elbow to elbow. If there was a choice, most people opted to ride as close to the front of the train as possible, where they believed the cars swayed less. Smoke and cinders were inescapable wherever one sat, even in the Union Pacific's most expensive private coaches. For Kellen, his choice of seats hinged on how much conversation and company he wanted. He had moved several times to achieve exactly this much isolation.

Apparently, so had the dead man.

Kellen stood, placed a hand under the stranger's elbow, and slipped his dime novel under the man's coat. "Press this against your wound," he whispered. "Let me help you sit."

Summoning enough energy to glance at the book's colorful cover illustration, the man grasped it with bloodstained fingers. "Hate to see Nat Church put to such a use."

Kellen offered a thin smile. "If you believe the stories, he's seen worse."

"Oh, I believe. Believe 'em all."

There was a pause, and Kellen thought he was going to say more, but a weak cough and a spittle of blood on the man's lower lip was all that followed. Kellen eased the man down on the wooden bench and helped him slide into the corner beside the window, the same space Kellen had previously occupied.

Kellen bent low and spoke quietly into the man's ear. "I'm going to get help."

"No."

"The conductor passed through here a few minutes ago. He can't be far."

"No." This time the objection was more forceful, not easily ignored. He turned his head toward Kellen's lowered one and stared him down. His soft grunt revealed mild surprise and a measure of grudging respect when Kellen didn't blink or back away. "Guess I ain't in a position to argue."

"That's right." Kellen started to straighten and move away, but the dying man reached out suddenly and grabbed his wrist. His strength made Kellen hesitate even while it filled him with a greater sense of urgency. Perhaps he had mistaken the hopelessness of the stranger's condition. He looked down at the white-knuckled fingers gripping his wrist. "What is it?"

"My valise." He jerked his chin toward the narrow aisle. "Put it here. Beside me."

Kellen's own valise was stored under the bench. He didn't bother offering to put the stranger's bag there. He picked up the bag, discovered it was heavier than he anticipated, and made a small grimace as he hefted it onto the bench. It occurred to him to ask what was in the bag, but engaging in conversation was probably not exactly what the man had in mind. "I won't be long."

The stranger shrugged. "S'fine. Don't have long."

Kellen knew that if the stranger was to have even a slim chance of surviving, he had to ignore that. He twisted his wrist, and the man's fingers fell away. Kellen stepped back into the aisle and confirmed his promise to return with a quick nod.

He found the conductor four cars forward. It took him more time than he had allowed for because passengers two cars ahead had opened up their baskets and were sharing food across the aisle and between the benches. The atmosphere in that car was as festive as a summer picnic, and he was encouraged by every traveler of the female kind to sample a slice of this and a square of that. Exigency warred with civility. He was polite but firm, then coldly polite, and finally merely cold. No one offered him anything on his return passage.

The conductor, a smallish man with widely spaced eyes and spectacles that sat too narrowly on the bridge of his nose, had his hands full keeping two women from clawing each other—or him. Lying in the aisle between the would-be combatants was a flattened black velvet bonnet, artfully decorated with black-and-white glass beads and a large black-tipped ostrich feather. Kellen assessed the situation as a standoff and concluded he could expect no help without intervening. While passengers on either side of the aisle called out their opinions and generally egged on the spitting and hissing females, Kellen slipped the toe of his boot under the bonnet's brim, gave a little kick, and sent the bonnet sailing toward the coach's ceiling. Both women leaped, and once they were airborne, Kellen reached between them, grabbed the conductor's arm, and yanked him free of the dispute.

Kellen couldn't be sure, but he thought he glimpsed a look of gratitude before the conductor began to make all the proper noises about not abandoning his post even as he was being dragged toward the rear of the car.

Between cars, Kellen explained the situation. He had precious few details to offer. No, he couldn't say who was responsible. No, he didn't know when the man was injured. Yes, he was certain it was a grievous wound. Yes, the man required a doctor's attention if one could be found.

The conductor, in Kellen's opinion, delayed their progress unnecessarily by insisting on proper introductions, and Kellen had the impression his name would find its way into an official report to the Union Pacific Railroad or, more concerning, to the local vigilance committee. He was tempted to ask Mr. Berg if he knew the names of the unbalanced women in the forward car. He resisted the question because Mr. Berg seemed as if he might be the sort of person to go back and correct this oversight.

"There is a physician in the next car," Mr. Berg explained. "Go on ahead, and I'll ask him to attend us. I won't be but a minute or so behind you."

Kellen didn't know what he would find by the time he returned to his car. When he didn't immediately see the stranger, he thought the impossible had happened and that somehow the man had moved on. That wasn't the case. As Kellen moved closer to his seat, he saw the stranger was doubled over, bent so far forward as to be invisible from the front of the car. Far from being dead, the man was purposefully rooting through his valise. Kellen had a distinct memory of setting the bag on the seat beside the stranger. Had it fallen to the floor?

"What do you need?" asked Kellen. "Let me get it for you." He watched the man remove his hand as quickly as a child caught in the act of swiping his finger through a freshly frosted cake. "Then let me get it out of the way." Kellen pushed it under the bench beside his own bag and sat down. "Conductor's bringing a doctor. Maybe you've got longer than you think." He helped the man straighten and situated him once more in the corner of the seat, allowing him to rest his shoulder against the side of the car. His head lolled against the window. Kellen removed his own jacket, folded it, and placed it under the man's head and shoulder.

"You want to tell me what happened?" Kellen asked.

The stranger lifted one ginger eyebrow. "You interested?"

"I am."

"Didn't seem like you might be. Runnin' off the way you did."

Kellen had to lean close. The man's voice was weak, softer than a whisper, and hard to hear over the steady clickety-clack of the train on the rails. He watched the stranger's lips and strained to hear.

"Thought you might be squeamish. Didn't think you were when I first noticed you, but you never know."

Kellen ignored that. "You're wasting your breath," he said. "Literally. Who are you?"

"Name's Nat Church. Heard of me?"

Arching an eyebrow, Kellen revealed his skepticism. "Nat Church." His wintry blue eyes dropped to where the stranger's hand disappeared under his coat. Somewhere beneath the heavy woolen overcoat, the man was still pressing a dime novel against his wound. *Nat Church and the Ambush at Broken Bow. Nat Church and the Indian Maiden. That* Nat Church?"

"That's right."

"Huh."

"You don't believe me."

"Sure don't, but I don't think it matters." Kellen watched the man who called himself Nat Church shrug and immediately regret the small movement. A grimace twisted Mr. Church's mouth into a parody of a smile. Kellen looked away and in the direction of the passenger car's door. Help wasn't arriving as quickly as the conductor had indicated. Perhaps the doctor was reluctant to offer assistance.

Several rows ahead of them, a father sitting with his young son glanced back. Kellen intercepted the glance, and the father immediately turned away, apparently as disinclined to become involved as the doctor. When the boy started to swivel in his seat, the father clamped a firm hand on the back of his son's skull and made him keep his eyes forward.

Another quick survey of the car told Kellen all he needed
to know about the likelihood that there would be help from
another quarter. The passengers studiously avoided his eyes
every time he attempted to catch theirs. Kellen could tell they
all knew now that something unpleasant was happening within
spitting distance of their seats, but their instinct was to maintain
that distance lest some spittle attach itself.

Their reaction struck him as odd. They were behaving counter to his experience. In his travels, he'd found that people in
the wide-open Western territories were more likely to step up
and lend a hand than city folk or the denizens of small towns
where the yoke of lawlessness was still a heavy burden.

There was a possibility, however, that explained it. Kellen
bent his head slightly and addressed Nat Church. "You told
them to stay away."

Mr. Church did not pretend that he didn't understand.
"'Course I did."

Kellen had the impression that Nat Church was not only at
peace with what he'd done, his fleeting smile seemed to indicate
that he was satisfied that Kellen had figured it out. "All right,"
said Kellen. He concluded there was no point in challenging
the dying man's assertion that he was Nat Church, in spite of
the fact that he looked nothing at all like the hero described in
all twenty-two of the wildly popular dime novels. The fictional
Nat Church was in his twenties, easily half the stranger's age.
Nat Church of the serialized adventures had hair as black as
tar and eyes so impenetrable that light was neither emitted nor
reflected. The man sitting beside Kellen had a face that was
infinitely more expressive, eyes that were as gray as the wiry
strands of hair at his temples, and a thin face whose deep lines
were a map of life experience. The hero of *Nat Church and the
Sleeping Detective* and *Nat Church and the Hanging at Har-
risonville* had wide shoulders and wore a beaten, buttery-soft
brown leather duster, not a woolen coat with the heavy collar
turned up to hide a pencil-thin neck; and Church, the hero,
sported scuffed brown boots with tarnished silver spurs, not
ones that were polished to a military shine. "There's no good
reason not to believe you. You're *the* Nat Church. Are you going
to let me see your wound?"

"Can't. Lift the book . . . I'll bleed out."

Kellen was certain that was going to happen regardless. There was nothing to be gained by hurrying the process along. "You were stabbed, is that right? Not shot."

"How you figure?"

Impatient with the man's need to hear an explanation, Kellen set his jaw for a moment. He said, "You didn't board the train injured. It's my habit to watch people at the stops, see who's coming and going. I saw you walking the platform; saw you waiting to climb aboard. Hands at your sides. Patient to take your turn. Watchful but not worried. I saw enough to be confident that whatever happened had happened after you stepped on the train. I didn't hear a gunshot. No one in this car reacted as if they'd heard one either. That leads me to conclude you were stabbed."

There was humor in Mr. Church's voice as he whispered, " 'Leads me to conclude.' You a lawyer?"

"No."

"Sound like a lawyer . . . maybe a politician."

"Neither."

Church nodded once. "Can't abide either one. Thought maybe I lost my touch for takin' a man's measure."

Kellen was curious about what made this Nat Church choose him, but he didn't take the dangling bait. It was sheer hubris to suppose that he was picked because Church sized him up and surmised something steady about his character. It was far more likely that he had been selected for what he'd been reading at the time. He might have been passed over completely if he'd been holding *The Pickwick Papers*.

"Who did this to you?"

Again, the small smile. "Ain't it the way of life that most things is done *by* ourselves, *to* ourselves?"

"Philosopher? The Nat Church I read about is none of that."

"Even a good writer can't put all of me on the page."

"I see. So are you saying you stabbed yourself?"

"Hardly. Not such a fool as that. Just tryin' to say that I had some part in it."

Kellen watched the man take a short, steadying breath, drawing air through clenched teeth. In spite of the pain, it seemed to Kellen that Mr. Church wanted to take his time, tell his tale slowly in the fashion of Scheherazade, as though he might be granted a night's reprieve if he could spin the ending to another chapter.

Kellen put his next question bluntly. "Do you know the name of your murderer?" He gave Nat Church full marks for not flinching. Perhaps he had something in common with the man he purported to be after all.

"Never saw it coming . . . crowded in the aisle . . . people trying to get settled."

"One car back? That's where I thought you boarded."

Mr. Church tried to suppress a cough but couldn't. He pressed the ball of his free hand against his lips.

Kellen passed him a handkerchief.

"Thank you." He wiped his mouth and crumpled the hand-kerchief in his fist. "Yes, one car to the rear. Did I say I never saw it comin'?"

"You did."

"Should have seen it. Half expectin' it since . . . since for-ever. Knew what I was up against. Wife would've tried to stop me." A short laugh had him raising the handkerchief to his mouth again. "Damn me if that don't hurt."

It hadn't occurred to Kellen until now that there might be someone to notify. "Who should I tell? How can I find your wife?"

"Can't. She's gone now. Same as me."

"There must be someone."

"Bitter Springs."

Not a person at all, but a place. Kellen's Western journeys had taken him past the town on several occasions. It existed on Wyoming's high flatland near the Medicine Bow Mountains, a survivor of the camps that sprang to life as the Union Pacific laid track from Omaha toward Utah. Instead of disappearing as so many of the camps did when the rails passed them by, Bitter Springs found commerce in cattle country and as a water way station for thirsty engines and their thirstier passengers.

Kellen had never seen anything from his train window that recommended Bitter Springs as a place of particular interest. Now he wondered what he might have missed by not spending a few days with the locals. "Is that your home? Bitter Springs? Were you going there?"

"Going there . . . not home."

"Expected?"

Mr. Church nodded. "Pennyroyal. Should find her . . . tell her . . . she's waiting."

"Penny Royal. All right. I'll be certain to—" He stopped, his attention caught by the coach door opening. Mr. Berg appeared on the threshold with a man Kellen supposed must be the doctor on his heels. The late arrival was explained by the doctor's condition. The man required the conductor's shoulder to keep him steady and upright. Kellen swore under his breath and got to his feet. "Right here," he said. He stepped into the aisle, backing up as he pointed to Mr. Church. He jerked his chin at the doctor but addressed his question to Mr. Berg. "You sure he can help? He looks as if he can hardly hold his bag any better than he can hold his liquor."

"Don't like the looks of you much either," the doctor said, answering for himself. He kept pace with the conductor and then switched places so he could sink onto the bench beside Mr. Church. He flipped the clasp on his medical bag and opened it, offering his resume to Kellen as he withdrew a ball of tightly wound bandages. "Woodrow Hitchens. Late of St. Louis. Graduate of Philadelphia Medical College, class of '60. Cut my teeth in the field hospitals at Manassas, Gettysburg, and Shiloh, to name a few that you might have heard of, you still being a whelp and all. That suit you?"

Kellen accepted the rebuke, knowing it was deserved. The doctor hadn't slurred a syllable. Liquor didn't account for the man's unsteady gait or the slight tremble in his hands. Some sort of wasting disease did. "Suits me fine," Kellen said. "What can you do for him?"

Dr. Hitchens gave the patient his full attention while Mr. Berg inched closer for a better look until Kellen put an arm out to ease him back. "You're going to have let me see your wound, Mr.—"

"Church. Nat Church."

"Well, that's something," the doctor said equably. "I've been known to enjoy your exploits. Especially liked *Nat Church and the Frisco Fancy*."

Kellen smiled wryly as Nat Church offered a modest thank-you. The man had no shame—perhaps another trait he shared with his fictional counterpart.

The doctor had some difficulty unbuttoning his patient's coat. Aside from the tremor in his hands, his fingers quickly became slick with blood. "Can't wait to read the new one. Have it on order."

"*Nat Church and the Chinese Box*," Church said as the doctor opened the coat at the site of the wound. "Got a copy for you right here."

The conductor blanched and sucked in a breath when he saw the bloody mess that was Mr. Church's midsection. He was relieved to have Kellen take a deliberate step forward and block his view.

Kellen couldn't distinguish between book, blood, and bowel. The doctor tossed the latest Church adventure to the floor, shoved slithering intestine back inside the gaping wound, and held one hand against Church's bloody flesh while expertly unwinding the ball of bandages in the other. When he had a wad the size and thickness of his palm, he used his teeth to tear it off and replaced his hand with it. "Mother of God," he muttered, looking back at Kellen. "This man's been gutted. Who did this?"

"He says he doesn't know."

Mr. Berg squared his shoulders and raised his chin a notch. It didn't add so much as a quarter of an inch to his height, and he still stood a full head shorter than Kellen Coltrane. He was either oblivious to this fact or undeterred by it, because there was a sharp edge of accusation in his tone when he asked, "Do *you* know?"

Kellen ignored the question. "Anything you can do, Doctor?"

"Put this away." Hitchens held out the unused portion of bandage to Kellen. "Take out the smallest syringe and give it to me."

Kellen followed the instructions, eventually taking the doctor's place beside Mr. Church and using his hand to keep the man's guts from spilling onto his lap. Hitchens wiped blood from his fingers and then filled the syringe from a vial of clear fluid that he extracted from the bottom of his bag.

Watching him, Kellen saw both resignation and determination on the doctor's face. It wasn't so different from what he observed in the man who wanted to be Nat Church.

"Morphine?" asked Kellen.

The doctor didn't answer. Without a word of warning or apology, he plunged the point of the syringe into his patient's thigh.

There was only waiting after that. Nat Church eventually closed his eyes. He slept. He died. And none of those who stood as witness to his end had an explanation for it.

They agreed that the bloody tin star the doctor found pinned to Nat Church's vest might account for some part of the answer. Kellen Coltrane was left to wonder what accounted for the rest of it.

ABOUT THE AUTHOR

Jo Goodman is a licensed professional counselor working with children and families in West Virginia's Northern Panhandle. Always a fan of the happily ever after, Jo turned to writing romances early in her career as a child care worker when she realized the only life script she could control was the one she wrote herself. She is inspired by the resiliency and courage of the children she meets and feels privileged to be trusted with their stories, the ones that they alone have the right to tell.

Once upon a time, Jo believed she was going to be a marine biologist. She feels lucky that seasickness made her change course. She lives with her family in landlocked Colliers, West Virginia. Please visit her website at www.jogoodman.com.